# The Short-Legged Fisher Boy of the Land of Left

For Braylen and Ansley —
we hope you enjoy
the adventures of
Jogai!

[ Hope we have a chance
to talk about this
sometime — n ]

Ard Webb
11/25/06

Jalinde C Webb
11/25/06

To order additional copies, please contact us.
BookSurge, LLC
www.booksurge.com
1-866-308-6235
orders@booksurge.com

# The Short-Legged Fisher Boy of the Land of Left

Ned Webb and Kalinde C. Webb

Cypress Creek Publications
2005

# The Short-Legged Fisher Boy of the Land of Left

*For*

*Gareth, Luke, Emma,*
*Granston, Katya, and Katelyn*

CHAPTER I

# The Festival is Only Two Days Away

"You coming, Togai?"

Togai let his head sink lower into the water but held onto the diving raft and looked up at his friend Dilo on the edge just above him.

"I told you once already. No."

From far up the pole ladder to the high board came Tatl's voice. "What's the matter, *Birdleg*? You afraid? *Everybody* dives off the high board before their eleventh Festival, and you've only got this afternoon and tomorrow left. I dived off two years ago, before I was ten Festivals old."

"No need to call him names or brag," Dilo said.

But Togai had already pushed away from the raft and the only sound that reached his ears was that of the splashy strokes carrying him upstream. He quickly slowed, though, and turned onto his back and began a leisurely hand paddle toward shore. No need to act upset. That would only lead to more teasing from Tatl and others around the raft. Besides, he wanted to see what Tatl would do.

Tatl was now at the top of the high board's ladder, posing and showing off his muscles, pretending to be clowning. But Togai knew Tatl wasn't clowning. Tatl liked it that he was not only bigger and stronger than any other twelve-old in the village but bigger and stronger than any thirteen-old as well.

Tatl took a step toward the end of the board, but stopped and shook his head 'no' with enough exaggeration to make his thick and

I

dark ponytail, which he was also proud of, swish from side to side and hit his face. When laughter came up from the many on and around the raft, he ran to the end of the rough-hewn board, leaped up and out, wrapped his arms around his bent legs and—amid cheers and his own high-pitched wail—came down, bottom first, *kerwhoosh*, with a huge spray and splash.

Hmpf, Togai thought. Tatl had taunted that by their eleventh Festival *everybody* had dived off the high board, but as far as Togai knew, Tatl had never *dived* off, just done that bottom-buster of his.

Togai let his feet down to the sand-gravel bottom and began wading toward shore, backward, so he could now watch Dilo.

Dilo, a bit of a showman too, crawled from the ladder onto the high board and, still on hands and knees, leaned to one side to peek at the water. But even as the first laugh came, he stood, took a few quick steps along the board and jumped high. He came down on the end of the board with knees bent and jumped again as the board shot him upward. At the very top of his arc he arched forward and, arms ahead of him, hit the water with almost no splash.

With noise from the raft returning to the normal laughing and splashing, Togai turned and headed for the willow bush where he always got into or out of the water. He sat on the bank beside the bush and looked back through its thin leaves and droopy limbs.

It'd be fun to be down there with the others, he thought, playing king of the raft or just swimming and diving, but…He looked down at his legs and straightened them so they came clear of the water. He sighed. His legs looked the same as yesterday. Even though the upper parts were about the same and normal looking, the lower part of his left leg was a little shorter than the right—and much thinner. Little more than skin and bone. He snorted. It did look like a bird's leg—and the little foot fit right in. No wonder the others called him names like "Stickleg" and "Funny Foot."

Shouts rang out. "Canoes!" "Canoes!"

Togai quickly leaned forward and pushed aside some limbs. As he expected, the first of the fishing canoes were just coming into sight around the first bend in the river. He smiled and felt his chest swell with pride. Once again his father's canoe was in front. For a long time he'd thought that the other fishers, out of respect, let his father—head fisher Togl—lead them in from their day's fishing on the ocean. But Kallo said the reason Togl's canoe was always in front was that he was the best paddler. And Kallo should know; he was three Festivals older and had actually fished once or twice with their father. Old Exl, their father's partner, was a good paddler too, and neither of them wanted to be beat. Even more reason to be proud of Togl, Lilu said, was that he was the most looked-up-to man in the village because the fishers, either with their fish or the fruits and vegetables they traded their fish for, provided most of what the village ate—and its clothes and tools and cooking utensils too. And Togl was the *head* fisher. The best.

Togai glanced across the river to where the canoes were headed, to the trading bank, which was already crowded with Zaprians. Off to one side stood some Chelk women and girls. Even if they hadn't been standing apart, even if they'd been mixed in with the Zaps, Togai would have known they were Chelk from their colorful dresses. He guessed they weren't waiting nearly as much for trading to start as for it to end. No doubt that after a long day of working for the Zaps they'd like to get in the canoes, get home.

And when the fishers arrived he'd be able to easily pick them out from the Zap men because all the fishers would be in short pants and sleeveless shirts, and the Zaps'd be in hats, long pants and long-sleeve shirts. To protect their delicate white skin from the sun, Kallo said—like it was a sissy thing to do.

Just a little way from his willow bush the dirt bank crumbled into a rocky, gravelly strand that widened quickly and ran down past the raft and on around a slight bend to the fish-holding pens, which Togai couldn't see. This wide and flat strand, where the fishers would land their canoes, now had a number of women on it, most young and most with small children they'd brought for a last play and bath before supper. Togai was almost certain his mother was in their hut, cooking. The hard work of fishing built a good appetite, and Lilu liked to have supper ready for Togl as soon as he came in.

The landing of the canoes was something of an end-of-day signal. By the time the fishers were halfway to Chelekai most boys and girls were running for home and young mothers were pulling their babes and toddlers from the water. All seemed happier than usual today, and noisier, Togai thought, but then, with the Festival getting closer, it seemed everyone in the village had been in a good mood the last few days, including him. He liked going to the Festival. Liked crossing the river and going into the City of Light, liked wandering around in its big central square, listening to music and watching people dance. He especially liked getting his near fill of sweet things he got to eat only once a year.

Even as the fishers began taking their paddles and nets from the canoes the store-hut keepers and fish handlers began taking away the traded-for goods and what was left of the day's catch.

When Togai saw Togl pull his fishing net from the water, where he'd thrown it to rinse some of the saltwater from it, he slid off the bank into the water. The racks weren't far away, and he didn't want to be seen. Togl had seen him once, there under the willow, and asked why. Togai had shrugged and said something like, "No reason." If Togl saw him other times after that, he never said he did, never again asked why.

Togai peeped through the willow's roots, watched Togl hang the net and turn back toward the canoes—and wished he were put together like that. Big, muscular arms. Sturdy legs. And hair! Most Chelks had pale to medium brown hair, a few dark brown. Togl's had once been really dark, Lilu said. It was now nearly grey, "ash" she called it—and there was a lot of it. Not in the sense of long though. Pulled back in a short pony tail—like most men in village—his hair was thick and full, made his head seem unusually large, made him seem even stronger, more robust. Togai guessed that even if Togl weren't the head fisher he'd still be the most respected man in all of Chelekai.

Togai watched Togl and Exl turn their canoe over and slide their paddles in under it, but not until the last of the fishers was headed for the village did they leave. At the opening in the willows where the widest and most used path to the village began, Togl said something

4

to Exl and paused to look back. He seemed to assure himself that all canoes, nets and paddles were properly tucked away for the night, and with one last glance at the willow, turned and started up the path.

Any other day Togai would have climbed onto the bank and run as hard as he could through the scattered willows and scratchy-limbed bushes to get home ahead of Togl. But this wasn't just any other day.

He quickly pushed away from the bank, glided to deep water and began swimming hard toward the raft, trying to go fast, yet smoothly. He didn't want Togl—or anyone else—hearing splashing and coming back to see who or what it was. From the river side of the raft Togai pulled himself up to where his eyes were level with its uneven, warped boards. With a glance up and down the beach and a careful look at the path opening, he pulled himself up and hurried toward the high board's ladder.

Though the ladder's steps, pieces of limbs tied between two upright poles, cut into his feet, he was quickly up to the board. But after one step onto it, he stopped. Things didn't look—or feel—like he'd thought they would. Not only did the board seem much higher, it didn't seem to be nearly wide enough to run on.

He wanted to walk out and take a look, but he was afraid if he did that, he'd never have enough nerve to go off. Besides, he didn't have time. He took a deep breath and started down the board with steps that were, at first, quick and sure. But the whole raft seemed to sway underneath him. He almost lost his balance and his jump for the end of board wasn't nearly as high or as sure as he had hoped or imagined it would be. He came down with his right leg bent more than his left, as planned, but already a little off balance, and with the board not bending as much as he'd thought it would—and springing back more quickly—he was suddenly shot up and off the board at an angle, with his feet wanting to go one way and his head and flailing arms another. He flailed and kicked to right himself, but quickly gave up on that. He tried to get his feet up and his head down so that he could at least say he'd made a dive. But, to his horror as the water came rushing at him, all he managed to do was get his head a little

5

lower than his feet—and though he was bent a little in the middle, he hit the water mostly sideways and nearly flat.

He came up gasping, hurting. But no air would come in. He tried to swim. But his arms wouldn't move. Turtles, he thought, if he drowned, he hoped he'd either sink or the river would carry him away. He didn't want to be found floating there, only a few strokes away from the raft, have people wonder, "How'd that silly Togai manage to do *that*?" He laughed at the thought. Then, when he realized he could breathe, he laughed again and started swimming as hard as he could toward shore.

Big, splashy steps took him through the shallow water and he headed toward the path into the village, knowing that almost surely he'd in some way have to pay for being late for supper but thinking it was worth it. It hadn't been much of a dive, but at least it wasn't a bottom buster. He laughed. He guessed from the whack he'd heard and the way he'd hurt the splash must have been pretty big. Big enough that anyone who'd heard the noise and turned in time to see the splash would have thought he'd done a bottom-buster.

Hurrying up the sandy path through the willows as fast as his gimpy leg would let him, he took a glance at the mountains, just now starting to turn dark under the setting sun. He'd heard other kids say that if you were late for supper Ogre would send his little Ogres of the Cold to get you. But he'd also heard Togl say that he suspected Ogre had better things to do than worry about little boys being late for supper and, besides, the Ogres of the Cold came down only when somebody got too close to the mountains or Maker or Mother Nature let them come down because someone in the village or in the kingdom had been really bad. Togl had never said what he would do if Togai or Kallo were late for supper—and Togai hoped he wouldn't find out now. One thing he was glad for was that the head fisher's hut was the one closest to the river. If it was on the far side of the village, turtles, he really would be late.

Just short of the last willow he stopped and pressed his hands down the legs of his cutoffs and squeezed the frayed and raggedy edges to get out as much water as he could. He ran his fingers through his pony tail and ran on. Lilu didn't like messy hair.

He jumped over the one step up to the porch and landed almost in the open door.

Thank goodness, Togl was at his usual place at the table—looking toward the fireplace, back to the door. To his right at the table was Kallo, who glanced up at the door with a raised-eyebrow, you're-going-to-catch-it-now look. Across from Kallo sat Lilu—stiff and straight-backed. Her eyes were on a full bowl of fish in the middle of the table, and she had her hands folded in front of her as if to make the point that they had been waiting very patiently.

Putting on his most miserable, sorry-as-can-be look, he went around behind Kallo—on purpose, so Lilu could see him—and sat down.

"You're late," she said. "And *wet*."

"Yes ma'am."

"You know how I worry about you. What were you doing?"

He looked down. He well knew how she worried about him. He shrugged. "Not much."

"That's not much of an answer," Togl said.

Togai looked up. Togl's face, as his words had been, seemed neither chastising nor harsh. Togai could never tell what his father was thinking.

"Was it something important to you?"

"Yessir."

"Important enough to keep us waiting—and did you think about that before you did it?"

Togai swallowed. "Yessir."

Togl nodded. "Then tell your mother you're sorry and don't let it happen again. All right?"

"Yessir." He glanced at Lilu. "I'm sorry."

Lilu gave him a hard look, but before she could say anything, Togl said, "Hungry, Kallo?"

"*Yes, sir!*"

Togl laughed. "Me too. I'll bet this is the best fish on any table in the village tonight."

"Hmpf," Lilu said. "I'll bet it's cold. Probably won't be fit to eat now."

Togl reached for the bowl. "Don't fret. The boys and I will take the top pieces, leave the warm underneath for you. Beside, we eat cold fish at the Festival, and it's always good, isn't it Kallo?"

"Sure is," Kallo said. "But for Festivals I think pickled fish is better." He looked at Lilu. "You taking any this year?"

"Of course," she said. "Other people like it too."

Togl nodded. "Old Exl says you make the best pickled fish he's ever eaten—and he's eaten a lot in his time."

"Did he really say that?" Lilu asked.

"Sure did. Speaking of the Festival, you making a new dress?"

"You know I am. You...I saw that! I saw you wink at Togai and Kallo. You're teasing. You know how much I like making Festival outfits. Even for fish-brainy men who say they don't want one."

"I've never said I didn't want one," Togl said. "I just wondered if you were making new outfits this year. I haven't seen any."

"I'll declare, fisher Togl. Of course you haven't. You never do. You know it's bad luck if anybody but the sewer sees a new outfit until the night just before the Festival." She twisted her hands together. "Ooh. I can't wait till tomorrow night when I can show them to you—and the next morning when you put them on." She reached and tousled Togai's hair. "I'll bet you can't wait either, can you, Little Turtle? You'll probably lie awake all night thinking about the Festival. All those new outfits. The eating and singing..." She glanced at Togl. "...*some* people dancing."

Togai had pulled away. He didn't like having his hair tousled, didn't like being touched, didn't like people thinking they knew what he was thinking. But he didn't say so. He simply shrugged.

"What I like," Togl said, "is coming back and putting notches in the table." He sat a little straighter and looked across the table. "How many you have over there, Togai? Two hands worth? I thought so." He smiled. "So, come Festival night we can add a toe, start you on a foot."

"Maker help us," Lilu said. "How time flies." She leaned and tousled Togai's hair again. "My Little Turtle is growing up."

"I just happened to think," Kallo said, "you won't be able to run in the children's race this Festival, will you? You going to run in the boys' race?"

Togai shrugged. "I dunno. Dilo and Tatl are going to."

"Well, I hope *you* don't," Lilu said.

"Why?" Togai said quickly, sharply—and immediately looked down, sure he'd be scolded.

"I'm afraid it'd be too hard on you. After all, it's all the way around the square, isn't it? And with. . .Well, you understand."

Even as Togai felt the resentment welling in him, he heard Togl say, "Oh, let the boy run if he wants to. You don't need to baby him so much."

As startled as Togai was, he guessed he wasn't near as startled as Lilu seemed to be. She had looked at Togl and opened her mouth as if to speak, then quickly looked down at her bowl.

Togai looked down too. He didn't know what to say or do. He had never before heard either parent say anything to contradict the other, not even in this mild a way. And though he felt a little sorry for Lilu, he was glad that Togl had said what he did. For as long as he could remember, Lilu had babied and worried about her "Little Turtle." Other mothers in the village, both young and old, seemed to feel sorry for him too. Most adults seemed to not know what to say or how to act when around him and would often look the other way when he was near.

Though young children, along with Togl and Kallo, seemed to not care—or notice—he had a short leg, older children certainly did. He well knew that from the names he was called and the teasing he got for such things as wearing long pants on hot summer days. But if he had a choice, he'd take the way boys and girls his age treated him over the way adults did every time. On any given day, the boys and girls soon tired of teasing and let him play with them as if nothing had happened. With adults, the feel-sorry-for demeanor and treatment never went away.

The meal ended in silence, and it wasn't long before Togai and Kallo went to their room and crawled onto their cots. Togai's was under the window, and for a while he lay there looking at the nearly full Festival moon which had their room and the village lit nearly bright as day.

The children's race, he thought, was not so much a race as it was a chance for boys and girls less than eleven Festivals old to have fun. He'd run in it many times. And the more crowded it was the more fun it seemed to be. Bumping into one another, stumbling and giggling and falling, they'd, as best they could, run, walk or toddle across a short open space to get to tables loaded with goodies. Didn't matter that Zap children got to go first in a separate race and could grab the juiciest pieces of melon and biggest pieces of cake. Everybody got something. There were no winners or losers. But the race for boys eleven to thirteen Festivals old, like the one for older boys and the one for men was a real race. The only prize was for first to the finish line.

He spoke into the stillness, "Kallo, do you have to wear shorts to run in the boys' race?" Kallo was three Festivals older and knew lots of things, though not as much as he sometimes thought he did. Though Kallo liked to say he was three Festivals older, because he was born just a few days before a Festival and Togai just a few days after one, Kallo was, in truth, only a handful of days more that two Festivals older.

"No," Kallo said with a yawn. "Why?"

"I was thinking about running in it. Like you said."

"What's shorts got to do with it?"

"You know...If I had to wear shorts..."

"Oh, yeah. Your leg. But what does it matter what your leg looks like if you run fast?"

"I don't know. You think if I tried real hard I could win?"

"No."

Togai propped up on an elbow and glared in Kallo's direction . "Why do you say no? I can run fast when I want to."

"I know. But..."

"You're like everybody else. You think I couldn't do it because of my leg. Well, I always beat Tatl and Dilo in the children's races."

"Oh, shut up and listen, fishbrain. First, you're only—or will be—only eleven Festivals old and you'll be running against some boys that are not only two Festivals older and bigger and stronger but also have probably run in two other Festival races. But the *main* reason I don't think you can win is I don't think *any* Chelk could. No Chelk has ever won a Festival race, far as I know."

"Not ever?"

"Not ever."

"Why not? Chelks can run as fast as Zaps, can't they?"

"Probably. But Zaps get to cheat."

"Cheat?"

"Yeah. They get to start in front—and other things."

"How come they get to start in front?"

"It's like the children's race. It's their race. They get to make the rules."

"Gee. If Zaps get to start in front, I'd have to be really fast to win, wouldn't I?"

"Yep. But it's not just a matter of being fast. You see, if you run, you'll find out that the thirteen-old Zaps will get to start in the very front. Being oldest, they should be the fastest—of the Zaps. Then come the twelve-old Zaps, and behind them the elevens. Last come Chelks, whether eleven, twelve or thirteen makes no difference. Then, when the race starts, the eleven-old Zaps block Chelks who try to pass."

"That's not fair."

"Of course it isn't. But that's why I think you couldn't win—and why the few Chelks who do enter races don't really try. Mostly, they do it to show off, seems to me. They go skipping around the course—prancing, I guess—trying to make people laugh."

"When you ran, did you do it just to show off?"

Kallo yawned. "No. I tried. Really hard. But just once. Right at the start I tried to get past the Zaps, but they crowded me up against the ropes—and some Zap watching the race stuck out his foot and tripped me. I jumped right up. I'd show them, I thought. Caught up real quick and tried to barge through the middle of the pack. But they elbowed and kicked and shoved and tried to stomp my feet with those hard shoes of theirs. Didn't take me long to figure about the only way I'd be able to get past was to jump over them, which I couldn't do of course. So I quit. Haven't tried since. You can have it."

"You mean they're allowed to push and shove—*and* stomp your feet?"

"Yep."

"But that really seems unfair, with them wearing shoes and us barefoot."

"Yep. But remember. They make the rules." He yawned. "I'm sleepy. Good-night, Togai."

Togai tried to imagine what the start might be like. The ropes. People on the outside. Zaprian runners in front of him. Again he turned toward Kallo. "You know, Kallo, I was thinking..."

"Go to sleep, Togai. You think too much."

## CHAPTER 2

# Togai's First Festival Race

The next day, with a morning of trying to help Lilu and stay out of her way as she hurried to get "oh so many things" ready for the Festival—and an afternoon of almost everyone on and around the diving raft getting more and more excited as the afternoon wore on—Togai pretty much forgot about the race. But on his cot that night, with the Festival and the Festival moon just about close enough to touch, he spoke into the stillness. "Kallo, I've been thinking..."

"Uh oh."

"No funning, now. Is there any way you can think of to get by the Zaprians? Surprise them in some way maybe?"

"Gee, I doubt it. The eleven olds know you're back there and that they're supposed to block you...But wait a skip. Maybe you could." Kallo sat up. "Yeah. Colatt ran the race the year before I did. He said all he wanted was to get the apple for the first Chelk, so he just ran along, easy, behind the eleven-old Zaps. He said that when they saw he wasn't trying to pass they stopped looking back and started to run harder, racing each other, trying to catch the older Zaps ahead. So, maybe if you took it easy at first, the eleven-olds in your race might think you weren't trying to race and after a look or two not look back again. Then, if you were fast enough, you might be able to dash by them before they saw you." He lay back and his wood-chip mattress rustled as he wiggled to renestle into it. "Might work. But I doubt it. 'Night, Togai."

Togai curled up on his own mattress, but thoughts of the race wouldn't leave his mind. After a while he said, "Kallo..."

"I know, Togai. You've been thinking. Forget it. Go to sleep."

Togai rolled over, but didn't stop thinking *or* go to sleep. At least, not right away. He looked up at the moon. He guessed there were lots of other kids in the village looking up at the moon and thinking about the Festival. He *knew* that if they were looking out at all they were looking in the direction of the moon and the sea. Not the mountains. Every hut in the village was built with its children's room on the ocean side lest a child come awake and, unlikely as it might be, catch a glimpse of Ogre. Ogre, it was said, rose from behind Round Mountain only in those rare moments when Maker happened to fall asleep. Some seemed to think that the worst that could happen would be that the child would be so terrified by the sight that he or she would never sleep again. Others said that Ogre, annoyed at being seen, would turn the child to stone—or send the Ogres of the Cold down on the whole village in retribution.

Togai had sometimes thought he might slip out some night, hide behind a dune—a place Ogre wouldn't expect a kid to be —and sneak a peek. But not tonight. He didn't want to risk spoiling anything. Tomorrow could be his best Festival ever.

When sleep finally came it seemed his eyes had barely gone shut when he heard Kallo say, "Wake up, Togai," and he looked out and saw a bright horizon streaked red and gold.

He staggered to his feet and reached for his new pants, on the stool at the foot of his cot where Lilu had so carefully placed them. He gave no thought to their being inside out. Chelks had long had to wear their clothes inside out whenever they were in the kingdom. Though he was barely awake and the light in the room was still dim, he thought his clothes were, as Lilu had promised, pretty. One pocket of the basically brown pants was bright red, the other orange. And the two seam flaps, from the light green waistband to the dark blue cuffs, were bright yellow. He thought his new blue shirt, also inside-out, pretty too, with its floppy yellow pocket and bright green collar.

He dressed quickly, and by the time the sun was half up he was well over halfway across the river and was looking down a line of canoes filled with noisy and colorfully-clothed Chelks. Behind them, only a few old canoes littered the bank—and no one was left in Che-lekai.

Togl, as head fisher, had the honor of having in his canoe—along with his family—Old Helu, the village leader. She sat just ahead of Togai and behind Kallo, who was paddling in the bow.

Togl and Kallo let their canoe slow and soon after it glided ashore, the others did. But as eager as all Chelks were to get to the Festival, Kallo was the only one who got out. They all knew that no Chelk should set foot in Zaphyr until the sun was fully up. When Kallo, pants rolled up and taking care to stay in the water, had pulled the canoe as far onto shore as he could, Helu stood, raised her hand and looked downriver to the sun. As she watched the sun creep higher, Chelks in the other canoes turned their heads back and forth in effort to watch her and the sun at the same time. Not until its clinging, gold-droplet tail popped free and a full circle appeared did she drop her hand—and in almost no time the canoes were as empty as the village and Chelks were filling the path-road to the City of Light.

In front was a small herd of small boys walking fast and talking excitedly, but just short of where the path-road passed through a grove of large oaks and widened into a street, they stopped and waited for their families to catch up.

At the last Festival Old Helu had told the villagers she was getting old and slow and that they no longer needed to wait on her to lead them into the city, to just go on in an orderly, quiet way. They did that now, family by family, and if they talked at all, they talked quietly lest they wake some Zaprian who might be sleeping late.

At the entrance to the city's large central square where, except for horse races, all Festival activities were held, Togai and Kallo followed Togl and Lilu as they turned toward "Left Corner." Zaprians had long referred to the side of the river where the Chelks lived as the "The Land of Left" and, in keeping with that, called the Chelks "Lefts" and referred to the lower end of the square, where the Chelks had to eat, dance and go to toilets, as "Left Corner."

As Lilu urged them to hurry so they could have her favorite blanket-spreading spot, Togai saw only a few Zaprians in the square and saw that most of them, as he'd expected, were men setting up booths or in other ways preparing for the Festival. Though it would be a while before the Festival actually started—the race for boys eleven-to-thirteen would be the first event—almost all Chelks wanted to get there early. Some wanted simply to sit and look and enjoy the beauty and richness of the City of Light. Some, but not so many, wanted to get work helping the Zaprians readying for the Festival. Women and girls could help the many and varied food vendors not only put out their goods but in some cases help in the cooking—of breads, muffins, pies, cakes, cookies, and candies. Men and boys could help farm families unload apples and pears, pickles and cheeses, jams and jellies, and jars of honey. The luckier men and boys might find work helping finish the bandstand or stage or helping set up booths for games, shows and for goods to be displayed and sold.

Most of the Chelks who worked at the Festival said they wanted to not just for what they could earn but because most of the Zaprians they worked for seemed kinder and more generous than at any other time. Some attributed that to a fun-time mood. Others said it was because, a long time ago, when King Andar had decreed that Chelks could come to the Festival, he had also decreed that Zaps had to be nice to them.

Kallo had carried the picnic blanket. As soon as he helped Lilu spread it, he asked, "May I go look for a job?"

She looked at Togl, and at his shrug she pulled a shirt and pair of pants from a big fishnet bag and handed them to Kallo. "All right. But I want you to change into last year's outfit first. Don't want you getting your new one dirty like you did last year."

Togai suddenly remembered. Last year Kallo had earned a big juicy pear just by helping a farmer carry a few crates into the square. Neither Tatl nor Dilo had said anything about working at the Festival, and he was pretty sure if Tatl had been planning to, he certainly would have said so.

He looked at Lilu. "May I go too?"

"Oh…I guess so. Your father said you might ask…" She sighed. "…so I brought your last-year's outfit too."

Togai looked at Togl. "Did you really say that?"

Togl laughed. "You doubt your mother? I was about your age

when I did my first Festival work. Makes you feel good to *earn* something on your own, especially the first time. So, when Kallo mentioned the race the other night, and I saw you were thinking about trying it, I thought you might be ready to try work too."

Togai smiled. His father, *head fisher* Togl had just said...

"Don't just stand there with your mouth open, fishhead," Kallo said. "The quicker we get changed and up in the square the better job we get."

About halfway up the square Kallo pointed to a narrow opening between two buildings. "Let's try that street. Lot of farmers park their wagons there to unload."

As they were about to start up the street, Kallo stopped and pointed up the square. "See those men? They're putting up ropes for the race course. They'll leave an opening here till the race starts. The course is almost a circle." He pointed. "Starts up there, just below the king's balcony, curves out, almost to the buildings on that side, then through Left Corner, and up this side—almost against the buildings—and on up and around to finish where it started, right in front of the king's balcony. Because that side over there is a little downhill, this up, you might want to take it easy down the other side. Save yourself."

Togai nodded.

They didn't walk far before Kallo stopped at a wagon where a man and woman were putting apples in a cart. Without looking up the woman said, "You boys lookin' for work or just lookin'?"

"Work, ma'am," Kallo said.

"Expect to be paid?"

"Uh, yes ma'am. Sure."

"Hmpf," the man said. "If the king'd let any horse but his drop apples in the square we'd drive our wagon out there, wouldn't need help."

"How about a apple apiece, two altogether, for the whole load?" the woman said.

Togai smiled. If she meant horse apples, it didn't sound like too good a deal."

"Uh, I..." Kallo glanced up the street at the many wagons along it.

"Okay," the man said. "An apple between you, *each* cart load?"

Kallo gave Togai a glance and nodded. "Agreed."

"You boys better be worth it. Now come here, I'll show you how. Reach in pick up two apples and place them in the cart..."

As she talked, Togai listened and looked. At first he thought her blue eyes and pale skin gave her a lifeless, dead-fish look, but he soon thought the look as cold and heartless, void of feeling.

"...very gently. Bruised apples don't sell. So, any load, you drop two apples and you get nothing for that load. Drop three, and I start taking apples away."

Togai didn't want to work for her anyway. He looked at Kallo. "That's not a good deal. Let's..."

"Wait!" The woman turned her cold look toward Togai. "You sure are uppity for a little kid, especially one from Left." She half turned toward Kallo. "Drop too many apples and I'll give you one apple each and send you away? Agreed?"

Kallo glanced at Togai then nodded. "Agreed. We'll do it."

Togai spotted a second cart beside the wagon and started toward it. "No, no," the woman said. "One cart at a time. When the first is full," she nodded at Kallo, "you pull it out to the square. My husband will go with you to show you our bin and to watch you unload. I'll stay here with your little brother—I guess that's what he is—and watch him while he loads the second cart, then come with him out to the square and watch him unload. One of us'll be with you all the time, so you can forget any thoughts you've had about stealin' or eatin' apples when we aren't lookin'."

Togai's head jerked around. "Chelks don't..."

Kallo's kick came hard and swift, but the words were soft. "Shhh. Get to work."

They tried to work quickly, but with the woman watching closely and almost constantly telling them to slow down, to be careful and not bruise the apples, the cart filled slowly.

Togai began worrying about getting the entire wagon load out to the square in time for the race, so was glad when Kallo turned to the man and said, "Okay. Cart's full. I'm ready."

"Oh, no," the woman said. "It's barely up to the top. Can't fool me. You're tryin' to make as many loads as you can so you can get more apples. Oh, no. Pile 'em up."

"But if we do that," Togai said, "we'll have to go really slow to keep them from falling out."

"I'll tie a piece of burlap over the top so they can't fall out," she said. "But you'll still have to go slow, so the cart won't bounce on the cobblestones and bruise the apples."

Kallo looked at Togai. "Don't worry. If we're not done in time for the race I'll finish by myself."

As Togai had feared, once the woman had him—the uppity little kid—alone, her nagging became even worse. He barely managed to get his cart loaded before Kallo and the man returned—and her harassment continued to the bin and through the unloading. Don't bounce the cart. Don't drop. Don't bruise. Don't, don't, don't...And though he rushed as much as she'd let him, he didn't get the cart unloaded before Kallo and the man returned to the bin.

Going back to the wagon Togai saw the upper end of the square was starting to fill with Zaprians and he again worried about time, but he found fun in hurrying over the cobblestones, making the empty cart bounce and imagining the woman was in it. During his second and third loads the square filled steadily and he became more and more worried. So he was pleased when he got back to the wagon for his fourth load and saw there were enough apples for only half a load or so. He hurried and was back to the bin before Kallo's cart was empty.

As Togai stepped up to help Kallo unload, Kallo said, "You hear the cheer?"

"No."

"The king's here. Came out on the balcony and waved. Race should start soon."

They finished unloading with Togai's putting the last apple in place with great, exaggerated care. Kallo smiled broadly, turned to the man and woman and said, "There. Done."

Togai had from time to time seen the woman pick out small apples and put them in a box beside the bin. Not to be sold, he guessed. She now reached into the box, counted out some, and handed them to Kallo.

Kallo's face reddened. He held out the apples, two in one hand, three in the other. "But..."

"We made *eight* loads," Togai said. "You owe us three more apples. *Good* ones."

"No," she said. "You made only..."

The man spoke up. "I keep tellin' you, Emona, these people can count."

"Oh, all right," she said, and reached for the box of small apples. "But only two more. That last load your little brother made wasn't a full one."

"It was still a load," Togai said. "As much as could be."

"Yes," she said, "but..."

"Oh, for Maker's sake, Emona," the man said. He gave Togai a big apple. "Here. Go."

"Yes," she said, "and good riddance."

As they hurried away, Togai muttered, "You going to let them get away with that? Paying us with *little* apples?"

"Yes. With somebody like her, better keep your mouth shut. You might wind up with nothing."

"Well, I..."

Loud and resonant words came floating down through the square, "Fiirrssttt caalll for boys race. Fiirrsstt call for boys eeeleven-to-thirrrteeeen fessstivals old."

"Oh, oh. Time for you to go," Kallo said. He slid the small apples inside his shirt and took the big one from Togai. "Don't worry about the apples," he laughed, "I'll keep yours safe and sound. *Both* of them."

"That'd be funny another time, Kallo. But right now I'm worried abut the race. So, quick. Where do I go? What do I do?"

Kallo pointed. "Start line's at the top of the square, but with so many people between here and there, simpler to just go over to the course and follow the ropes around. No way you can miss the start line, just below the royal balcony, runners milling around. Then, just do what the starter says. He'll have a yellow armband. Better get going, now. Sometimes they're slow in starting, sometimes fast. Remember now, this is your first race. Take it easy. Who knows? You might not even be able to run the whole way."

Oh, yes I will, Togai thought. Yes I will.

As Kallo suggested, Togai went to the side of the square to follow the course up and almost immediately wished he hadn't. Zaprians lining the course were giving him curious, puzzled looks. Some stared, gawked, and he tried hard not to limp. In the bend toward the start/finish line, the crowd seemed to close in and he felt hot, sick, felt he might throw up. He was about to turn back when he saw Dilo and Tatl—a few steps back of the last of the Zap runners—and he hurried on.

As he came up, he was struck by how long and slender the Zaps' legs were. And how pale. A near sickly pale. But at least each one had two good legs, two that matched.

Dilo looked at him and nudged Tatl. "I told you he'd be here."

"Bet that really worries the Zaps."

"Laassstt caall for fiirrsstt boys' race. Laasst call for first boys' race. First call for secconndd. Fiirrsstt caall for seccconndd."

A man wearing a yellow armband standing near the front of the pack raised his hand high, and with a look back along the spread of runners said, "Give me your attention." When he spotted Togai, he laughed and dropped his hand. He laughed again, gave a disbelieving shake of his head and said very loudly, "I know you boys don't worry much about those *runners* from Left, but I think I should warn you. This year there's three of those ponytails back there—and one of 'em's wearin' long pants." At this, a loud laugh went up. "Pants inside out, of course," the starter said, and the laughter got even louder.

Togai wanted to find a hole to crawl in. All the laughter had seemed to come from the Zaprians crowded in behind the course ropes in both directions. As far as he could tell, only two runners even bothered to look back, and they were in the group of four just ahead of him. Kallo must have been right, he thought. None of the runners toward the front seemed to care there were Chelks behind them.

The starter again raised a hand high and said, "Okay. Listen up." He held out a big cow bell. "When I ring this bell, go! Once around the square. First one back to the starting line wins. Any questions?"

No one said anything.

*Clang Clang Clang* and "Go!" came at the same time, and all the Zap runners took off.

Togai had the urge to sprint after them, to quickly pass a few Zaps, if nothing else, to show those people who laughed—and the starter especially—that a "ponytail in long pants" could indeed run. Fast. But he wanted even more to show Kallo he could run the whole way. So, he'd use Kallo's advice to prove Kallo wrong. The best way to prove he could run the whole way and run fast? Togai smiled. Win the race.

Almost exactly as Kallo had predicted, one of the Zaps in the group just ahead of Togai glanced back and said to the others, "The only Left that's even close is..." His head snapped back and he took a longer look. "Goodness. It's the one in long pants and he's *limping*." He laughed. "No need to worry about him. Let's go." And all four looked ahead and began to speed up.

This was the chance Kallo had said to look for!

Togai began to sprint, and even with Zaprians in the crowd yelling warnings he was beside the four before they knew it. The two outside ones tried to get in front of him, but one stumbled over the other's feet and Togai sped past. The leather shoes seemed to make the Zaps slow and clumsy. In his bare feet he felt light and free, elated. He ran on, hard, determined to catch the next group of runners no more than two canoe lengths away. He'd show Kallo. He'd show Tatl. He'd show them all.

Warnings from the crowd and the runners Togai had passed caused the runners just ahead to look back. To his surprise, they didn't slow at all, just kept running. Togai took that to mean they were more interested in beating each other than slowing him down. Encouraged by that, he tried to go faster. But his breath was coming harder, and his pants were beginning to stick to his getting-wet-with-sweat legs.

By the time he was a fourth of the way around the course, he knew he couldn't win. He was tiring, and his left leg was beginning to hurt. A lot. He hadn't counted on the extra strain being put on it by the curve of the course. Just to go straight, even at an easy run, he had to put extra pressure on his left leg. To go fast and turn right both was a real effort. Sharp pains were jabbing him in the side and his left leg and left foot were beginning to cramp. He knew he couldn't keep going, at least not at the same pace, and though he knew Kallo and other Chelks were just ahead in Left Corner, he began to slow.

Kallo had seemed ready to clap and cheer him on, but now all he heard from his brother was a weak, "Hang on." From other Chelks he heard nothing. Maybe they weren't even watching.

Just after that, the Zaprians he had passed began to pass, and each one either tried to elbow him or stomped at his feet—or both. Somewhere past halfway he slowed to a walk, and as he did he heard snickers. He looked for a place to duck under the ropes and get off the course, but the only people he saw were Zaprians, and not one had a friendly face. Togai wanted to cry, but he was ashamed to with people watching, so he bit his lip and kept walking. Every step or two he'd glance back, and when he saw Tatl and Dilo coming—skipping and laughing—he tried to walk faster. But they soon caught up. They stopped laughing.

"Want us to walk with you?" Dilo asked.

"Yeah, *walk*," said Tatl.

Togai gave Tatl a sharp look, then glanced at Dilo. "Thanks, but no. Go on."

As they again picked up their skipping—and laughing—Togai forced himself into a jog and somehow managed to stay not far behind them all the way to the finish.

When he got back to Left Corner, Kallo tried to console him. He told Kallo he didn't need consoling, what he needed was a stronger left leg.

CHAPTER 3

# Old Zoltai

The rest of the day was misery for Togai. He didn't want to walk around the Festival alone because he was afraid Zaprians would remember him and laugh at him. He didn't want to do things with Tatl and Dilo because Tatl was sure to tease him. He didn't want to spend time in Left Corner because, other than Kallo, Togl and Lilu, any Chelk who seemed to know he'd been in the race didn't seem to care how he felt—and Lilu seemed to care only that all those people saw her Little Turtle in last year's outfit and he'd made himself sick running too hard and wouldn't eat the picnic food she'd worked so hard on. He wanted to tell her what really made him sick was her calling him Little Turtle and treating him like a baby, but he didn't.

He was glad when he saw the Chelks packing their things and hurrying toward the river so they could all be out of Zaphyr by sundown. He was glad because he wanted to get away from people, all people, and as soon as he was home and had changed from his Festival clothes, he left and headed out through the scrub in the direction of the mountains. He knew he'd have to be back by dark because tomorrow was a Praise Maker Day—and the once-a-year Growing-Up Day too. But he didn't mind. It'd also be his bedtime and he'd not have to talk to anybody.

Alone now, he felt the day's pent-in emotions start to rise, as if wanting to be let loose, and Togai began to run. He turned behind a small dune and, unable to see well in the dim light with his eyes filling with tears, he stumbled and fell. He began to sob, and the emotion flowed from him like water would from a broken barrel. Soon, though, he was only sniffing, and as he rolled to one side and wiped his nose on the back of his hand, he was startled by a voice.

"Great ax handles, boy, you sound like you lost your best friend."

Togai jumped to his feet. Someone had seen him, heard him cry. But who? Where?

In a frantic turn of his head he saw, sitting about halfway up the dune, Old Zoltai. Once head woodcutter, Old Zoltai was now one of the village Fire Keepers—and smoke from his big, Fire-Keeper pipe curled around his head.

Togai sniffed. "Oh, Old Zoltai. It's you. What are you doing out here?"

"Enjoying the quiet—till you came along."

Zoltai was known for being cantankerous. A bit odd too.

"Sorry," Togai said. I'll leave."

But before he could turn: "Saw you run today."

"Really? I...I didn't run near as well as I wanted to. Wanted to run better, but..." He paused. He hoped Old Zoltai would say something nice. But when no words came, he turned to leave. Zoltai wasn't known for being very talkative either.

"I was thinking," Zoltai said, and Togai stopped, "that if maybe you came out here to a dune, ran around it with your short leg on the downhill side, it might get stronger. Another thought I had was, seems like you might be feelin' a little sorry for yourself, cause of what happened. Now, I know I got no business choppin' into your tree, but..."

"Save your words," Togai said. "I've heard it all before. Too many times. Shouldn't feel sorry for myself, should just be grateful to Maker to be alive. Blah. Blah. Blah. Truth is, you probably think I'm a pathetic cripple. Well, I..." Togai suddenly stopped and bit his lip. Oh, what had he done? All Chelk youngsters were to be respectful to their elders. *Always.* And if Old Zoltai told Togl or Lilu what their second-born son had just said, well, that second-born son might wish he'd never been born.

As Togai was wondering what he could possibly say to get himself out of this mess, he heard Lilu's call, "To-gai! To-gai!"

"I better go now, uh, sir." And with an apologetic look at the old man, which he doubted could be seen in the near darkness, he ran off toward the village.

As Togai's footfalls faded, Zoltai took a long pull on his pipe and let the smoke out so slowly he could feel it drifting around his cheeks and up through his eyebrows. He picked his cane up from the sand and leaned heavily on it while getting to his feet. He leaned on it often coming down the steep dune, but once he was on level ground his gimpy steps gathered speed. He didn't want to offend Maker by being out after dark, or worse, be caught by the Avenging Witch.

For as long as Togai could remember, he had come awake on Growing-Up Day in a good mood, looking past the dull ceremonies of the morning to an afternoon of visiting and eating and playing. But this Growing-Up morning he awoke with concern. He quickly put on his new Festival outfit and, though he had little appetite, hurried out to sit down with the others for their usual skimpy, Growing-Up Day breakfast. He dreaded the walk to the river where the ceremonies would start, for he was sure that somewhere along the way Old Zoltai would either be waiting or would catch up to tell Togl and Lilu what had happened. But he had barely reached for his bowl when Lilu leaned to look past Togl and out the door. "Turtles," she said, "there goes Old Zoltai already. I think he's the first one to the river every Growing-Up Day—and most Praise Maker Days too."

Togai froze. Uh oh. Zoltai *would* be waiting. No doubt about it. But before he could start to worry, Togl said, "Well, with his leg the way it is, he needs an early start."

Togai quickly leaned to look past Togl—and when he saw Old Zoltai limping, cane in hand, the words *pathetic cripple* rang in his head. Why, oh why had he used the word "pathetic"? He'd been feeling so sorry for himself he'd forgotten about Old Zoltai's leg, about the accident. Great turtles! The old man had tried to be nice to him and he'd responded with surl and insult.

With barely a glance at either Lilu or Togl—he seemed to be talking to the corner of the table between them—Togai, said, "Be okay if I take a piece of Festival bread and leave? I want to be at the river when Tatl and Dilo get there."

Togl shrugged.

Lilu nodded. "Okay. Just don't get dirty before the ceremony starts."

"I won't," he said and took a torn hunk of bread. His first impulse was to hurry, but he didn't want to arouse suspicion. What was more, he needed time to think of what to say.

Togai had heard the story many times. Zoltai's leg had been crushed when Zoltai, head woodcutter at the time, had run to push a young woodcutter from the path of a falling tree and had himself been hit. Everyone said it was only because Maker was watching over him that Zoltai wasn't killed or didn't die afterward.

Togai shook his head. Why was he always feeling sorry for himself because he had a little leg and couldn't run like other boys? Old Zoltai had been through a lot more and limped for a much longer time, and he didn't seem to feel sorry for himself. Was there a lesson there?

As he ran up beside Old Zoltai, he slowed. "Could I talk to you, sir? Please."

Old Zoltai, startled it seemed, turned to look, but when he saw it was Togai his look hardened and he hurried on toward the river, his steps more resolute and less uneven than before.

Togai knew there'd be no talk between them, not this day, but as he came to a stop he called ahead, "Are you going to tell my father?"

Zoltai didn't hesitate—or slow or look back. "No!"

CHAPTER 4

# Togai Runs

Togai's relief barely lasted through the Growing-Up ceremonies. For the rest of that day and the next two, he worried that Old Zoltai might change his mind and tell Togl. Not until the third day had passed did he begin to believe that Old Zoltai was, as Togl liked to say every Chelk was, an honorable person true to his word. With this added respect for Old Zoltai and the soreness gone from his legs, he decided to jog into the scrub, somewhere well away from the village, and—it was the least he could do—give the old woodcutter's run-around-a-dune idea a try.

At first he ran the way Old Zoltai suggested, but he soon found that running with his short, left leg on the downhill side actually put most of his weight on the right leg and made it do most of the work. So he turned and ran with his left leg on the uphill side, and was elated. His left leg was now doing more work than it ever had. This was it! This was the way for him to make his leg stronger, become a better runner, beat the Zaps!

That night, with their room lit by the just-risen nearly full moon, he began telling Kallo what he'd done, but he'd barely started when Kallo sat up and looked at him. "You were *practicing* running?"

"Sure. Why not?"

"I don't know. It seems like a race is supposed to see who's the best natural runner. So, practice seems like, well, like cheating."

"Didn't you say the Zaps got to cheat by starting in front and that wasn't fair?"

"Yeah."

"Well, I don't think it's fair either. So why would it be so bad if *I* cheated a little by trying to make my leg stronger?"

Kallo sighed and lay back. "I guess it wouldn't. I just never heard of such."

"Do you think Zaps practice?"

"Now how could I possibly know that, Togai? Don't you ever run out of questions? Go to sleep."

"All right, but do *you* think it's fair I have to race people with two good legs?"

"Not really. But what are you going to do? Get 'em to have a race for people with a short leg? You'd almost surely win that. You'd be the only one in it."

"Not funny. But come on, now. You think it would be bad, be cheating, if I tried to make my left leg stronger?"

"Oh, I guess not." After a moment Kallo sighed and added, "You know, Togai, maybe sometimes you don't think too much."

Almost every afternoon after that, after morning chores and lunch, Togai would go out to the dune and run around it. But he also spent time running on level ground because he knew that was how he'd have to run in the race.

He hoped no one, especially Tatl, would notice when he showed up late for afternoon games or was hot and sweaty when he got there. But it was hard to keep a secret around such a small village, and it wasn't long before he was being called new names. But "Sidehill" and "Sand Dune" were a lot better than "Stick Leg" and "Birdleg"—and he kept running.

His right leg grew noticeably larger, as did the *upper* part of the left. But no matter how many times he ran around the dune, the lower part of the left stayed small and thin. But in no way did Kallo make fun of Togai. Now and then he would even challenge Togai to a race, to test and encourage him.

One day when they had gone to gather firewood, Kallo pointed ahead and said, "Race you to that tree," and without another word took off running. Togai had learned early on that his stronger right leg made him want to curve to the left, especially when he ran, and by now it was quite natural for him to aim to the right of whatever he wanted to run to so his tendency to curve would get him there with less strain on his legs, especially his left. So, as Kallo took off straight toward the tree, Togai aimed a little to the right of it and started running. As he saw that once again Kallo was going to beat him to whatever they were racing for, he realized he was going to have to get a lot stronger and faster to have any chance of winning the Festival race—and an idea suddenly hit him.

The idea was so stunning that it knocked everything else from his brain and he forgot he was running—and stumbled and almost fell. *Yes!* Yes, he could win the Festival race. If he could get fast enough. If he had the nerve. If there was a certain rule missing.

From then on, he practiced differently. He still ran some on the dune, but more and more he simply ran on the flat, in his natural, curving way, the way he had run when he raced Kallo to the tree. A disappointment was he didn't seem to get much faster, but to his surprise—could he be sure?—he seemed to be able to go farther and farther before he tired or ran out of breath.

One day when he came in from running Lilu looked at him and said, "Goodness, Togai, you're soaked with sweat." She sighed and shook her head. "Those long pants must be so hot, and you try so hard. Would...would you like for me to cut off some old pants, make you some shorts for the race?" She smiled brightly. "I could make them pretty."

Togai shook his head. He couldn't stand the thought of a square full of people gawking at him.

Kallo spoke up. "You *could* run a lot faster."

Togai glared. "I know that."

"And you'd have a lot better chance to..."

"I know. I know. But...I don't want to talk about it any more." He turned and stomped out, as best he could stomp, with a *CLOMP, kelunk, CLOMP, kelunk, CLOMP, kelunk.* He heard Kallo snicker. When he was well away from the hut, he snickered too. He wasn't good at stomping.

That night, as soon as Lilu had given him and Kallo their good-night kisses and left the room, Togai slid as far as he could to the head of his cot to take advantage of what little breeze wafted through the window. On warm nights like tonight, he wished their window opened toward the mountains and their generally cooler breezes. But older Chelks said that would put him at mercy of the Ogres. He often wished he didn't have to listen to elders, do what they said. Listening to them had a way of spoiling fun things.

He sighed and looked up at the stars. He knew they had come up from the Far Edge and would move across the sky to disappear behind the Mountains of the Cold—and go on down under the earth and come up again. Some said that Maker had put in stars because He wanted to add sparkle to the night sky. Others said the stars were from when Maker one night, angry with Himself for what He had done to Ogre, threw the moon against the mountains and little pieces went everywhere. When His ire was gone, He tried to collect the widely scattered pieces so He could put the moon back together. He soon decided though that it'd be less work to make a new one, so He did. Besides, He kind of liked the little lights.

Togai heard a noise, and when he caught a glimpse of someone in the doorway he quickly closed his eyes and pretended to be asleep. After a light footstep came the sound of a chair scraping the floor. He peered through a slit in one eye and saw Togl sitting down near the foot of the cot. Togai closed both eyes tight. What had he done wrong? What did Togl want? He lay still, afraid to breathe. Was Togl saying something? He strained to hear.

"Legs? Legs? You awake?" Togl barely whispered.

Turtles! Togai thought. Is my father, the head fisher, talking to my legs? He'd heard that his father could talk to fish, but to legs?

"I just wanted to ask how things were with you two," Togl said, again in a voice Togai could barely hear. After a moment or two of silence, Togl said, "Yeah, I agree. If a boy makes you run every day no matter how hot it is, he ought to be grateful enough to suffer a little embarrassment to make it easier on you."

Togai again opened an eye a slit. Togl was leaning forward as if listening intently. "Yeah, that's right." He nodded. "You could probably win if he was wearing shorts...What? Yeah, I'm tired too. Good night."

When Togl had left the room, Togai peeked down at his legs. Could they talk? Surely not. They couldn't even think, could they?

As soon as he was up the next morning and could talk to her without anyone else hearing, Togai said to Lilu, "Would you still be willing to make some running shorts for me?"

"Of course, Little Turtle," she said, and gave him a hug. "Of course."

"And some long pants big enough to wear over the shorts?"

"Why? I can carry the shorts for you in a bag. You can change before the race."

"I...I'd have to change in a toilet. And since the only toilets for us to use are in Left Corner, I...I'd have to walk all the way up the square..." He bit his lip. "...with all those people..."

She pulled him close. "My, dear, dear Little Turtle. Don't worry. You'll have your big pants—dyed extra pretty."

## CHAPTER 5

# Togai's Twelfth Festival of Kings

When Togai saw touches of gold and red tinting the eastern sky, he smiled. At last, it was here. Festival Day. He guessed that many Chelk youngsters had, as he had, often been awake during the night, looking for some sign of the sun and thinking about what the day would bring. But he'd not, as most probably did, thought about clothes or cookies or dancers or singers or walnut-honey candy. He'd thought about the race.

Slowly, so his cot wouldn't squeak or his wood-chip mattress rustle, he rolled over and peeked at Kallo, still asleep little more than an arm's length away. Good. He wanted to be fully dressed and ready to go when Kallo woke up. Kallo had said they could get a better job than last year if they got into the square earlier. Togai had the idea that, if Lilu would let them they could put their work clothes on underneath their Festival clothes and save a lot of time changing. For once Kallo seemed to think his little brother had a good idea. Togai now sat up, quietly, carefully, lowered his feet to the floor and stood.

Though Lilu had made his new pants big enough to go over his running shorts, he had to tug to get them up over his old pants. Lilu had said she'd dye them "extra pretty," and she had. One of the inside-out pockets was bright yellow, the other bright blue. The exposed seam flaps, down both sides, from the dark red waist band to the dark blue cuffs, were a vivid green.

As soon as he was dressed he hurried outside. The sun was already hitting the mountains, giving them a soft and yellow glow. In this light, even the Horns of the Ogres looked soft and non-threatening. It was going to be a good day.

As soon as their picnic blanket was spread in Left Corner, Togai and Kallo, with Togl laughing and Lilu protesting, pulled off their new clothes and hurried away.

"I want to be back with plenty of time to change for the race," Togai said, "so I hope we find something that doesn't take as long as that apple job last year."

Kallo laughed. "Yeah. And with somebody a lot nicer than that Emona apple woman. I guess she hadn't heard old King Andar said the Zaps were supposed to be nice to us." He pointed toward the upper end of the square. "Let's try the big bandstand. I heard that most of the work is done the night before but that the pay for any work that's left is good. I think we're ahead of everybody else, but let's hurry."

And with that, they began to run.

A gruff, burly man looked them up and down. "Yeah, there's some work to be done on the floor, yet, so..." He glanced at the stage. "How about two tokens apiece—for caramel apples—to hand up boards when the carpenters need 'em?"

Quickly, almost eagerly, Kallo said, "We'll do it."

Seeing Togai's puzzled look, he whispered, "Tokens are what Zaps themselves get paid for work. When the Festival starts you can take yours to a booth and trade 'em in for a couple of caramel apples."

Togai still wasn't all that sure about working for "tokens," but it didn't really matter. He could go back and tell Lilu and Togl he'd helped build the main stage!

As Togai walked and carried and handed, he kept thinking about what it would be like to be a performer on the stage, a juggler or an acrobat, and have people watch. Even better would be to be up there as race winner and hear people cheer.

Not until the last board was laid and the carpenters were leaving did the burly boss give Togai and Kallo their tokens. As the man walked away, Kallo said, "Let's go. I'm getting hungry."

"Uh, no. You go on. I think I'll stay up here awhile."

"Hmmm. Not much chance of another job now—and I thought you wanted to have plenty of time to change."

"Oh, I've got enough time. If I go back now I'll want to eat. Better not. Not before the race."

"Good thinking," Kallo said. "I'm glad I'm not racing. I'd rather eat!" And with a laugh he turned and was soon running toward Left Corner.

Turning slowly, nonchalantly, Togai looked for Zaprians. There were some at work on booths down past the middle of the square, some farmers hurrying back and forth with carts, and some musicians off to one side just starting to practice. None of them will ever notice me, he thought. And he eased over to the stage and went up its steps.

The stage, not much higher than his head, hadn't seemed high at all when he was handing up boards. Now, on it, it seemed really high. You can see everything and everybody from up here. What's better, they can see you! He was tempted to wave toward Left Corner and yell. But better not, he thought. Best to be quiet, not attract attention, just enjoy the view, look around.

He turned and saw that the stage was set directly in front of, and not far from, the Royal Balcony. Of course. So the king could have a good view. Or was it? Maybe it was the performers who wanted it there—in hope the king would watch.

"Hey! You! What are you doing up here?"

Togai turned quickly. One of the carpenters who had worked on the stage was coming up the steps. He looked directly at Togai. "I said, what are you doing up here?"

"Nothing, sir. Just looking."

"I think I left my hammer. You take it?"

Togai trembled. The man had eyes just like Emona. "No, sir. I didn't take it." The man took Togai by the shoulders, looked him up and down, and turned him around. "Hmmm. Guess you didn't." He snorted. "With your pockets inside-out, skinny as you are, not much place to hide anything. Especially a hammer. Now get off the stage."

When he was about halfway to the steps Togai heard the man call out, "And don't come up here again. Don't you know? Lefts aren't allowed on the stage."

Togai stopped and looked back. "Not even if I win the race?"

The man laughed and pointed. "You? A Left? Win? With a foot like that?"

CHAPTER 6

# The Race

As soon as Togai was back to the family blanket in Left Corner, he took his Festival outfit and running shorts to a toilet and changed, making sure he got his tokens deep into the inside-out pocket on his shirt. When he came back, Lilu said, "What'll you do with your new clothes when you pull them off? You just can't leave them lying on the ground somewhere. They might get stepped on—or taken."

"I'll take care of them," Kallo said. "I want to go with him anyway."

"Good." She wagged a finger at Togai. "And you. You find some place to hide to change."

Togl, Kallo and Togai all three laughed, but Togai had the thought that his mother needn't worry. The last thing he wanted to do was pull down his pants in front of a bunch of Zaps.

Togai was surprised at the change that had taken place in the short time he had been gone. Zaprians were now streaming in, talking and laughing and jostling in a friendly way for the few generally shady places around the edges of the square and for, though sun-exposed, places next to the bandstand, stage, and dance areas.

Kallo stopped to watch some acrobats warming up. Togai did too, but only for a few moments. He needed to find a place to change and went on slowly, casting glances here and there. When he spotted the puppet booth, off to itself and seemingly deserted, he looked back at Kallo, pointed to the booth and jogged toward it. Though there was a curtain across the back, it hung open enough that he could see there was no one inside. Not even any puppets. He looked around. There was no one near, no one watching.

Just as he was wondering if he should go in, he heard, "Fiirrsstt caall for boys race. Fiirrsstt call for boys..."

He couldn't wait. He ducked into the back of the booth and pulled the curtain shut.

He heard Kallo run up. "Get out of there! You can't..."

"Shhh," Togai said. "Someone might hear you. I've already got my shirt off, and..." He grunted. "There! My pants too. Anybody watching?"

"No."

"Good," Togai said and quickly crawled out and handed Kallo his clothes.

"You want my lucky scorn rock?" Kallo asked, and held out a glossy gray stone.

"No," Togai said. He'd agreed with Kallo. Wearing shorts would help him run faster. Carrying a rock, even one that was supposed to be lucky, wouldn't.

"I better go now. Where'll you be after the race?"

"I don't know. Stay somewhere around the finish line. I'll find you. Okay?"

Togai nodded and jogged off toward the edge of the square. He was glad there weren't many people here, near the middle of the course, to see him in what he felt was his near-nakedness. There'd be Zaps enough to gawk—maybe ridicule—up near the starting line.

Once on the course he jogged up to where he could see runners milling around, but since none of them were Tatl or Dilo, and since the second call had just been sounded, he turned and started back the way he had come. A little bit of warming up might help. He ran fast for a little ways, stopped and jogged back around the curve, this time lifting his knees extra high.

A man and woman were watching him. Just as he passed he heard her say, "He's the first Left I ever saw doing warm up stuff. You think he actually be thinking about winning?"

The man snorted. "Don't be ridiculous. With that leg and no shoes?"

Togai pretended not to hear. This wasn't the first time today he'd heard someone scoff at the idea of his winning. The Zaps wouldn't think it was so funny if he did win. And he just might if his plan worked. But right at that moment a tall lanky Zap broke away from the front of the milling Zap runners and sprinted out along the outer rope. Togai watched the runner slow down, turn and come sprinting back, knees coming high, long legs working smoothly, almost effort- lessly it seemed.

Turtles! Togai thought. He looks serious, and good. But so am I. I know it. Still, maybe I ought to do some more warm up.

But no sooner had he turned and started to sprint back around the turn than he heard, "Thirrdd and fiinnaall call for fiirrsstt boys' race. Thiirrdd and fiinnall caall"—and he came to a stop and walked back toward the start-finish line.

A man Togai recognized as the starter from last year slipped under the outside rope and said, "Sorry we're runnin' late, boys. We'll try to catch up." He took a couple of steps to a wiggly chalk mark and pointed down to it. "Okay, thirteen-olds. Line up here, just behind the line."

The slender Zap Togai had been watching was quickly there, first to the line.

"Good, good. No pushing now. Two deep if need be. Now the twelves. Fine. Good. Now the elevens. All right. Good. And one Left?" He looked past Togai. "No. We'll have three."

Togai turned and saw Dilo and Tatl skipping toward the line. He shook his head. Clowns. Just clowns.

The starter raised one hand high in the air, held up a cow bell in the other. "When I ring the bell, go! One time around the square. First one back here to the starting line wins. Any questions?"

Togai held up a hand. He trembled all over. This was the mo- ment he had been waiting for.

The man sighed and lowered his hands. "Yes? What is it?"

"The race is to see who can get around the square fastest?"

The man shook his head and, with what seemed to Togai a gen- uine amused smile, said, "Well it's certainly not to see who can get around slowest."

Togai heard laughter in the crowd. The boys in front of him looked back, puzzled, as if to ask, "You serious?"

Togai looked at the starter. "So, the race is simply to go around the square, one time?"

This time the man sighed, impatient. "Yes, son. All boys' races are just one lap. It's not two laps until you get to be a man—and for you that might be a long time."

Titters went through the crowd.

Laugh, Togai thought. I can outrun any of you. No matter how many laps around the square.

The starter held up his hand. "Oh. I almost forgot." He looked up, at the Royal Balcony, Togai assumed. "With a plea for Maker's blessing and in the name of the King..." He held the cow bell high over his head. "Runners ready?"

"Ready," some of the Zaprian runners called out, and as they leaned forward, so did Togai.

*Clang! Clang! Clang!* came the sound, and the runners were off! Togai's first step was almost a jump, and he quickly veered to the outside. But he had no intention of trying to pass the Zaps just ahead of him. As soon as he had taken one full step across the starting line, he turned and started back the other way.

The starter's mouth dropped open, but no words came. And as did Dilo and Tatl, Zaps behind the ropes stared in disbelief. One called out, "Stupid Left. Don't you know which way to run?"

But Togai cared about none of that. He was thinking about his plan. The starter had clearly said that the first one to go around the square and get back to the starting line was the winner. The point was, he hadn't said which way to run.

Togai felt good, confident. Going this way, with the course's natural turn to the left and all the training he had done, he was running much more smoothly and faster than he had last year.

And though he was running fast, the story that a Left was headed the wrong way was spreading even faster.

He heard several calls of "Here he comes! Here he comes!" and a woman said, "Goodness! He really is running the wrong way." Such calls or comments he didn't mind. He didn't like calls of "Dumb Left!" and "Horse Tail!" But he couldn't think about what people thought or yelled. He had to concentrate on running, on trying to keep a smooth and measured stride, to not run too hard early in the race, save something for the end.

Though people lined the course, Togai could easily tell from the two and three-story buildings where the corners were and he knew from last year's race that halfway was at the lowest part of the course's curve, where it passed under a huge wooden shoe hung high from a building. He wanted to get to halfway mark before the Zaps did, but as he neared the building three of them suddenly appeared right in front of him, led by the one he had watched warm up. Though they were startled and their steps faltered, Togai was the one who swerved.

He was disappointed and was tempted to start running harder right away, but they had seemed more out of breath than he, seemed to be laboring more. Had the main benefit of his practice running been to make him stronger? Could it be that the Zaps were tiring faster than he was and if he just kept pushing he could make it to the finish line first? Buoyed by that hope, but still mindful of needing to be strong at the end, he tried to go a little faster.

Silence greeted him in Left Corner. Only a few Chelks even looked up. Was it their usual indifference to the race, Togai wondered, or shame of him? As soon as the last of the Zaps were past he moved back toward the inside rope but looked ahead for Tatl and Dilo. Be terrible to collide with one of his friends and be knocked from the race.

About the time he saw them he knew he was back in the Zaprian part of the crowd. Even if he couldn't have seen the pale faces, he would have known from the big and flowery hats. Ever since King Andar's law about Lefts not being allowed to wear hats, Zaprian women had taken special delight in wearing the biggest, gaudiest hats they could make or buy. But big as the hats were, Togai could still look over them and see the Royal Balcony above the start/finish line. Three people were on it now, but that thought barely registered in his mind. The balcony marked the end of his journey. The place where he could stop and rest, where he'd find victory or failure.

Had Togai looked, he might have been able to tell that the people on the balcony were King Praidar, Princess Prandina, and the young Prince Zarian. Though they'd had breakfast in Pran Castle, the carriage ride into town had been a long one, and the king was just sitting down to a snack when the cow bell clanged and cheering broke out.

But it wasn't the usual start-of-race cheering, Prandina thought. Was there also some laughter, jeering maybe? She looked at her father. "May I take Zarian out on the balcony and watch the race, Daddy?"

"Sure, Princess," he said. Almost anything Prandina wanted to do was all right with him, as long as he approved of it.

Prandina knew her father wouldn't let them go down to the plaza to watch. Three or four Festivals ago he'd let her go onto the plaza for the first time ever—and she'd gotten too carried away. The children's race looked like such fun she'd pulled away from her nanny and jumped into the race and run. And laughed and tripped and fell just like any other kid. The king had been furious. Had sent her and the nanny back to the castle. Would have fired the nanny and kicked her out of the castle had Prandina not pleaded with him.

On the balcony Prandina held Zarian so he could see over the railing. She looked out and sighed. She'd like to be down there, in the crowd, cheering and cutting up. The only friend or playmate she'd ever had, other than Zarian, had been a servant girl who often acted more like a nanny than a playmate.

Her gaze was drawn to the big pack of runners streaking down the left side of the square and the ripple of yelling moving along with them. She realized there was also yelling coming from the right, and as she looked at that side of the plaza, she thought, "Goodness, is that runner really...it's a Left!...running the wrong way?" She almost laughed. Who could be so stupid? But kinder thoughts soon came. Maybe he wasn't in the race at all. Perhaps something had happened to scare or embarrass him, and he was running back to Left Corner to be with his people. And those Zaprians along the course are jeering. I feel sorry for him, poor thing.

But when Togai passed halfway, went through Left Corner and kept going, she called out, "Daddy, you might want to come and watch. Something interesting's happening."

The king came out wiping his mouth with a napkin big enough for a small child to sleep under. "I hope it's interesting."

She pointed. "See that Left running there, all alone?"

"Yeah. But what's so interesting about a Left running by himself? Is he showing off some gaudy new outfit—or just showing off?"

"I think he's actually racing, against the others, those over there."

The king glanced in the direction she pointed and then back at Togai. "Well, he's running like he's in a race. But who with, and where to?" With a disgusted wave he turned toward the apartment. "I've got better things to do than watch such foolishness."

For Togai, every step seemed to bring the balcony closer, and with every step he tried to go faster. In spite of all the training he had done his left leg and foot were starting to cramp. His stomach was churning, empty, and seemed to be trying to pull the rest of him into it. He wanted desperately to stop, but couldn't stand the thought of doing that with so many Zaps watching, waiting, ready to jeer.

Just as he was thinking one more hard step would be his last, he saw an official run across the course pulling a string behind him. Togai felt a surge of energy. It had to be the finish line. He didn't have far to go! But wait. The crowd near the official was cheering wildly, and the official was looking down the course and pulling the string taut. The leading Zap runners had to be getting close! Togai knew that they'd be close to the inside rope, so he aimed for the middle of the string and tried to make his aching legs go faster.

Just as he caught a flash of arms and legs, he saw officials at both ends of the string glance back toward him. If he hadn't been hurting so much he'd have laughed. The officials—with runners coming at them from two directions—began looking back and forth, wildly, as if they didn't know what to do.

With only steps to go Togai closed his eyes and strained with every muscle. He felt the string stretch across his chest and a moment later felt a tug as the leading Zap—the tall, lanky boy he'd been watching—hit it. Suddenly Togai wasn't hurting or tired. He had touched first! He had won!

He tilted his head back and laughed, or tried to. It was hard to laugh while sucking in great gobs of air, and it hurt too. But that was all right. He had won, had beat them all.

With Zap runners still coming in, red faced and breathing hard, Togai stayed near the outside rope and jogged in the direction they were coming from. Oh, how he wished Kallo or Togl or Lilu or anyone he knew was here to see and share this with him. He was the first Chelk to ever win a race!

But when he turned and started back toward the finish line, with so many people lining both sides, he suddenly wished he was completely alone. No Zaps or anybody else. He could do whatever he wanted. Jump or skip or shout or just close his eyes and feel good. And he now realized that it wasn't important that he was the first Chelk to win a race. What was important was that he had done what he set out to do. He'd practiced and sweated. His plan had worked. He'd been first around the course and he had won.

He stopped short of the finish line. He didn't want to get into that group of sweaty Zap runners, most still breathing hard, who were milling around and, while trying to get their breath, talking to each other and to the officials. Togai had expected one of the officials to come and say something to him about his winning. But not one of them seemed to be paying him any attention at all. In fact, they all seemed to be ignoring him. He knew that Chelks weren't supposed to speak to Zaps unless spoken to, but this was a special situation. He started toward the nearest official, but the man turned toward the crowd and pretended to look for someone.

Togai knew he'd really be in trouble if he tugged on the man's shirt, so he walked around and stood directly in front of the man. But the man—who had the same cold, blue-eyed look as the carpenter and Emona—didn't seem to notice Togai was there, didn't seem to care. Togai jumped up, to get into the man's line of view, and said, "I won, didn't I?"

The man ignored him.

Togai jumped up again—and again and again—as the words came bouncing out. "I crossed...the finish line...first...so I won... didn't I?"

The Zap runners and the Zaprians in the crowd near the finish line began to laugh, and the man laughed too. He sneered at Togai. "No, horse-tail boy. You didn't win. You're disqualified for running the wrong way."

Kallo ran up just in time to hear the last sentence and without hesitation blurted, "But the starter didn't say which way to run. I know. I was listening. My brother won!"

From back in the crowd came a man's shout, "Where'd he learn to run? Backwards Land?"

Several people laughed, and the laughter became howls when someone else shouted, "Yeah. That's where he learned to dress himself too!"

The official now glared at both Togai and Kallo, but before he could say anything there was a loud "Harrummppff" from right above them.

CHAPTER 7

# Togai's Up-close Look at the King, Puppets and People

Togai, as did everyone near the starting line, looked up. Looking down from the royal balcony was the king. He held a napkin. Beside him was a little boy and a girl Togai assumed to be Princess Prandina. She looked to be about the same age as Kallo and, though surely a Zap, had rich, creamy skin and live blue eyes, eyes that showed curiosity, concern even. He wondered how a girl that pretty could be the daughter of such a stern looking, pot-bellied old man.

"Be nice if a man could enjoy a little repast in his own kingdom," the king said.

The official's face reddened. "I'm sorry, Your Majesty. But these impudent Lefts are arguing that there's no rule about which way to run."

"And there's not," Togai said and looked up. But before he could say more Kallo clamped a hand hard over his mouth.

The king glowered. "If there wasn't, I declare it. Now start the next race. *Quietly*, please."

Togai could feel his chin start to quiver under Kallo's hand. Not wanting to let anyone see him cry, he pulled free of Kallo and ran back along the course as fast as his tired and cramping legs would allow. He had trained so hard, been so proud of his plan. Now, nothing. He brushed away some tears. Like Kallo said, the Zaps make the rules.

Knowing Kallo was close behind him, he hobbled on as fast as he could to a place where there weren't many people and ducked under the ropes.

The king, his mind on the big piece of walnut cake he'd left soaking in cream, had turned to go back to it, but when he saw that Togai was limping he stopped and stared.

"What is it, Daddy?" Prandina said. "You look worried."

"Nothing," he said. "Nothing." But he continued to stare, thinking about something he'd heard long ago.

"Stop," Kallo said. "I have your pants and shirt."

But Togai hurried on, dodging people, looking for a place to hide. A place where no one could see him cry, where no one could see his leg and know he was that "Dumb Left" who ran the wrong way. The puppet booth! That's where he should go.

He forced his aching legs to run, around the bandstand and the staring people getting settled there, and on toward the puppet booth. Though he saw there were now two stools alongside it, he ran around to the rear, lifted the curtain and ducked inside.

He heard running footsteps and Kallo's voice. "Turtles, Togai, somebody's been here. Get out of there before they come back."

Togai peeped out. Kallo was four or five steps away, looking first one way, then another.

"Give me my clothes!"

"No! Get out! The puppet master comes back and catches you in there he'll turn you into Ogre soup."

"*Give me those clothes.* They're mine."

"And I'm your big brother. You need someone to watch out for you. I stood up for you up there at the finish line. But why'd you do that? Where'd you get such a crazy idea?"

"Oh, just one day when I was running. I got to thinking..."

"Darn you, Togai. One of these days your thinking is going to get you into real trouble. You coming out or not?"

"No. Not till I get my long pants on."

"All right then, *fishbrain.* Here. See if I care if you wind up Ogre soup." That said, Kallo threw the rolled-up pants and shirt toward the booth and ran for Left Corner.

Togai scooped the roll into the booth and closed the curtain as he backed in. He sighed and sat back, and in the quiet and stillness, looked around. From a low shelf below the opening to the stage and from two side shelves, limp, slumped puppets stared at him, their polished-stone eyes questioning. He stared back.

He'd never seen them up close before. Though he'd been to many puppet shows, he'd always—as other Chelks had—had to stand behind the Zaprians, who got to sit up front, close to the stage. And though he'd seen them only at a distance, he knew every puppet. Over there was the Night Hag—with her one, claw-like hand, green eyes and red hair. She roamed the Zaphyr countryside at night, looking for children who had been naughty or who had disobeyed their parents. Beside her was the Avenging Witch—who also had green eyes and red hair but whose hands were ordinary, though withered and gray like those of an old woman. She could cause curses and send down the Ogres of the Cold, but only on the Chelk side of the river. Now that he could see the two up close, side by side, and see they looked very much the same, he wondered why Zaprian children laughed at the Avenging Witch but shuddered or even cried when the Night Hag appeared.

Across from them were the farmer with his little pitchfork, and his wife and daughter. And over there...Togai hesitated. He hadn't yet touched a puppet, but now he picked one up. It was the one everyone laughed at, the bumbling fool who helped the farmer, the one that was always falling down or stumbling over a milk bucket or doing some other dumb or stupid thing that raised the farmer's ire and caused the farmer to stick him in the behind with the pitchfork. Now, for the first time, Togai realized it was meant to be a Chelk puppet. It was big and fat, with a brown, leathery face and long, dirty yellow hair that tumbled from under a straw hat. Its inside-out clothes were brightly colored—and ragged and full of holes.

Beside it was the Chelk-woman figure, the one who worked for the farmer's wife. Even bigger and rounder than her bumbling husband, she had jowly cheeks that hung down over her gaudy but dirty inside-out dress. She was always spilling or burning something and being chased around the house by the farmer's wife, who was forever screaming at her and hitting her over the head with a broom. A head that, Togai now noticed, had only stubble for hair.

He shook his head. "Do they think we really look like this?" It was true Chelks were of more sturdy build than Zaprians, but he could think of no one who was fat—or dirty. He could remember thinking that Zaps laughed more than Chelks at puppet shows and could remember thinking that maybe that was because they could see and hear better. Now he understood why.

Togai jerked his pants on. He couldn't wait to get out. Not that he was afraid of being turned into Ogre soup. He just didn't want to be in a place were he might get whomped on the head or jabbed in the behind with a pitchfork.

Thinking he'd have a better chance of not being noticed when people were distracted by a race, he waited until he heard cheers from the direction of the finish line and slipped out. Because of the calls he had heard, he knew that the race just ending was the men's race, which was the last of the races. He was glad. That meant other Festival activities could get started.

He felt his shirt pocket to make sure the caramel-apple tokens were there and thought that now would be a good time to use at least one of them. If he hurried he could get to the apple booth before the race crowd did.

He started across the square and hadn't gone far when he met four small children and two women, all Zaps, coming directly at him. The children were in front and kept coming as if they expected him to step aside and let them pass—and he did. They went by without so much as a glance at him, as if he weren't there at all. So accustomed was he to such behavior, both by himself and the Zaps, he wouldn't have given the incident another thought had not one of the women looked back at him and laughed. She then leaned toward the other, and though their faces were hidden by their big, floppy hats, he could hear them whispering and giggling.

They're laughing at me because I ran the wrong way, he thought—and he started after them, to catch up, to explain, to tell them how he had *not* run the wrong way. But just as he came up behind them and was wondering how to get their attention—he wasn't supposed to speak to a Zap first and wouldn't dare touch one, especially a woman, on the shoulder—he heard one say, " I just can't believe the clothes those people wear, can you? I guess they have to wear them inside out, but why in the name of Maker do they dye them those awful colors?"

The other laughed. "Maybe they think the bright colors will hide their fishy smell."

Togai stopped and looked down. He kind of liked all the different colors. Did the Zaprians not think such clothes pretty? Clothes that Lilu and other women of Chelekai took such pride in making? And...he sniffed...did he smell of fish?

A lot of Zaps were now wandering between booths and stands, buying, trading, eating, laughing—and listening to and dancing to music that came from the bandstand. But Togai didn't really care whether the Zaps were eating or dancing or whatever. He just wanted to get back to Left Corner—*after* he got his caramel apples. Like the Zaps or not, they made good caramel apples, and he wanted his. He'd earned them.

It took him some looking to find a booth, but when he spotted one he hurried up to it, holding the tokens tightly in his fist. The booth had a low and narrow front counter and was barely big enough to hold one man, a few baskets of apples, a pot of caramel on a small stove, and, on a small table, a tray of coated apples, upside down with stout-looking sticks in their cores.

Togai looked at the apples and, hand shaking, put his two tokens on the counter.

The man looked at him, seemed about ready to say something when a little girl came running up. A typical Zap with dark hair pale skin and blue eyes. But Togai thought she was kind of pretty. Her eyes sparkled.

She dropped a token on the counter and looked up at the man.

He laughed. "You want an apple?"

She nodded eagerly. "Yes."

"What kind? Red or yellow?"

She thought for a moment, then pointed. "That one. That big one on the end."

With a firm thumb-and-fingertips hold on the end of the stick the man carefully lifted the apple from the tray and patiently held it, apple part up, until the little girl had a good hold on the stick and one finger against the side of the apple to keep it upright.

"Thank you," she said, and the man smiled as she walked away.

The man glanced around, as if to make sure no other Zap was coming, and looked at Togai. "Yes?"

Togai pick up his tokens and held them out to the man. "I'd like..."

"Where'd you find those?"

"I didn't find them. A man gave them to me this morning. For working on the bandstand."

"Hmpf. That'd be my brother-in-law. My overly generous brother-in-law." He turned around, and after looking over the apples picked up a small one—with his fingers, not the stick. He pulled the stick out and, after setting the apple on the end of the counter away from Togai, licked his fingers. "Ummm. Good," he said and held out his hand. "That'll be two tokens."

Togai looked at the apple. "But...the little girl...and this morning the man said..."

"You must have misunderstood. And the little girl's someone special. It's two tokens for you—or any other Left." He snapped his fingers and again held out his hand. "*Two!* Then take your apple and get outta here before all the caramel runs off and I have to clean up the mess."

Togai looked at the little finger-marred apple and let the two tokens drop on it. "Keep the tokens," he said, "the apple too."

Though Togai hurried toward Left Corner with short, fast steps he watched carefully as Chelks and Zaps passed one another, saw the way Chelks—every time—moved to one side, naturally, without thought.

He saw a Zap clown in baggy, inside-out clothes. He was holding a long rag-doll fish up to a man and saying, "Oh, mister, sir, will you give me a rotten carrot for my nice fish? My children really like rotten carrots."

Even before Togai heard the man and the clown laugh, he began to walk faster. He was almost at a run when he heard a yell, "Togai! Togai! Come get in line."

It was Tatl, in line with other Chelk boys at the rear of a booth. Togai thought it was the biggest booth he had ever seen, for sure the longest. As he walked toward it, someone from within called out, "Next!" and as the door at the back opened and Tatl went in, Dilo came out, dripping wet.

"Jumpin' turtles," Togai said. "Your mother'll tie you up in a fish net. How'd you get so wet?"

"It's fun," Dilo said. "All you do is sit on a little platform and get dumped in the water—and you get paid for it! Three times and you get a piece of candy."

"A platform?" Togai asked.

"Yeah it's new this year," Dilo said. "Go up front, have a look. I'm getting back in line."

At the front of the booth was a large group of noisy, laughing men and boys. Zaps. Togai moved on by them to where he could watch and, he hoped, not be noticed.

Over the booth was a large sign, 'Zaprians Only.' Togai couldn't read. No Chelk could. But they all knew what the signs 'Zaprians Only,' 'No Lefts,' and 'No Lefts Allowed' meant.

At the back of the booth, ten or more long steps from the front, was a large vat of water—and above the water, more than a man's height above, was Tatl. He was sitting on the edge of a small platform that was held up by three ropes. Two went from the back corners up to an overhead beam, where they were tied in place. The third ran from a front corner up to a pulley and down to a swivel contraption that Togai couldn't see clearly. What he could see clearly was that attached to this, by a long wooden arm, was a target with the face of a Chelk painted on it.

The barker gave his spiel, in a sing-song voice: "Step right up, step right up, show your skill. I have a fresh dry one, just for you to spill."

Many of the Zaps laughed. Soon afterward came a loud "thunk" when a fist-size rock thrown by a muscular young Zap hit the target.

Tatl fell—*kersplash!* Howls of laughter erupted from the Zaps. Tatl came up sputtering—and laughing—and Togai turned away. He was glad Tatl and Dilo were having fun. But he couldn't stand to watch. Couldn't they tell—or didn't they know—the Zaps were laughing *at* them?

Soon he was almost running—to get away from Zaps. And as soon as he came into Left Corner, he began to think he might want to get away from Chelks too.

He heard a man call out, "Here comes Wrong Way Togai. Hey, Wrong Way, how'd you find your way back?" As he passed a dance circle of young Chelks, laughter came when a girl said, "We'd ask you to dance, Togai, but you'd want to turn the other way."

Even Lilu seemed to be down on him. When he walked up, she kept fussing with something in the picnic baskets as if she hadn't seen him. But he knew she knew he was there. She had a peeved, I'm-not-about-to-speak-to-you-until look. He guessed that, today, it was until he apologized for having embarrassed her and all of Chelekai. But, right now, he didn't care what she or anyone else thought. He looked at Togl. "May I take the canoe? I want to go home."

Lilu's head jerked around. "Go home? How could you possibly want to...Oh..." She held out her hands and started toward him. "You look so sad."

He turned away.

Lilu came up beside him, one hand still out, waiting for some sign he wanted to be comforted. "Poor Little Turtle. Are you upset because you made a mistake and ran the wrong way?"

"Yes," he said. "That's why." He didn't have the heart to tell her that Zaps laughed at the clothes she made, at her, at him, at all Chelks.

He turned and looked at Togl as if to ask, Are you going to answer my question or not?

Togl nodded. "Sure. Take the canoe."

Simple. Straightforward. A man's answer. Togai liked it. No "Why? Aren't you feeling well?" or "Are you sure you want to?"

"What'll we do?" Lilu said. "And do you think it's safe for him to go alone?"

"Oh, there'll be plenty of room for us in other canoes. And as far as it being safe..." Togl smiled. "I reckon a boy who can swim across the river and back without stopping ought to be able to make it okay one way in a canoe. Now there's an idea. Why don't we let him swim. And since you wouldn't want him to get his new clothes wet, he could take them off and..."

"Oh, you men," Lilu said and started walking away. "Take the canoe, Togai. Take the canoe."

Togai sighed. "Thanks, Papa. I guess I'll go now, but...but first, may I ask you something?"

"Sure."

"When you trade with the Zaps, you ever take tokens for your fish?"

"No," Togl said. "Why?"

"Oh, I was just wondering."

"Want to guess why I don't?"

"Because...because you never know what you'll get for them?"

Togl nodded. "Yeah. That's right. I reckon you grew up some today."

Prandina looked across the gently swaying carriage at her father. He'd seemed distracted, troubled even, ever since the end of the first boys' race. Even riding Noble Cloud in the parade hadn't cheered him up—and if anything could make him feel better, it was riding Noble Cloud. She'd thought she'd wait until the Festival was over and they were on their way home to ask, to say anything. But he now seemed more withdrawn than at any time during the day—just sitting over there, staring out at countryside he'd looked at no telling how many times. If he still seemed withdrawn tomorrow, she'd say something. For now...She shifted, being careful not to disturb Zarian who had fallen asleep with his head in her lap, then wedged a small pillow into the corner near her and put her head on it. She'd sleep too. It had been a long day.

When it seemed to the king that Prandina was asleep, he slid a little from the corner, stretched out his legs, and put his head back on the seat. But he didn't fall asleep. Once again he let his thoughts drift back to a time long ago, to something he'd heard—and something he'd read.

Old Rono, his head cook, had worked in the castle kitchen for as long as he could remember. One morning—he was six or seven Festivals old at the time—while she was serving breakfast his father had said, "You seem a little worried, Rono. Anything wrong?"

She mumbled something about everything being fine but his father said, "Come on, now, I can tell. What is it?"

She twisted her hands nervously in her apron. "I'm not sure I should say, Sire. Not in front of Prince Praidar."

"Don't worry. He'll be king someday." He laughed. "He needs to learn a king's life isn't all milk and cookies as you'd have him believe."

"Well, Sire, people say my dreams mean something and that I can sometimes see into the future. Last night I had a strange—and very scary—dream. In it an Ogre of the Cold, in the form of a little man, or a boy, with a shriveled leg came down from the mountains into Left. He then swam the river and stole something of great value from the castle, and took it back into the mountains where it could never be recovered. I...I'm sorry, Sire."

"Why be sorry, Rono. It was only a dream. We all know that no one, nothing—at least not anything that walks—has ever been able to get into or come out of the mountains." He laughed. "But I have to admit, I'm curious about one thing. In your dream, what did the man-Ogre take?"

Her answer, Praidar remembered vividly. She had looked down at the floor. "I'm not sure, sire. But I think it was a person. A child maybe."

As far as Praidar could tell, his father didn't give the dream a second thought. But he did. To him it became a story, not a dream, and many times when he had the chance he'd ask Rono to retell it. She would. And he'd ask her questions and try to get her to tell him more about the short-legged Ogre and where and how it got back into the mountains. But she'd always say she'd told everything she knew, could tell him no more.

Actually, his father did think about the story—at least once more. One day Praidar was intently listening to Rono tell the dream again. His father walked in, seemed to get very angry, and forbad Rono to tell the dream again. With no more retellings, the dream fell from mind until he was sixteen Festivals old and happened to read a story written by old King Rotar. It reminded him of Rono's dream, but because Rotar had dismissed the story as having come from a lunatic, so did he—and he hadn't given either story another thought. Not until today. Not until he saw the short-legged boy from Left.

He opened one eye to look at Prandina and Zarian—and shuddered. Though he'd given no thought to Rotar's tale until today, he thought about the other thing Rotar wrote every day.

## CHAPTER 8

# Growing-Up Day and Scorn Marks

Togai slowly opened his eyes and, since the eastern sky wasn't really bright yet, thought he might again be the first one up. But some slight sound told him he wasn't and he rolled over to look. Togl was in a chair by the table and Lilu was drawing her big handlewood comb through his hair, trying to pull it back into a tight pony tail.

"Ow," Togl said. "My eyelids are coming off."

"Not my fault your hair's thick. Got to have you looking nice. Not every day a boy grows up."

Togai glanced at Kallo's cot. Kallo was already up, putting his shirt on, smiling. Of course, Togai thought. He'd almost forgotten. It was Kallo's Growing-Up Day. For many Chelks the day after Festival Day was almost as big as Festival Day itself. For those youngsters who had just turned fifteen Festivals old and their families it was an even bigger day, maybe the biggest of a lifetime. Growing- Up Day. The day the new fifteen-olds chose—or were assigned—his or her lifelong job.

As Togai, Togl and Lilu joined other Chelks in the long column forming along the river bank and turned their backs to the brightness of the east, Togai felt some pride. They were, this day, near the front.

At the head of the column, ready to lead it back into the village after the Praise Maker ceremony, was Old Helu, the Dilkina, village leader and head of Council. Behind her were the nine growing-uppers, four boys and five girls—in two rows, girls first. Next were the other members of Council and, in short rows behind them, each growing-upper's hut family. And that's where Togai felt pride. Because Togl was head fisher—and Kallo was one of the growing-uppers—Togl, Lilu and Togai were right behind Council, only a few steps from the growing-uppers. Behind the last family came the rest of the village in no particular order.

Togai had heard Togl tell many times how the Chelks had arrived at the work system they had and how the village's way of life had come to be. Early on the Chelks discovered that the rock and sandy soil of Chelekai and the sea that bordered it could support only so many people. Because of that, every man-woman pair made it a goal to have only two children. Though some couples ended up having three, some had only one, or none, and so the numbers were maintained.

Early, too, the people of Chelekai discovered the number of fishers, wood cutters, net menders and so on that were needed to keep village life running smoothly and agreed that in each family the first-born child could choose to do what the parent of the same sex did. Any children after that had to choose from whatever jobs Council said needed to be filled at the time.

As Togai looked ahead at Kallo, he felt some envy and guessed that practically every boy in the village did too, maybe even some men. Since Kallo was the only growing-upper who was the first-born of a fisher, he was the only one who could choose to be a fisher. Not only that, by being the son of head fisher Togl, he was likely to some-day be head fisher himself.

Togai felt the envy would be there because even though fishing, with its getting up early, paddling out to sea, and casting a net all day long, was the most demanding of all jobs—and most dangerous too—almost any man or boy would choose to be a fisher. Fishers were the most admired men in the village. Chelks knew they needed canoe builders and paddle makers and net makers, and woodcutters and tool makers and the many women who cooked and sewed, but they needed fishers most of all. Fishers fed them. If it weren't for the fishers, they'd die of starvation—or have to trim their numbers so low there'd barely be anyone left.

Just as Togai was thinking how pretty the mountains were, their usually white tops pink above slopes of soft yellow, sunlight hit the nearest hill and started down it. Spreading, it gained speed, came swooping toward him and before he knew it he felt warmth on his neck and saw his shadow on the back of the man in front of him.

Old Helu climbed to the top of a little sand pile and turned. Her words came clean and clear into the quiet: "Before we begin our Growing-Up Walk, let us take time to be thankful to The One of All Possibility, The Maker of All Men and All Things."

Without having to be told, Togai turned with all the others to look back along the river to the sun coming up out of—or maybe out of—that great unknown where Maker lived.

Togai waited to hear Old Helu start, then, as the sound rose all around him, lent his voice to the near-synchronous chant:

"In humble thanks for what and all You have done for us so far, we respectfully ask You to continue. Fishes and turtles give us, wisdom too. Protect us from Ogre, and may, this particular day, our work choices be pleasing to You."

In a few moments, the stillness was broken by a muted stir as bare feet began to turn in worn sand. As the column moved toward the village Togai was struck by the contrast between how Old Helu— the only woman ahead of him—looked and what he'd just seen when he had turned and looked back. Like looking down a flower bed of floppy-brimmed hats. A reason many Chelk women liked Growing-Up Day so much was that on this side of the river they didn't have to pay any attention at all to an old king's decree to not wear hats. Over here, at home, they could wear as many hats as they wanted, as big and as colorful as they wanted. And that's the way they made them, big and colorful.

Old Helu stood out, though. Really stood out. Not only did she have no hat, she had no hair. In the tradition of dilkinas for as far back as anyone could remember, she had—for Growing-Up Day— cut her hair right down to a scalp that was, Togai thought, sickly gray.

And hanging from her neck on a seaweed rope was an ornate emblem carved from the shell of a sea turtle. It had a zigzag, wave-like, shape and had been polished smooth by the handling of many dilkinas.

Though Togai couldn't now see them, he knew there were two other "seawave" representations on her. One was a deep scar. A burn, high on the left side of her head between ear and forehead. The other was in the middle of her forehead, freshly painted in dark red dye.

The hair of the growing-uppers behind her had also been cut as closely as possible. But only one side. Left for girls, right for boys. Though the near-white color of their scalps reminded Togai of the bellies of floating dead fish, he couldn't wait until his would be like that.

In going through the village the column passed between small piles—one pile to each side—of axes, saws, hoes, knives, turnips, nets, blankets, and, at the end, between two racks of smoked fish, two canoes, and two large paddles upright in the sand—all to show appreciation for the workers who made, used or produced them.

The Council hut was at the far edge of the village at the bottom of a gently sloping dune so that on important occasions everyone in the village could have a place to sit and be able to see and hear all that went on. The families of the growing-uppers were given places of honor at the bottom of the dune. Because Togl was given the high-honor middle places, Togai—between Togl and Lilu—was in the very middle, down front. On a bench directly in front of him, in front of the Council hut, were the Council elders. About four steps away and a little to his right Old Helu stood, waiting patiently for everyone to get onto the dune and be seated. A little to his left, on two benches set at an angle to the dune, were the growing-uppers, girls on the front bench, boys behind them.

"For many of you," Helu began, and waited for silence, "this may not be as much fun as Festival Day, but it's certainly more important. This is the day our young adults—our growing-uppers—become full adults and either choose or are assigned their lifelong tasks."

She turned and spoke directly to the growing-uppers. "Because every task is absolutely necessary for our survival and we all depend on each other to do his or her job well, our future and our well-being are—or soon will be—very dependent on you and the decisions you make or that are made for you today. Since we cannot expect a child to make or accept decisions that last a lifetime and affect us all, we show that we think you are now adults and expect you to accept responsibility and act accordingly by honoring you with the symbol not only of adulthood but of our very souls, our history, of what we have been and will become—the red scorn."

She pointed to her forehead. "No one but the Dilkina can wear a forehead scorn, not even if it'll wash off, as this one will. And, of course, only the Dilkina, or someone who has been Dilkina, can have the permanent, burned-in scorn, as I have. Why this mark bears the name of *scorn* or why it has the shape it has, we probably will never know."

Togai watched and listened. In three years he'd be going through this. Helu went on to say that some thought the mark was called a scorn because of the scorn—*and the love*—Maker felt for the Chelks when He caused their island home to sink but let them escape and led them to Zaphyr. Some thought "scorn" showed the fishers' defiance of storms and the woodcutters defiance of hail and lightning. Whatever else it might mean or stand for, its bestowal on a young Chelk meant he or she had stepped into adulthood.

Helu walked to the end of the girls' bench. An elder handed her a small, stone bowl, and she asked the first girl to stand and face her parents.

"Do you, Ilil, daughter of Inyl and Malai and on the honor they have taught, accept the responsibility of adulthood and promise to use all of the will, strength and wisdom Maker gave you to live and work for the good of us all, including yourself?"

"I do."

"Do you also promise that though you become an adult, you will continue to live with your parents and to honor and obey them as a child would until the day you marry and have a hut of your own?"

"I do."

Helu dipped her first finger into the bowl. With it, tip now dark red, she carefully drew the zigzag flourish on the side of the girl's head in exactly the same place as her own scar scorn.

"I now declare you an adult."

The girl remained standing, as did the others as Old Helu worked her way down the bench, asking the same questions, getting the same responses, and painting the red scorn on the side of each one's head.

At the end of the bench she paused and looked back. "Sometime in the next few days, come to me so I can replace your temporary scorn with a permanent, tattooed one. The boys—the young men—will not have theirs replaced. If one of you is given the honor of becoming Dilkina, the tattoo will be burned into your head."

Togai looked at Lilu and whispered. "Do you have a tattoo?"

"Shhh. Yes. It's very pale. Under my hair. I'll show you sometime."

At a nod from Helu, the boys had stood and they and the girls moved in a circle around the front bench and stopped and sat down. Boys now on the front bench, girls in back.

Kallo, by design, was now at the end of the bench away from Old Helu and the last to get his scorn. When he was asked to stand, Togai sensed Togl straighten, heard Lilu sniffle.

When she had finished the ritual with Kallo, she asked the boys to be seated and an elder took the bowl from her. She faced the crowd.

"One way we keep up our skills," she said, "is the tradition of son following father, daughter following mother. It is in the home, from early childhood on, that a constant loving association of student and teacher allows knowledge and skill to be passed from one generation to the next.

"The first-born are the lucky ones, the ones who have that lifetime of home training. But our well-being depends as much on the second-born, for they will go on to learn some new skill, from some caring teacher, and I beseech them to learn it well. Someday they will have a first-born to teach.

"Now, as always, we start with selections of the first-borns. This year we have only one first-born son. He is Kallo, the first son of Head Fisher Togl."

When she turned and nodded at Kallo, he stood. "Kallo, now that you are a full-fledged adult, please tell us what you have chosen to do."

Kallo, in the way he had been instructed, looked first at the villagers, then at the Council of Elders. "I...May I ask a question?"

Old Helu seemed surprised—and Togl and Lilu looked at one another.

"Why, yes, I suppose so," Helu said.

Kallo took a deep breath. "Is it all right for a first-born to give up his right to choose?"

Togai felt Lilu and Togl jerk.

Old Helu frowned. "You want to give up your right to *choose*?"

"Yes—if I can give it to Togai."

Exclamations of surprise and excited talk came from all over the dune, and Togl gave Togai a sharp look. "Did you know about this?"

Togai shook his head. He was bewildered. He had no idea what was going on.

Helu looked hard at places on the dune where people were talking and whispering and didn't speak again until quiet returned. "Kallo, as far as I know, no one has ever before made this request. I feel that since it's your birthright, it's yours to do with as you will. But since some on Council and some in the village might not agree, please tell us why you want to pass your birthright on to your brother."

Kallo looked down. "It's...it's because of his leg. When his Growing-Up Day comes, there might be a shortage of woodcutters, and if he had to spend his days standing on steep hillsides, cutting down trees and dragging them to the river...well..." He looked up. "You understand."

Togai looked at Lilu. She was trying to wipe the tears from her face. Old Helu turned and looked at the elders. "As I said, I think it's his birthright to do with as he pleases. You?"

Each one nodded agreement, but a few also shook their head as if they thought Kallo a fool.

"Does anyone wish to make a comment or dissent?" Helu asked and let her questioning look drift over the dune. Just as she seemed ready to turn to Kallo, hurried whispering broke out on one side of the dune. As many did, she craned to see who it was.

Chulo, an old fisher, stood. "Forgive me and my son for whispering. May I now speak openly?"

Fishers said Chulo's canoe talked more than he did, so when he asked to speak, the villagers knew he had something to say. Old Helu knew it too. "Chulo's words are always welcome," she said.

Chulo cleared his throat. "Since Kallo has given up his choice as a first-born, will he now be the first of the, uh, second-borns to choose?"

Helu glanced back at Council, then looked at Chulo. "Yes."

The old man put his gnarled hand on his son's shoulder. "Galu and I thought that's what you'd say, and he agrees with my proposal. My joints have stiffened so much that I can no longer work the way I used to. I would already have given up throwing nets and started mending them if Galu had a son to take my place. But he doesn't. So, I want to let Council know I'm retiring, right now, which means there's an opening for a fisher. That means, if Kallo wants, he can use his second-born choice to fish with my son, and when Togai comes of age he can use his Kallo-given first-born choice to, as is our fishers' tradition, fish with his father."

As Lilu started crying others started cheering.

Togl scooped up Togai in one arm and carried him out to a smiling, laughing Kallo and scooped up Kallo in the other arm. Tears were running down Togl's face. "If ever a man was blessed, it's me. Now I'll get to fish with both my boys."

Togai was happy too. He'd get to be what he thought he'd never be and every boy wanted to be—a fisher. He'd get to fish with Togl, and, better than anything else, Togl seemed truly happy he'd some day be fishing with his short-legged second-born.

CHAPTER 9

# Keys to the Kingdom?

In a roomy hallway closet between the king's study and the no longer used "royal" bedroom, a wide-eyed Zarian was looking up at Prandina from their nest of blankets and pillows. She was reading,

"And then the vengeful Night Hag was cast out of the castle, never to return again, and the Royal Family lived in peace forever hence. The End."

Prandina yawned, but Zarian clapped. "One more story, Dina! One more last story. *Please!*"

"Okay, sweet Zee. But only one more and it's nap time for you. With all the Festival goings on yesterday, you were up early and didn't get your afternoon nap either."

She started telling "The Ogre who Liked Apples," but before she was half way through it he was asleep. She liked the feel of his tiny, warm body near hers and had barely snuggled down beside him and closed her eyes when she heard booted footsteps on the cold stone from the far end of the hallway. Her father. He was back from his ride!

Her first impulse was to jump up and run to greet him, but in moving quietly so as to not disturb Zarian she got her head outside the door barely in time to see the door to the study close. Why'd he close the door? She'd never seen him close it before. Why now?

She carefully crawled over Zarian to the back of the closet. In some earlier game in the closet she'd seen some loose mortar between two stones close to the floor. She'd tugged, and when a long piece came out she had a mouse's-eye view of the study. Now, as quietly as she could, she slid the piece out and peeked through.

Her father was bending over his desk and...Why was he lighting a candle? In the middle of the afternoon? In a room with a big window?

She watched as, candle in hand, he started across the room toward a display case and a bookcase set against the far wall. In the space between the two was a full-length, life-size portrait of King Rotar, builder of the castle. She guessed her father was going to the bookcase to get a book, but he went to the glass-fronted display case instead. With his free hand he reached up and ran his fingers along the top edge of the case. She assumed she found a key, for when he brought his hand down he went through the motions of putting a key in a lock and turning, the case door popped open. Though he partly blocked her view, she knew—from having looked in it many times—that the case held, among other things, a tarnished crown, some ceremonial swords and daggers, a few really old books, a huge iron key, and a small music box.

He knelt on both knees, set the candle on the floor, and reached into the bottom shelf. She heard a clunking and got a glimpse of the huge iron key as he pulled it out.

Because his broad back was toward her, she couldn't see what he was doing, but after a few moments in which he seemed to be doing some twisting with his hands, she heard a *clank* as, she guessed, he placed the key on the stone floor—then a lighter *clink*. What was that? She watched, fascinated, as he leaned over and began trying to do something to the front of the portrait. She put her hand over her mouth to stifle her giggling. She'd never seen her father like that before—big rear in air, face almost touching the floor. Not a very dignified royal position.

But her urge to laugh suddenly went away. The portrait swung open, frame and all. Like a door. Behind it was an opening! An opening to a small, dark room.

Her father picked up the candle and, with a grunt and a push of a hand on one knee, stood. He pushed the portrait back to where it was fully open and took a step into the small, narrow room. Facing the wall to his left, he reached up high and pulled down a book.

He came out, closed the portrait-door and, book in hand, came to his desk and sat down. She couldn't see the book, but from his motions and concerned look, she could tell he was searching for something. Finally, with a sigh, he stopped turning and settled back in his chair to read.

She lay on her back and sighed too, realizing she'd nearly been too afraid to breathe. He was so close—and the study so quiet—she was afraid to put the chunk of mortar back in place lest he hear the scraping noise. She reached for a pillow and carefully placed it over the hole, then crawled back to where Zarian was and snuggled in beside him. She hoped he wouldn't awaken for awhile, and that when he did he'd stay quiet.

But more than worry that her father might hear them—why would he think she'd seen anything even if he did find them?—she was worried about *him*. He'd seemed distant, even unhappy, ever since the race yesterday. Now, a day later, he had shut himself in and taken a book from a hidden room. Why? Did the book have anything to do with yesterday? Yesterday with the book?

She awoke with a start—and immediately but carefully rolled away from Zarian. On stomach and elbows she crawled to the back of the closet, carefully moved the pillow away from the chink, and peeked. The study was empty, dim in the late afternoon light. The bookcase and cabinet and portrait stood the way they always had—but she knew they'd never look the same to her again.

The king had told himself he was going to stop thinking about the boy with the limp, about the dream and the tale he'd read, but in his ride it all kept coming back to him and he'd decided to re-read the story and, if nothing else, assure himself that old King Rotar didn't put much credence in the story.

As he remembered it, a few days after his fifteenth Festival his father had called him into the king's study and, to his surprise, closed the door. His father, Prandar, had leaned back in his big chair of kings and pointed to one side, the one where there was a door, a display cabinet, a portrait, a bookcase, and another door. The other side wall was a bare stone wall. Behind the king's chair, in a corner, was a big window that gave a view of the distant mountains.

"That far door," the king said, "as you know, leads to the Room of Records. Not just births and deaths and marriages and so on, but records on weather, crop yields and plantings that go I don't know for how far back. Dull, but stuff you may need to know about, especially if there's a prolonged drought or something." He pointed to the door next to the bookcase. And as you know, that leads to the Room of Writs and Decrees, where there are records of most—but not all—of the many decisions and decrees down through the years. There's a lot of useless stuff on where the queen should stand in a receiving and so on, but you *should* read back through the decrees and get to know them. Why? Because no king has *ever*—at least not knowingly—*ever* reversed a decree. Not one of his own or of any other king. We cannot have kings arbitrarily deciding which decrees to enforce, which not, or when. People would get the idea that no law had to be obeyed and pretty soon our whole society would fall apart. Understand?"

"Yes, sir."

"Now, I want you to swear, in the name of Maker and at risk of eternal torment by the Nether Ogre, that you will never tell anyone other than the son who is to succeed you what I next tell you."

Praidar took a deep breath. He knew his father was a stickler for such things. "I swear, in the name of Maker and at risk of eternal torment by the Nether Ogre that I will never tell anyone but my successor what I am about to hear."

"Good. Now swear it two more times, word for word."

Twice more Praidar swore what he had just sworn, and when he was finished his father showed him, first, where a small key was hidden, then showed him how to use that key to get to a second, the second to a third and, last, how to use that third key to get into a hidden room, a room that no one but a king, or the person due to replace him, had ever been told of or allowed into.

Starting with the three-time oath swearing and with the revelation of each key Praidar had become more and more excited, but he'd been sorely disappointed when the door to the hidden room swung open. The room was tiny and dark and from it came a musty smell. From what he could tell in the dim light, it was no more than a library. A really tiny library.

He guessed his disappointment showed for his father said, "I know it doesn't look like much, but..." He stepped into the room and, candle held high, gestured for Praidar to step in. There was barely room. So close behind Praidar could feel its cold was a wall of solid stone. Just in front of him were two tall bookcases, one about three-fourths full, the other empty.

His father gestured with the candle. "These are the Books of Kings, written in their own hands. Their innermost thoughts and fears, their dreams and wishes. Comments on why they made some of the decrees they made. And most important, the decrees they made that apply *only* to us kings and are only for kings or queens to know about."

"Queens?"

"Yes. Zaphyr has had a few ruling queens, but since most reigned only until they had a son old enough to pass the crown onto, what little they wrote is scattered here and there inside the kings' books." He chuckled. "I guess women would rather talk than write. Now, I admit some of the kings were pompous and verbose and not near as smart as they thought, but would you like to read in some of these books, learn some history that will someday make you a better king?"

Praidar shrugged. "Maybe."

"I wasn't really *asking*. I *want* you to read. So, read some every day. Since the old books deal with problems of long ago and are in crude handwriting with words strangely spelled, I suggest you start with the recent ones. Particularly your grandfather's. He was an unusually wise man. But..." He looked directly at Praidar. "One last thing—or I keep the key to the portrait door in my pocket. I ask you to promise me, not swear, just promise, that as you start reading you will not read the first or last page in any book. Promise—and double promise?"

Praidar nodded. "I promise. Double promise."

Each day after that, for two moons or more, Praidar would go into his father's study, close the door and, after using the three keys to get into the secret room, take a book from it and settle down to read. He soon came to the conclusion that most of what he was seeing—skimming—must have been written by old men with nothing better to do than write down any thought that popped into their heads, no matter how trivial or vacuous.

So, one day when he went into the Room of the Books—as he had just heard his father call it—to get a book, he had a thought. Why not start at the beginning?—and from the very top shelf he took the very first book. Moldy and bulky it was, with thick pages that were swollen and yellowed with time and looked ready to crack at the slightest touch. He slowly opened the book, just enough to see that, indeed, as his father had said, the handwriting was crude and the words strange. A few more barely-open peeks convinced him that though he might be able to read it if he really tried, he didn't want to bother.

With that thought, he put the book back and, on a whim, took the fourth. At first, it too looked too difficult to read, but after some careful opening and looking he came to a page that, somehow, seemed more readable. On it, in crude block letters, was:

*Writ of Keng Rotah, Aith Keng of Zaphyr*

*The tale I now put to papyr ha not been writ before. My vatter Rotar tol it me yust for he die. So, tho Rotar say story not sposed to be writ down and tho I not sur story tru, I want to writ it down in case I die 'fore I can tell whoer be keng aftr me (lik amos happn Rotar and me) (I ha no son yet). Now, repeet: Rotar tell me story always pass on keng to keng, by telling, not writin, caus frst keng (not rilly keng, first leedr) say it not sposed to, yust for kengs (leedrs) eers only. Also not sur story tru caus Rotar probly crazy at tim. Strang thigs happn. Try kill my mutter one niht. He wak up, thenk she Niht Hag, try trow her out windo. Copl tims try kil sef. Wunz clim up to ruf of castl stark nakd, I cawt him yust for he trow sef off. And reesn he di suddn, he try jump frm windo onto stalyun— no clotes on—miss and brak bons in legs, stuff insid too (bleed lot frm mout). He tell me tale yust for di (lik sposed to, I gess).*

# THE SHORT-LEGGED FISHER BOY OF THE LAND OF LEFT

*So, heer wat my (crazy?) vatter tol me yust as e abowt to di.*

Now, many years later, after Praidar had re-read what Rotah wrote, he sighed, closed the book, and got up and went to the window. As he looked at the mountains he thought. Did he believe the Rotar tale now? Probably not. He probably wouldn't have paid it any attention anyway had it not been for Old Rono's dream. Had he not remembered her dream he probably wouldn't have looked in later books to see if other kings had passed on Rotar's tale—and they hadn't, at least not in writing. Rotah's own son, Rotanor, hadn't put the Rotar tale in writing, which almost surely meant he didn't believe it either. As for Old Rono's dream, Praidar thought, it probably wasn't unusual at all. Many people probably dreamed, even had nightmares, about Ogres in some form coming down from the mountains to do evil. So why not a crippled old man? Some people thought cripples were cursed anyway, not necessarily evil themselves, but carriers of evil.

But it wasn't the Rotar tale that had disturbed him, it was the decree by Rotah that came right after it. A shudder had run through him when he'd first read it and suddenly realized why his father didn't want him to read the first or last pages of Books of Kings.

Back then, when he'd first read that decree of old Rotah's, he'd not thought he'd be personally affected by it—and he'd never truly believed there was any substance to Rotah's tale or to Old Rono's dream. He sighed. He'd been wrong about not being affected by the decree. Would he be wrong about the tale and dream too?

CHAPTER 10

# The Smokehut

When Togai awoke the morning after Growing-Up Day, Togl and Kallo were gone, and he wished he, like Kallo, had his scorn and was starting his life-long work as a fisher. But he knew he had a lot to learn first.

Chelekai had no schools, but each workday morning the boys and girls of the village from seven to eleven Festivals old had to gather at the work hut either to choose or be assigned a morning chore—with seven-olds being given the easiest chores, eleven-olds the hardest. At age twelve boys and girls were called "learners" and stayed learners until their Growing-up Day, the day after their fifteenth Festival.

While the fourteen-olds had to work until noon, the twelve- and thirteen-olds could be allowed to leave their jobs as early as mid morning, depending. Chelks believed that children should become responsible adults, but they also believed that children should be allowed time to play.

Though a first-born was almost certain to take as life-long job what the father or mother did, each boy and girl had to get some instruction in—and use—every skill needed to keep the village functioning. While boys spent most of their time learning canoe-building, tool making and so on, they also had to spend some time learning gardening, sewing and smoking fish, just as girls had to spend some time learning to make paddles and sharpen axes. The idea was not so much that everyone needed to know how to do every job but that everyone have an appreciation for what it was others did to make all of their lives easier. Only fishing and woodcutting—since they would require full days away from the village—were excluded from what the learners had to do.

Unlike the younger, "chore" children, learners didn't show up at the work hut each day to learn what their morning job would be. Since their jobs ran a full moon, from Maker Day to Maker Day, the morning after each Maker Day they would come to the work hut to choose from among the jobs they hadn't been trained in. The first to arrive were first to choose, which almost always meant that the last job left was the one nobody wanted to do. And this choose-work morning, Togai, still sore from the race, was the last learner to the hut.

As he came limping up, Old Helu gave him a look of sympathy. "Guess what, Togai."

"The smokehut?"

"Yes."

Oh, no, Togai thought. For a whole moon he'd have to work for Old Zoltai. The man everyone said was impossible to please. The Man he'd insulted a year ago. Why hadn't he gotten up earlier, walked faster? But the dread of what he was about to face slowed his walk even more.

The smokehut was near the river, not far from the holding pens and smelly tables where the fish cleaners did their work. Well before he could see the hut, though, Togai could hear the *thwhacks* and *cheunks* of an ax, so close together they had an almost angry sound. As he came into the clearing around the hut he saw Zoltai take a cut at a limb sticking up from a large tree trunk. The limb dropped with one blow. Zoltai picked it up and laid it across the trunk. One-handed— *thwack*—and he cut the limb in two! The less solid end, with its many small branches and twigs, he flung onto a large pile of similar limb ends, the brush pile as Togai would come to know it. The pole-like end, as long as a canoe paddle and bigger than Zoltai's arm at its butt end, Zoltai tossed toward the hut, onto a scattered pile of similar pieces. Off to one side and running off toward the river was a strung-out pile of trees and tree tops.

As Togai walked up, Old Zoltai glanced at him. "You're late."

"Yessir."

"Last in line?"

"Yessir."

Zoltai snorted. "That figures." He pointed to the pile of limbs, bent, crooked, straight. "Those need to be moved over there," he nodded, "to the fire pit, by the hut. Lay 'em as straight as you can, like the ones I've already put there. Just more work for me if you jumble 'em up."

"Yessir," Togai said—and walked to the end of the pile closest to the smokehut and pulled a cut limb from the pile by its thin end and started dragging it toward the hut.

"Great sufferin' axes, boy!" Zoltai yelled. "We'll never get anything done that way. Take as many as you can get your hands and arms around. Drag 'em if you have to. But for the Great Woodcutter's sake—and mine—take more than one."

"Yessir," Togai said. After some fumbling and trying, he started toward the smokehut dragging four limbs—each held or clasped by its thin end, one in each hand, one under each arm.

"Hurry, boy," Zoltai said. "You can't keep up with my cutting going that slow."

Togai responded quickly—and almost as quickly realized that though the sand felt good to his sore feet the limbs were already cutting into his sides and underarms. He'd have to find another way to drag or, tomorrow, stuff some rags down the sides and into the arms of his shirt.

The fire pit was about thirty steps away, Togai guessed, and as he hurried and winced his way toward it he took in what he saw. The smokehut was on a low mound at the far end of the covered pit, and he was guessing there was space beneath the floor for smoke to come into and then spread up though cracks into the smokeroom.

He stopped at the end of the "pit"—a long, tunnel-like thing of stone that ended in a high chimney that rose right beside, maybe partly in, the smokehut. It all seemed to make sense, but what puzzled him was a ladder against the chimney. Had the masons been working on it?

"Don't stand there gawking, boy!" Zoltai yelled. "Get back here. The women'll be bringing yesterday's catch soon."

Togai knew that no one had fished yesterday, or the day before either, but figured he'd best not say that to Old Zoltai. If the main holding pen hadn't broken open, the fish workers would have the last workday's catch to clean and cut into strips for hanging on the smoke racks. He tried to hurry, but found, to his surprise, the muscles in his right leg were even sorer than the ones in his left. He winced every time he tried to take either a fast or a long step.

Zoltai looked at him. "You're limping a lot. Sore from the race?"

"Yessir. Some." But he limped all the time. Had Old Zoltai forgotten that? Or was Old Zoltai being sarcastic, trying to get back at him for the "pathetic cripple" remark?

He bent over the pile of poles and, after some sorting, was soon headed toward the fire pit dragging four as fast as the underarm chafing pain would allow. He didn't like this adult world. He wasn't used to being around adults who were harsh with him, treated him like an adult. He wanted...Turtles! What *did* he want? He used to feel sorry for himself because adults treated him like a baby. Now he was feeling sorry for himself because he wasn't.

Togai carefully placed his poles on, in his opinion, Old Zoltai's too-carefully aligned poles and hurried back. He expected Old Zoltai to give him, if not a sharp comment, a critical look. But the old woodcutter had his head down and was working as if Togai weren't even there. They worked that way for awhile, Togai sorting and pulling and placing, Zoltai lopping and chopping and, as far as Togai could tell, never looking up. He guessed Zoltai was just plain disgusted with him—with him *and* his work.

Togai saw that the pile he was taking from was even larger than when he'd started. Working as fast as he possibly could, he hadn't been able to keep up with Old Zoltai. He was ready to give up even trying when he heard Old Zoltai say, "I see women coming over from the cleaning pit, so I better get to the fire. I'll take a few limbs as I go—but you'll have to get the rest."

"Yessir," Togai said.

On the next couple of trips Togai watched Zoltai methodically throw limbs far back into the fire pit, then take chunky blocks of wood from a separate stack and—cringing from the heat—toss them into a fire that was now roaring. Seeing Togai watching, Zoltai nodded toward the block pile, said simply, "Green wood. Makes better smoke."

Zoltai then slid some flat stones that had been leaning against the side of the pit across the entrance, almost sealing it off, and limped around to the chimney and started up the ladder leaning against it. By the time he was at the top, smoke was pouring out. Togai watched as Zoltai, head in smoke, straining and coughing, slid a big, flat rock around to where it covered the opening and almost completely cut off the flow of smoke. By the time Zoltai was back on the ground, trails of smoke were beginning to show here and there along cracks in the smokehut walls.

Togai guessed the rock must have been balanced on the chimney top, half or less of the rock hanging over, but through it all, he had kept working. No way he wanted to give Old Zoltai reason to again accuse him of dawdling.

As Togai placed the last limb of the batch he'd just dragged down, Zoltai glanced at the sun and said, "You've been here about long enough. Go back," he pointed, "gather me up a big arm load of little limbs and bring 'em back here and stack 'em, there, alongside the fire pit. For restarting the fire tomorrow morning. And that burlap bag, there? Take it back to where I was chopping, fill it with good-sized chips—they burn good too—and bring the bagful back here and put it against the pit, beside the little limbs. That done, you can go. You older, I'd get you to help me cut and split a few of the trunks I've cut the limbs off of, but..."

"I could stay. I'm not tired."

"No. Council doesn't like it if I work you young ones too hard."

"But..."

Zoltai's voice had an edge. "Don't talk back. Just do what I say."

"Yessir," Togai said, and hurried off. When he had placed the arm load of limbs and the sack of chips beside the fire pit, he went back to where Old Zoltai was, again, chopping and, again, adding to the layer of chips around him. Togai stood directly in front of him, close enough to be seen but not close enough to be hit. For several, heavy, grunting strokes Zoltai ignored him. When he glanced up, it was only long enough for an annoyed look and a forceful nod toward the village.

Togai walked away slowly. He was discouraged. Not only had he been late, he'd not worked well and had talked back, sort of. Old Zoltai had either forgotten about his leg or was still angry for what had happened a year ago, or both. Whatever, it hadn't gone well. The old man didn't seem to care much about his feelings, just whether he was on time and how fast he could drag limbs.

With that thought an idea came, and instead of going straight home he turned toward the river. He might be able to find what he was looking for in one of the old canoes.

That night, when he and Kallo went outside to wash up for supper, he whispered, "After we eat, will you help me do something?"

Kallo looked at him. "You been thinking again?"

"Will you help me or not?"

Kallo shrugged. "If I can, sure."

"And will you also wake me up tomorrow morning when Togl wakes you up?"

Kallo laughed. "Gladly."

Togai guessed that if he got up when Togl and Kallo did, he could beat Old Zoltai to the smokehut. Very few people were up and about before head fisher Togl.

CHAPTER 11

# The Books

Prandina stood at a window that let her look almost directly down on the castle gate. As soon as she saw her father go out, she turned and hurried down the hall. Being on Noble Cloud, he was likely to be gone a long time. And with Zarian downstairs taking a nap, now was her chance. From the moment she'd seen her father go into the room behind the portrait-door, she'd wanted to go in too, see what was in it.

She left the door to the study open. If she got caught with it closed, she'd really be in trouble. Too, with the door open, she'd be much more likely to hear anyone coming.

One thing she had wondered about was whether her father's opening the display case and taking out the big key had anything to do with his opening the portrait-door. She got down on her hands and knees and looked closely at the bottom of the portrait's frame where he seemed to have pushed or pulled or twisted or whatever. In each corner was a carved rose, and as she began trying to push, pull and twist one of them she spotted—in the shadow below it—a small slot, almost surely a keyhole. She glanced at the large key in the case. Longer than her forearm and hand it wouldn't even start to fit into the tiny slot. But her father must have had some reason for taking it out. Could it, somehow, be the key to a little key?

She went over to the ancient and heavy king's desk, took the footstool from near it—the one she had sat on many times—and placed it near the spot where he'd stood to get the key from above the display case. She could only hope he'd put it back where he'd found it. She stood on the stool, reached up and began to feel along the case's ledge—very carefully. If she knocked it off, its ringing clatter on the stone could bring some servant to look.

Little puffballs of dust floated down. She sputtered and blinked, closed her mouth and eyes and kept feeling. Just as she was wondering if he'd put the key back on the ledge, she felt something small, cold and hard. Carefully she slid it to the edge, pinched it and pulled it down. Her heart was beating with such a thump she could hardly hear. She held her breath and listened. Nothing.

With some jiggling of the key and a good tug, the case opened. She picked up the large key. It was heavier than she had thought it would be, and she sat on the stool and put the key across her knees so she could look at it closely. Nothing obvious. No little key tied to it, stuck to it. Did it come apart maybe? Her father had seemed to be working on it, tugging at it. But it looked solid. She turned it on end to look at it—and suddenly stopped. Was that a click? She turned it up the other way. Yes. No doubt. A click. But where was it coming from?

She turned her head and, with the big, loop-handle end close to her ear, shook it. No noise. Quickly she turned the key to where the other end was close to her ear and shook. Yes! A little clattering. There was definitely something inside. The big key had to come apart, but where?

She held it so that light from the window fell on the toothed end and, turning it slowly, looked carefully. She was about to think it was one solid piece when she saw a thin line, a tiny break where the round, main-shaft part stuck out over the flat, toothed part. Did the end piece pull off? She tugged. Nothing moved. She tugged harder. Again no movement. Her father had...Did the end screw off?

She held the toothed part with one hand and tried to turn the end piece with the other. Nothing happened. She tried to turn it the other way, harder. The end began to turn. Easily. In only a couple of turns the end came off—and a tiny key slid into her lap.

Hands trembling, she picked up the key, and was just bending to set the big key aside when she heard from far down the hall the call of a tiny voice, "Dina! Dina! Where are you?"

Quickly, hands shaking, some fumbling, she began to put the little key back into the big one. The portrait room would have to wait for another day.

CHAPTER 12

# There Is Nowhere but Here

As had happened a few mornings before when he had been excited about the Festival and the race, Togai slept little after the first streaks of light hit the sky, and he came fully awake as soon as Togl came in to awaken Kallo. When Kallo, remembering he had promised to awaken Togai, reached across the space between the cots to stick a wet finger in his brother's ear, Togai grabbed the hand and jerked Kallo off his cot. They both laughed, and Kallo pulled Togai to the floor. But that ended the fooling around. Each dressed quickly and went out.

"Maker's blessings!" Lilu said when she saw Togai. "What are you doing up?"

He shrugged. "Just wanted to get up."

"You want your breakfast now?"

"No," he said. He pointed to the paddle of fish she had just set on the table. "Could I just take a piece of fish and go?"

"I guess so...but..."

But it was too late. Togai had quickly scooped up a hot piece of fish and, flipping it hand to hand, was already going out the door.

She looked at Togl. "Goodness. What was that all about?"

Togl smiled. "Growing up, I reckon."

Togai went around the corner of the house, took a couple of quick bites, picked up a thin bundle he had hidden there before he went to bed, and headed for the smokehut. The soreness, especially in his short leg, seemed to lessen with almost every step, and more than the taste of hot fish, he began to enjoy the quiet and stillness. Maybe this was why Togl liked getting out early.

He was just swallowing the last of the fish and still wiping his hands on his pants when he came to the edge of the smokehut clearing. Good. No sign of Old Zoltai. Though Togai's intention—hope—had been simply to get to the smokehut before Old Zoltai to, maybe, make up for being late yesterday, an idea now came as to how he might make an even better impression, and he hurried on.

In the clearing, in the place where Zoltai had done his chopping yesterday, were two treetops that, Togai guessed, Zoltai had dragged over to be ready for his ax attack first thing. He thought Old Zoltai would really be impressed, if when he first stepped into the clearing he saw Togai not only already there but also hard at work lopping off limbs! But where was the ax?

He dropped his bundle. Now...where would an experienced woodcutter like Old Zoltai leave his ax? Where he'd use it next, of course. He walked in between the two tops and just as he bent to look back into the tangle of limbs he spotted the ax under and lined up with the trunk of the nearest top—put there, Togai guessed, so it wouldn't get dew on it and start to rust.

He pulled the ax out. It was heavier than he'd thought it would be. Let's see, he thought. Zoltai stood on one side, cut on the other. Sure. Less chance of hitting your leg—or cutting a toe off.

Just as he raised the ax he heard, "What in the name of the Blessed Woodcutter are you doing?"

Togai turned and saw Old Zoltai coming rapidly across the clearing, cane barely touching the ground. Where was the cane yesterday? Togai wondered. He hadn't seen it at all.

Zoltai stopped in the opening between the two trunks. Togai felt trapped.

"Can't you hear?" Zoltai asked. "I asked what you were doing.'"

"Uh, I was just going to cut off some limbs, try to make up for yesterday."

"Never, never use another man's tools without his permission. Especially his ax. Didn't you know that?"

"Uh, nosir. I didn't."

"Well you know now. I know we Chelks share everything, sort

of. But would your mother like it if she cooked some fish and I just walked in and took a piece?"

"I guess not."

"Well, that ax is *mine*. I do my work with it, take care of it, keep it sharp. What if you hit the ground with it, maybe a rock, put a nick in it?"

Togai looked down. "I don't know."

"I bet that's the truth! Well, enough talk. Let's get to work. Just don't let anything like this happen again."

"Yessir."

As Togai carefully let the ax lean against the tree trunk, Zoltai said, "You might as well learn the whole routine. Let's go down to the fire pit and get the fire restarted."

Zoltai stopped in front of the pit and tossed his cane to one side. "Help me move these rocks and get a few pieces of wood thrown in before the coals die down. Make the big fire later. But be careful with those rocks. They're probably hot."

Though Togai moved quickly, Zoltai grabbed one of the big flat slabs of rock blocking the pit opening and dragged it around to the side before Togai could do anything. Togai reached for the second but quickly pulled his hand away. It really was hot, just like Old Zoltai had warned. He started pulling off his shirt to wrap around his hands, but Old Zoltai said, "Never mind," and quickly took hold of the rock and pulled it around to the side.

Togai began re-buttoning his shirt and Zoltai brusquely brushed past him and quickly threw a few small pieces of wood—right past Togai—deep into the pit.

"Well," Zoltai, said, "you were a big help on that," and he turned and started toward the chopping area at a fast walk, limp barely noticeable.

Back at the treetops Togai picked up the bundle he had dropped near them and stepped back to wait for the first limbs to come off.

Old Zoltai pointed to the bundle. "I see you have some stuff wrapped in an old shirt."

"Yessir."

"Yeah, some boys do that. Bring an old shirt, some rags. Not tough like we were when I was growing up. Not as smart either. Not as many bring a shirt or rags as ought to."

He pointed toward the nearby treetops. "Drag over a couple more tops while I get started, then you start dragging. Like yesterday, when I get enough cut, I'll help you drag and then we'll start the big fire. Now get moving."

Togai dropped the bundle and hurried toward the tops. If things go the way I want, he thought, you'll be trying to keep up with me.

He dragged a big top over and hurried back to get another. By the time he was back with it, Old Zoltai had built up a pile of ten or more of the pole-like, trimmed limbs.

Togai picked up the bundle. Now, he thought, let's find out who has to keep up with who.

The outside, the wrap part of the bundle was an old shirt with the sleeves tied together. Togai quickly untied them and pulled out two lengths of rope, each a little longer than he was tall, each with a loop in the end of it that Kallo had tied for him. Working quickly, he pulled four limbs from Old Zoltai's pile, looped one rope around their ends, stuck the end of the rope through the loop to make a noose and pulled the rope taut. Quickly he did the same with four other limbs, took two rags from inside the shirt, wrapped those loosely around his wrist and hands, then, with his back toward the limbs, picked up the end of each rope, and with little flips and double twists of his hands, quickly had the ropes looped around his wrists and firmly grasped in his hands. He began pulling, and though he had trouble at first with the limbs jerking from side to side, they fairly quickly fell in line and before he knew it he was almost running with them toward the fire pit.

When he came even with the front of the fire pit, he stopped, turned and with two quick tugs and jerks had his ropes free—and in almost no time was running back toward the chopping area.

Old Zoltai was staring, mouth open—and Togai looked down so Zoltai wouldn't see him laugh.

Once back to the chopping area, he found only six pole-limbs piled there, and though he didn't dare look, he could tell from the sound that Old Zoltai was chopping furiously. Togai quickly made a looped bundle of four for one hand, and as soon as he had two more for the other hand he was again away in a limb-dragging run.

When he got back, there were only three limbs, and Old Zoltai was coming toward him, huffing and puffing and dragging another top. "I'll get the tops, if you want," Togai said, and hurried past Zoltai to get one to drag over. After that, Togai dragged both limbs and tops, mixing green and seasoned, while Old Zoltai sweated and swore as he chopped.

Just as Togai was beginning to sweat heavily and breathe hard—and wonder how much longer he could keep up the pace—Zoltai stopped his chopping and looked toward the fire pit. "Looks like we've got about enough for today. Let me get enough lopped and trimmed for you to drag down—and a few for me, then we'll go down and start the fire. All right?"

"Yessir."

Zoltai was just about to toss a limb into the pit when he stopped and sniffed. "Hmpf. Shouldn't be smelling smoke." Quickly he looked up at the chimney. "Drat, boy. You got me so flustered this morning I forgot to move the cover off the chimney."

"Let me do it," Togai said.

Old Zoltai gave him a hard look. "No. That rock is heavy. You'd have to strain to slide it—and what if you slid it too far? It'd fall, and we'd have to, Maker forbid, ask for help to get it back up there."

When Zoltai was back from moving the rock, he said, "I could see over on the river the women have just started cleaning yesterday's catch. So, since we don't need to start the fire yet, want to go to that stump over there and sit a spell? Room for both of us. Sawed off the stump myself, from a big oak that floated down in a flood."

Togai hesitated.

"You don't have to, but I can't let you leave this early. People would think my head had lost its hone."

Togai shrugged. "Don't have anything else to do."

Zoltai started away and snorted. "Glad the idea of my company excites you so much."

Zoltai sat facing the mountains, and since Togai didn't want to seem rude by sitting on the other side, sat on the same side. But not too close.

After a while, Old Zoltai said, "You're the first boy who ever showed up early, and I *never* had one get ahead of me dragging before. Where'd you get the idea for the ropes? Some woodcutter tell you?"

"Nosir. Just thought of it."

"Good idea. Should have thought of it myself a long time ago. Woodcutters have long used ropes, with harnesses, for dragging logs and treetops. Yep, should have thought of it myself."

A silence fell, and when it seemed the old man didn't have more to say, Togai said, "I'm sorry about almost using your ax this morning...and about other things too. Uh, like last year, at the dune. I didn't mean to be disrespectful. I...I'd forgotten about your leg, and, uh, I'm sorry. Sorry. I'm not very good at apologizing—and I've got a lot to apologize for."

"Most of us do," the old man said. "But let that be a lesson to you."

"A lesson? What be a lesson?"

"Forgetting about my leg. If you'd try to forget about your leg and not be so touchy about it, most people would forget about it too, and..."

In spite of what he'd just said about being disrespectful, Togai blurted, "That's easy for you to say. Your leg's a sign of honor, an accident. I was born this way."

"And born lucky too."

"*Lucky*? How can you say that?"

"In all our history no one else has had an older brother willing to give up his first-born right so his little brother wouldn't have to be," Zoltai chuckled, "be a *woodcutter* like me. Also, Lilu and Togl love you. You're a good runner. And smart. So don't feel so sorry for yourself. Things could be a lot worse."

Togai sighed. "I guess you're right, but..." He was encouraged by Old Zoltai's smile. "Can I tell you something, Old Zoltai, something I've not told anybody?"

"Sure."

"You won't tell? Not anybody?"

"Not a soul."

"After the race, after I thought I'd won, I came home early and I...I thought about running away."

"Running away? Where to?"

"I don't know. Someplace. Somewhere."

"Somewhere? Maybe you're not as smart as I thought you were. There is no other place. Just here. Surely Togl has told you if you take a canoe too far out on the ocean you'll fall off the Edge. And even if the Ogres would let you try, you couldn't climb those high rock walls to get out of the valley. I know. I've seen them. Even if you could climb the walls—and *if* the Ogres let you past Ogre's Horns, let you up the mountains somewhere—you'd just fall off the other side. So, where could you run away to?"

Togai shrugged. "Maybe into Zaphyr. I could hide in the woods, sneak down to the king's orchard. Not really steal. Just pick up fruit they left on the ground."

"Hmpf. You get caught in the king's orchard, somebody'd be picking up your head."

CHAPTER 13

# Rotah's Book

Prandina knelt and with a shaky hand pushed the small key into the slot in the portrait frame. Her heart was in her throat and, bent the way she was, with its every thump she felt she might choke. As soon as Zarian had gone down for his nap she had hurried up here. She thought the king would be out for a good while riding, but she couldn't be sure—which was why she had planned ahead, knew what she wanted to do, was ready to move quickly.

She turned the key—hard. The portrait-door popped open and though it banged against her head she paid it no mind. She quickly reached for the lit candle she had set on the floor, stood and stepped into cooler air that had a strong, musty odor. The yellow candle light showed a tiny room, narrow and no more than three of her natural steps long. On one side were two bookcases that reached almost to the ceiling—which was lower than in the study—but only one bookcase, the one nearer the door, had any books in it.

Holding the candle high at first, then moving it down, she saw that the top shelf and the next three were fairly well packed with books—all about the same size—while the fifth shelf, next to the bottom one, was about half full. The bottom shelf was bare. Having taken all that in at a glance, she reached out and pulled in the stool, the one she had stood on to get the first key and sat on to get the third. She now stood on it again and looked at the upper left corner of the case. That's where her father had looked and reached, high enough, it seemed, to make her guess she'd need the stool. But which book had interested him so much? They all looked about the same and, on that shelf at least, old. There seemed to be some writing on the spines, but it was all faint and, in this dim light and at this distance, impossible to read. She hadn't counted on that, but then, titles wouldn't have helped her.

Was there a clue to which book her father had taken—other than it seemed to be from the left corner of the top shelf? Noticing a layer of dust on the shelf that was about level with her shoulders, she held the candle higher—and stretched and stood on tiptoe so she could look along the top shelf. Yes, there, a streak in the dust that led right to a book.

Slowly, carefully, she pulled the book out along the same streak. With a little jump and a few quick steps she was at her father's desk—in his chair!—book in front of her. She took a deep breath and looked down at it. Since there was only that one streak in the otherwise thick layer of dust on the shelves, she was fairly sure that was the first time in a long time her father had looked at any of the books. Question was, why this one, why now? But first, assuming this was the right book, where in it had he looked?

The musty smell and moldy feel of the book's dark and cracked leather cover had already told her it was old. Now, the many little cracks and splits in the dark yellow of the uneven page edges told her that the book's inner parts might be even older than the outer.

But where to start? Would the top edge—like the shelf edge, maybe—show some break in dust? With one finger she slowly turned the book to where she could see the top, and lo, a frayed ribbon marker attached to the spine led down into pages near the end of the book.

Now even more nervous, hands even more shaky, as carefully as she could she lifted the book open enough to get her index finger in between the pages where the marker was. That place secure, she turned the book to look at the spine. The lettering was very faint, but if she used her imagination and let her mind fill in gaps and cracks, she was pretty sure the large letters at the top of the spine made *Book of Kings*. Below that, smaller, was...what? A number? Number seven? No. Four. Then *The*...followed by something ending in *ing*? And below that...*Rotar* and *Rotar*? Didn't make sense.

Almost certain from what she'd seen and felt that both the

book's cover and pages were easily torn, she used her free hand to carefully lift the cover and peek in. As she had hoped, the first page was a title page.

*Book of Kings*
4
*The Writings of*
*Rotar and Rotah*

Better, she thought, this made sense. Then, for the first time the thought hit her. Of course. It all made sense. It was Rotar's portrait on the portrait-door. He'd built the castle and put the secret room there, hid it behind his own portrait.

Carefully, cautiously, she opened the book at the marker, where her finger was, and saw—in crude block letters:

*Writ of Keng Rotah, Aith Keng of Zaphyr*
*The tale I now put to papyr ha not been writ before. My vatter*
*Rotar tol it me. . . .*

With even more fascination than her father had when he first read Rotah's words many years before, she read on—of the tale that was not 'sposed to be writ down.'

But of all the things she read, what surprised and shocked her most was the decree Rotah revealed and had put on paper for the first time ever. Though she read and re-read the entire entry, each time she read the decree she was shocked by it, found it repugnant, impossible to believe. It just couldn't, couldn't be true. But there it was. And at the end of the entry was a rough but flowing, script-like 'Rotah,' underscored with a big 'Z,' written with a flourish, as if the writer were very proud of what he'd just written.

Almost surely her father had known about this story, this book, for he had gone directly to it, but why now? Why the day after the Festival? Or did the Festival have anything to do with it? And had he actually read, or re-read, this particular entry? Maybe he had looked elsewhere in the book, just happened to put the ribbon where she found it. But she didn't think so. What she'd read was so revealing, so dramatic, so. . .so awful she didn't want to believe it.

Suddenly she sat upright. Had she heard the thud of hooves?

Hurriedly, but carefully Prandina put the book away, but even as she did she was thinking she wanted to read more. But when would be the best time to come? When her father was away? During the night when everyone else in the castle would be, she would hope, sound asleep?

CHAPTER 14

# Zoltai's Yarns

The next morning, Togai and Zoltai arrived at the smokehut at about the same time, again worked hard and well together, Togai with his ropes, Zoltai with his ax. And as had happened the day before, when everything was ready for the fire, Zoltai pointed to the stump and offered a short rest.

For a while they seemed content to enjoy the quiet and the warmth of the early morning sun. Zoltai spoke first. "Why were you thinking about running away?"

Togai took a deep breath. "Partly because of the race, but...Did you know Zaprians laugh at us—because of our clothes and, and... the way we smell?"

Zoltai sighed. "Kind of. Do you know why we have to wear our clothes inside out?"

"Nosir."

"Well then, I bet you don't know how it came about we are even allowed to go to Festivals—or how the river came to be named 'Forbidden.'"

"Nosir, I don't."

Zoltai took a deep breath. "Well, you should know. Togl should have told you because the heroes of the story—at least the Festival part—are fishers. The whole thing happened like this.

"Back before the time of King Andar, the Twelfth King of Zaphyr, Chelks weren't allowed into the kingdom at all on Festival Day but could go there any other day some Zap wanted them for work— as long as they were out of Zaphyr by sundown. Zaps, though few seemed to want to, could come into Chelekai anytime they wanted.

"King Andar had a high-spirited and adventuresome young grandson, Arandar, that the old king, it is said, loved more than his own life. One day, when the river was swollen by heavy spring rains Arandar took a dare from a cousin and paddled a small raft they had made over to our side to—part of the dare—dive from a high tree that leaned out over the river. Arandar made the mistake of not tying the raft to a tree—or not pulling it far enough on shore—and just as he was diving it went bobbing away. He tried to swim across the river to Zaphyr but, like the raft, was swept downstream by the swift current. The cousin came running to the castle, crying and telling what had happened. Through the night men of the kingdom, carrying torches and calling Arandar's name, searched up and down the river banks. The next day the Chelk fishers found the boy's body floating in the sea and returned it to Zaphyr.

"The king told the fishers—it's supposed to be the first time a Zaprian king ever spoke to a Chelk, maybe the last, too—he was so grateful that they had found Arandar and kept him from floating over the edge and dropping into the eternal fires of the Unknown Under that they—and all Chelks—could come to the Festival for as long as he was king.

"In contrast—in his grief—Andar decreed no Zaprian ever again go into—or onto—either the river or the ocean, which is how the Forbidden River got its name. He further decreed that no Zaprian could ever again swim or even try to learn to swim. Not anywhere. Not even in a pond."

Zoltai jumped up. "Axes, boy! If the fish women got here and we didn't have the smoke going, they'd tell everybody we'd been lollygagging."

As they started toward the fire pit, one favoring his right leg, the other his left, Togai said, "Tomorrow, will you tell me the story of why we have to wear our clothes inside out?"

"Maybe, if we have time. But I'm not big on woman talk."

When Togai got to the smokehouse clearing next morning and saw Old Zoltai wasn't there he hurried toward the fire pit. Good, he thought. Get the early fire going, save some time for stories—maybe.

Might even make a good impression on Old Zoltai. But no sooner had he rolled the slab rocks away from the opening that he saw Old Zoltai hurrying toward him, a scowl on his face. Uh, oh, Togai thought. "Am I doing something wrong?" he asked.

"No, boy," Zoltai said, and huffed right past him. "You keep working. I forgot to uncover the chimney before I left yesterday."

Bending and tossing small pieces of wood as far back into the pit as he could, Togai found himself wondering what story Old Zoltai might tell next, but the next words he heard from Old Zoltai were, "Owww! Great cursed axes."

Togai quickly looked up. Zoltai was bending over and grimacing, left hand on the top rung of the ladder, right clutched to his chest.

"What's wrong?" Togai yelled out—just as Zoltai dropped his left hand to the next rung and quickly took a step down.

"What's wrong?" Togai yelled again.

"Nothing, boy. Nothing. I always come down a ladder this way."

Togai ran to the ladder and watched Zoltai carefully come down, one step at a time, holding to rungs only with his left hand and keeping his right hand tucked tightly against his chest.

"What happened?" Togai asked as Zoltai stepped off the ladder.

Zoltai held out his quivering right hand for Togai to see. Blood oozed from split finger tips and nails and the fingers themselves were bloody and raw all the way back to their middle joints. Zoltai closed his left hand over the bleeding right, and, in obvious pain and bending nearly double, put them both between his legs and closed down on them tightly.

"Like I've done so many times...was holdin' onto the chimney with my right hand, kind of lift-slidin' the damper rock around with my left. Let it slip. Ooo. Dummy!."

"Want me to run and get Old Helu to come and put a poultice on it?"

"No. But do go tell her I'll need a couple of the older boys to work for a while—that'll be *woodcutters*. I won't be able to hold an ax for...for I don't know how long."

"I could..."

"No. I know you could try—and you'd try hard. But I'll need someone to do all the chopping, do a lot of the things I do after you leave. So, run along. Hurry. And tell Helu to send them right away. We've got wood to cut, a fire to make."

It wasn't long before Togai was back—and soon after, Old Helu with a poultice and two woodcutters to be, Caldo and Sodl. Their looks showed they'd much rather have been left in their canoe-making training, hard as that work was, rather than come back to Old Zoltai.

As Togai had feared, Old Zoltai offered no stump break that morning—or the next or the next. With Caldo and Sodl there he became once again the hard-to-please taskmaster he was reputed to be. Togai hoped the hand would heal so he could again look forward to and enjoy an invitation to sit on a stump and listen to a Zoltai tale. But the hand didn't heal, and the only amusement Togai got from the rest of his one-moon training with Zoltai was hearing Old Zoltai chide Caldo and Sodl for not being able to cut limbs fast enough to keep one little fisherboy busy.

Still, when Togai would look back, he'd remember that first moon of his first training year as the happiest he ever lived. Everyone in his family was in a good mood. Especially Togl. No man had ever had two sons become fishers. Anywhere in the village anyone in the family went, they'd hear talk about what a brave and loving thing Kallo had done. Though at times Kallo would be embarrassed, he liked all the attention and praise he was getting. If that weren't enough to keep him in good spirits and make him fun to be around, each night he'd come home eager to talk about what he was learning from Galu and Chulo and what had happened during the day.

One night at supper he again had Togl and Lilu and Togai laughing so hard they thought their sides would split. He was telling how—in trying to impress old Chulo and Galu with how far he could throw the net—he snagged old Chulo and not only got off balance and fell out of the boat but almost pulled old Chulo in with him.

Togai was still laughing when he saw Togl looking at him with an amused, pleased look. But it seemed to Togai that Togl was amused and pleased not as much by Kallo's tale as by the way Togai was laughing at it.

"You like that story?" Togl asked.

"Yessir," Togai said—and tried not to giggle.

"How would you like to go fishing with me tomorrow?"

"Really? Could I?"

"Yes."

"Jumping water lizards. Wait'll I tell Tatl and...What about my training work?"

Togl smiled. "I've already talked to Old Helu about it. She said okay—but to not ask too often."

"Will Old Exl be with us?"

"No. He wasn't feeling well today and thought a day off would do him good. So this seems a good chance to get you started, that is, if you want to be a fisher someday."

"Oh, I do. Of course I do."

That night, soon after the hut had gone dark, Togai spoke softly from his cot. "Kallo, will you tell me again how I got my name and how Papa and Old Exl became partners?"

Kallo yawned. "Sure. Lilu says I was just a baby at the time. Papa was fishing with his father, our grandfather. Exl was fishing with his young son, who was not much older than I am now. One day a big storm came up, with a lot of rain and wind, and they tried to hold the two canoes together so they wouldn't capsize. But they both got turned over and Grandpa drowned while trying to save Exl's son, who drowned too. So, ever since, Papa and Exl have fished together."

"What was Grandpa name?"

"Oh, Togai. You know. You just want to hear the story again. His name was Togai—and Papa and Lilu named you after him because everyone loved him so much."

## CHAPTER 15

# Fisherboy

Though Togai tried as best he knew how to help Togl get their canoe ready, with all his fumbling and stumbling they were still the last to dip their paddles. Going downstream on the river's smooth, early morning surface was fun and exciting. He'd been in a canoe many times, with Kallo and alone, moving slowly, awkwardly, the canoe seeming to go wherever it wanted to go. This was the first time he'd ever tried to paddle with a good paddler behind him—and with the strongest and very best behind him now, they seemed to be flying, just skimming along, barely touching the water.

Excited as he had been, though, it was nothing like the excitement when they rounded the last bend and the ocean was right there before them, a strange gray-green, stretching as far as he could see in all directions. At last he was going to do something he'd often thought about and long wanted to do. Go onto the ocean. But when they hit the first big wave and the bow of the canoe shot up and came down with a jar and splash that left him wet with spray and his teeth hurting, he thought that maybe fishing wouldn't be as much fun as he had thought it would be. And he was right. It wasn't.

He spent most of the day trying, as he was told to, to stay by Togl's side, watch and try to imitate every move that Togl made while at the same time, not get in the way or step on anything or fall out of the boat. Too, Togai discovered, there was no shade on the ocean, and because the unrelenting sun kept him hot and thirsty he drank a lot—which meant he needed to pee a lot. Trouble was, in the bobbing, pitching canoe he couldn't pee over the side without getting more on himself than in the ocean.

But he still enjoyed every moment of it. He'd bet no other 12-old had ever been on the ocean before—fishing! He couldn't wait to tell Dilo and Tatl.

The fish that Togl caught—Togai didn't catch any—they put into holding nets, one on each side of the canoe, to keep them alive and fresh. About the middle of the afternoon Togl glanced at the sun and said, "We'll need a head start on the others if we want to do any trading—so help me dump the fish back into the canoe, put in some water, and we'll head for shore."

Fish and water in, Togai knelt in the bow and winced. His knees were raw and achy from the morning paddle. He wanted to stand and bend over, or something, but knew if he did the other fishers would laugh at him. So, he gritted his teeth and began to paddle—and discovered another agony. His arms and shoulders were sore, too, and what was worse, the canoe—with its part load of fish and water—was more sluggish, harder to paddle. No wonder Togl and the other fishers had big arms and shoulders, which he'd long admired. Now he wished he had something else the fishers had: thick knee calluses.

So, though there were often tears in his eyes, he fought to match Togl stroke for stroke, even if many were weak and ineffective. He was glad when finally he could look upriver and see some Zaprians on the trading bank and others coming down from the City of Light. "Slow down some," Togl said, "let the others catch up. Coming in, you paddled better than I thought you would."

Wow, Togai thought. Buoyed by the unexpected praise, he said, "If we kept paddling, we'd be first there, and you'd get best bargains for your fish."

"Yes. But that wouldn't be fair to the others, would it?"

Though Chelks weren't allowed in Zaphyr except to work for a Zaprian—or go to the Festival—the rocky strand where the canoes landed was considered part of the river. It was slightly below the bank where the Zaps stood, and the Chelk fishers could get out and walk on it to trade with Zaprians who, by old Andar's decree, had to stay on the bank.

When their canoe touched, as Togl had said to, Togai jumped

from the bow—as much as his aching knees and cramped legs would let him jump—and pulled the canoe onto the strand.

Togl was quickly out and as he waded up alongside the canoe he reached in and pulled out two sea bass. He held one out toward Togai. "Here, you might as well start learning to trade."

Togai had already taken a look at the Zaprians, standing there with their to-be-traded jars of honey, loaves of bread, baskets of fruits and vegetables and bundles of old clothes. He looked down. "I don't want to."

Togl's mouth started to open, but he said nothing.

"Could I just hand fish to you as you need them, Papa?"

Togl nodded. "All right. But pay attention. You'll have to learn sometime."

When trading ended and Togl waved for the other fishers to go on, Togai thought his father was just being nice to them, saying they didn't have to wait. But after just a few strokes toward Chelekai, Togai realized that Togl, in the stern, must be barely paddling. Only when the other canoes were well ahead did Togai feel the surge of Togl's powerful strokes.

"Why'd you not want to trade?" Togl asked.

The question and its tone took away Togai's thoughts of getting home to food and bed and sleep. Never before had Togl spoken to him in such a direct way. Togai took a deep breath.

"The…the Zaprians were standing on the bank. And I didn't want to look up at them—or have them looking down at me."

"And why is that?"

Togai didn't want to answer, but…

"Because, Papa, because they laugh at us. Do you know they laugh at us?"

Togl's answer was slow in coming. "Yes. Sometimes, anyway."

Togai felt his mouth go dry. "Why then, Papa, if you know the Zaps look down on us, do you trade with them?"

Togl sighed. "You know how it is over here, the poor soil we have. Can't get fruit trees to grow. Best gardens give us only a few little carrots, some potatoes, onions, not much more. So, we *have* to trade with the Zaps. No choice if we want to eat—eat reasonably well, and I think we all do. So we trade—our fish, which we have plenty of, for their fruits and vegetables and other things, which they have plenty of. So we both benefit."

"I guess, Papa. But it seems they don't give us very much for our fish. Is that because we need what they have more than they need—or want—fish?"

Togl sighed. "Togai, sometimes I think you're already all your fingers and toes old. I've been fishing with Old Exl for I don't know how many Festivals and he's never asked anything like that. But you're right. Zaps make the point that they don't actually *need* our fish. They tell us that some farmers from the far side of the valley eat a lot of eggs and cheese when they can't come for fish—or run out of dried fish. What it comes down to, Zaps could live without fish, they just don't want to."

"They seem to have lots of cows and chickens. Could they eat them?"

"I guess they could, but why would anyone eat a cow that can make milk or a chicken that can lay eggs? That'd be silly. Main thing, though, Zaps know Maker didn't make animals to be eaten."

"Well, didn't He make fishes?"

"Yes. To eat."

## CHAPTER 16

# Dreams and Disappointments

Prandina yawned and looked at the candle. It had burned almost to the bottom and she'd have to go soon. It didn't matter. She was about burned out herself.

After that first read in the Rotar-Rotah book she'd been really eager to get back to it, to find out if Rotah said more about the tale, maybe even look and see what was in the next book about it, if anything. She wanted to look in the next book anyway to see if its writer—or writers—had followed Rotah's decree and passed it on, that dreadful, awful thing.

So, after a good afternoon nap with Zarian, she had come back the next night—and then the next two or three—to scour the rest of Rotah's book and go onto the next one. To her disappointment she had found Rotah said nothing more of the tale—and that the book after his, that of kings Orand and Oprand, had nothing at all about it. She had looked through the book page by page, and if either one had read the tale or heard of it, he obviously hadn't thought it worth passing on. She was sure, though, that Orand had read Rotah's book—or the last page of it anyway. For there, as Rotah had decreed, on the first and last pages of the Orand-Oprand book was Rotah's decree, repeated. That was a big disappointment to her. She was even more disappointed when she looked ahead to her father's book, to the one he was still writing. And there the decree was, first and last pages. The decree lived.

Prandina had thought that would satisfy her curiosity about the tale, but now and then she'd get the urge to take just one more look—and spend part of another night looking through a book or two and again blowing out the candle, disappointed.

One good thing to come of it was that, oddly enough, it brought her and her father closer together. Wondering if he might be aware of Rotah's tale, but afraid to ask directly, she thought of a devious way to find out—with some risk that she might make him suspicious.

Such thoughts in mind, one morning she went into her father's study, past him asleep in his chair, and over to the window. She waited a moment and scraped her foot. He quickly sat up.

"Just resting my eyes. What you looking at?"

"Oh, just looking up the valley. Seems so pretty. But I've never really seen it. Could I ride up there with you someday?"

Praidar came and put his big arms around her. "Of course. But I didn't think you liked to ride."

"That's been true. So far. But since you seem to like it so much..." She intentionally didn't finish.

He laughed and leaned past her to look out the window. "Pretty day, but a bit cool. The Ogres may be down low, so we shouldn't go up too far, but...How about this afternoon?"

She turned and gave him a hug. "Oh, could we, Daddy? Could we?"

They rode up far enough for her to get a distant view of Sky Falls. And though her father had kept them in the middle of the valley, well away from the high rock walls that bordered it—to avoid irking any Ogres, she guessed—she had a good enough view to see why Rotah would doubt his 'vattar's' tale. Before they turned and started back to the castle, she pointed and said, "Goodness, that rock wall over there looks smooth and almost straight up. Anyone ever climb it?"

She held her breath.

Her father gave her a puzzled look, then said, "Goodness, I can't imagine—given the Ogres and all—anyone would even dare try. I've been up close and taken a good look at those walls." He laughed. "Why, even a fly with some of Old Rono's cookie dough stuck to his feet would have a hard time climbing those walls."

Prandina laughed heartily and long, pretending more glee than she felt so she could look right at him and study his face. All she saw was amusement, no hint of suspicion or puzzlement. And nothing in his words gave the least hint he'd ever heard—or read—Rotah's tale.

After that, they began to take rides together every other day or so and only occasionally would she think about the books or what Rotah had written. Now, having come back for one more 'last time' look, she decided it really would be her last. Rotah's tale seemed to have died with him. She just wished his decree had too.

CHAPTER 17

# Does a Festival Count if You Don't Go?

In spite of all his aches and pains after one day of fishing with Togl, Togai would have jumped at another chance but none came. All other work days his first year as a learner he went to one of his training jobs. And though he always had other boys and girls his age around him, any one of those mornings he spent learning to mend a net or chip away at a log to make a canoe he would gladly have traded for another day in the canoe with Togl or another morning alone with Old Zoltai.

As Festival time neared, almost no one believed him when he said he didn't want to go. Even Old Xalu was going, people said—and she was the oldest person in the village and could barely walk. If someone asked why he didn't want to go, he'd say he didn't like Festivals anymore, too much noise and carrying on. Tatl was the only one who said he thought Togai wouldn't go, said that when others were around. Said if he'd run the wrong way, he wouldn't want to go either. Not ever.

Togai knew he shouldn't lie, but he didn't want to tell anyone—especially Lilu—he didn't want to go because Zaps thought that Chelks were dumb and smelly and wore awful clothes. He guessed other Chelks must know how the Zaps felt but kept their mouths shut and kept going to Festivals anyway. Not talking about the Zaps' attitude he could understand. Enduring it, no.

Festival morning, Togai heard Kallo getting dressed, but didn't get up until Kallo went out. Slowly he put on some pants, then a shirt. He wanted to put off going out as long as he could.

"Togai, for Maker's sake, hurry up," he heard Lilu call, then, "Togl, you and Kallo take these things and go on. Togai and I will catch up. *Togai!*"

When he came out she looked at him in disbelief. "Where's your new Festival outfit?"

"I...I said I wasn't going."

"Yes, but I...You just don't appreciate anything I do for you. I spent all that time..." She jerked a picnic basket from the table but after only a few steps stopped and looked back. "All right. Stay if you want. But don't you *dare* get out of sight of this village. You hear me?"

"Yes ma'am," he said, and though he dreaded that Togl might come back to get him, he sat down at the table. It would be worse if Togl had to come looking for him.

When the sounds of people passing stopped, Togai went outside. The village looked deserted, but from the river came voices and laughter and clunks as Festival goers plunked paddles and picnic baskets into canoes and shoved off. The voices and laughter grew faint, and he began to look around.

Strange, he thought. He had a whole day to do whatever he wanted—but what? He started up through the village, but with the door to practically every hut open he quickly began to feel as if he were snooping, prying, and he turned toward the river.

Just inside the willows that bordered the strand, he peeped out. He could see no one on the path to the City of Light—which meant no one could look back and see him, which meant that, now, he really did have the place all to himself. All of it. All of Chelekai.

He waded in shallow water along the river's edge, idly poking a toe at crawfish as he went, and he laughed as each leapt and scurried away backwards. He imagined they were quite afraid of the strange snub-nosed monster attacking them.

His aloneness made him daring. Lilu didn't say he had to keep his clothes on. He waded to shore and, quickly down to bareness, ran back in, splashing and laughing, and dived toward deep water. Slowly he swam down to the raft, pulled himself up and lay by its edge, enjoying the warm feel of the early sun on his back and looking down into the river's stillness. A school of minnows swam by, in white clouds and blue sky it seemed.

He rolled and looked up. He couldn't see any of the horses or fishes or turtles Dilo was always saying he could see in clouds. But he didn't care. At a glance he already knew lots of fishes—and soon would know lots more. In just two more Festivals he'd be fifteen and...He suddenly sat up. Turtles. What if this one didn't count because he didn't go? What if Council said he was still only twelve Festivals old and would have to go to three more before he could become a fisher? Elders were reasonable, weren't they? Surely they wouldn't do that. Wasn't it simple? By tomorrow, thirteen Festivals would have passed since he was born. What if he'd been sick and couldn't go? But they probably wouldn't accept sickness as a reason. He didn't think any Chelk had ever been sick at Festival time.

He sat straighter and listened. What was that? Hammering? And music? Creeping spiders! The Festival! The very thing he was trying to avoid..

He dived from the raft and swam to shore. In almost no time he was dressed and running, upstream and upwind, along a path that followed the river. When he could no longer hear any hint of music or laughter, he slowed and began looking for trout and turtles.

By the time he remembered Lilu's order to stay in sight of the village, which he took meant being able to see at least one roof or chimney, he couldn't. But it didn't matter. It was a silly rule. He could climb a tree and see a rooftop or a chimney anytime he wanted to. And if he stayed by the river, he couldn't possibly get lost, could he? He looked back. The river disappeared around a bend, but it *had* to take the same course going back it did coming up, didn't it? Maybe he should climb a tree and look just to be sure. No. Sometimes you had to trust your thoughts. So he went on, further than he'd ever been, seeing things he'd never seen.

Togai enjoyed ambling along, looking at farms, at white houses on slopes well above the river, above orchards and fields and meadows. And after a while...Turtles! What was that? It had to be the king's castle—almost as big as the hill it was on! Turtles. Half the huts in the village could fit in it. How could one man, one girl and a boy need so much space? What could they possibly do with it? He laughed. Get lost? Play hide-and-seek?

CHAPTER 18

# Extra Portrait? Missing Book?

About the time Togai left the raft and started upriver, Prandina arrived at the Festival. By the time he was ambling, enjoying his first view of farms, she was pacing—in the Royal Apartment—already bored and a little angry. She had hoped that, being a Festival older, she might be allowed to go down on the plaza, maybe take Zarian with her, see clowns and a puppet show up close. But when she'd hinted at that her father had said no, certainly not with Zarian. If she wanted to see clowns and puppets up close, he'd get them to come to the castle. She was tempted to say she'd really like to see that, like to see puppets *walk* to the castle, but she didn't.

The main thing she was angry about was not getting to ride in the parade. She'd hoped that since she'd ridden several times with her father, he'd know she could ride around the plaza twice without falling off. But when she'd asked him, he'd said no. He said he wanted to take Zarian with him on Noble Cloud, the way he used to take her. He said he wanted Zarian to get used to being in the parade, wanted people to get used to seeing their next king at the front of it. That hurt Prandina, but she was happy for Zarian. She could well imagine the delight that would be in Zarian's eyes when he was lifted onto Noble Cloud, easily imagine the bewilderment and joy he'd feel on seeing the crowd and hearing their cheers. Easily—for that was the way it had been with her.

Though it meant she had no one to play with, she was glad Zarian had gone down for a nap. He'd need to be rested for the ride in the parade. She yawned. Maybe she needed a nap too.

"Ffiirrsstt calll, boys' race. Ffiirrsstt calll…"

She looked at her father. He didn't even look up from his walnut cake, just shrugged and waved toward the balcony.

Prandina hurried out and looked down at the gathering runners. Shoo. The little short-legged fisherboy who brought so much excitement to last year's race wasn't there. She waited patiently, and when he didn't line up for the second race, went in. Maybe he was too embarrassed by what happened last year, or maybe he too had a strict father and had been told he couldn't run.

The troubadours, her favorites, and clowns and minstrels wouldn't be coming soon, so...Maybe she'd walk down the Hall of Portraits to one of her favorite places, the big window at the end.

There, she sat on the window's low, wide sill, and as she looked up at the mountains she had a thought she'd had many times before, that huge as the mountains were, as much as they seemed to go on forever and ever, they were just a part of something bigger—*inside* whatever it was Maker lived in. She put her face close to the window and looked as nearly straight up as she could. Was Maker up there now, just outside the sky—or was He the sky? Was He looking down now? If He was, could He see her? See her face, her eyes? Know she was thinking of Him?

She sighed and started down the hall. She had noticed several different times that the portraits at this end of the hall were the oldest and much alike. Each was of some unsmiling man, hand on sword. Trying to look menacing, she guessed. Hmpf. She wondered if that was why there were no portraits of queens. Queens didn't carry swords? Wouldn't look menacing?

She knew that downstairs, on one side of the entrance, was the oldest known portrait of a king. Of which one, she couldn't remember. Across from it was one of her grandfather, Prandar. Her father's would replace it sometime. He always said he wanted his to be of him on Noble Cloud.

The portraits up here, in the Hall of Portraits, weren't hung straight across from one another, and she guessed they alternated, one side to the other, in order of reign. First, to her right and closest to the stairs was, according to the nameplate, Valderan. To her left, and next, came Protan. Neither name she recognized. Then came Rotar. Yes. Maybe she was influenced by what she'd read, but he did look a little crazy. Next was, of course, Rotah. She paused. Rotah looked like his writing. Crude, craggy, rough. And...what was that? She took a closer look. On the hand resting on his sword? A scar. A big one. Like a Z, but with more zigzag. Like a bolt of lightning. Hmmm. Wonder how he got that? In a real sword fight?

She went on..."Rotanor." Yes, she thought, a good name for Rotah's son...and then Orand...and Opran and...Wait! Those names. Orand and Opran. Weren't they the names on the book after Rotar and Rotah's? Wasn't it the Orand-Opran book she so carefully searched through after reading Rotah's tale? Sure it was. She'd spent so much time reading it, seen their signatures so often at the end of things they'd written, how could she forget. Quickly she looked at some more names. She was sure she had seen some of them but—wait! Were the portraits actually in order? She bent and looked closely at Rotah's name plate. Yes, there it was. In small letters under his name, "Aith Keng of Zaphyr." And the others? Yes! With quick close looks she saw, under Rotanor's name, "Nith Keng of Zaphyr"—and under Orand's, "Teth Keng of Zaphyr."

But she hadn't seen a book with Rotanor's name on it. Not at all. She was sure about that. Absolutely certain. But where was it? Had it been destroyed for some reason? Probably not. She doubted any king would destroy another king's book. Might even be a decree against it. Would be much easier to tear out some pages. The logical explanation was that the missing book had simply been put back in the wrong place, out of order.

She began running for the dimness at the end of the hall—as if getting back to the royal apartment would help the Festival come to an end. She couldn't wait for stillness and darkness to engulf the land and she'd be the only one in the castle still awake.

## CHAPTER 19

# The Stone Fingers

Past the castle the river had become narrower, swifter and rockier, with banks higher than Togai's head. He glanced up at the sun. He hadn't brought anything to eat and was getting hungry, but he'd really like to see the high walls Old Zoltai had talked about. Maybe if he climbed the bank...

He started to climb. Wait! What was that noise? A murmur? A stirring caused by the Avenging Witch? Maybe some sign from the Ogres of the Cold?

No. It seemed more steady, more like a roar from something big, distant, not a swarm of little Ogres. Or could it be some big guardian of the river he'd never heard of?

He took a deep breath and headed upstream, picking his way among the rocks but staying close to the water's edge. He'd go on. At least to the next bend.

With the roaring getting louder, Togai looked as far ahead as he could with every step. But though the roaring had gotten much louder, when he could see around the bend all he saw was another bend. Close. It wouldn't take long to get to it. He hurried on, and when he was near the bend, he moved close to the bank and—with the roaring now really loud—cautiously peeked around.

He gasped. Not far from him the river was tumbling and bouncing down a high wall of rocks and boulders that stretched from bank to bank. He ran-stumbled to the base of it and looked up through mist and spray. Surely this wasn't the Sky Falls he'd heard about. It was only three or four times as high as his head, not sky high.

Togai studied the rocks and boulders at the end of the wall close to the bank. They were wet and slick looking, but...He looked up. He had no idea what he'd see from the top of the bank, but whatever it was, it'd be a view he'd never seen before. He took a deep breath and reached for the top of the first boulder.

As he pulled himself onto the bank he almost fell backward. He'd never seen anything so big. Only three or four stone-throws away rose a sheer rock wall of red-brown, the same color as the jumble of huge boulders that lay beneath it. It was even bigger than the king's castle, but as big as it was, it was only the stub end of a long finger of stone that ran on and on for as far up the valley as he could see. And the side of it, like that of a huge square finger, was practically straight up and looked apple smooth.

Beyond the far side of the boulder field rose another fingerlike ridge, maybe higher than the first. Clearly there was a valley or ravine in between the two, but how wide and deep? And did it have a river in it?

Togai started across the boulders, warily jumping from one great stone to another. He knew the Ogres of the Cold jealously guarded the mountains—but did the ridge and boulder field count? It was warm and sunny here. Maybe it was the high, far-off mountains they guarded. Or maybe they didn't think anybody—especially a little boy—would come up here on Festival Day.

When he came to the edge of the boulder field, he was breathing hard, partly from effort, more from excitement. Below him was a narrow ravine with a dry creek bed at the bottom. On the other side of it were the straight-up and solid walls of the other ridge he'd seen. Far down the widening ravine, beyond the hills at the end of it, was a gray haziness that he was sure was the ocean.

On the other side of the second ridge were two other, higher ones. The closer one, like the first two, ended in a pile of boulders, but the last and highest one ran all the way to the ocean.

He now turned and looked up the ravine. The ridges seemed to blend together in a broad stretch of stone, like fingers on a hand, a hand that extended from great bluffs and cliffs. He could imagine that woodcutters might now and then stand in the edge of the ravine to cut down trees, but he doubted any ever walked in the ravine. Certainly not this far up.

That thought in mind, Togai quickly worked his way down through the boulders to the dry creek bed and turned toward the mountains. He felt small. On both sides the sheer red walls loomed over him. He'd like to get on top of one, but the ridge sides were as steep and slick as the sides of a bald man's head. At the end of the ravine, though, where the finger ridges came together there was, as between fingers, a depression where the wall was much lower—and maybe not as steep. He hurried on.

The ravine came to an end at a steep dirt bank covered with bushes. From the bottom of it he looked up—and was disappointed. The curving-inward wall, though lower than the side walls, was still higher than any tree he'd ever seen—and almost as straight up. But it did have a small crack in it that widened as it came down. How much, he couldn't see because of the bushes, so he started up through them for a better look.

The ground felt cool and damp to his bare feet, and as he pushed past the last bush he saw that at about level with his knee the crack was wide enough for him to crawl into. He quickly dropped to all fours and as he peeked in felt cool air waft past his face. For as far back as he could see the crack was lined with moist, almost drippy round stone and...Jumping turtles! Was there light back there? In solid rock?

Ogres didn't make fire, did they? He took a deep breath and crawled in. Though his back and shoulders would fairly often rub against the many protruding wet rocks and though his hands were almost immediately wet and cold, he kept crawling—keeping a steady and wary eye on the faint light ahead. Further in, the crack got a little roomier, and he thought he could see that it ended in something like a chimney, which the light was coming down.

He took a few more fast, crawling steps to the edge of the patch of light and, holding his breath, cautiously stood and looked up. Yes. Just like looking up a chimney. About a tree height above him blue sky showed through a small opening. On every side, from where he was all the way up, he thought he could see rough, bumpy stones sticking out, and just as he was wondering if he could use them to climb up to the opening at the top, the sky lost its color and the chimney darkened.

Turtles. Were the Ogres of the Cold coming for him? He quickly dropped to his hands and knees and scurried toward the opening as fast as he could. Just short of it, he stopped and peeked out. Far down the ravine, the hills and ridge tops and sides were in bright sunlight. Whew. Nothing more than a cloud passing in front of the sun, he guessed. But, turtles! The sunlight was far down the ravine, shadows were long. If he didn't get home before sunset, before his parents, he'd wish the Ogres *had* caught him.

As fast as he dared, Togai ran down the dry creek bed and—rather than climb up to and across the boulder field and take the long winding path back along the river—scrambled over the hill at the end of the first ridge and on through the scrub back to the village. Another reason for not going back along the river was to not run the risk of being seen by anyone coming back from the Festival, especially Lilu or Togl.

When he ran up to the hut, all that remained of the sun was a sliver of red and he could hear voices coming up from the river. Quickly he found a rag and wiped the mud and dirt from his hands and knees and elbows and tossed the rag under his cot. He barely made it to his chair at the table when Lilu came striding in, several steps ahead of Togl and Kallo. Her nose was in the air and she had a peeved look as if to say she hadn't had any fun all day and it was all his fault. He was about to say he was sorry when she glanced at him. Her look softened and she hurried toward him. "Oh, my poor, poor Little Turtle," she said, "have you been sitting there like that all day?"

He shook his head. "No." He knew his voice was trembling, and he hoped she wouldn't ask him what he'd done. He looked down, afraid he might cry.

"I was afraid this would happen," she said, and leaned down and kissed him on the forehead. "Maker forbid! You're all sweaty. Do you not feel well?"

"Not really," he said, which was true.

"I hope you're not getting sick," she said—and went to the fireplace and lifted the lid of a crock. "Now I know for sure you're not feeling well. It doesn't look as if you've touched the fish and cabbage I started this morning. Kallo, will you put the picnic leftovers on the table?"

"Nothing near the edges," Togl said. "I need to cut our Festival notches."

The Festival notches! Togai thought. He'd forgotten his concern about being counted a Festival older. He quickly got up from his chair, to let Togl sit there if he wanted to, but Togl sat down at Lilu's place, his big knife in hand. "We'll honor your mother by doing hers first," he said.

Togai looked over Togl's shoulder. The notches were in groups of five. Many Chelks said *ha* for five, the number of fingers on a hand. Some used *to*, the number of toes on a foot. Two *has* were ten, and a *hato* was twenty, for the total number of fingers and toes. Chelks had little need to count above four hatoes, for it was rare anyone got older than that.

Togai watched Togl add a small, clean notch to the notches already cut into the table at Lilu's place—and wondered whose notch Togl would cut next. He bit his lip and tried not to show he was nervous. He couldn't wait to find out whether he'd get a notch or not, but he was afraid to ask about missing a Festival. His thinking was, maybe if he didn't bring it up, no one else would think about it.

"Now, mine," Togl said, and moved around to his place. "Great water spouts!" He looked carefully at the edge of the table and tapped along it with his knife. "In three more Festivals I'll be two hatoes old."

Lilu laughed and kissed the top of his head. "And still the best fisher in the village."

His notch cut, Togl moved to Kallo's place.

Togai watched and waited, practically holding his breath. It seemed Togl would never get Kallo's notch cut.

"Now for the youngest," Togl said and started to move to Togai's place but stopped and looked at Kallo. "Oh, I almost forgot. Did you ask Old Helu about missed Festivals?"

Kallo sighed and looked down. "She said, 'No Festival. No notch.'"

Togl shook his head. "Fish floater. That means an extra year of training jobs before he can fish."

"Enough, you two," Lilu said. "He feels bad enough as it is."

Kallo and Togl both laughed, and Togl moved around to Togai's place and began cutting a notch.

Togai laughed, and when they sat down to eat he not only ate all the pickled fish and cabbage Lilu put in his bowl but more than his share of the leftovers.

When he had finished, Lilu patted him on the head. "I knew you'd feel better when we got home. You must have missed us so. I'll bet you can't wait for next year's Festival."

Togai smiled. She was right. He couldn't wait. Not to go to the Festival but to again, he hoped, be the only person in Chelekai and have another chance to go to the mountains. He just wished he knew more about them, and he thought he knew the best person in the village to tell him.

CHAPTER 20

# Is Rotanor's Book There?

As Prandina stood on the stool and held the candle up, her hand was shaking nearly as much as the first time she'd looked at these books. That shaking had been from fear of being caught. This was from excitement of discovery—or not. Almost as exciting, more intriguing, she thought, would be to discover that the Rotanor book was missing. If it was, why, where was it? And as she had that first time, she stood on tiptoe and craned to look, resisting the temptation to hold onto the top self lest, in doing so, she'd leave streaks or handprints her father might see.

In the wavering yellow light she looked closely at the book she'd looked in first, the Rotar-Rotah book. Yes. Though hard to see, It was as she remembered, Book 4. Shadows on the ceiling danced as she moved the candle to the next book. The lettering on its spine was also faint. She hadn't even looked at its spine before, nor at the spine of any other book. She had simply assumed they were in order. Now, if she looked carefully, she could make out *Book of Kings* followed by, further down, as she remembered, *Orand* and *Oprand*. And the number? She held her breath and strained to see. She sighed. No doubt about it. It was a six. A book was missing, Book 5. But where was it? She looked at the next—and the next and the next. All the way down to the end, they were in order, Books 7, 8, 9...13.

Quickly she lowered the candle and looked at the lower shelves. As she'd expected the books looked newer and newer, from left to right, from shelf to shelf, and had spines easier to read. All were in order, and there was no sign of the missing book.

She sighed and was about to step down from the stool when she thought of the books that came before number 4. Though there were only three, could one of them be Book 5? She had to strain harder to make out the words and numbers, but after some squinting and carefully rubbing-away of dust with her finger, she was convinced. Book 5 was nowhere on these shelves.

Disappointed, Prandina stepped off the stool and stood in front of the bookcases that held all but one of the Books of Kings. Where could Book 5 be?—if it was still somewhere to be.

CHAPTER 21

# Maker and the Ogres

By early afternoon of the next day, Growing-Up Day, almost all Chelks were having a good time, visiting the homes of the growing-uppers, giving best wishes and partaking generously of fresh foods and the many good things left over from the Festival. After just one stop, Togai asked Togl and Lilu if he could wander around on his own. With a warning for him to be nice and to eat something besides honey cake and candy, Lilu said he could go.

He wandered out, as if he had no place to go, but soon headed for Old Zoltai's hut. He doubted any of the growing-uppers or anyone in their families had bothered to invite Zoltai. Togai guessed Old Zoltai didn't care, was probably home. Alone. His wife had died some years ago, and they had no children.

Zoltai wasn't on the porch, and the only answer to Togai's call was an echo.

Togai thought about the dune, but on a hunch headed for the smokehut. As he came into the clearing he saw Old Zoltai bent over, burlap bag in hand.

"You ever get tired of picking up chips?" Togai asked, hoping his words sounded friendly, like the banter among men.

Zoltai straightened, looking a little startled. "Might as well. Nothing better to do. Besides, you must've done your turn at the woodpile by now, must've learned to save chips."

Togai smiled. "Yessir. I learned that. But not at the woodpile. From you."

"Hmpf. Didn't think you'd remember."

"Oh, I remember a lot from working here. More than just the

work." He smiled and nodded toward the stump. "Want to rest a spell?"

Old Zoltai chuckled. "Why? You tired from all the work you've been doing today?"

Old Zoltai started walking. Togai fell in alongside but when they neared the stump took a few steps ahead and around to the far side of the stump so they'd be facing the mountains. And when they were seated, he intentionally said nothing. He wanted to learn about the mountains, but he didn't want to seem eager, risk some slip of the tongue that'd indicate he'd been anywhere near them.

After a silence, in which only the distant hills were reflected in the woodcutter's old and watery eyes, Togai cautiously said, "Did you like being a woodcutter, Old Zoltai?"

"Oh, yes, boy. If it weren't for us woodcutters the village wouldn't have canoes, or paddles, or wood for cooking. Lots of things."

"I know," Togai said. He pointed to the farthest hill they could see. He knew it was on the river, just across from Zaphyr. "Have you been to that hill?"

"Sure. Lots of times."

"Is that where Sky Falls is?"

"No. Sky Falls is way further up, very end of the valley."

"Does water really fall from the sky there?"

Zoltai chuckled. "No. It just looks that way—from way off anyway. Saw it lots of times, when I worked in the harvest. I was younger then, of course."

Togai thought for a moment. "Well, if it looks like it comes from the sky but it doesn't, where does it come from?"

"Well, the Ogres of the Cold think the high ridges that border the valley are theirs, but just above Sky Falls, where we can't see, is where the Mother of Rain and Water makes water and pours it down over the falls so we'll have the river and so the sea won't get too salty. She uses big cauldrons to turn white cold to water, and you can tell when she's doing that. The mountains get hazy, maybe even foggy, from the steam coming up."

"Did the Maker of All Men and All Fishes make all the good

things, like her—but the evil things too. Like the Ogres of the Cold?"

"Yes. Had to. Togl being a fisher, you've probably heard a lot about the Evil Eel and the Black Turtle, but...would you like to hear the story of the Very Beginning?"

Togai merely nodded. He knew that Zoltai, like most old people, didn't need much encouragement to tell stories. But he didn't mind Old Zoltai being that way. He liked Old Zoltai's stories.

Zoltai took a deep breath. "Back before time began the Maker of All Men and All Trees was the only thing there was."

"Is He the same as the Maker of All Men and All Fishes?"

"Yes. Many call Him the Maker and Controller of All Things, sometimes just Maker, but whatever His name, before time He was all there was, and when He became bored being alone, with nothing to do or look at, He decided to make Himself a brother and a sister. He made the sister first, Mother Earth. Right away he saw that she would be quiet and timid and maybe not a lot of fun, so He made His brother, Ogre, more spirited and mischievous. But back then the Maker of All Men and All Trees didn't have much experience making things, and Ogre turned out mean instead of mischievous—though Maker didn't know that until the contest."

"The contest?"

"Yes. The brothers spent all their time playing rough and tumble games that Mother Earth didn't like, and one day she went to her brother, the Maker of All Trees, and asked Him to think of a game she could play too. He told her, 'I've been thinking of making people, but I don't yet have a place to put them, so, I'll make a big sky and divide the space below it down the middle. You can take one half, Ogre the other, and you can have a contest making a place for people to live. When you're finished, I'll choose which half I think is better and put the people I make there.'

"Well, Ogre began working on his half. He made it cold and harsh and rugged, a place where only people who were big and strong and mean like him could ever hope to live. The first thing Mother Earth did was make the sun and gentle breezes. She then made the

Mother of Rain and Water and asked her to help. Together they then made the ocean—so people could have fish—and began making trees, and fields for orchards and crops. When Ogre saw what they were doing, he became jealous and angry and..." Zoltai looked at Togai. "Lot of parents don't tell this to their children. Too scary. Want me to go on?"

Togai quickly nodded.

Zoltai pointed to the mountains. "See those two white-top peaks straight up the valley, far away? The two highest ones?"

Though Togai guessed he had looked at those two peaks at least once every day of his life, he now looked up the valley as if he had never seen them before. "Yes."

"Well, those once were—actually, still are—Ogre's horns. And the peaks off to the side? Along the skyline? Those are the spines on his back."

Togai shuddered. That was the first time he'd ever heard that.

"And why is Ogre there? Angry and jealous at what Mother Earth had made—and was making—Ogre lay down up there, where you see, at the very edge of what she was making and began to pull it toward his mouth. He was going to swallow her creation so she couldn't have it and he wouldn't have to look at it anymore. His first pull brought up great piles of rock and dirt, the lower mountains you see there in front of the Horns. And just as he started to reach out again with his great stony fingers, the Maker of All Men and All Trees saw what he was doing and hit him a fierce blow on the head.

"But Ogre was mean and tough and again reached out. This time Maker stomped on his hand and arm and hit him really hard. Ogre had reached out all the way across the valley with his right arm, and when Maker stomped on it, He bruised it badly. That's why the far side of the valley is blue rock. And in stomping on the hand on this side, where Ogre was pulling things up to his mouth, Maker broke off some of the fingers. That's where the hills came from—and the 'Finger Ridges,' too, which you can't see from here because of the hills."

Togai's eyes opened wide and he blurted out, "You mean they

really are fingers?"—and immediately wished he hadn't. Would Old Zoltai notice?

Old Zoltai didn't seem to. "Yes, they really are fingers. And you can tell Ogre is not completely dead yet because the rock in them is still red."

Togai nodded. He remembered the red well.

"Maker raised His hand for one hard and final blow to kill Ogre but Mother Earth said, 'Please spare my brother's life.' Maker said, okay, if that was what she wanted, but He'd tie Ogre down, right where he was and take away all his powers so he'd never again be able to do harm to the nice and pretty place she was making.

"Though Ogre was severely stunned and unable to move, when he heard Maker say that, before Maker could take away his powers, he quickly used up what little energy he had left and breathed out the Avenging Spirit and the Ogres of the Cold—and told them to forever protect his body and make life as miserable as they could for the people he knew Maker was going to put in the valley."

Togai pointed. "So those pointy mountains we can see there on the skyline are all part of Ogre's body? And there between the horns, is that the top of his head?"

"Yes."

Togai shuddered. "Where are his mouth and eyes? Down behind that round mountain?"

"Can't say about the mouth, but the eyes are. I've seen them."

"Really?" Togai said. How could Old Zoltai—or anyone else—have seen Ogre's eyes if no one had ever been into the mountains?

"Yes," Zoltai said. "Part of Ogre's punishment is that he's not supposed to move. Not even his head. If he does and is seen by Maker, Maker will turn him into dirt for trees to grow on. But in spite of that threat, sometimes when the Maker of All Men and All Trees is sleeping—and Maker sleeps only when all people in the valley are asleep—Ogre will lift his head enough to peek over that low mountain and try to figure out some way to get the valley to his mouth so he can do what he started to do with it. Eat it."

Togai was hardly breathing. "But if Ogre only lifts his head when everyone is asleep, how could you..." Togai stopped. He knew he wasn't supposed to question his elders.

"Easy. You see, Ogre's so big and made of stone, he can't move very fast, and *if* you do happen to wake up at the right time and look—most people are afraid to do this—you can see his eyes before he can duck down."

"See his eyes? In the *dark*?"

"Yeah, parents aren't just talking when they tell children his eyes are a scary, fiery green. I've seen 'em."

Togai nodded. Too many times he'd heard Lilu say why his cot was where it was. "And do you believe the Ogres of the Cold try to protect Ogre?"

"Of course, boy. Woodcutters are on hills next to Ogre's fingers almost every day, but don't dare go up between the fingers or out onto the boulders at the end of the fingers."

Togai swallowed. How did he get away with doing what wood-cutters wouldn't do? Did the Ogres not know he was there—or were the woodcutters and other people wrong about them?

Old Zoltai looked at Togai, eyebrows raised. "Want to know what made woodcutters such strong believers?"

Togai's eyes opened wide. "Sure."

"Just over that farthest hill there, beside a low waterfall, is the crushed end of one of Ogre's fingers, and once long ago two young woodcutters—wanting to show they weren't scared by the stories they'd heard—went out on the boulders and threw rocks at the end of the finger. The next day, though older woodcutters tried to get them not to, they did the same thing, and while they were out there danc-ing around and mocking Ogre, the Ogres of the Cold—from a dark cloud that looked like a rain cloud—spewed down hard pellets that stung the young woodcutters and sent them scurrying for the trees. The Ogres even tried to pelt the woodcutters who were watching, but the trees protected them, and later the spirits of the forest turned the pellets to water."

Old Zoltai took a deep breath. "The next day, the Ogres came and covered the grass and flowers of the valley with a blanket that was white and cold and brought great pain to the feet of people foolish enough to walk on it. But as had the spirits of the forest, Mother Earth soon turned the blanket of white to harmless water—and made the flowers bloom and the grass grow again. The Zaprians suspected that some farmer had offended the Ogres by going too close to the mountains. Even to this day, the Ogres will sometimes send a blanket of white cold into the upper parts of the valley to warn people to stay away—which is why no one lives up there." He turned toward Togai. "No Chelk has ever told a Zaprian what the woodcutters did, so don't you. I wouldn't have told you, but you're the first boy to ever ask me about the hills."

"Oh, I won't tell anyone," Togai said. "I promise. Uh, you also said woodcutters wouldn't go between the fingers? Why? What's between them?"

"Not much. They're like little valleys. But dry. Some woodcutters call them 'canyons.'"

Togai hoped his words didn't stick in his throat. "If you went up one of those, uh, canyons, do you think you could get into the mountains?"

"Oh, no, boy. No. Great axes, no. The Ogres of the Cold wouldn't let you."

Togai had some doubts about what Old Zoltai had said, but that night—and for many nights afterward—he would suddenly awaken from dreaming that, in the darkness, huge stone fingers had grown down around the village and had begun pulling it toward Ogre's mouth—and in that mouth was a great green fire.

CHAPTER 22

# One Child Grows

For several days after discovering that Rotanor's book was indeed missing, Prandina gave a lot of thought to where it might be. Most likely, she guessed, was that some king had absent-mindedly stuck it in with some other books, maybe into the big bookcase in the king's study. But it wasn't there—or in any of the small, rarely used bookcases in the castle. Thinking it might be in her father's desk, she'd even dared look there one afternoon when he was out riding, to no avail. Though after that she'd occasionally look in a closet or some other stray spot she happened to think about, she began to believe that the only place it could be—if it was anyplace at all—was in the Great Hall of the People, most likely in the Royal Apartment where some king took it and forgot to bring it back. She sighed every time she'd think about that possibility. Unless something really unusual happened, she'd not be back in the Great Hall before the next Festival.

Resigned to a long wait, she found pleasure in riding Little Whi-Face, an after-Festival gift from her father—especially when they rode together. Where didn't matter. Up the valley to look at the mountains or down or across it to look at farms. At first Praidar seemed to think it beneath her to talk to farmers—or their wives or children—but he seemed to become amused by her questions and antics. Once he even got off Noble Cloud to watch while a farmer's wife showed her how to milk a cow, another time waited patiently while Prandina helped a little girl gather eggs, then laughed when the little girl offered him a small one for his breakfast.

In time he began to tell her about farms they passed, which

fields had the best wheat, carrots, apples, potatoes. Things, he cautiously once said to her, a king should know.

As the days grew shorter and cooler, he didn't seem to want to ride as much and would let her ride alone, always with the admonition to "be home by dark." She took 'dark' to mean just that, and many times when she was letting Whi-Face amble along in the stillness and quiet of twilight, she could well imagine she was the only person in the world. Not far from the castle one such night, though, haunting single notes from some distantly strummed lute reminded her there were others in the world, and she turned Whi-Face alongside an orchard and stopped at the edge of it to listen. Not far away was a farmhouse that she'd have trouble seeing were it not for a yellow glow from one window that gave it a warm and inviting look. She began to pick up some singing, faint at first, only a word now and then. Another voice came in and soon the two male voices were singing quite loudly. As if practicing? Yes! She and her father had seen them in the orchard one day. One of the old troubadours and his troubadour grandson, who, as often happened her father told her, had come to live with his grandfather so he would be ready to take over the farm when the grandfather died. As she nudged Whi-Face toward the castle she thought it would be nice to be a troubadour, by a warm fire, sharing something with someone, someone who enjoyed what you did.

As the grays of winter gave way to the blossoms of spring, Prandina rode more and more with her father and knew this would have been the happiest time of her life had it not been for the lack of any sign of a corresponding blossoming in Zarian. Though large for his age, his words were simple, his pleasures childish. Seeing the effect that had on her father added weight to her sadness. Often, when Zarian would be getting more food on him than in his mouth or when he'd lean over his plate and, legs swinging wildly, ask her a question such as, "Prina, you tell me again the story of Ogron the Friendly Ogre?" she'd see her father staring sadly, as if he couldn't—or didn't want to—believe that Zarian was staying a child. Times like that she wanted to cry, and sometimes when she couldn't be seen, she did.

Though Prandina noticed no changes in Zarian, it seemed practically everyone in the castle was noticing changes in her.

For some time Old Rono had been beaming over how well she'd been eating and was encouraging her to eat even more, saying a growing girl needed extra milk and cookies to fill out her dresses. As opposed to Rono, the seamstress Wono scolded her for growing *too* fast. Wono had already started making Festival clothes and the last time Prandina had gone for a fitting, Wono had looked at the length of the dress and said, "Witches, child, you keep growing and I'll have to start over."

One day about half a moon before the Festival she and her father were in his study, she reading, he writing. She happened to look up and he was looking at her, studying her. "Something wrong, Daddy?" she asked.

He sighed. "No. Just thinking. It's kind of sad, for any man, I guess, to see his little girl grow up." His voice quavered. "I'm glad you're so attentive to Zarian."

CHAPTER 23

# Ogres Revisited

Even though in some of Togai's dreams Ogre's giant fingers would come groping for him and him alone, more often than not he'd be able to go back to sleep and dream, not about the fingers closing around him but about what it would be like to stand atop one. The few day times he'd felt a cool breeze and looked up in fear Ogres of the Cold were coming after him, he'd wound up looking at the mountains and wanting to go there.

After cool weather passed and the village hadn't been dragged away or covered in white cold and the worst thing that had happened to him was being caught in a cold rain, Togai began to think he'd gotten away with something. And if he'd gotten away with it once, couldn't he again?

So, when Lilu asked if he'd rather she pretty-up blue pants or brown pants for his new Festival outfit, he told her he didn't think he would go. Again she didn't believe him. She said he'd change his mind because he'd remember how alone he'd been last Festival Day when she came home and found him ready to cry.

Festival morning, when he said, with finality, he hoped, that he truly wasn't going, she glared at him and said, "Why do you have to be so different?" She turned to Togl. "You talk to him."

Togl shook his head. "No. I don't see any reason to make him go." He glanced at Togai. "Sometimes it takes courage to be different."

By the time the last canoe was on its way toward Zaphyr, Togai was jogging easily toward the mountains. Tied around his waist in a cloth was a piece of fishcake he'd snitched from the picnic basket.

Though he stopped at the top of the hill next to the boulder field to catch his breath and to look and listen for signs of Ogres and stopped again a few more times on his way up the first canyon, he was soon into the crack at the end of it and crawling.

In the narrow chimney, he stood and looked up. The chimney seemed cooler and dimmer than it had last year—because, he hoped, the sun wasn't very high, not because Ogres were near. He shivered. He could see knobs and cracks and little ledges to about halfway up. Whether there'd be good footholds and handholds all the way to the top, he'd simply have to find out. He got a good grip on a narrow ledge, put his left foot on a rounded bulge, took a deep breath, and began to climb. To his surprise he discovered that he felt more secure using his left foot to brace against footholds than his right, especially when the crack or protruding rock was small. He laughed. Finally, something his stiff little left foot was good for.

In places where the chimney was really narrow, he found a variety of ways he could press his back, legs and arms against the chimney sides and feel safe. Much easier and sooner than he'd thought, he was at the opening. Cautiously he peeked over the edge and looked all around. Seeing nothing that looked like it could be an Ogre of the Cold—whatever one might look like—he climbed out of the chimney and stood.

Off to each side the high stone ridges he'd been seeing all along still rose above him—and came together a good ways on at the end of the cupped valley they formed. It was, truly, as if he were in a depression between two giant fingers. Except for some small boulders and pieces of rock scattered here and there across the depression, it was all smooth, solid rock. Though the ridges to each side of him were still nearly straight up, the slope up the depression to where the ridges joined was a gentle one—and he began to run.

The sun warm on his back, the stone cool and smooth beneath his callused feet, he ran as he'd never run before—with a great sense of elation and freedom, of likely being where no Chelk had ever been before, even dared imagine it possible to be.

Softly and swiftly he went, his equally swift but silent shadow just ahead of him. The shadow, though in some ways a welcome companion, wobbled unevenly and reminded him of his limp.

As the floor of the depression rose, with the ridge bottoms spreading to meet it, the sides became less and less steep. When Togai thought the slope up the left ridge was gradual enough, he turned and started up it. It was still so steep that he had to slow to a walk and now and then even had to lean forward on his hands to keep his balance and pull himself up.

Just as he was beginning to wonder if he'd ever get to the top, his steps began to get easier, and he soon was running again—out across the ridge's rounded top toward the Valley of Zaphyr! He had never been so high. No Chelk had. No Zaprian. No one ever.

He suddenly stopped and looked toward the mountains. The Ogres of the Cold. Surely they could see him, here, high, out in the open. He got ready to run. But no. There was no cloud anywhere, no feeling of cold. Just bright sun. Where were the Ogres? Why didn't they care?

He turned and a few more steps took him to the very top of the ridge, to the middle of its rounded top and he looked down the valley and gasped.

All that he was familiar with—the village, river, city—all that he had long been close to and that had always seemed so large, now seemed small and far away—and far below. He had the feeling that if he just ran a few steps and spread his arms he could soar out over the valley and the hills and the village and...

Turtles! The ocean! Other things had looked smaller to him. But the ocean looked much bigger. How could that be? He'd been on it, and though it had looked big, it hadn't looked *that* big. He'd heard Togl—and lots of other people too—say that fishers were afraid that if they paddled out too far they'd go over the edge. But from what he could see, they'd have to paddle a long, long way.

The valley, too, looked much bigger than he'd expected it would. The wall on the other side, Ogre's bruised right arm, Old Zoltai had said, was indeed blue and high—and long. It ran on and on, away from him, letting the valley widen and, as it did, disappear in the hazy distance.

At the upper end of the valley was...

*Great turtles!* It was Sky Falls!

What startled him, took him aback, was not Sky Falls, impressive as it was, but that he was seeing *above* Sky Falls—and not seeing any signs of cauldrons or a fire or anything that looked like it might be an Ogre of the Cold. No. Everything looked normal. Like things he'd seen before—only prettier.

The falls was a green arcing plume, white at the edges that fell down through a rainbow mist. Beyond it was a lake, and running away from the lake was a deep valley with slopes that changed from tree-lined to barren, from boulders to rocky spires. And, in the distance, above it all, were the massive white-topped mountains.

He looked up the ridge he was on. It ended in a boulder field at the base of Round Mountain, which rose to the left. Above it showed the white tips of Ogre's horns. Old Zoltai had said that when Maker slept—which was only when everyone in the valley was asleep—Ogre would raise up and look at the valley with his fearsome green eyes.

Togai looked up. Still no hint of a cloud anywhere, not a touch of cold. The Ogres had left him alone, so far. Would they let him go further, get all the way to the top of Round Mountain, take a peek, see more of Ogre's face than anyone had ever seen before? He again looked for clouds—and began to run.

He was tempted to stop at Sky Falls, take a close look at it and the lake and valley beyond, but he ran on. The air had cooled some and a few dark clouds now showed on the far horizon.

He slowed at the edge of the boulder field, picked his way across it and was soon moving up the face of the mountain—but not as quickly or in the way he wanted to. Because it was much steeper than he had imagined, and because he kept sliding back in its loose dirt, he decided to cross at an angle, work his way up to an edge and peek from there. But that tack put a lot of strain on his left leg, so, when he came to a rocky gully that led up to the mountain's ridge-line, he gladly took it.

With the better footing, he soon came to the end of the gully— just below a low ledge of crumbly rock. He didn't want to climb onto the ledge and look over, too much chance of stepping on a loose rock and sending it clattering down the slope and warning Ogre. Being very careful, he crawled along behind the ledge out to its end and lay there, barely breathing, trying to get up his courage.

Holding his breath, heart beating wildly, he moved his head just enough to get one eye beyond the last rock at the end of the ledge and immediately jerked back and lay on his back. But why? He hadn't seen anything out of the ordinary. The Horns of the Ogre had loomed over him much higher and much larger than he'd thought they would, but he hadn't seen any eyes—or a mouth or a nose. Nothing like that. Just mountain.

If Ogre's eyes seemed big from down in the village, they'd look absolutely huge from this close, wouldn't they? But if Ogre only stirred at night when Maker was asleep, maybe he was sleeping now, in the daytime, had his eyes closed. But what about the mouth? The one he wanted to eat the whole valley with. It'd be really huge, impossible to hide.

Carefully he peeked again. Still no eyes, nose or mouth. Nothing like a face. Just a slab of boulder-strewn blue-gray rock rising above a small lake. He turned and sat with his back against the ledge. He yelled. Nothing. He yelled again, as loud as he could. All he heard was faint echoes. No snarls. No growls.

He stood and looked. No fiery eyes. Just a stone mountain in stony silence. Nothing that looked alive or like it had ever been alive. Could Old Zoltai have been wrong? Simply awakened from a bad dream and imagined he'd seen fiery eyes?

No doubt the Ogres existed. Too many people had seen what they could do. So, since people knew Maker wouldn't make anything evil and that Ogres of the Cold had to come from someplace, maybe someone came up with the story of Ogre to explain where the Ogres came from—and people believed it. But...Why hadn't he thought of this earlier? When Chelks came to the valley, they didn't know anything at all about it—or the mountains or Ogres. So everything Chelks believe about Ogre or the Ogres they must have learned from the Zaps. But where'd the Zaps get the idea? Why make Ogre up? Could there be a reason?

Wispy gray clouds now flitted around the horns. Clouds further back were darker, thicker. Could it be that whatever was beyond the mountains was what the Ogres really wanted to protect? Togai wondered. But what was beyond the mountains, on the other side? He had been told it was nothing, that the world ended at the mountains. He had assumed people didn't mean right at the skyline. He had assumed the mountains had something on the other side to hold them up, like a pile of sand would—and then, well, just nothing. After all, everything had to end somewhere, didn't it?

He looked up at the saddle-like depression between the Horns, and wondered what the world, or whatever it was, would look like on the other side. What did nothing look like?

The slope up to the saddle didn't look really steep. The sun wasn't overhead yet...He set off at a jog.

At the shallow creek that flowed from the lake he knelt, dipped in his hand and—after a cautious sip—lay down and took in great gulps of the cold, clear water, the coldest, best tasting water he had ever had.

The water—and a now more adventuresome spirit—gave him an appetite, and as he started across the creek he took his first bite from the hunk of fishcake he had carried around his waist. The creek was spread in shallow sheets over the smooth, blue-gray stone that seemed to be everywhere, and by the time he was on the other side he had finished the fishcake and his feet were numb. Just as he was thinking that the blue stone of the slope was even colder than the creek, low clouds moved between him and the sun and he began to shiver. Were the Ogres of the Cold at last trying to make him turn back?

The clouds seemed to be racing him to the saddle. By the time he was halfway up the slope they were halfway down the Horns.

He strained to run, but not until the slope lessened did his effort and leaning into the wind produce anything like a run, and even then it was slow and halting. Just ahead, in the flat, wisps of cloud were appearing and disappearing, darting here and there around the tops of the tallest boulders. He aimed for the nearest big one, hoping it would give him some protection from the wind.

He knelt behind it, quickly blew warm air into his hands and peeked out. Though he couldn't see far into the patchy grayness that came streaming up the slope toward him, he could see far enough to tell that this back side of the gap between the Ogre's horns looked pretty much like the front side—boulders scattered over a gentle slope of blue-gray rock that quickly steepened and dropped off. But into what?

Shivering, teeth chattering, eyes smarting in the wind, he was about to duck back behind the boulder when an opening suddenly appeared in the swirl ahead of him. He stared. Could he really be seeing what he thought he was seeing?

CHAPTER 24

# What's that noise?

Though Prandina was now on the balcony, looking laughing and smiling, last night she'd been worried when her father told her that he was going to let Zarian ride in the parade alone. She'd replied, quite genuinely, that she was concerned. Zarian had 'ridden' his pony only a few times, and that was with one of the stable boys leading it. Her father had said not to worry, they'd put him on Docile. Even Old Rono could ride Docile. Prandina was still a little worried though. Music playing, people cheering, clowns running around. Who knew what might happen?

In spite of her concerns, she was eager for the parade to start. First, she wanted to see the delight in Zarian's eyes when the music started and Docile took the first of many plodding steps to stay alongside the high-spirited Noble Cloud. Even more, and she felt guilty about this, she was eager for the parade to start so she could dash back into the Royal Apartment and begin searching its study for the missing *Book of Kings*, the one that would have—or should have—Rotanor's writings in it.

That morning, while her father was in the study, where he seemed to spend most of every Festival day, she had used the ruse of playing hide-and-seek with Zarian to search every nook and cranny in the apartment—outside the study—big enough to hold or hide a book. So now, not having found the book, she was eager to get into the study and look there, where, all along, she had guessed the book would be if it was in the apartment at all.

Though in some ways she wanted to keep watching, as soon as her father and Zarian had turned down the side of the plaza and she could no longer see Zarian's face, she turned and hurried into the apartment and into the study.

Contrary to what she'd done in the castle, she left all doors open behind her so she'd be able to hear the music and cheering as it followed the parade. That would give her plenty of time to get back onto the balcony to wave to her father and Zarian as they came by on the first of their two—with Zarian riding—sure-to-be slow trips around the plaza.

Though she thought she'd have plenty of time, she quickly set to work. Having been in the study many times, she knew where she wanted to look and in what order. Though she thought the desk was surely the most likely place for the book to be, she put it last on her list of places to look. She wouldn't feel she were snooping if she looked in the open bookcase or in other exposed places around the room—even behind a portrait if the room had a portrait. But she'd feel she'd betrayed some implied trust if she even took one peek into her father's desk, let alone searched it. So, she would look in the desk last, when there was no other place to look.

The bookcase had only a few books in it, none of which, she saw quickly, was the missing *Book of Kings*. No wall picture had a hole or a door behind it, and even on her hands and knees she could see nothing other than dirt and dust under the desk or any other piece of furniture. Feeling a little uneasy, she opened a large cabinet but found no books in it, just ledgers with scraps of paper stuck into them here and there.

That left only the desk. She put her hand on its middle drawer and paused to listen. The music, though faint, seemed to be getting fainter, from near Left Corner, she guessed. She looked down at the drawer and feeling as if she were about to spy on her father in his most private moments, pulled, hoping it would slide open easily. And it did. So did the first side drawer—and the next and the next and the next. Not a book in any of them. Just more ledgers and loose papers and, in the top right drawer, some fresh crumbs.

She sighed. She wanted to cry. She had so hoped...

What? Had the music stopped? Yes. And...was that yelling and shouting?

She ran out. At this distance she couldn't make out any detail at the far end, but it seemed there was a lot of confusion, with people running here and there. As she watched, men and boys from farther along the parade route began to run toward the lower end—and near her, in the upper end, people began pointing toward the lower end and talking excitedly. One woman put her hands to her face and began to cry.

What had happened?

Fear gripped her. Was it something to do with Zarian? Had he fallen off Docile, been trampled by Noble Cloud?

CHAPTER 25

# Did I see what I thought I saw?

Togai blinked in effort to clear his watering eyes and looked again. But the opening was gone, disappeared. Had he really seen something green? A far valley with fields maybe? He shielded his eyes with his hands and stared through narrow slits between his fingers. But the grayness kept streaming toward him, growing darker with no hint of thinning anytime soon.

He shook from head to toe. He had never been so cold. He had to get back to where it was warm. If he ever came here again he'd want to wear warm clothes, maybe even shoes and some of those things the Zaps called socks.

He turned and ran toward the slope he had come up. The wind that had long tried to push him back was now pushing him forward, and despite feeling miserably cold and stiff, he laughed and gave a little jump.

'Nothing' couldn't be green, could it? Oh, what a day—and he was already feeling better. In the far distance was the village—*in full sunshine.* He laughed again, almost gleefully this time. *If* Lilu asked if he'd gotten out of sight of the village, he could tell her at the very farthest he'd been from the village he could still see it.

Though both his feet were stiff with cold, where he could run without much risk of falling, he ran—and he ran down that first slope without any thought that he was running down Ogre's face and might be swallowed whole or burned to a crisp by fiery eyes. No longer did he think of the Horns and the jagged peaks of the skyline as parts of some long-ago beast turned to stone. They were just mountains. Mountains he knew how to get into.

He slipped and slid down the face of Round Mountain. About the time he got to Sky Falls he came into sunshine and looked up. The sun was still mid-afternoon high, and he slowed some. He didn't need to rush, but he didn't want to dally either. He'd like to be in the hut—clean, dry and rested—when Lilu came in.

Togai trotted up to the chimney, thinking he'd sit on its edge and take his time looking for good footholds and handholds—to be safe and to give his legs a rest. But just as he started to sit, he saw, by his right hand, three straight lines—marks—etched into the rock. And almost as soon as he saw them, he realized, straight as they were, connected as they were—he shivered with the thought—they couldn't be natural. They must have been put there by somebody. He bent for a closer look. Chiseled, probably.

His body shook.

He wiggled around for a better look. About as large as his hand, it was three lines connected like...like...Turtles. Like the scar on Old Helu's head, like the mark she painted on every growing-upper's head.

He leaned back on arms trembly and twitchy. Turtles. What was going on? Had some Chelk been up here before him and to leave proof—or show contempt for the Ogres—put his mark here? The mark of the Dilkina?

But if some Chelk had been here before, why were Chelks so afraid of the mountains, think there was no way into them? Had this Chelk, as he had, been afraid to tell?

He was giddy with questions of who, what and when, of why and why not, but he started down the chimney. He'd have time enough to think later, but he doubted he'd come up with any answers.

And just as he thought he had questions enough, in the bottom of the chimney he stepped on something in the mud and sand, something that didn't feel like a rock. He knelt and, with some digging and tugging, pulled out a round object that filled his hand from wrist to fingertips and, in the dim light anyway, looked too round to be natural. Too heavy, too.

He kept pitching it ahead of him as he crawled through the tunnel, and once he was outside and able to stand, he began scraping mud and dirt from it. Though all he could see and feel was rough and flaky rust, he was sure it had been made perfectly round. But what was it? What had it been? He held it up in the light and looked more closely. A wheel? No. A pulley! That's what it was. A pulley. He looked back up at the finger over him. But why would anyone have a pulley up here? What could they have possibly wanted it for, used it for?

He sighed. He didn't have time to stand here and think, needed to get moving. He glanced at the—he was sure—pulley and, not knowing what else to do with it, tossed it in the bushes. If he ever wanted to look at it again, he knew where to find it.

Once again he set out running but a ways from the village, realizing he was sweating and grimy-dirty and, with the sun still well above the horizon, turned toward the river, the closest point. He didn't even hesitate at the bank; he just dived right in and, while under, tried to scrub his face and get some of the dirt from his hair. In shallow water he stood and washed as he waded. Back on the bank, walking slowly along it to give his clothes time to dry, he sensed something wrong, something not right. But what? He stopped and listened. He was only a little upriver from the City of Light and ought to be hearing Festival noises, but he wasn't. Why not?

He began to run. As he rounded the bend that brought the trading bank across from the village into view, he saw a long line of girls and women and men and boys in brightly colored outfits hurrying down the path from the City of Light to the river. And...was that crying he heard?

He was on the strand by the time the first canoes were halfway across, and as they came toward him he could see children puzzled and scared-looking, men and women somber and ashen. Dilo was in the bow of the first canoe, and even as Dilo jumped out and bent to drag it onto the gravel, Togai ran up and asked, "Something happen?"

Dilo looked up. "Yeah. We've been banned from the kingdom."

## CHAPTER 26

# Noble Cloud and...Something like a Z?

With growing apprehension Prandina watched from the Royal Balcony as more and more citizens of her father's kingdom hurried as best they could toward the lower end of the plaza. Boys ran. Men, some with small children on their shoulders, trotted, and the very old tottered, helping each other. Many in the upper end of the plaza had stayed. She called and waved, hoping to get someone's attention and learn what had happened. But no one heard, no one saw. Everyone seemed to be looking the other way, gesturing, pointing, talking.

She resisted the urge to run down and try to find out, maybe even go on to the end of the plaza. But she reasoned that it would be better to stay where she was, where, surely, Zarian or her father would be brought as soon as practical if either was ill or hurt. Oh, she hoped it wasn't Zarian. Not that she wanted her father hurt, but as strong and hardy as he was, he'd be able to recover from an injury much quicker than Zarian would. Too, if Zarian were hurt, he'd blame himself.

Just as she was about to yield to temptation and run for the plaza, the hubbub died down and she saw, far toward the end, the crowd parting. And coming through the lane opening up...Was that her father? On Docile? Holding Zarian?

She watched, and soon had no doubt. Yes. It was her father and Zarian on Docile, and as the crowd thinned she could tell her father was trying to urge Docile into a gallop. Her heart beat faster, and she strained to get a good look at Zarian. By the time they were close enough for her to see that Zarian, at worst, was only confused, she could see that her father's face was red, his jaw set.

When they came into the apartment, her father carrying Zarian, he let Zarian slide to the floor and, face now filled with anguish instead of anger, sat down in the first chair he came to. He covered his face with his hands and sobbed, "Noble Cloud's dying. Noble Cloud's dying."

She gasped—and sadness and despair swept over her as she watched her father press the palms of his hands hard against the sides of his head.

"Noble Cloud is..." He sniffed. "Aah. He's probably dead by now. Some...some crazy Left dashed from the crowd and slit his throat."

She'd never before seen her father cry, and his hurt made her hurt. She wanted to console him, but didn't move, said nothing. She was afraid he'd take anything she did as a sign that she thought he, the kingdom's most powerful man, needed help, needed consoling.

He sniffed again. "Cloud...brave Noble Cloud...staggered a few steps and fell, blood squirting everywhere. Some farmer in the band ran up and tied the sash from his uniform around Cloud's throat, but I could see the blood was still gushing out, could still hear Noble Cloud wheezing. I couldn't bear watching." He covered his eyes, and his shoulders shook with silent sobs.

Prandina turned to Zarian. "You all right, Sweet Zee?"

He smiled. "Got to ride horsey."

With all that was going on in the apartment she'd been only vaguely aware of an occasional, distant shout from the plaza. Now she became aware of a babble of voices that seemed to be getting closer.

She ran out to the balcony and saw coming toward her up the plaza—ahead of a broad band of people—seven or eight of the Royal Guard. The two in front held a man between them—a shabbily-dressed Left, the first shabbily-dressed Left she'd ever seen. Each guardsman had a hand clamped on one of the Left's hands, the other jammed up under an armpit. They were almost running, carrying the Left along. His feet barely touched the ground.

From behind her came her father's bitter words. "That's the man. That's the man that cut Noble Cloud."

The guardsmen stopped a few steps from the balcony and a man Prandina recognized as the Captain of the Guard stepped forward.

"How fares Noble Cloud?" the king asked.

"He..." The captain took off his hat and glanced down. "He is dead, sire."

The king glared and, shaking from head to foot, pointed at the Left. "Take...take that vile creature to the execution chamber. Double lock the door and have two men guard it until further word from me."

"Yes, sire," the captain said. And with a gesture from him, the two guardsmen holding the now struggling Left forced him toward a passageway that led in under the Great Hall.

The king's voice trembled. "Why would that man want to do such an awful thing? Did he say?"

"No, sire," the captain replied. "I think his name is Calo, a demented carver who lives outside the Lefts' village. The few Lefts who would talk to me said they hadn't had good fishing lately and this carver blamed it all on demons. And when you and Noble Cloud came by, those standing near this carver said he muttered something about it wasn't right that any animal should look so perfect or be so admired in a world gone mad—and suddenly lunged out and..."

The king angrily waved his hand. "Enough. Who he is or why he did it doesn't really matter. He did it." He looked at the captain. "Do the Lefts have a chief, a leader of some kind?"

"I don't know, sire, but I could find out."

"Go then," the king pointed, "and bring back the nearest thing to a leader the Lefts have. If no one is brave enough to admit he's the leader, order them all to come."

"Yes, sire."

As the crowd parted to let the captain and his men through, the king strode back into the apartment.

Prandina started to follow him but decided to stay on the balcony. The more time he had to himself, the better. Besides, she wanted to keep up with what was happening. Soon she was watching the Royal Guard coming back through the plaza with, she could hardly believe her eyes, a woman in the middle of them. A large number of Lefts followed close behind, and as the back line of the vast spread of Zaprians filling the upper end of the plaza parted to let the Guard through, the Lefts stopped some distance back and spread out across the plaza.

Talk spread and became louder as the Zaprians realized that the leader of the Lefts was, presumably, a woman. A fairly old one.

Prandina guessed her father must have heard the increased noise for, when she turned to call, he was already on his way out.

The group of Guardsmen stopped and those in front stepped back, leaving the captain and a woman just below the balcony, looking up.

The king looked down and, though clearly still angry, there was disbelief in his voice. "Are you their leader?"

"Yes, sire," she said, and pointed to a hand-size, thick emblem hanging down the front of her dress, something like a Z. Prandina stared at it. Where had she seen a symbol, a figure, shaped like that before?

"What is that?" The king said. "Looks like a piece of turtle shell to me. What's it for? Good luck? Something to protect you against your Avenging Witch?"

Prandina saw several Zaprians look at each other and smile. She knew that while Lefts greatly feared their Avenging Witch, most Zaprians thought of her as a joke, a creature that, though supposedly powerful enough to move mountains in Left, couldn't cross the river to be seen in Zaphyr. But, given the seriousness of the situation, no one laughed.

"No sire. It is to show I am not so much a *leader* as the Chelk who conducts ceremonies and helps, when need be, settle disputes. I also have such a mark cut into my scalp."

The king snorted. "Well, I really am impressed. I guess I should have worn my crown."

At this, the king's second obviously sarcastic remark, many in the crowd did laugh. But not Prandina. She was looking at the old woman's head, thinking about the jagged mark that must be hidden there—and suddenly she remembered. One of the portraits in the Hall of Portraits showed a jagged mark on the king's hand, a mark with shape a lot like the old woman's turtle-shell emblem. Or did it? Was she imagining things? She'd like to check, but she couldn't go, not now.

Praidar held up his hand. When silence came he glanced down at the Captain of the Guard. "As soon as I finish my next comment, ready the Royal Coach for our return to the castle."

"Yes, sire."

The king held out one arm, looked over the crowd toward the far end of the plaza and said in a loud, clear voice, "I hereby decree that from this day forward, until Maker dries up the river and takes away the mountains, if any Left so much as sets foot in the Kingdom of Zaphyr, that foul and smelly creature shall have its throat cut and be left to die, die slowly, the way Noble Cloud did."

With excited talk breaking out behind her, the old woman whose name the king didn't know stood below the balcony, stunned. But there was no one to protest to. The king was gone—and had pulled Prandina with him.

In the apartment, without a word, the king dropped Prandina's hand, scooped up Zarian and started down the long Hall of Portraits. Though he was walking fast and Prandina knew she was expected to keep up, she slowed as they neared the end of the hall—where there was good light and where she thought she'd seen the portrait with the mark. Right and left she looked....Andar, no. Opran, no. Orand, no. Rotanor, Rotah's son, no. But...Yes! There it was! On Rotah's hand!

She paused. If she looked closely it indeed looked like a scar. And if she tilted her head a little to one side, looked very much like the old woman's turtle-shell symbol.

"Prandina!"

"Coming, Daddy," she said, but didn't move so fast she couldn't get a good look at the portrait of Rotah's father, Rotar. Goodness, he too had the scar. Why?

Going past the last three portraits she didn't even try to read the names, just looked at the on-sword hands. All three showed the scar!

She wanted to look at the portrait of Keng Baldor when she left the building—but her father was holding the door open, looking back.

CHAPTER 27

# Prandina's Discovery

Togai had long thought that this day, Dilo and Tatl's Grow-ing-Up Day, would be a fun one. Both their families had invited him to their celebrations. But as villagers gathered at the river for Praise Maker ceremonies and the start of the Growing-Up Walk back to the village, the only smiles Togai saw were on the faces of small children and the growing-uppers and their families. But even in the eyes of the adults of those families, he saw no joy. He at first guessed people were sad because Carver had been sentenced to be executed. But the talk was not of Carver. Typical was an old woman saying what a shame it was that Noble Cloud was gone, that Festival parades just wouldn't be the same anymore—and her middle-aged son replying, "So what? We won't be there to see anyway."

Togai had wondered, even yesterday, why people weren't more concerned about Carver. Was it because no one knew him well? Was it that people cared only about what affected them directly? He guessed he was that way too. He'd awakened several times during the night, but he hadn't thought about Carver. He'd thought about what he'd seen—or thought he'd seen—in the mountains. He was sure he'd seen Sky Falls and what was supposed to be Ogre. But had he really seen something beyond the Horns? Something green? And what about the scorn mark? Sitting up there, looking at it, he'd convinced himself it was very much like Old Helu's mark, like the turtle-shell emblem, but was it really?

He'd seen Old Helu's head last year and seen the mark she paint-ed on Kallo—and thought he remembered exactly what the scorn looked like, but did he?

As the long line for the walk back into the village began to form, he stayed with Tatl and Dilo near the front—next to Old Helu—long enough to get a good look at her, long enough to convince himself that the one he'd seen by the chimney, except for being larger, was as much like Old Helu's scar and turtle-shell emblem as one could chisel into stone. Someone, maybe someone still alive, had burned the scar into her scalp. But who had made the mark above the chimney—and when?

Prandina had spent more of the night awake than Togai had.

Togai's thoughts had *kept* him from sleeping, but Prandina had stayed awake because she wanted to. And while only part of Togai's thoughts had whirled around what Old Helu's symbol looked like, almost all of Prandina's had. Ever since she'd seen that the old woman's symbol and the hand scar of early kings looked very much alike, she'd wondered "why?" How could that be? How could it have happened?

Immediately she had wondered if she might find, if not full answers, at least some insight or clues in the Books of Kings—which was why she wanted to stay awake. So that, when the castle was quiet, she could sneak up to her father's study and get into the secret room. Trouble was, the castle didn't get quiet.

She lay awake for a long time, waiting for her father to go to his room, but when he did, silence was not what came down to her. It was footsteps. Booted steps. Pacing. Striding. And not just in—or from—the bedroom, but up and down the hall and on the stairs. Once she'd even heard a distant boom as the castle's huge front door swung shut. She was fairly certain he was upset about Noble Cloud's death, and probably would be for a long time. Sadness alone, though, she thought, wouldn't be keeping him awake, wouldn't make for restless roaming. It was probably anger.

The last thing she could recall hearing before she fell asleep was his booted steps in the hallway above her. And it was bootsteps there that brought her awake as the first hints of sun were lighting her wall. This time the steps had a strident ring, a purpose to them, and as they ended—at what she was sure was the hall window that opened toward the stables—through her window came a loud and insistent, "Saddle Black Thunder."

In a short while, after many other sounds, came the sound of hooves at gallop.

She could sneak up to the study now, she thought, but Old Rono for sure was already up and stirring—and Zarian would be soon. No need to rush. She was afraid that this day she'd have plenty of time to sneak into her father's study.

At breakfast she asked Old Rono, "Did you hear my father leave this morning?"

The old woman frowned. "Of course, child. You know I can't sleep past sunup. Besides, the king wanted his breakfast early and a, uh, lunch to carry with him. And, uh, he said not wait supper on him. He might be late getting back."

Prandina hesitated. "Did he say where he was going?"

"Uh…" Rono nervously twisted her hands in her apron. "Into town, he said. Uh, some business he had to take care of."

Prandina usually really enjoyed Praise Maker Day, when Zarian's nanny and most other castle workers had the day off and she could have Zarian all to herself. But today she was glad when right after lunch he said he was ready for a story and a nap, and as soon as he was asleep, she hurried up the stairs, confident that on such a pretty Praise Maker afternoon the only other person in the castle was early-rising Old Rono, who was probably asleep too.

Though Prandina hadn't been in the secret room for almost a year, she remembered her routine well and in almost no time was in the little room, holding a candle and stepping up on the stool she'd used many times before.

She looked up and gasped. Where were the books? The entire top shelf was gone! Why would her father…? She giggled and put her hand to her mouth. There were no books missing. She'd simply grown a lot, grown enough to put her eyes about level with the bottom of the top shelf. She no longer had to look up the way she used to.

With the eerie sensation that she should have to be stretching, she pulled the fourth book—the Rotar-Rotah book—from the shelf. But as she was turning to step off the stool, a second eerie feeling hit. Something was different. She'd seen something she hadn't seen before. But what?

She stood on tiptoe and held the candle closer to the books. She'd always thought they were loosely packed. Easier to get hold of and pull out, she'd assumed. Now, down the space where book four had been she could see there was another book back there, turned sideways.

Forgetting all previous precautions about not disturbing dust, she quickly placed book four atop the bookcase, shoved six and seven—and others—hard to one side, and reached back.

Hands shaking, she pulled the book out and held the candle close to its spine.

Yes! It was the missing book! *Book of Kings 5*, the *Writings of Rotah and Rotanor*

Heart racing, legs trembling, she carried *Book 4* and *Book 5* out to her father's desk and carefully put them on it. She sat on the edge of his big chair and pulled the just-found *Book 5* in front of her. What she was looking for could well be in *4*, she thought, but first she wanted to look in *5*. It was as if she had found some of the kingdom's memory, memory it didn't even know it had lost. Truth was, though, she thought, what was in the Books of Kings always had been and always would be lost to the people.

Afraid she might tear something her hands were shaking so, she used one finger to lift the old and stiff front cover just enough to peek in. Carefully she turned to the first page of writing—the familiar handwriting-printing mix of old King Rotah—and opened the book enough to start reading. Something about looking for a place to build a new castle. On the next page, to her surprise, was a detailed, well-done sketch of a castle. She looked more carefully. It was *this* castle, the one she was in!—as it might be seen from down by the river. Did Rotah, who seemed barely able to get legible words onto paper, draw this precise, really pretty picture? She was about to turn to the next page when her eye caught a glimpse of what she guessed was a signature, at the bottom of the sketch, almost hidden in the crease of the book.

Carefully opening the book a little wider, she peered into the crease. Yes. It was Rotah's signature all right, the one she'd seen so often in *Book 4*. A crude, blocky "Rotah" with a flourish under it, a large Z-like mark, seemingly added with a slashing motion, as if Rotah really meant what he'd just written or, in this case, drawn. This added flourish wasn't flat, though, like a Z, it was more of a zigzag and had a squiggly tail.

She looked again—and her mouth came wide open. Take off the squiggly tail and the mark looked a lot like the scar shown on Rotah's hand in the portrait—a lot like the symbol the old woman from Left wore around her neck!

She began to turn pages more rapidly, looking for signatures. For several pages almost every page had a signature somewhere on it, each with the squiggly-tailed Z. Then came a stretch of five written-on, unsigned pages, followed by a signed one that had only a few lines at the top. Below the signature and the squiggle Z, filling the rest of the page was a huge X, a sure sign that Rotah was about to write a decree. Quickly she turned the page, and saw:

*DECREE*

> *I herby decree that frum this day frward, no keng or any purson about to becum keng shall cut into his hand—or his son's hand—the jag Z-Mark of Zaphor long worn and used by leders of Zaphyr. Furter, from this day on, no keng, includ me, shall use that symbol as part of sgnatur. . .*

Prandina's eyes jumped to the end of the decree. Yes, there it was, Rotah's signature—but no squiggle-Z flourish under it. She came back and finished reading:

> *. . .or in any form put on clothes or papyrs or anywhere.*
> *Furmor, this day on, no purson in Zaphyr can use or show that symbol in any way. In short, that mark banned from Zaphyr furevr.*
> *Rotah, Aith Keng of Zaphyr*

Prandina wanted to laugh. Finding out things was fun. Now she knew why the Z abruptly disappeared from the portraits. But why did Rotah ban its use? What turned him against it? She guessed the pages she'd just turned past might have the answer. She turned back and began to read:

> *Becus Mother Natur send good and timely rains early summr make crops unusual bountful, best evr sum say. But Ogres, jellus maybe, make late summr unusual cool so crops late cummin in. Becus that, firs tim evr, far as I know, let Lefts come in to hep with harvst after Festival...*

With the strange spellings and crude handwriting, Prandina had a hard time reading what Rotah wrote, but the gist of it was that a few days after the Festival, Rotah had gone riding to check on the harvest and had happened to see a young Left working in an orchard who, it seemed, had a really bad cut on his half-shaved head. Curious and a bit concerned, Rotah had ridden over for a better look and was shocked when he saw that the boy's head was not cut but had a Z painted on it in red. Infuriated, the king covered his scar and demanded to know how the mark got there, and why. The boy's father, seeing the boy was bewildered and scared, cautiously intervened. The king, to his great chagrin, soon learned that Lefts, *all* Lefts, got that mark as a sign of growing up, had for a long time. But the man didn't know for how long or where it came from.

Rotah had ridden away feeling humiliated and angry. At first he tried to think of some way to punish the Lefts but decided that would only serve to let the people of the kingdom know that the symbol of their kings had been desecrated. Then the thought came that so many Lefts had used the symbol, for so long, the solution was to forbid its use by kings or any other Zaphyrian ever again. After all, its use by Lefts had soiled it forever.

What luck she had found this book, Prandina thought. She now had an answer to her question of why kings had stopped using the symbol. But could it happen that Lefts were using a symbol that was the same as—or very close to—a symbol that, supposedly, was known only to Zaphyrian kings?

She read on and quickly discovered that, not surprisingly, Rotah had wondered the same thing. And what he reasoned was that since Lefts had been coming to help with the harvest for so long, for almost as long as they'd been in the valley, surely some Left—or Lefts—must have noticed the scar on some king's hand and, seeing it as a mark of distinction or honor, appropriated it for their own use. "Made them feel nobul an importnt," Rotah wrote.

Prandina shook her head. This hadn't turned out the way she had hoped it would. Reminded her of when she got her first pony. She'd so looked forward to it, but when it came it was short and fat and just plodded along. Same with her answers. They just plodded. Dull, simple, logical. Not at all mysterious or exotic.

Though she still had more than a page to read in the long passage before Rotah's decree, she'd about lost interest and was about to close the book when the word "troobdor" caught her eye. She again bent over the book and began to read.

> *Not sure what I bout to write is fatual, just want try to tribute a little sumthen to histry fore I cum part of it. I put this together from bits and pieces, sum from books of kengs, mostly from tale my vattar tell and from old troobdor song, and tho, I repete, I can't vouch for it, I believe it tru. The tale is. . .*
>
> *Original leader Zaphor have a Z on forhead and when he name dauter to susseed him (he not have son?) he burn Z into her forhead and decree (maybe just say) (if anythin written down it musta got lost or burned) that all rulers of Zaphyr after that have to have Z burned in forhead too. As say bout other tale erlier, not sure cus of condition of vattar's mind that tale tru and kind of doubt til one day out ridin happen come cross one of old troobdors, ax him if know any old songs. He say <u>all</u> songs he know old. I mean real old, like back firs leaders, I say. He tink, say yeah, member one his granvattar taught him, and he sing*
>
>> *They say young Zee thought her pretty as could be*
>> *But all the people feared. . .*
>>> *their queer-looking Kween Delkineer*

*They say it wasn't her fault she looked horrid*
*Was cus of the mark..*
*old papa Zee put on her forhead.*


*That set me tinkin bout other tale my vattar tol, so I cautius ax*
*old troobdor if he know or ever hear any songs bout mens cumin out of*
*mountains—and he look at me like I crazy. But his song convens me the*
*Z tale tru. So (back to tale)...When it cum time for Zaphor's dauter*
*(I guess her name Delkineer) to burn Z into her son's forhead, befor he*
*cum next leader (not have kengs back then eethr), she cudn't do it. She*
*order, insted, that Z be <u>cut</u> into his <u>hand</u> and that from then on the new*
*leader get same mark. But since that order or decree not writ down and*
*since that was before purite of mark spoiled by Lefts using it, I think it*
*best to take it off future kings. What's honr or distinction in havin mark*
*like Lefts? And if the original leader's daughter can change own vattar's*
*order from <u>burnin</u> a mark into forhead to <u>cuttin</u> one into hand, surely I*
*can do way with it altogether to spare future kengs of Zaphyr ridicule.*
*Peepl not like it their keng use somethin Lefts use. So, I will make decree*
*to forbid futur use of mark, but until I do, one more time and still writ*
*with pride, this is*
    *Rotah, Aith Keng of Zaphyr*


And below that was a large, squiggly-tailed Z, the last, she was
sure, he or any other king ever wrote.

## CHAPTER 28

# The Edge

Togai was glad to see night come. He was tired of hearing people complain about not getting to go to Festivals ever again. Their talk had spoiled Growing-Up Day, and he welcomed the chance to curl up on his cot and think about what he'd been wanting to think about all day—the mountains and the mark he'd seen. He had no doubt now that it was the same as Old Helu's, guessed whoever had done it must have been, like he was, afraid to say he'd been up there.

He fell asleep imagining he had climbed to the top of the chimney, hammer and chisel stuck in his clothes, and was sitting there, hammering carefully, slowly cutting the symbol of scorn deep into Ogre's finger. He began to feel, in under him, the finger start to twitch, as if it were itchy, wanting to scratch, when, suddenly, a blast of cold air swept down from the mountains and up the chimney came a moan, as if from Ogre's mouth far away. He dropped the hammer and chisel and scrambled down the chimney and out the tunnel—and ran down the canyon with Ogres of the Cold nipping at his back, grabbing his shoulder.

He sat upright, startled and scared—but relieved. It had only been Togl shaking him.

"Get up," Togl said. "Old Exl's here. He ate too much at yesterday's Growing-Up parties and doesn't want to fish today. Want to take his place?"

"Sure," Togai said and quickly rolled from the cot. He didn't know why Togl bothered asking. He knew Togai wouldn't turn down a chance to fish, and "No" wasn't an acceptable answer.

Once outside, he was puzzled why Old Exl was still there, even more puzzled when Exl joined them to walk down to the river. He soon had an inkling. They—that included Kallo—had no more than started across the strand than Exl pointed across the river and said, "Just like we thought would happen."

Coming down the road-path from the City of Light were two men on a horse-pulled cart. The horse and cart were black. The two men wore black clothes.

Kallo looked at Togl. "Think Carver's body's in the cart?"

Togl nodded. "Zaps don't want him over there."

"You think they'll dump him in the river?"

"Let's hope not," Togl said. "Let's hope they don't dump him anyplace."

The cart stopped at the bank, and one of the men stood and cupped his hands to his mouth. "Will you come and get the body?"

Togl waved and yelled back. "Yes!" He turned to Kallo. "Get a Going Away canoe and tie it to mine. Take Togai with you and show him how. Hurry."

As they ran up the strand, Togai asked, "You think Togl will take me to get the body?"

Kallo nodded.

Togai felt his mouth go dry. He couldn't imagine touching a dead body. Especially Carver's. He was sure he'd throw up.

But it went better than he thought it would. All he had to do was stand in the water and hold the Going Away canoe against the bank while the Zaprians let the body slide out of the cart and Togl and Kallo guided it into the canoe. An added blessing was the body was wrapped in heavy black cloth and he didn't have to look at it.

By the time they were back across the river the rest of the village was there, along the strand and bank all the way down to the first bend. Though the villagers may not have known Carver very well and though many would remember him as the one who took away Festivals, he was still one of them and deserved a decent burial. Besides, no one wanted to risk offending Maker by not treating one of His creations with proper respect.

Old Helu came to Carver's Going Away canoe and placed in it

what was said to be Carver's favorite piece, a horse with a kingly figure on it. She stepped back, and the fishers headed downriver, canoes single file. Last were Togai and Togl, towing Carver in his Going Away canoe.

At the fishing grounds, the other fishers formed a lane and held their paddles upright as Togai, Togl and the Going Away canoe passed.

"Keep paddling," Togl said quietly from the rear of the canoe. "I'll tell you when to stop."

"How far do we go?" Togai asked.

"Out past where we usually fish, nearer the Edge, where it'll be easier for Maker to find Carver."

"And what will Maker do with him—and the canoe?"

"Take both of them over the Edge, to where He lives."

Togai wanted to know how Togl knew that, but didn't ask, just kept paddling. The sun wasn't even halfway up the morning sky when Togl said, "This is far enough. I'll untie Carver's canoe and we'll turn. But don't look back. What happens from now on is between Carver and Maker."

Once they had turned, Togai asked, "How did you know how far out to go?"

"Out to where the village was starting to disappear from sight."

Togai had already noticed that from the tops of swells he could catch glimpses of the village but that from the troughs he couldn't even see chimney tops. "What makes the village start to disappear?" he asked.

"It's Maker's way of warning us. If we go out on the ocean too far, out past where we're not supposed to, Maker starts to take the land and village away. But if we come back, closer, Maker is pleased and restores the village and the land."

"Has anyone ever gone out far enough to make the village disappear completely?"

"Yes. Once, many generations ago, the fishers, all of them, got careless and chased a school of Great Yellowtail out too far. A storm came up and blew them even farther out, and they had to paddle frantically to get back before night and restore the village."

"What happened to the people when the village disappeared?"

"Nothing. Maker was merciful. Since they had done nothing wrong, he didn't make them suffer and restored them to life as if nothing had ever happened. They couldn't even remember they had disappeared."

Talk of the Edge, The Great Edge, reminded Togai of a story he had heard before, but he wanted to hear it again. "Tell me again, please, Papa, how we got to be here, in this particular place?"

"Maker first put us on a place out near the Edge, close to where the sun comes up."

"And how do you know it was near the Edge?"

"Because one night the sun lost its way and tried to come up underneath our island—people could feel it bumping around under there—and made the ground so hot it gushed up out of the mountain there and we had to leave. As we paddled away—we were lucky Maker had let us know which way the Edge was—we could see Maker slowly pulling the mountain down, to give more room for the sun to come up.

"Maker let us drift for a long time. One day, when we had proven we were good enough fishers to live on almost nothing, he began to build this place, and as we paddled toward it, it rose out of the sea—and we landed near where our village is now. And though it was in a place where gardens did not grow, He—and we—knew we would not starve."

"Why did He make us land in Left, instead of in Zaphyr, where we could grow gardens?"

"Because he had just made the Zaprians. Though the land was fertile, they were near starved when we landed, and we had to keep them alive with fish."

"Really?"

"I'm sure of it. It is a tale that has been handed down from father to son and from mother to daughter for as long as anyone can remember. Maker knew we were tough and resourceful, but not the Zaprians. That is why Maker put them where they are."

Togai thought for a moment and nodded as if he understood, but he didn't.

At lunch time, when the fishers gathered their canoes around Togl's almost all the talk was about Zaprians coming to the river to trade. Or not. Many fishers were afraid the Zaps wouldn't come because they'd think the fishers wouldn't come—out of fear of violating the king's decree even if they stayed in the water or the canoe to trade. Other fishers were afraid that Zaps wouldn't come—even if they thought the fishers would—out of anger over Noble Cloud being killed.

But that afternoon, when they came around the last bend and could see the trading bank, Togl laughed. "So much for the Zaps not coming. I think there are more there than I've ever seen before. They must want to load up on fish in case the king does shut off trade."

Since Togl knew about Togai's not liking to talk to or look up to Zaps, he let Togai hand him fish while he—keeping both feet in the water—did the trading.

As Togai watched and handed, he realized that though Togl didn't like the Zaps either, he was good at dealing with them and at keeping his feelings hidden. One of the men Togl traded with was the man who had supervised construction of the platform Togai and Kallo had worked on at the Festival.

"We were a little afraid no one would show up to trade," Togl said to him.

The man laughed. "We were afraid *you* wouldn't show up and that we wouldn't have any fish to eat—ever again."

Togl laughed. "We were afraid we wouldn't have anything *but* fish to eat."

Several Zaps laughed. Togai watched. Each side was doing the same thing, trying to keep the other in a good mood so the other would be easy to bargain with.

That night, though Togai was really tired, he lay awake. So much had happened in the two days since he came back from the mountains he'd barely had time to think about being there. He certainly hadn't told anyone what he'd done, what he'd seen and not seen. And he doubted he would. Main reason was no one would believe him and he'd forever be laughed at. He wasn't even sure he believed it himself, and now, with the ban on going to Festivals, he might never have another chance to go back and look again. On ordinary days, because of chores, he'd not have enough time. Even if he did, the woodcutters were always in the hills somewhere and he was likely to be seen. On Praise Maker days, he'd be expected to be in the village with everybody else.

A few nights later, Lilu said, "I'm really going to miss the Festival. Used to, my spare time, I could think about the Festival, sew and plan. But now..." She sighed. "There's just not much to look forward to. I so wish the king would lift his ban."

"So do I!" Togai said with great enthusiasm.

"We don't need your sarcasm," she said.

"I wasn't being sarcastic. I really do wish the king would lift his ban."

"Sure," she said. "Everybody knows you didn't go to the last two Festivals."

Togai said nothing, but he'd really meant what he said. He'd give anything if Chelks could go to Festivals again and give him other chances to get into the mountains.

Next morning Togai was at the work hut early to start his last year of training work. Net making and mending was one of the jobs he hadn't trained in yet, so, thinking the work shouldn't be too hard and thinking that, as a fisher, he should know as much as he could about nets, he chose that. And it did turn out to be easy. Old Gluml, the woman in charge, began teaching him the basics but about midmorning seemed to grow as bored as he was and though he was now a fourteen-old and was supposed to work until noon, she let him go.

But after being in the mountains and having helped tow Carver's body out to where Maker could get it, he couldn't get excited about anything around the village, especially with Tatl and Dilo "grown up" and not there to play with. With little chance of getting to the mountains again, the only thing he had to look forward to was becoming a fisher. So, he thought, if he was going to be a fisher, why not the best?

He'd been embarrassed by how puny his throws had been compared to Togl's and the other fishers. He needed to be able to throw farther and to make the net spread more. But he didn't want to stand on the strand or get in a canoe and go out in the river to practice. The other boys and girls would laugh at him. The fishers would be sure to hear and some would tease him. No. He needed a place where no one could see him. Why not go upriver? Go far enough, up to shallower water, might even catch some river trout. Fishers said river trout were hard to catch because they were so skittery and could see anyone close enough to throw a net. So, if he could net some trout, even if only two or three, maybe they'd think he could be a good fisher someday.

With that thought in mind, Togai quickly ate lunch and ran down to the river. As he had hoped, given it was near noon on a cloudy, cool day, no one was there and he soon had a spare net—pulled from a drying rack—draped over his shoulder and was hurrying upriver along the bank. He guessed he'd have to go past the king's castle before he came to rapids or other water shallow enough for him to be able to see river trout—and hope they didn't see him first.

Near the castle he became so interested in looking at it that he almost didn't notice the long sandbar near the bank on the castle side of the river. He stopped and looked. He was pretty sure it hadn't been there two Festivals ago, the first time he'd gone to the mountains, but there it was. He could imagine spring floods coming down, cutting into the far bank, swirling around and depositing the sandbar. What intrigued him were the ripples that broke above it and along the sides, signs of swift and shallow water. A good place for trout to be—if he could just get over there with the net.

He didn't dare try to swim with the net. Once wet, it'd probably be heavy enough to pull him under. Even worse, he might get tangled in it. But if he had a board or...He dropped the net and ran back to where he'd seen a good-sized limb that had washed ashore. In almost no time he had the net on the limb and was in the river, swimming and pushing the limb and net ahead of him. He landed at the downstream end of the narrow strip of sand and gravel, took the net from the limb, and walked as quietly as he could up the middle of the strip to its end. He was disappointed. The dropoff on each side was steep. He could see bottom for only a few steps out. And though the water was indeed shallow above the sandbar and though he could see bottom, the ripply water made it impossible for him to tell whether any of the wavery dark shapes he saw were fish or rocks. Oh, well, he thought. He had come mainly to practice. Might as well throw and hope for the best.

No sooner had the net plopped into the water than he heard the sound of a horse galloping. He looked up and saw—coming at a fast pace toward him across the broad, grassy field that stretched all the way up to the castle—a figure on a small brown horse. Quickly he began pulling in the net and at the same time turning to see how far it was back to the limb. But then he thought: Why am I worried? Zaps can't swim. The worst that can happen is I get yelled at. But for what? I'm not in Zaphyr, I'm in the river.

So, with that thought, and acting as if he didn't care that a horse and rider were coming, he finished pulling in the net and threw again. Though he had told himself not to look, when he heard the horse stop he turned his head slightly to sneak a peek out of the corner of his eye and was startled.

It wasn't a king's aide or the king himself. It was the Princess Prandina! He took a full look. He had never seen a girl or a woman on a horse before. The princess wasn't much more than a good net throw away and was now leaning forward close to the horse's neck and looking a little to one side, watching carefully as it came down the steep, dried-mud path from the top of the high bank to a little sand flat. As she got off to let it drink, she took off her hat and dark hair, much shinier and longer than any he'd ever seen, cascaded down her back. Togai was sure he had never seen anything—or anyone—so pretty. He wanted to tell her that. But when she glanced at him across that narrow stretch of water he quickly looked away. He was certain that she, like most Zaps, would think him ugly or dumb or both. Even worse, she'd think of him as one of those people who had killed her father's horse.

But as he began pulling hard on the net, wanting to get away as quickly as he could, she said, not something nasty, but, "How's the fishing?"

"I..." His tongue didn't want to move. It had been two Festivals since he'd spoken to a Zap, and he'd never heard of a Chelk actually talking with anyone in the royal family—except for Old Helu just the other day, and that was different. He sneaked a glance across the narrow strip of water and was again startled. She had knelt by the horse and was now looking up at him. He'd never had a Zap look up at him before. "I...I haven't caught anything yet," he said.

"Are you the Left who finished first in a race two or three Festivals ago?"

He was dumbfounded. Not only did she remember him, she was the only person other than Kallo and Old Zoltai to say he'd won the race—and she was the king's daughter!

"Why...Why, yes. I am," he stammered.

"I thought so. But I haven't seen you in any races since, have I?"

"No. And you probably won't see me or any other Chelk in another race. Not ever again."

Her hand flew to her mouth. "Oh, I'm sorry. I forgot about the banishment. And...and I was right there on the balcony. I..." She paused. "I saw your leader. She had this piece of turtle shell, shaped like a Z..."

"Shaped like a what?"

Prandina blushed. She'd forgotten something else: Lefts were illiterate. "Uh...a zigzag," she said, and with one finger drew a Z in the air. "And your leader *said*..." Prandina took a deep breath. "...she *said* she had a mark like that cut into her scalp. Does she *really*?"

Togai thought it a bit odd that Prandina would now have, as he had just had, an interest in Old Helu's symbol. But he guessed Prandina, being a girl *and* the daughter of a king, had probably never, ever had a scratch or a bruise and couldn't imagine *letting* someone cut her. Squeamish girl. "Sure," he said. "I've seen it."

"Do you, uh, know where she—or your people—got the idea for that symbol?"

Togai shrugged. "I don't know. As far as I know, the Dilkina has always had it."

A strange look came to Prandina's face. As she stood, she asked cautiously, carefully, trying not to show too much interest, "What did you call her?"

"The Dilkina. That's what we call her, sometimes. Most of the time we..." He saw Prandina was getting on her horse and he looked directly toward her. "Did I say something wrong?"

"No," she said, and turned the horse away from the water. "I just remembered something, I think. Sorry. I need to go." She leaned over the horse's neck and urged it up the bank. As it broke into a gallop she turned and called back, "I hope you catch a bunch!"

Togai sighed. And he didn't catch a bunch of anything. Just two little catfish. No trout. But he didn't throw the catfish back even though they were small. He'd heard Old Fanl liked river catfish. Maybe he'd give them to her if she'd promise not to tell.

On his way back to the village he noticed dark clouds out over the ocean. He began to hurry, but his worst fears were realized. A few fishers who had come in early because of the threat of bad weather saw him trying to sneak the net back onto the rack. What was worse, they saw the two little catfish before he could throw them in the river.

All during supper Togai was afraid Togl or Kallo—or both— would start teasing him. When neither did, he guessed they hadn't heard about the fish. But later, when he and Kallo were in their room and he asked, "Kallo, do you think Zaprian girls are pretty?" Kallo said, "I don't know. About as pretty as catfish, I'd guess."

## CHAPTER 29

# Whence "Dilkina"?

As Prandina expected, her father was in his study when she got back from the river. But soon after darkness and quiet had fell over the rest of the castle, she lit a candle, tinkered with keys both large and small, and was soon at her father's desk—Rotah and Rotanor's book open before her.

Quickly, though carefully, she turned to the passage she'd read just a few days before—and read it again:

*They say young Zee thought her pretty as could be*
*But all the people feared. . .*
    *their queer-looking Kween Delkineer*

*They say it wasn't her fault she looked horrid*
*Was cus of the mark. . .*

Yes, Prandina thought. That was what she had remembered. *Delklneer. Kween Delkineer.* A leader. The fisherboy runner—did he say his name?—said Lefts called their leader "the Dilkina." Could be coincidence, she thought, but more likely, just as some Lefts could have seen the Z on the hand of a king and adopted it for their use, they could have heard a troubadour sing about the Kween Delkineer, maybe heard 'Dilkina,' and decided to call their leader that. But what about the tale Rotah's crazy old father told? Could there possibly, just possibly, be another explanation?

CHAPTER 30

# You Can Lead a Horse to Water but. . .

Next morning, as Togai had hoped, it wasn't long before Old Gluml began to yawn, and after she had dozed off a few times, she again told him he could leave early—and he did. Eagerly. He had told himself he wanted to get upriver so he could fish, but the real reason, he knew, was he wanted to see Prandina again.

And he did. She was riding in the field below the castle when he got there. And it wasn't long after he was on the sandbar that she guided her horse down the bank to the river's edge.

"Hi," she said, and slid down the side of the horse as it began to drink.

"Hi. That the same horse as yesterday?"

"Yes." She laughed. "I call her Whi-Face. Not many horses have a white spot like that. You not notice?"

Togai blushed. He guessed he hadn't.

"You come here to fish every day?"

"No. Yesterday was the first time. And I'm not really fishing. Just practicing." He glanced at her. "My father's the *head* fisher."

"Oh. That's nice. We Zaphyrians don't. . ."

"*Zaphyrians?*"

She laughed. "That's what we call ourselves. Whatever, we—to you—Zaprians don't eat fish from the river."

"I know. That's one reason we *Chelks* don't fish the river. That, and if we did, we'd soon catch all there. We're good fishers."

She smiled. "You must be," she said, and climbed back onto the horse and started to turn it but stopped. "Say. Did you say your leader was called the *Dilkina?*"

"Yes."

"Do you know why she's called that? Where the word comes from—or what it means?"

"Uh...no."

"Well, if you happen to find out, let me know, will you?"

"Sure," he said. "Sure."

At the top of the bank she reined in Whi-Face and pointed toward the mountains. "Goodness. Look at those dark clouds. We may be in for a storm."

Togai glanced toward the mountains. But he had already started pulling his net onto the sandbar and folding it. As soon as Prandina had asked about *dilkina*, he knew he had something better to do than fish.

When he had the net properly hung on the drying rack he headed for Old Helu's hut. He stepped onto its little porch and would have knocked but the door was already open. "Come in, Togai," she called to him. "I don't get many young men callers. What brings you here?"

"I, uh, why are you called *Dilkina?*"

She gave him a puzzled look, "What?"

"I mean, what does the word mean? Where'd it come from?"

She gave another puzzled look, then shook her head. "I don't know, Togai. Where does the word *fish* come from?"

That night, the last thing Togl did before he sat down to eat was go to the door and again look toward the mountains. He came back and sighed as he sat down. "We've been watching the clouds build all day. I'm afraid this is going to be a bad one."

And during the night it came. Wind and heavy rain. At dawn, though Togai wasn't sure just when that was, the rain was still coming down hard. Normally he would have been glad, for hard rain meant no chores and extra sleep. But this rain brought no extra sleep, no extra dreams. It brought thoughts of "Would a princess ride on a rainy day?" Even with doubts, he was soon up, moping around, looking out, hoping the rain would stop.

Togl was gloomy too—until around midmorning when the sound of rain on the roof changed from a steady drumming to a pattering. He went to the door and came back smiling. "I believe it's going to clear off. We ought to able to fish tomorrow."

Togai thought: *I'm not waiting until tomorrow*, and soon he had a net over his shoulder and was hurrying upstream along the bank. Dark clouds still scudded above the mountains, but he didn't care. He was on his way to see the Princess, enjoying splashing through puddles and feeling cool mud ooze up between his toes. But when he came to the bend where he should be able to see the little island, he couldn't. If it was there, it was under water. Muddy water. Fast-running water. Turtles! If she came down at all, they'd not be able to talk. They'd have to yell. Loudly. Loud enough to be heard above the rushing water.

He folded the net and put it on a rock so it wouldn't get muddy and sat down on it. Waiting for even a distant glimpse of her was better than anything else he could think of doing—and he had plenty of time. The sun was still getting higher. But so was the river. From lots of rain in the mountains, he guessed.

The sun moved slowly, on past its noon high, and just as he was thinking Prandina might not ride, she came around the corner of a low building at the back of the castle on—even from this distance he could tell—the white-faced horse. Since the field at the bottom of the hill was practically a lake, he expected her to turn across the top of the hill, toward the woods or upper valley in hope of finding relatively dry ground, but she kept coming, down the hill, straight toward the river. He jumped up. Was she hoping to see him—or was it *dilkina* she was interested in?

He watched, barely daring hope she wanted to see him. Just as the horse got to the bottom of the hill and started its high-step splashing across the field she looked up and waved. He waved and moved a little closer to the bank. He'd have to yell to let her know he'd talked to Old Helu. He sighed. If the sandbar had been washed away, and it probably had, he might never again be able to 'talk' to her.

She reined in Whi-Face just short of the bank and leaned forward to peek at the river. Whi-Face, seeming to take her standing as a signal to move, took a cautious step forward. The normally hard-packed dirt path was now slippery mud and Whi-Face slid down it, forelegs stiff and straight in a frantic effort to stop. The rushing water grabbed—in terrible, slow order—hooves, legs and chest, pulled them down and under and twisted Whi-Face to one side. The princess fell, with hands out and head back, eyes wide and full of fear of the swirling water that was about to take her and her horse bobbing away.

CHAPTER 31

# Whim of the Current

Even as they were falling, Togai was running. He knew she couldn't swim. No Zaprian could. A sense of desperate urgency made him run as he'd never run before. He barely looked at the path, paid no attention to rocks or mud or overhanging branches, just kept looking at Prandina—and thinking: I've got to get ahead of her! I've got to get ahead of her! His heart sank with her as she went under, but she soon came up flailing, flailing wildly, trying to get to the horse which was now off to one side. Why, oh why, Togai thought, hadn't the king changed those decrees so she'd know how to swim?

"Paddle!" he yelled as loudly as he could. "Try to paddle." But he doubted she heard. About the time he was even with her, she went under again, and just as the river made a bend in front of him, he dived as far out as he could and came up swimming hard and calling to her. Somehow, above the raging water she heard his yell, but as she was turning to look for him her head struck a big willow limb. Togai grabbed her just as she went under. Instinct made him put his left arm around her—so he could swim on his side with his stronger right leg deeper in the water. But as good a swimmer as he was, he had to fight to keep their heads above the swirling water, swirling water that carried them first toward one rapidly passing bank then the other. He caught up with a bobbing log and was just about to catch his breath when the far end hit a rock. The jolt sent the log's bark tearing into the skin under his arm and along his side. He tried to hold on, but couldn't, and once again it was only his strength that kept his and the princess's head above the choppy, turbulent flow. Struggling the way he was, fighting the way he was, Togai was tiring rapidly, and as the realization came that he couldn't possibly keep them both afloat until the river widened and they were in calmer water, he saw a place where the water had run over the bank and out into a meadow. It had to be shallow there, not as swift. But even as he forced his aching and scraped right arm to pull them that direction, he knew they were headed for Zaphyr, the side of the river that meant death to any Chelk. But he couldn't worry about that, not now. From the time he was very small he had heard his father and other fishers say that the first duty of any fisher was to save anyone in the water. Now he had to save the princess.

He managed to get to water he could stand in, but with the current tugging at his legs and the slick grass underfoot, he kept slipping and falling. When he finally got her onto grass at the water's edge he knew that he should run on downstream to calmer water and swim across to Chelekai. But he couldn't leave her—not in mud and grass, not unconscious. Not near rising water. He knelt and slid his arms under her and somehow managed to get to his feet and start for a house and barn on a low hill. Her thoroughly soaked dress seemed to weigh as much as she. It dragged the ground and he tripped over it often. The muscles in his arching back and already tired arms began to quiver and seemed ready to burst into flame. He wanted to call for help, but he was afraid to. Why give the Zaps warning? Just get the princess into good hands and run for the river.

Only when he was close to the house and had spotted a cart by the barn did he call out.

A man and woman came running out of the house, but as soon as they saw him they stopped and stared, mouths open in disbelief.

"It's the princess," Togai gasped as he struggled to make the last few steps toward them. "She needs help."

The man ran toward the barn. "I'll get hay for the cart. Put her there." As he ran he called back to two boys who had come out of the house. "Grannon, get out the mare. Hitch her to the cart. Hurry. Rednar, take my horse and ride as fast as you can to tell the king— and tell the neighbors along the way. Hurry, now."

The woman stayed several steps away but watched closely as Togai gently placed Prandina on the ground beside the cart.

When he stepped back the woman saw the lump on Prandina's forehead, the dress muddy and torn, and she screamed, "What have you done? What have you done? Get away from her, you animal! Get away from her!"

Togai turned to run, but the man was blocking his way. He had an angry look and he carried not hay but a pitchfork, a pitchfork pointed at Togai's chest.

As soon as a neighbor arrived the farmer handed him the pitchfork—and soon had the mare at a trot, pulling him and a hay-nestled princess toward the City of Light.

A ways behind and on foot came Togai—attended by a growing number of farmers with pitchforks.

The king passed on his black stallion, riding hard, and when Togai and the farmers came to City of Light's central square, they were met by a large crowd headed by King Praidar. He was still on the big horse, now blotched and streaked with drying foam and looking more gray-brown than black. The king pointed and ordered Togai carried to the cross that had been erected where Noble Cloud died. Togai felt rough hands grab his legs, and he felt that he might be torn apart as he was dragged through the jeering crowd. Some said he deserved to die, that he had tried to drown the princess—and worse. The dragging stopped. With men all around him, he could see little of what was happening. His hands were tied behind his back and he could feel ropes being tied around his ankles. Suddenly he was jerked upward, feet first, and he winced as his hands and the back of his head hit the cross's upright. He cried out and tried to lift his head, but it was pushed back against the beam. Upside down, hands and feet tied, head held down, panic engulfed him. He couldn't move. He felt absolutely helpless, desperate. The world seemed nothing but feet and legs. A quiet came—and the feet and legs moved back to let him see those of a prancing black stallion.

"Is the executioner ready?" the king asked.

Togai heard, "I am, O King."

The man who had been holding his head down stepped back, and Togai was able to lift his head enough to see—a little to one side—a hooded, thick-armed man in a sleeveless black robe.

The king opened his mouth to speak but saw the crippled-looking foot and the small lower leg of the youngster hanging upside down in front of him. Could this be the Left who ran the wrong way in the race, the one who reminded him of Old Rono's dream? He tilted his head to better see the face. "Are you the Left who ran the wrong way?"

Togai was tempted to say he didn't run the wrong way, but, for some reason he couldn't explain, he said, "Yes."

"Yes, Sire," the executioner growled.

The king took a firm grip on the saddle horn to steady himself. Thought of Old Rono's dream had made him dizzy. What if this crippled boy really was a boy of prophecy? Did he, the king, or anyone else, have a right to interfere? He hesitated. People were watching. He had to act. He looked at the executioner.

"Do you have the knife of the demented carver who killed Noble Cloud?" the king asked.

"Yes, O King. I do."

"Begin the execution."

CHAPTER 32

# Prandina Chooses

As Togai watched the executioner walk toward him he heard the king say, "Remember. Cut him so that he bleeds slowly."

"As you command, O King," the executioner said—and stopped with his feet almost in Togai's face. He muttered, "Maker forgive me," and stepped around behind the post. Doesn't want blood spurting on his clothes, Togai thought.

Togai felt the man grab a handful of hair, felt his head pulled hard down and back, felt his neck stretched taut, felt a knife's cold blade against it.

He closed his eyes and clenched his teeth. He felt he'd throw up. He didn't want to die.

"No, Daddy, no!" It was Prandina. "Wait! *Please* wait."

He opened his eyes just in time to see Prandina run up and, almost exhausted it seemed, fall against the horse and reach up to grab the back of her father's coat. "Please don't kill him, Daddy. Please. He saved my life."

"He may have saved *your* life, but he disobeyed *my* law. He must die." He pushed her away with his leg and pointed to the executioner. "Proceed!"

Once again Togai felt his head pulled back, felt his neck stretch. He clenched his teeth and tried to force air out through his nostrils. He didn't want to drown in his own blood. He could again feel the knife against his throat.

Just as the executioner said, "Now, O King?" Togai felt a bump—and suddenly the princess was seated beside him, her arm around his head, her face close to his. "Kill him if you must," she said. "But kill me with him."

A murmur ran through the crowd.

"Silence," the king said. He wasn't used to being defied, least of all by his own daughter. But he was the king. He had to act, be decisive. But what about the dream, the prophecy?

He sighed and pointed his riding crop at Prandina. "The choice is yours. If he goes free, you go with him—across the river, never to return."

She stood. "Then lower him. I'll leave if I have to. I cannot let him die."

The only possession Prandina was allowed to take with her, the only possession she had when she and Togai stepped out of Kallo and Togl's canoe into Chelekai, was the torn and muddy dress she wore.

When the Chelks heard what had happened, they were all—especially Togl, Lilu and Kallo—grateful to Prandina.

Though grateful, only a few villagers actually offered to help 'the princess.' Some just didn't want to. They asked, why help the daughter of the man who would no longer let them come to Festivals, who threatened them with death if they so much as came into his kingdom? But most didn't offer because they were ashamed to let a princess see, let alone share, what they wore, ate and, most of all, what they lived in.

Old Helu, whose husband had been long dead and who lived alone, took charge. With apologies to Prandina for the simple nature of her hut, she asked Prandina to live with her and asked that girls and women about the princess's size bring dresses. Only a few did. Even Lilu, saying again and again how grateful she was, offered nothing of her own—but vowed to make the princess a new dress as soon as suitable material could be obtained.

Prandina thanked all those who offered a dress, but took only two, both old and faded. She had long heard how poor the Lefts were, and her first look at the village and villagers up close told here they were worse off than she could possibly have imagined. Right away she told Old Helu she didn't want to be a burden or get special treatment. She wanted to live as the villagers lived.

What she really wanted, *needed*, she said, was shoes. Though some children in Zaphyr went barefoot until they were eight or ten Festivals old, none did after that age—and Prandina had *never* gone barefoot. Her shoes had, of course, been lost in the river, and even the short walk she made from the river into the village had left her tender feet sore and bruised. Old Helu tried to find shoes for her, but since very few Chelks wore or had shoes—certainly no young people—the only ones she found were not only too big but so old and hard that Prandina soon said she'd rather go barefoot, would use a walking stick and walk on the sides of her feet until the bottoms toughened.

The morning after Togai and Prandina rescued each other was a sunny and normal one for Chelks. Adults went back to jobs that had been interrupted by the rain. Children of chore and training age went to their morning tasks. All adults, that is, except Lilu, all 'children' but Togai. Togai's arm and back muscles were so sore from swimming with and carrying Prandina—and his back so scraped and raw from being dragged across the square—that Old Helu had agreed that he could stay home and that Lilu could stay and take care of him.

Togai had thought he'd like that. But not long after Lilu had pampered him with a big breakfast, Old Helu came in carrying a small pot filled with a dark ointment. She said it would cure anything and told Togai to lie face down on his cot. As she slathered his back with it, he had the thought that, from the way it burned and smelled and made his eyes water, it probably would cure anybody of anything—if it didn't kill them first. When he started to sit up, she said no. He had to lie there. All morning.

One good thing about her visit was that before she left he heard her say to Lilu, "After what the king did, I couldn't imagine liking anyone in his family. But, I might like Prandina. She seems so interested in *us*, been asking questions ever since she got up."

That reminded Togai of something he wanted to tell Prandina and he smiled, even though his back was on fire and he could barely see through watery eyes.

Just as he was thinking he couldn't lie there any longer he heard a clatter in the outer room and turned his head enough to see Lilu standing by her overturned chair. She had her hand to her mouth and was staring at the doorway.

Came Prandina's voice, "I have some bark tea for Togai, from Old Helu. She didn't want me to walk, but I wanted to see him. May I come in?"

"Yes, please," Lilu said. "We're honored."

Togai closed his eyes. What would the princess think? The tiniest room in the castle was probably bigger than the hut. For all he knew, her bed was.

"There's not much room in there," Lilu said. "I'll put a chair in the doorway." She gave a nervous laugh. "You don't want to be very close anyway. Whew. That smell."

Prandina laughed. "I'm used to it. Old Helu put a thick layer of her cure-anything paste on my feet last night and bandaged them well." She lifted the hem of her long dress just a little and looked down. "See? Helps me to walk too."

She sat down. "Togai, I...I want to thank you again for saving my life. It was a brave thing you did."

He blushed. "No. You were the brave one. You saved me. I should be thanking you."

She laughed. "Well, if you hadn't saved me, I wouldn't have had to save you."

"I...I..." He didn't know what to say. The thought of her...He didn't even want to think about it.

She stood. "Well, I better go. Old Helu says she doesn't want me walking much for a while. But, well, I just had to come over."

Before he could think of some way to say what he wanted to say, or even know what that was, she was gone.

CHAPTER 33

# The Village Needs a New Hut

A few mornings later, though Togai didn't feel ready, Togl insisted he go back to work. But Old Gluml took pity on him and let him go early. He'd not seen Prandina since her visit that first day, so he took an unnecessarily long way home through the village, hoping that if he went by Old Helu's hut he might at least catch a glimpse of the princess. He walked slowly past, even stopped twice to bend and look at something imaginary on the ground, but he got no glimpse, heard no call.

He was feeling down until he came to where he could see his hut at the edge of the village and saw Prandina walking toward it, very gingerly, with a long, thin bundle hanging from one hand. Oh, she's bringing me a present, he thought, and hurried on. "Hi," he said, as he came up beside her.

"Oh!" She looked around quickly. "You startled me. I...I was paying so much attention to where I stepped I didn't hear you."

"Sorry." And though he told himself he shouldn't, he looked at the bundle.

She held it up a little and blushed. "Oh, that. It's...it's a lunch Old Helu let me make. I was hoping I might talk you into something—you feel like it, of course."

"Oh? What? I feel pretty good."

She glanced cautiously at the hut. "I was wondering if you'd take me for a canoe ride, teach me to paddle?"

Given she'd almost drowned only five or six days ago and, as far as he knew, still couldn't swim, Togai was surprised. He'd have guessed she wouldn't want to be anywhere near the river for a while. But he didn't care. It was a chance to be with her.

They were slow in getting to the river, but once there Togai was soon helping her into the bow of a small canoe and pushing them off. "It's easy," he said. "You just kind of reach out with the paddle and..." As she looked back, Togai continued. "You pull the water back alongside the canoe. Do it a few times on one side, then on the other. I'll tell you if you need to switch."

She had only made a few strokes when she again looked back. "Do you think we could paddle up by the castle, to where you were standing when I fell in?"

"Sure," Togai said, puzzled. "It'll take a while, but if we stick to calm water, stay out of the current, we can do it."

"Please understand, I'm not complaining. You...you *Chelks* have been very generous. But I'd really like to have my own things, especially shoes. I was thinking that if I got out on the bank—the Chelekai bank—someone in the castle might see me and come down. Maybe I could talk them into getting some things for me—if they're not too afraid Daddy would catch them. But..." Her voice quavered. "...what I'd really like is a picture Daddy had painted of me and my little brother, Zarian. He was on my lap and...and if I just had that picture, maybe I wouldn't miss him so."

Togai wanted to ask what a picture was, but he didn't. He felt sorry for her. He could imagine how he'd feel if he was suddenly taken away from Kallo without a chance to tell him goodbye. How he'd feel about a father who had sent him away, he wasn't sure.

Prandina turned out to be a better paddler than Togai had thought she'd be. And though she paused now and then to look at her hands, which he could see, were getting raw and blistered, they made good time.

They had barely climbed onto the bank—on the Chelekai side—when they saw something white wave from an upper window in the castle. "Goodness," Prandina said. "Someone must have seen us coming up the river."

"I guess," Togai said. "But since it might be a while before anyone comes, want to wait under those willow trees?" He had heard that Zaps had to be careful about being in the sun too long lest their skin get red. He'd rather Prandina stay the way she was, with skin that reminded him of something he'd only seen a few times, a mix of cream and honey.

As the sun crept higher, Togai wondered if someone had really waved to them. Maybe they were just—he'd seen Lilu do it—shaking a dusting cloth out a window. Though he was happy just being near Prandina, he didn't really like sitting, waiting. He wanted to get up, walk around. Something. But he knew that the less he and Prandina moved the less the chance of being seen by someone who'd run and tell the king.

Prandina sensed his restlessness. "Let's wait until a little after noon," she said. "Daddy will often go for a ride—or take a nap—right after lunch, and if he does either, that would be a good time for someone to slip out and come down here."

The sun moved past the midpoint of the sky and Togai was about to suggest they leave when three young women come out of a clump of trees off to one side of the castle. Each was carrying a large bundle, each kept looking back as if afraid of being seen. Prandina stared as they came down the hill. Suddenly she laughed and clapped her hands. "It's Grestina and Patya…and Obena!" She looked at Togai. "They're—they were—my handmaidens."

By the time the three were coming down the now dry bank path, where Whi-Face had slid into the water, Togai and Prandina were landing on the new and narrow gravel strand there. Prandina seemed to forget she had sore feet, and as they dropped their bundles and ran toward her, she jumped out of the canoe and ran toward them.

Even as they were laughing and jumping up and down and hugging, Prandina asked, "How's Zarian?"

"Patya reads to him every day," said Obena, "and I play with him a lot. But he keeps asking, 'Where Dina? Where Dina?'"

Prandina began to cry. Grestina, who to Togai looked the oldest but not much older than Prandina, pointed to the bundles. "The king ordered Eano to burn all your things, but we saved some dresses and shoes. We thought…"

"What about the picture of me and Zarian?" Prandina asked. "Did it…"

She stopped abruptly. They could all hear the thud of a horse's hooves on grass.

Grestina pushed Prandina toward the canoe and almost screamed at the others. "Quick! Get the bundles. Throw them in the canoe —or in the river."

But before anyone could take more than a step the king brought his hard-breathing horse to a stop at the top of the bank. He looked down at the handmaidens and shook his head. "I thought something like this might happen." He lifted his riding crop to point at them but caught sight of Togai, in the canoe, using his paddle to hold it firm against the bank. "I should have known it'd be you," he said. He shifted his look back to the handmaidens and pointed his crop. "Though I didn't give the order directly to you, you knew I ordered the princess's things destroyed—and your disobedience leaves me no choice. Each one of you...Grestina...Patya...Obena..." He pointed at each as he named her. "...is hereby banished from Zaphyr. Under penalty of death, do not let your face be seen on this side of the river ever again! Now go!"

Togai had feared that the king might declare Prandina was on Zaphyr soil and take her away and have her punished. But Praidar had acted as if she weren't even there, hadn't so much as looked at her, yet as he spurred the horse away he yelled back, "Take those clothes with you. I don't want anything left on this side of the river to remind me of my daughter."

CHAPTER 34

# A New Hut Goes Up

Many of the Chelks were upset, especially with Togai. Before the princess, they'd never even seen a Zaprian on their side of the river. Now they had four who were gong to live with them! Right there in the village. The Chelks liked to think of themselves as tolerant and generous, but they also believed in accountability and their generosity had its limits. In a special Council-village meeting that night it was agreed that since Togai was, in a way, responsible, and since his family was responsible for him, he, Togl and Kallo should together—in their spare time and with help of the village carpenter—build a hut for the princess and the handmaidens.

Another agreement was that the princess and handmaidens could share in the village's food as long as they pitched in and did their fair share of the village work.

But to everyone's surprise it quickly turned out that the handmaidens might be more of an asset than a burden.

When the fishers went to trade the next day, the parents of the three handmaidens were there. They were worried about their children, wanted to hear how they were, and had some food and clothes for them which they hoped the good fishers would be kind enough to deliver.

Most of the fishers had children and, since they could understand a parent's concern, answered all the questions they could. Most, too, offered to take to Chelekai whatever the parents wanted them to take. But Galu wasn't one of them. On the way across the river he said, loud enough for all to hear, "King Praidar not only bans us from Festivals, he sends his own daughter and three others for us to take care of. Why should we be nice and deliver whatever they want delivered? Why? Pray tell me."

"It doesn't hurt to be nice just to be nice," Togl said. "But Obena's parents also offered me a small basket of apples to deliver some vegetables and clothes to her—and I took it."

"I got a jar of honey for my delivery," said another fisher. "A big jar."

"I got walnuts," said a third.

Galu now had a sheepish look. Chelks were accustomed to sharing things that could easily be shared. "I don't much like honey," he said, "but, uh, could I have a apple or two—and maybe some walnuts."

Togai had gone to the river to meet Togl and Kallo so he could walk with them to work on, as he thought of it, 'Prandina's hut.' When he heard what had happened, he was glad for the handmaidens, but it made him sad that no one had sent anything for the princess.

Realizing there were a lot of things to be delivered to the handmaidens, and that the handmaidens *and* Prandina were staying with Old Helu, Togai was just about to volunteer to carry something when Togl said, "Make yourself useful. Grab that bag of potatoes there."

"Yessir," Togai said quickly. And as he followed Togl toward the village, he thought, *All right. I didn't have to ask!*

The handmaidens began looking into their bags and baskets and bundles and oohing and aahing practically as soon as Togai, Togl and others set them on Helu's porch. Since Helu and Prandina had come out too, Togai would have liked to stay a long time, but Togl said brusquely, "Let's go. We've got a hut to build."

As they walked away, Togai heard Prandina say in a mild voice, "You think, since the Chelks are sharing with you, you might share with them?"

The next afternoon, even as Togl and Exl's canoe was gliding in, Togai was asking, "Anything for the handmaidens today?"

Old Exl laughed and shook his head. "Not from us. Today, *everybody* wanted to bring something over—especially when they heard the handmaidens were going to share. You never saw such paddling when we started in this afternoon. Your dad says we're going to have to work out a system to take turns."

In a few days, though, when the parents were satisfied their daughters had the clothes they needed and weren't going to starve, the flow of goods slowed. But from the very first, parents and daughters alike had realized that the fishers could carry messages—both ways. And so it was, the homesick maidens were coming to the river every day hoping they'd get more than something to wear or eat.

One day when Togai was waiting—with the handmaidens not far away—he got the impression the fishers' canoes were coming for shore a little faster than usual, with Kallo and Galu's leading the way and aiming for the handmaidens. Though Kallo and Galu slowed to let Togl and Exl's canoe touch first, Kallo jumped from the bow in one big bound and landed right in front of the three girls.

"Guess what," he said. "Your parents want us to bring you over so you can visit. One of them had the bright idea that as long as you stayed in the canoe you wouldn't really be in Zaphyr, so..."

But he didn't get to finish. The three banished handmaidens erupted in squeals of delight and began jumping up and down and hugging each other.

Togai walked around to where Kallo was.

"You can't do that," Togai said.

Kallo's smile faded, but before he could say anything, Galu brushed in beside him. "Did you say we can't do that?"

"Yes," Togai said.

Galu took a step closer and glared down at Togai. "You're not the head fisher," he said, "and certainly not the Dilkina. You can't tell me what I can or can't do."

"Easy," Togl said. "I don't think my son would say that without a reason." He looked at Togai. "So, what is it?"

Togai looked at the handmaidens. "Don't you remember? The king said, 'Under penalty of death, do not let your face be seen on this side of the river ever again!'"

Grestina's hand flew to her mouth. "Oh, Maker help us. He did say that."

Galu sneered. "What difference does it make? He can't get over here to punish you."

Togai looked at Togl. "No, but he could do something to the parents, maybe stop Zaps from trading."

Kallo spoke up. "They could sit with their backs toward shore."

Togl shook his head. "No. Togai's right. We know what the king meant, and we can't risk angering him. Any man who would put a knife to the throat of a boy who had just saved his daughter, then banish that daughter, such a man would do anything."

He looked at some of the fishers. "You want to risk losing trade with the Zaprians?"

Most shook their heads, no, but he had already turned to the handmaidens. "And he could shift the death penalty from you to your parents. Want to risk that?"

With Obena and Patya about to cry, Grestina answered, with a quavering voice. "No."

"Well, I want to hear what Old Helu has to say," Galu said, and stalked off.

"Fine," Togl said. "Go hear."

Later, just as Togai and Kallo were getting up from their chairs and saying goodnight to Lilu and Togl, there came a knock at the door. It was Old Helu.

"Come in," Togl said.

She gave Kallo and Togai a hesitant glance. "No," she said to Togl. "It's late. I shouldn't have come, but...if you'd have time for a word out here..."

"Sure," Togl said, and stood. "Go on to bed, now, boys. It's late."

They both hurried in. Togai could tell from the way Kallo quickly lay down—and lay very still—that he too wanted to hear what Helu had to say. But strain as he might, lie as still as he might, the only words Togai made out were Old Helu's, "Good night."

The next thing Togai heard was some footsteps and Togl chuckling. "All right, you two, I've never heard it so quiet in here after you went to bed, so I won't even ask if you want to know what Old Helu said. Galu *insisted* she meet with Council—which is his right. The short of it is—no surprise—she and Council quickly agreed: no taking the handmaidens over—upside down, backwards or with a sack over their faces. No way at all. So, go to sleep now. And don't talk, Togai. Kallo has to fish tomorrow," he chuckled, "with Galu."

Not far away, Prandina and the handmaidens were also settling in for the night—in their new hut. It had been built much faster than anyone expected, most of all, Kallo.

As they had started home well after sundown that first afternoon of work on the hut, Kallo was complaining. He said that at the rate they were going—they'd only gotten one corner post in—they'd be a year getting the hut built, if then. And why hadn't some of their friends come to help? Especially Togai's. He'd gotten them into this mess.

Togl said to be patient. It'd go much faster once the posts and floor beams were in. Kallo's complaining continued for the next two work sessions, but his outlook and attitude changed dramatically during the fourth. That was when the princess and the handmaidens showed up, said they'd help.

Togai was annoyed because Kallo seemed so glad the princess was there. He was even more annoyed when almost all of the village's young men and many of the older suddenly wanted to help. Togai wasn't sure if they hoped to be rewarded with some of the goodies being sent over from Zaphyr or, for the young, make a good impression on the princess or one of the handmaidens. With so many scurrying around trying to impress Prandina, Togai was afraid she wouldn't even know he was there.

He became more concerned about her noticing him when Patya, youngest of the handmaidens, seemed to want to be wherever he was, help him with whatever he was doing. He was really glad, pleased, that in only a few days after Patya began hanging around him, Tatl began hanging around Patya, offering to help her even if she was doing something for Togai. Tatl made a show of lifting heavy things—and more than once Togai overheard him tell Patya that he was a woodcutter and though his specialty was cutting down trees—*big* trees—he was a good carpenter too, could make her a chair, maybe something special she wanted.

Togai didn't know it, but he wasn't the only one in the village annoyed. Many of the women were upset with their husbands and sons and husbands-to-be because they were building for the women from Zaphyr the biggest and finest hut ever built in Chelekai.

Though the women—and old men—didn't stop making comments about how big the hut was and though many villagers resented having to baby-tend the daughter and three subjects of a king who wouldn't let them come to Festivals, as the hut went up, so did liking for Prandina and the handmaidens. Not only were the four working hard on the hut, they were cheerfully doing their share of the village work. And their attitude, Old Helu was quick to say, was due mostly to Prandina.

To anyone who would ask, Old Helu would say that from her very first day in Chelekai, Prandina had said she didn't want to be a burden. And when her handmaidens came and wanted to continue being her handmaidens, Helu said Prandina had laughed and said they couldn't tend to her, she didn't need tending to and wasn't going to be there to be tended to anyway. She was going to be working. And so were they. What impressed Helu most was that Prandina also told the handmaidens that now that they lived in Chelekai they needed to act like Chelks, think like Chelks, learn Chelks' ways.

Lilu liked Prandina too. The first Praise Maker Day Prandina and the handmaidens were in Chelekai, Lilu got three of her friends to join her in inviting the four girls, one each, to their homes for the Praise-Maker meal. Since Togai had saved Prandina and, especially, since she had saved him, Lilu was given the rightful honor, they said, of inviting "the princess."

After Prandina had praised Lilu's meal and helped her with the clean-up, they came out to the porch where Togl, Kallo and Togai were. After a little while Prandina said to Togl, "Old Helu said you'd tell me the story of where Chelks came from if I asked." She smiled. "The fishers' version anyway."

"Uh, be glad to. You want to hear it now?"

"Sure."

"Well, a long time ago…"

As Togl told the tale about the Chelks living on an island that grew hot and erupted and sank into the sea, Togai, though he'd heard it many times, found himself really enjoying it. Today Togl was much more dramatic than he'd ever been before.

After Prandina left, Lilu said, "That's really nice of Prandina to ask about us, and I think she's not just being nice, I think she really is interested. Old Helu says she's asked her all sorts of questions about where the scorn came from and about being Dilkina, even about where the word came from. I think that's one of the reasons Old Helu likes her."

"Lot of people do," Togl said. "Even Old Zoltai likes her. And know why?" He smiled. "He says she's a lot like Togai."

Kallo looked at Togl in disbelief. "*Togai?*"

"Yes. Zoltai said she asked him lots of questions about the mountains."

CHAPTER 35

# A Canoe-Raft Festival?

Togai was dejected when work on the hut ended because he thought that would end his being around Prandina, but with the hut finished and the late afternoons free, he began to see her not just more but closer too—and right there in his own hut! Trouble was, that led more to bitterness than joy.

Almost every afternoon soon after the fishers were in, Prandina would drop by, "just to visit," she'd say, but would usually, to Lilu's delight, ask for Lilu's advice on something to do with sewing or cooking. And though she'd ask Togl and Kallo and Togai about fishing, it seemed to Togai she was interested only in what Kallo had to say, about anything. But maybe it was the *way* Kallo said it. Sometimes he'd get to talking about something and she'd ask him to walk her home just so she could hear the end of it.

Togai thought he'd be able to tell her things a lot more interesting than anything Kallo could ever tell her. Things about the mountains. Maybe he *would* tell her someday, maybe someday when Kallo wasn't around.

Sometimes Prandina would stay for supper, and after she'd shared a supper one early-summer evening, they—as many villagers liked to do that time of year—moved their chairs outside so they could enjoy the nice weather and chat with anyone who happened by. By now they were so comfortable with each other that each was content just to sit there and enjoy the quiet, thinking his or her own thoughts and letting others do the same. After a long but comfortable silence, Lilu sighed and said, "Oh, I do miss the sewing."

"The sewing?" Prandina asked.

"Yes." Lilu sighed again. "Used to, evenings like this, I'd sit out here and work on our Festival outfits. But..." She quickly looked at Prandina. "Well, I miss the Festival."

Prandina smiled. "I can understand how you might feel about my father. Truth is, I'd like to go to the Festival too. But, say..." She paused to think a moment. "Did you ever think about having your own festival? Over here?"

Lilu sat up. "No. I never thought about that. But...but I don't see how we could. We could make good things to eat, and new outfits and so on. But we wouldn't have any music, and without music..." She shook her head. "It just wouldn't be the same."

"You can hear Festival music over here," Togai said. "Down by the river. If you're quiet."

"How do you know?" Prandina asked.

Togai started to answer but Lilu interrupted. "He didn't go to the last two Festivals. He stayed here. *Alone.*"

Prandina looked at Togai. "Why? Were you sick?"

"No," Lilu said. Togai wished she'd let him answer. "He just didn't want to go. But let's not talk about festivals. Upsets me."

"But, if you can kind of hear the music on this side of the river, shouldn't you be able to hear more on the other side?" Prandina asked, of no one in particular.

"You'd think so," Kallo said.

Prandina looked at Togl. "Could the diving raft be towed to the other side of the river?"

Togl shrugged. "Take work, but sure, it could be done."

Prandina's face brightened and she looked at both Togl and Lilu. "So why not tow the raft over and use it to dance on? You could put canoes around it, maybe put boards between them, have a canoe-raft festival."

At first, not many in the village were for "Prandina's Festival," as it was being called. Most pooh-poohed the idea, said it wouldn't work, said that even if the raft could be taken over and re-anchored, you'd not be able to hear the music—and even if you could, who'd want to dance on a raft or have a picnic in a canoe? But when Prandina said it shouldn't be thought of as Prandina's Festival but as the "Chelekai Celebration," the idea began to catch on. And when she pointed out that Chelk women could wear flowery hats, something they couldn't do in Zaphyr, the idea really caught on—and more Chelks than not began thinking that having Prandina around might not be so bad after all.

Though now free to do differently, the women of Chelekai decided they'd keep making—or remaking—festival outfits as they'd always made them, colorfully trimmed and inside out. Then, when Prandina said she'd also make her "Chelebration" outfit colorfully trimmed and inside out, her popularity really soared. "She's becoming one of us," many said.

Each night, the more Lilu would say about the raft festival and how well women in the village liked the idea and how wonderful they thought Prandina was, the happier—sillier and more stupid, Togai thought—Kallo seemed to get.

Though Chelks who claimed, too often and too loudly, other Chelks thought, to be most devout said that for full and true observance of Praise Maker Day one should be inside by sundown the night before, most villagers let their youngsters, once twelve Festivals old, stay out until the newly-full moon was a forearm high. The first Praise-Maker eve after Prandina had suggested the canoe-raft Festival and had the whole village talking about it or her, Togai was in bed soon after his forearm-be-home time, and though he knew some boys and girls his age would slip out after their parents were asleep, he wouldn't. He'd wait until he was 'grown up' and, like Kallo, could stay out until the moon was overhead. He wondered where Kallo was, what he was doing. He was probably with Prandina, and though they hadn't acted so gushy about each other the last few days, they seemed more serious. He wondered what they'd do if they were out late together. Walk? Talk? Go for a canoe ride?

Yes. That's what he'd do if he had a chance to be with her. Take her for a canoe ride. He'd do the paddling, go downriver, and there in the river's broad mouth where the water would be smooth and calm, he'd let the canoe drift, let her look back toward the mountains. That would be a good time to tell her about the mountains and what he'd done.

He drifted into a dream. He dreamed he had left the others on the porch and after he was in bed he heard Prandina say, "Togai didn't seem himself tonight. I think I'll tiptoe in and see if he's feeling okay." Out in the main room a board creaked...then another.

He came half awake. Was he dreaming? No. There it was, another creak. Was Prandina really coming to see him? He sat up in his cot and tried to get his eyes open. He heard scratching—and a whisper.

"Papa? Papa?"

Suddenly he was wide awake. It wasn't Prandina's voice. It was Kallo's! Why was Kallo scratching on Togl and Lilu's door, trying to wake Togl? He heard the door come open and could tell by the different creakings that Kallo and Togl were moving toward the front door.

Togai took two, careful, tiptoe steps to the doorway of his and Kallo's room and peeked out. Kallo and Togl were sitting on the front step, and in the light of the full moon their dark features had an eerie whiteness to them. Their voices were so low Togai could barely tell they were talking. He cupped a hand to his ear and leaned forward. At first he heard nothing, then came Togl's words, careful and cautious, "Does she feel the same way about you?"

"Yes, Papa."

"And...?"

"She...she wants to get married too."

Togai bit his lip.

Togl sighed. "I was afraid this would happen."

"Afraid?"

"Yes. You may think your mother and I are too old, but we haven't forgotten what it's like to be young and in love—and we aren't blind. We've seen the way you and Prandina look at each other. A lot of villagers have."

"But that seems to make you sad, Papa. If you remember how you were, shouldn't you be happy for us?"

Though Togl's voice was low, the words were distinct, stern. "You don't understand, son. The king may have banished Prandina, but she is still his daughter—and if she were to marry one of us, he would be really upset. So angry, I bet, that he'd stop all trade between us and the Zaprians."

"So what? We don't need their old honey—or raggedy clothes or wilted turnips."

"Oh, son. You and Prandina might be willing to do without a lot of things that come from Zaphyr, and do without for a long time. But would it be fair to ask others to do that? Now, we *might* be able to get by without getting vegetables and such from Zaphyr, but what would we do when all our axes and saws became dull and broken? How could we then cut trees for canoes and paddles? How'd we get wood for fires?"

"We'd find a way."

Togl put a hand on Kallo's shoulder. "Do you want to be head fisher after me?"

"Yes, Papa. Ever since I was a little boy, more than anything else, I've wanted to be head fisher after you."

"Then you cannot marry the princess. We older people have seen how you and other young men have looked at the princess and the handmaidens, and we've talked about what would happen if—when—questions of marriage came up, especially if the princess was involved. And I can tell you, much more than they fear what the king might do, the people of Chelekai, especially the fishers and their wives, fear that such a marriage would offend the Maker of All Men and All Fishes. If the Creator of All had intended for Zaps and Chelks to marry, He would not have made us different and put a river between us."

"Are you saying that if the princess and I marry, the other fishers will not have me as head fisher?"

Togl nodded. "That is what I am saying."

Kallo sighed. "I'm sorry, Papa. I don't want to disappoint you, but I would give up anything to marry Prandina."

Togai tiptoed back to his cot, and when Kallo came in he pretended to be asleep. He didn't want to hear Kallo say he was going to marry the princess. He didn't even want to think about it. How could she marry Kallo? It wasn't Kallo who had pulled her from the river. It wasn't Kallo she saved from the executioner.

Next morning, at the end of the Praise-Maker ceremonies, Old Helu said, "Before you go. Around mid-morning you'll hear the conch blow. Head fisher Togl has asked me to ask Council to meet with the fishers, the princess, and her former handmaidens."

Whispers of excitement and expectation ran through the crowd.

"And please tell anyone you know who's not here so that when they hear the conch blow they'll know it's not an emergency but, as usual, they're free to come or not."

When Togai got to the dune for the meeting—with Togl, Lilu and Kallo—he guessed the message must have been passed on. The dune was practically covered.

At a nod from Old Helu, Togl stood and faced the dune. "I'm guessing from the talk I've heard that by now most of you know that my son, Kallo, and the Princess Prandina want to marry—and know that it would not be our custom to try to stop that. But I also know that many of you, especially fishers, fear that if Kallo marries Prandina, King Praidar will stop the Zaps from trading with us. Some have asked, though, how would he find out? Couldn't we keep it a secret? Well, almost every day we fishers carry messages from the handmaidens to their parents and there's hardly a day goes by that some Zaprian doesn't ask, 'How's the princess?' So, to keep the king from finding out, all of us, handmaidens and fishers alike, would have to agree to not mention the marriage to anyone in Zaphyr."

Togai, who had been angry all morning, was now really angry. He was tired of lots of things, especially kowtowing to the king. "It'll not work," he said.

The Chelks—Togl most of all—were stunned. No son—especially a second-born—should ever question a father, certainly not the head fisher and certainly not in front of Council and the entire village.

Hurt showed in Togl's eyes. His response was quick and sharp, almost angry. "What do you mean, *not work?*"

"I mean, Papa, that the fishers—especially you—won't be able to keep it a secret. I know you and Lilu have taught me and Kallo to be honest and truthful, like all Chelks are taught. Maybe to be too honest, too truthful. So, the first time some Zaprian asks you about Prandina, you might be able to say, 'Oh, fine.' But if the Zaprian is looking at you, he'll know right away you're hiding something and ask more questions. And pretty soon the whole story...."

Togai was interrupted by the sound of Patya crying.

Togl gave her an exasperated look and asked, "What is it, Patya?"

"My mother is making me a new dress," she said, "and if the king stops trading..." She sniffed. "...I won't be able to get it."

"Oh, great suffering turtles," Togai said—and stood, something that surprised the people even more than his speaking out. He looked directly at Patya. "Half the village knows that on Praise Maker days you and the other handmaidens sneak upriver and hide in some willow trees across from where Grestina's parents live—and that your families hide on the other side and you talk back and forth. So, quit feeling sorry for yourself and this afternoon tell your parents to send whatever it is you most want as soon as they can. Just don't tell them *why.*"

Even as Togai stalked off, trying his best not to limp, he realized he wasn't really angry at Patya—or the king. He was angry at himself for listening to Patya, for caring what his brother or Prandina did or didn't do. He should just forget them. Forget them all.

It didn't take many steps for his anger to cool, though, and he began to think. He'd just humiliated his own father, the most respected man in the village. How could he have done that? What would Togl say to him? Do? Turtles! What if, come his Growing-up Day, Togl took revenge and gave him a lifetime's humiliation by refusing to take him as his fishing partner, even to let him be a fisher? Ever. Oh, Togai thought, what have I done? He wanted to cry, wanted to run back to the meeting and say how sorry he was. But he couldn't. It was too late. He hurried out into the scrub. He'd find a bush or something to hide behind where he could see the hut, wait till Lilu had time to get there…Turtles, it would be their Praise Maker meal, their much-looked-forward to Praise Maker meal—and now he'd spoiled it.

Togai watched and waited and when he went in the other three were already at the table. Lilu and Kallo grim-faced. Togl back to the door. Walking quickly, he went behind Kallo and sat down. He kept his eyes on the middle of his bowl, afraid to look at Togl.

He waited for someone to say something. No one did. He swallowed. Were they waiting for him to speak first? His mouth was going dry. He didn't know what to do.

He closed his eyes and was just about to get up and leave when he heard Togl say, in words clear and distinct, "Who do you think it was you disgraced today? Me or you?"

Togai swallowed. "Both, I guess, Papa."

"That's what I thought too," Togl said. "At first."

Togai glanced at Kallo who, though looking down, showed as much surprise as Togai guessed he did.

"Though you were wrong to speak to your father that way—especially in the presence of others—you were also right. Your words showed wisdom. And though your words stung, many things are more important than personal feelings. So, to show I forgive…You *are* sorry for the *way* you said what you said, aren't you?"

"Yes, Papa. I am."

"So, to show there are no hard feelings, will you fish with me for a while? Old Exl cut his hand really bad yesterday and…"

"Oh, yes, Papa," Togai said and sat up straight. "Does this mean I can still be a fisher and fish with you come my Growing-up day?"

Togl chuckled. "Yes. But you ever talk back to me again the way you did today—out there in front of the other fishers—and I'll throw you in the ocean."

A few days later, as Togai and Togl and the other fishers paddled toward the Zaphyr side of the river for the start of trading, Togl reminded them again, "If anyone asks about the princess, just say something like, 'Fine, as far as I know,' or shrug like you don't much care. Whatever you've been doing. Just don't lie. And if any of the handmaidens' parents are there with a lot of stuff, don't act like you think that's anything special."

Togai looked at the collection of people on the bank ahead. "Do you see any of the parents today, Papa?"

"No," Togl said, "and I'm a little surprised. They're usually pretty prompt in trying to bring whatever the girls ask for—and I know they went upriver to talk, Praise Maker Day, like you said they should."

"You think they said anything about Kallo and Prandina?"

"Whew. I hope not. We told them not to."

After they landed, Togai a few times looked up and down the bank for sign of anything other than normal trading and—not seeing any—guessed none of the parents were there or would come. Then, as trading seemed to be coming to an end, he saw a wagon pulled by two horses coming down the path-road from the City of Light. He handed Togl the next fish and pointed. "Wagon coming, Papa. The people in it, parents maybe?"

Togl leaned so he could look past the man on the bank above him. "Yes. That's Patya's parents on the seat and..." He squinted. "Grestina's and Obena's parents in back. It's all of them."

Togai watched the wagon stop some distance from the bank. All but the driver got off and came over to the bank, as if intending to trade. A man who had just climbed on his horse called out, "Oh, hi, Crodar," and rode over to the wagon. He seemed about to speak when he suddenly stood in his stirrups and looked in the back of the wagon. "My goodness, Crodar. What's all that stuff for? There are bundles enough of shoes and dresses—and dishes?—to last those girls for years."

"We, uh...Oh, those are just some old things we wanted to get rid of."

The rider took another look in the back of the wagon, wheeled the horse around and came back to the bank. He looked down at a woman. "What's going on, Yana? I've known you and Crodar—and Grestina's and Obena's parents too—for a long time, and I'll bet there's not another shoe or dress left in any of your houses."

The woman gave a quick, nervous look at the Zaprians near her. Whether it was because or in spite of the fact that some of them were watching her closely, Togai didn't know, but she motioned for the man on the horse to lean down.

As he did, she stood on tiptoe and began to whisper.

Slowly he raised up and looked down at her as if he couldn't believe what she had just told him. But his look of disbelief lasted only a moment. Suddenly, even as he was turning his horse toward the city, he was yelling to the few Zaprians still scattered along the bank—and at that moment, word that the princess would marry a Left began to spread through the kingdom as fast as people could run and horses could gallop.

As the fishers paddled away from Zaphyr, most felt that it would be their last time. They were sure that the king would stop all trade—and in Chelekai that night, the only laughter heard was that of small children.

But next day, as the fishers paddled upriver from the ocean and the trade-bank came into view, as many Zaprians as ever were there. Maybe more. Most wanted to trade. Some came only to hear for themselves that it was true, that the king's banished daughter would marry a fisher. What was his name? Coolo? Cuckoo?

And from those Zaprians willing to talk—and some were quite willing to talk with Lefts now that there was gossip to be exchanged—the fishers learned that though the Zaps couldn't wait to tell each other about the princess's marriage, they didn't want the king to hear about it. They didn't want trade stopped any more than the Chelks did. If trade stopped, what would they have for supper? Chicken? Heaven forbid. And the king could only blame himself if he didn't hear. He had decreed that anyone who used Prandina's name or talked about her in any way in his presence would be banished. This was one decree everyone in Zaphyr wanted obeyed. If someone disobeyed, no one would have fish to eat. Well, actually, the one who disobeyed would—from a wooden bowl in Left.

Since only a handful of Zaprians were ever anywhere near the king, the rest could talk as much about the princess as they wanted, and talk they did. A much discussed question—puzzle—was "How could the princess possibly marry one of those awful Lefts?" All could see how a Left might be attracted to a Zaprian. But how could a Zaprian *ever* be attracted to a Left, let alone want to marry one? The whole idea was preposterous, disgusting even.

Chelks talked about the upcoming marriage too, and most said it shouldn't take place. Many said much the same thing Togl had said to Kallo only they said it more strongly. They said it was obvious Maker didn't want Chelks to marry Zaps. He'd put a river between them and made them different colors so they could tell each other apart.

Togai tried to stay away from such talk. He didn't want to hear anything bad about Prandina, or anything good either. Truth was, he didn't want to hear anything about her at all.

Night was worst. All Lilu wanted to talk about was the wedding. Though she would have preferred that Kallo marry a Chelk, she put his happiness first and began to do all the things mothers in Chelekai were expected to do before a wedding. She thought that, given the situation, she should make Prandina's get-married dress—and Kallo's get-married outfit, of course. But when the handmaidens volunteered to make the dress, Lilu's biggest concern became the wedding blanket.

It was a custom in Chelekai for every adult in the village to give the bride's mother a small piece of cloth, usually a colorful strip from some old Festival outfit, that the bride's mother, in this case, Lilu, would use in making a 'unity' quilt for the couple so that, on cool nights or when they simply looked at it, they would be reminded that while, indeed, they were united to love and protect each other they were also a part of a larger group united to provide and work for the good of all.

What quickly began to bother Lilu was that many in the village were refusing to give their piece of cloth because they were strongly against the marriage. They didn't want to anger either the king or Maker, especially Maker.

Old Helu averted the blanket crisis—a crisis in the eyes of Lilu, anyway—by going to villagers who hadn't given their piece of cloth and saying that since Kallo and Prandina were going to get married anyway, why not give the piece of cloth? The king would never know, and Maker, surely, was more interested in the fabric of the community than one thin quilt.

Togl's problem was bigger. Not only did he have to make sure the new couple had a bed to put the quilt on, he had to make sure they had a place to put them. Since it was customary for Chelks to build a hut for newlyweds if no suitable old one was available, and no one was, Togl assumed that one would be built, as usual, with the village carpenter taking charge and others in the village pitching in. When he went to Helu to talk about it, she said pushing people to give a piece of cloth was one thing, a whole hut another. So, don't worry, she said, I'll let the girls live with me, Kallo and Prandina can have the hut built for her and the handmaidens.

Pleased though Togl was, Helu's offer of the newest and biggest hut in the village to the couple that might bring all kinds of problems made most Chelks resent them even more.

The most devout Chelks were usually in their huts by sundown the night before a Praise Maker Day—and loudly said others should be too—but even they made exceptions for weddings and other special occasions. And this Praise Maker Eve, perhaps like none ever before in Chelekai, was a special occasion.

As the tint above the mountains faded from red to pink and to nothing, a golden-red one appeared in the east, and when the moon—one that would be full—showed above the horizon, Kallo and Prandina started their walk into town. Their path, from the river side of the village all the way through to the dune and Council hut, was lined with villagers. Many were there reluctantly, and might not have been there at all had not Kallo been the head fisher's son and Old Helu said it was important for all to be there. Though they'd all seen big, golden-red moons, most agreed this was the biggest, reddest they'd ever seen. Blood red, some said, and wondered if Maker was already sending a sign.

Close behind Kallo and Prandina came Togai and the handmaiden Obena. Togai was glad he was supposed to have a solemn face. It hid what he was really feeling. For one, he was upset he was even involved. He'd rather be waiting at the dune with Togl and Lilu. There he could have given the whole time to sulking, sulking about Kallo and Prandina. Especially Prandina. She'd made the choice. He guessed he was supposed to feel honored. Kallo had chosen him to be his 'helper-ever,' and Prandina had asked him, since he was her 'dearest friend' and her father wasn't there, to fill her father's place in the ceremony.

As the four walked through the village, the villagers lining the way fell in behind them and followed at a respectful distance. At the bottom of the dune Old Helu waited. To her one side stood Togl and Lilu. To the other, in place of Prandina's mother, who probably wouldn't have been allowed there even if alive, was the handmaiden Grestina.

Kallo and Prandina stopped in front of Helu, with Togai and Obena a step or so behind them.

Togai could hear the light crunch and swishing of sand and hear some murmuring as the villagers closed in behind them. When all was quiet, Old Helu looked at Prandina and said, "We don't have the Zaprian custom of the father giving away the bride. We feel the bride is not anyone's to be given away. But the 'father' does take part in our ceremonies." She glanced past Kallo at Togai. "Togai, would you step forward please."

Togai gulped. No one had told him about this. Not at all sure he was doing what he was supposed to, he stepped up beside Kallo and gave Helu an uneasy look.

She smiled, as if to say, don't worry, you'll do fine. "Do you, Togai," she asked, "solemnly pledge to, as best you can, fulfill your duty as the assumed father of the bride?"

Togai tried to remember other weddings he'd been to. "I do," he said in a weak voice. He had to force the words out. He felt he was about to choke.

Old Helu smiled again. "This is your 'father-promise' stick," she said, and handed Togai a well-seasoned, sturdy stick about as long as his arm. She nodded toward Kallo, and Kallo got down on his knees.

*Oh, yeah,* Togai thought, *I'm beginning to remember.*

"Do you, Togai, promise to defend your 'adopted' daughter against abuse by this man?"

"I do," Togai said, with a little more assurance.

"Then hit him on the right shoulder to show you mean it."

Togai tapped Kallo on the shoulder, as he had seen many fathers do.

"A second time: Do you, Togai, promise to defend your 'adopted' daughter against abuse by this man?"

"I do," Togai said.

"Then hit him on the left shoulder to show you mean it."

Togai gave Kallo a good rap.

"For the third and final time, Togai, do you promise to defend your 'adopted' daughter against all abuse by this man?"

"I do," Togai said. This time, his voice was firm and clear.

"Then hit him on the head as if you really mean it."

*Thuuu..whack!* Togai's hand stung from the force of the blow.

"Ow!" Kallo said and looked up and gave Togai a puzzled look.

People in the crowd began to titter, and Togai leaned down and whispered to Kallo, "And I *really* mean it."

Helu took the stick from him and, still smiling, nodded for Kallo to stand.

When Kallo was on his feet, a now somber Old Helu asked, "Do you, Kallo, promise to never abuse the woman Prandina and to be ever loyal to and protective of her?"

"I do."

"And do you, Prandina, promise to be ever faithful to this man Kallo and to work with him to make your life and his life and that of your children as happy as possible?"

"I promise."

Old Helu took a step back. "The village accepts your promises, and we expect you to keep them. But, as is our custom, to make your marriage final..." She nodded to Prandina. "Prandina, you walk in that direction around the dune. Kallo, you walk in the other direction. When you meet on the other side, at the marriage rock, kiss if you will, then climb to the top of the dune where we can see you. That will make your marriage and your promises final and we will all go to our huts and stay in them until dawn.

"However, if you do not appear, we will know one of you has had a change of heart. During your walk if either one of you has doubts or is not sure of this marriage and do not want to go through with it, simply stop and wait. If one of you gets to other side and the other does not appear, simply wait there until the moon is well overhead.

"The rest of us will have long before that realized that one of you had a change of heart and would have gone to our huts. Since none of us can ever know which one of you—or if maybe both—decided to call off the marriage, neither one of you should ever be embarrassed if that happens. Marriage is not to be taken lightly. It'll be far better waiting alone for a small part of one night than to spend all the others in unhappiness.

"So, go. We will wait here, hoping you will appear. But whether you do or not, all of us wish that from this moment on both your lives are full and happy."

Togai sighed as they left and watched Prandina until she went out of sight behind the dune. When he looked the other way to see if he could spot Kallo, he saw no sign of movement at all.

Though he'd just seen Prandina disappear, he looked toward the top of the dune. About half the moon now showed above it, its color now more gold than red, its hue more warm and inviting than threatening. He guessed that everyone there was looking up, wondering if Kallo and Prandina would appear. He'd also guess that most were hoping Kallo and Prandina wouldn't appear—but he doubted anyone else was hoping for the same reason he was.

He watched—and sighed. How long had it been? How long should it take? He hated to wish his brother bad, but he hoped that right now Kallo was sitting out there by the marriage rock crying his heart out.

Togai glanced around. People were getting fidgety. Were they thinking Kallo and the princess should have appeared by now? He looked again. Still no one at the top of the dune. His mouth went dry, and his heart was beating faster. Had Prandina finally realized the way he felt about her when she saw him hit Kallo?

He closed his eyes. *Stop, Prandina. Please stop.*

He heard a shouted *"Look!"* and, almost immediately, near him, a disappointed "Turtles!" He opened his eyes and saw two figures in silhouette against the moon. Around the head of one, he was sure, was a golden glow. He sighed, and like the others, turned quietly and headed for the hut he called home, to leave the night to Kallo and Prandina.

Many villagers had trouble sleeping that night. Togai, because of thoughts about Prandina and Kallo, the others because they were afraid Maker might not let the sun come up.

CHAPTER 36

# Maker Let the Sun Come Up Anyway

Not every Chelk was on time for every Praise-Maker sunrise service. Some of those who saw they wouldn't make it on time stood in a window and when the sun came up said a few words in praise of Maker and went back to bed. A few didn't bother to get up at all—especially cloudy Praise-Maker mornings. They figured that if they couldn't see the sun come up, Maker couldn't see them. The 'do-gooders' of the village tried to keep up with who the 'slackers' were and would tell Old Helu. And if she didn't chastise them, the do-gooders would.

But this Praise-Maker morning everybody was there, on time. Many came early. Many in the village felt that Maker was sure to retaliate in some way. The most common suspicion was that He'd not let the sun come up. Because of that, all had come, even the worst slackers. No one wanted to risk adding to Maker's ire.

Though the eastern sky had been getting brighter and brighter and showed streaks of red and gold, most villagers were relieved when rays hit the heads of those ahead of them in line and they all turned to see the rising sun in all its glory.

Many uttered "Praise Maker," but many of those same people began to wonder if Maker might let the sun come and punish them by letting Ogre loose—and they looked anxiously toward the mountains. But after a few days in which there were no tremors, the Horns didn't move, and there were no dark clouds or far-off storm rumblings, not even high winds or noticeably cool nights, all but the worst worriers stopped worrying. Maybe Maker wasn't as upset about a Chelk and a Zap marrying as they'd thought He'd be. Some of those who thought most about such things decided they had been—and still were—correct. It was true. Maker didn't want or like Chelks marrying Zaps, but He liked Prandina. Yeah, that was it. Most agreed. Maker likes Prandina. And most villagers, seeing that's how things were, began to like her too and to accept the marriage, especially when they saw how happy Kallo and Prandina were.

This caused a problem for Togai. It seemed that Lilu couldn't wait for Togl to come in from fishing so she could tell him all the nice things she was hearing about Kallo and Prandina, especially Prandina. During supper she'd tell him all those things again, and if she ran out of saying what she'd heard today, she'd retell what she'd heard yesterday—and the day before that. Oftentimes Togai would go to bed early and cover his head so he couldn't hear. But, then, sometimes he'd uncover his head so he *could* hear. And he hated himself when he did. Night after night he'd lie there alone in his dark room wondering why Prandina had married Kallo, why she hadn't waited, why Kallo hadn't shown more feeling for his little brother? Such nights he'd ache all through his chest and back. Then one night it hit him. What he wished was that Kallo was there to talk to.

In spite of what he now realized must be a deep and true love for his brother, he couldn't forgive him for taking Prandina and didn't want to be near him—or Prandina. If they came to the hut for an ordinary supper or a special Praise Maker lunch, Togai would eat quickly, say little, and leave to see Dilo or Tatl or do some other trivial thing he happened to think of. Better they think him rude than for him to ache.

Still, Togai often wished he had some time to talk to Prandina alone. He'd been intrigued when he heard she'd asked Old Zoltai about the mountains. Why? Did she *know* something about the mountains? Some secret? He doubted it. He didn't know how to go about asking her questions without rousing her suspicions. But he'd like to try. Or was he kidding himself? Was he simply looking for an excuse to talk to her? It didn't matter. She was always with someone and he'd not have a chance to talk to her anyway.

He tired of hurting, of hurting needlessly, and tried to think of good things, fun things. And what he found himself thinking about most was his Growing-up Day, when he along with the other growing-uppers would be the center of attention. He'd like that, enjoy it. He'd be in such a good mood by then he might even enjoy the Chelebration the day before, even if many still thought of it as "Prandina's Festival."

CHAPTER 37

# The First Canoe-Raft, Chelebration

As Festival Day approached many Chelks still thought Pran-dina's idea for the canoe-raft Chelebration wouldn't work. And for a while that Festival Morning, the pooh-poohers looked like prophets.

Togl and other fishers had trouble getting the diving raft across the river and getting it re-anchored, and the pooh-poohers who watched from the Chelekai shore had several occasions to laugh when a Festival-clothed fisher fell into the water trying to put boards between the easily capsized canoes. But toward mid-morning, once things were in place and those on the raft began calling back, saying they could then hear sounds from the Festival and when the breeze was right smell fresh-baked bread, the few canoes left in Chelekai be-gan to stream across filled with pooh-poohers and the bulging picnic baskets they'd packed just in case.

With the arrival of the pooh-poohers, the already noisy and crowded canoe-expanded raft became even more noisy and crowded. The most noise and laughter came from the side of the raft where the village carpenter had rigged up a hit-target, dunk-boy contrap-tion. Unlike the one at the Festival in Zaphyr, a boy got dumped in the river, not a tub, and the people throwing the rocks were Chelks. Never before had the Chelks been allowed to throw—and those lucky enough to get in line early and get a chance were having great fun— but the crowd watching and the boys getting dumped seemed to be having even more.

As noon neared, the dunking game was closed, rowdy boys were told to settle down, and mothers began stuffing their small children and babies with food to keep them quiet. Noon was when the band started playing dance music, and as brown faces watched the sun's slow movement. the only sounds were the gentle lapping of water and the muted bump of canoes. More and more looked upward, squinted, and shielded their eyes. The sun seemed to pass midpoint—but no sound of music came from the City of Light, and disappointment filled faces.

Togai was watching Lilu. Just as he saw a tear run down her cheek he heard a whoop. And another. And all of a sudden it seemed half the people were standing and cheering and the other half were shushing and telling them to sit down and be quiet.

As quiet returned and faint strains settled into straining ears, cheering again broke out. To Togai's surprise, Togl jumped onto the raft and held up his hands and called out. "Quiet, everybody! Please! If anybody at all is going to enjoy the music, we're all going to have to be quiet. So, why don't some of you who want to dance—we'll have to take turns—get up here and get started. The rest, if you want to laugh and clap, do it in your head."

Togai thought that was funny. He didn't know how one could laugh—or clap—inside one's head. But when the dancing started and he saw non-dancers smiling and moving their hands as if to clap, he guessed that, in one's head, one could do almost anything.

The dancing started. Two lines of Chelks faced each other, women on one side, men on the other, partner facing partner. The two lines moved toward each other, in light and skipping steps, bowed and backed away, then moved toward each other again, with partners circling partners and skipping away—feet swishing on the smooth boards of the raft in near-perfect accompaniment to the ghostly music of the now distant and almost forgotten City of Light.

Since Togl was head fisher and had overseen assembly of the canoe-raft and because it had been Prandina's idea, Togl and Prandina—and Lilu, Togai and Kallo—were given a spot for their picnic blankets right beside the main raft. Lilu and Prandina had been all giggly as they helped each other spread blankets on the wobbly, uneven boards. Lilu had insisted that Prandina put her and Kallo's blanket closer to the raft, and Togai was glad. That way he wouldn't have to sit next to Prandina or Kallo. He could sit as far out toward the end of Lilu's blanket as he could get. Frog warts! He wouldn't have to sit here. He could go sit with Dilo. But if he went over where Dilo was, he wouldn't be able to see Prandina.

Now, as the dancing began, he saw Prandina lean back toward Lilu. "Why are they dancing that way?" she whispered.

Lilu looked puzzled. "What way?"

"Not touching. Why don't you do the Prandar twirl?"

"We aren't allowed to."

"What do you mean, 'aren't allowed to'?"

Lilu shrugged. "Just that. We aren't allowed to dance Zaprian dances."

"Well," Prandina said. "You're not in Zaphyr—and this is not a Zaprian Festival. Want to learn the twirl? It's a lot of fun."

For a moment Lilu stared in near disbelief, then laughed and said, "Yes! That would be fun"—and she leaned and whispered to Togl

When the first dance ended Togl jumped onto the raft and held up a hand. "Prandina says she is willing to teach anyone who wants to learn the Prandar twirl. Anyone want to?"

At first, people on the raft and those around it seemed puzzled, but when they began to realize what he had said, a woman called out, "I'd like to." Then came, "Yeah, me too!" "It's about time," and "I'd like to Prandar twirl on the king's head."

Togl nodded to Prandina and stepped off the raft.

As she stepped onto it, Prandina said, "Let's see, to teach, I'll need a partner." Smiling, she looked all around, acting bewildered, as if she had no idea of whom to pick—and smiling, amused looks spread through the crowd. She stopped turning, looked momentarily at Kallo, then suddenly pointed at Togai.

Even as Togai's heart began beating faster, even as he was cherishing—yet dreading—dancing with her, she said, "No, you're too young."

*I wasn't too young to pull you out of Forbidden River and carry you up a hill,* he thought.

"Hmmm," she said. "Who…" She looked directly at Togl, and with many in the crowd smiling and beginning to chuckle, she said, "No, you're married. Besides, you're too old."

That brought laughter, which became even louder when she looked at Kallo and said with a sigh, "Oh, well. I guess that leaves you."

"But I can't dance," he said.

"That's why I picked you, clumsy," she teased. "If you can learn, anybody can."

Again, most people laughed, and the laughter continued as Kallo, Prandina beside him, tried to get his feet to follow hers as she talked and demonstrated. But when she turned to face him and showed him how to put one hand on her forearm and another on her waist, a silence fell. The Chelks, save Togl, Lilu and Togai, had never seen a Chelk touch a Zap or a Zap touch a Chelk, not even during the wedding. Was the world turned upside down? Forever?

The handmaidens had, by invitation, spread their picnic blanket next to Prandina and Kallo's, and after showing Kallo a few more steps, Prandina looked in the direction of the handmaidens and said, "Hey, you three. You know how to do this. Get a partner and teach him how to do it. And the rest of you…" She looked all around the raft. "Watch, then try it yourselves. You can do it."

That said, Prandina then guided Kallo smoothly through the first steps of the dance, as smoothly as if they'd danced together all their lives.

Because he had brought them into Chelekai, Togai felt a little protective of the three handmaidens—maybe like a brother would— and watched with interest as the two older ones, Grestina and Obena, got up and went to the edge of the raft. Grestina asked, "Anyone want me to teach him this dance?"—and glanced shyly in the direction of young paddle-maker Colatt.

In a flash Colatt was up and coming toward her. To Togai's surprise, Dilo was just behind him, obviously intent on asking Obena to teach him.

Wondering where Patya, the youngest, had gone, Togai turned to look and discovered she was barely a step away, looking down at him. "Want me to teach you the twirl, Togai?"

"No," he said.

"Why not? It'll be easy. Fun."

Togai felt his face getting warm. How could he tell her Prandina was the only one he wanted to dance with? "I, uh…" He nodded toward his leg. "I don't…"

"I have two good legs," came a sharp voice. "Want to teach me?"

Patya and Togai looked up. Standing at the edge of the raft was Tatl. Glaring.

Patya gave Togai a quick look and with a toss of her hair started toward Tatl. "Well, I'm glad somebody wants to dance with me."

As Tatl helped her onto the raft, he looked at Togai and smirked.

By the time the third dance started, the raft was covered with couples dancing—or trying to dance—what they had renamed the Prandina twirl. Whether actually doing or trying, they were all smiling and seemed to be having so much fun that even the oldest Chelks were saying they'd try it too—if they could find room on the raft.

Since they weren't 'in' Zaphyr, the Chelks didn't have to be 'out' by sundown, but as the sun dropped toward the horizon and sounds of the Zaprian Festival faded, they began preparing to move, as they now called it, the Chelebration raft back to Chelekai.

Had any one of them, perhaps some keen-eyed fisher, bothered to look back toward Zaphyr, across the broad meadow and up into the woods that bordered it, he might have spotted a figure on horseback. He might even have been able to tell—or guess—that the figure was that of the king. But even had he the eyes of a sea eagle, he'd not have been able to see the sadness in King Praidar's eyes.

Praidar had been there a while, watching, thinking. He'd heard early on that the Lefts were going to have some kind of a canoe-raft Festival. He hadn't really believed it but had ordered the criers to announce that no one was to leave the Festival to come to the river, even far enough to see. But he wanted to see for himself. At least that's what he'd told the Captain of the Guard. Down deep, he knew he wanted to get a glimpse of Prandina. But he hadn't seen her. Even with the crowd on and around the raft thinning, he couldn't pick out a dress that wasn't one of those gaudy-awful Left things, which surely Prandina would never wear.

Slowly, so as to not attract attention, he turned the horse back into the trees, toward the City of Light. He sighed.

He missed Prandina. Had all along. Even in the square that day as he was banishing her and the fisherboy he'd felt remorse. But she'd given him no choice, put him on the spot, made him act quickly. There, in front of so many of his subjects, he couldn't appear weak or indecisive. He had to be forceful, kingly. He couldn't let it appear a child could tell him what to do. So, he'd acted hastily—and regretted it ever since. Deeply.

Worst thing was, the people of the kingdom needed Prandina. But he couldn't let her come back. Not now. To let her come back now would be to admit he'd made a mistake—and he couldn't do that. He had to have a reason, an excuse, and he was sure it would come. It wouldn't be too long—certainly not more than a Festival or two after this one—that people would realize that that blubbering child they saw on a plodding horse just couldn't be their king. They'd want Prandina back—and be grateful to Praidar when he let her return.

He sighed. He'd have to bide his time. He just hoped it would pass quickly.

After many young girls and women—young and old—had stopped on their way off the raft to thank Prandina for her canoe-raft idea and for teaching them the Twirl, Lilu leaned toward Prandina and, with Togai watching, whispered, "I think they're really beginning to like you. Several told me they really liked the outfits you made for you and Kallo."

Prandina leaned close and with an impish look whispered, "Don't tell anyone, but next year I'll have to make three outfits."

Lilu gasped—and put her hand to her throat. "Oh, blessed turtles!" Suddenly she jumped up. "Togl? Where's Togl?" she cried.

By the time the raft was re-tied to its old moorings and the last canoe pulled ashore, the only hint of day was a sliver of light above mountains mostly dark. The path to the village was botchy with shadows and ghostly silver in the light of the just-risen moon, and as the last villagers started up it, though footsore and burdened with picnic baskets and with blankets and children draped over their shoulders, they didn't hurry. They were content to let the day last. They hadn't had Zaprian honey candy or roasted walnuts, or been able to see the jugglers or hear the minstrels, but most all felt it had been the best Festival ever. They'd been free to do what they wanted, dance the dance they wanted to dance.

CHAPTER 38

# Togai's Growing-Up Day

To savor and extend the good feelings of the first Chelekai Celebration for as far into Growing-Up Day as they could, many villagers stayed up late. But it wasn't long before the talk in most huts changed from Festivals and celebrations to something else—after some neighbor would knock and ask—or whisper across from the next hut—"Have you heard that Prandina is pregnant?"

But Togai heard none of it. After Togl and Lilu had taken turns cutting the hair off half his head as closely as they could, with Lilu crying and saying too many times, "I can't believe my Little Turtle has grown up," he had gone to bed. He knew most people had liked the Festival, that some had even thought it was the best one ever. But he hadn't liked it. Not at all.

Oh, Prandina had been nice, had talked to him, but she hadn't asked him to dance. Maybe she hadn't asked him because of his leg, maybe because she thought he'd be embarrassed trying to dance in front of all those people. He didn't like her even thinking about his leg. But even if she was, that was no excuse. She could have asked him after the raft was full of dancers and no one would have noticed. And he didn't like to see her dancing with Kallo. Maybe next Festival he'd stay home, sneak off to the mountains. Yeah, that's what he would do. So what if the Ogres got after him and he fell or got hurt, or got lost and didn't come back. Prandina would be sorry then. Kallo too. He sighed. But why worry about what happened today—or what might happen this day a year from now. Tomorrow was his Growing-Up day. Tomorrow he'd get some attention. Lots. He was sure of it.

Though he was awake and up well before sunup, he dressed

slowly and waited until he saw lots of people on their way to the river before he came out and told Togl and Lilu he was ready to go. Almost immediately he was disappointed, almost immediately the resentment of Kallo and Prandina returned. Instead of people coming up and saying nice things to him they seemed to be shying away. And though they talked in low voices, so Togl and Lilu wouldn't hear, he guessed, he picked up enough words to know they weren't talking about him or Growing-Up Day or any other growing-upper. They were talking about the baby, Prandina and Kallo's baby. And no one was happy about it. Some were sure that as soon as the king heard about it the least he'd do would be to end trading. Others said, don't worry about the king, it's Maker who'll *really* to be upset.

During the usually happy march back through the village to the dune, the growing-uppers were the only ones who seemed truly happy. Even their parents had somber looks.

And it was that way all the way through the Growing-up Ceremony. Togai, from where he sat down front with the other growing-uppers, saw very few smiles. Most people looked as if they were just waiting for the ceremony to end.

Since Togai had Kallo's first-born right but since he was, nonetheless, a second-born, Council decided he should be the last of the first-borns to choose, or the first of the second-borns, whichever way one wanted to look at it. So, after the only true first-born there, Choai, the son of woodcutter Hewl, said he wanted to be a woodcutter, Togai was tempted to say he wanted to be a woodcutter too. Or something else. Just as long as it wasn't what his brother was.

But he knew he couldn't do that. Couldn't stand the thought of hurting Togl. Besides, he really did want to be a fisher. So, when it came his turn, he said what was expected. He said, "I want to be a fisher. Like my father and grandfather—and my brother too."

Lilu had made a lot of food in anticipation of a lot of people stopping by the hut, but few came. Old Exl, a few other fishers and their wives—and Old Zoltai. But no one stayed long, and seemed to have only polite things to say. Togai could see Lilu was about to cry, and he was glad when Tatl and his parents showed up. Lilu liked Tatl's mother, but they were soon off in a corner and it wasn't long before Lilu hurried into her and Togl's bedroom and closed the door. Tatl's mother then turned and congratulated both him and Togl—and told Tatl and his father it was time to go.

Kallo, Prandina and the three handmaidens had been there the whole time, with Prandina and the handmaidens in and out between the porch and the main room, eating and talking—mostly about the baby—and in general acting as if they couldn't be happier.

Their attitude—their happiness—made Togai angry, and the next time they started in, he stalked out, right past them, and went out behind the hut. He sat down, with his back against the wall, and put his head in his hands. He'd been born with a bad leg. The Zaps had taken a race away from him, and Kallo had taken Prandina. Couldn't anything go his way?

A footstep caught his attention and he looked up. It was Prandina.

"You not feel well? Eat too much, maybe?"

"No," he said quickly, and started to get up. "I'm fine."

"Stay where you are," she said. "If you don't mind, I'll sit down with you. The shade looks good."

"Suit yourself."

She sat and smoothed the lower part of her colorful Festival dress over her legs. "Truth is, even when we first got here I thought you might be sick. You just didn't seem very happy, it being your Growing-Up Day and all."

"I'm fine. Don't worry about me."

"But I do worry. You've seemed, um, kind of resentful toward Kallo and me ever since we got married, especially me. Even when you do speak to me, you're terse, seem almost angry sometimes. So, I've been thinking, want to talk about it?"

"About what?"

"About your feelings."

"Why? If you cared about my feelings you wouldn't have married Kallo."

"Oh, Togai," she said, and touched his arm. "I was afraid that was what it was."

He jerked his arm back. "Afraid? Were you afraid when your horse fell in the water? I saved you. You saved me. How could you marry Kallo? Is it because you think I'm just a boy, just a kid—or because of my leg?"

"Oh, no, Togai. It's has nothing to do with your leg *or* your age. It's simply that there's this very special feeling I have for Kallo, the kind you'll have for someone someday. But I also have a special feeling for you, a very special feeling. One I could never, ever, have for anyone else."

"Really?"

"Of course." Again she put her hand on his arm and this time he didn't pull it away. "You saved my life, Togai. So this special feeling I have for you, your place in my heart—in my life—could never be taken by someone else—or lessened by what I might feel for someone else." Her hand tightened around his arm. "You're very, very dear to me, very special, and always will be."

It pleased him to hear her say that. But all of a sudden it didn't really matter. Now that he'd said what he wanted to say, let her know how much she and Kallo had hurt him. It was done with. Finished. He knew Prandina would always be something special to him. From now on it just wouldn't hurt. He hoped.

"I feel better now. Thanks." He gave her a sly look and smiled. "Now that we're just *friends*, could I ask you something?"

She gave his arm a squeeze and laughed. "Sure."

Keeping his eyes on her, Togai carefully asked, "Why are you so interested in the mountains?"

Even more than surprise, Togai thought he saw concern in her eyes, but she responded as if completely baffled. "The *mountains*? Why would you think I'm interested in the mountains?"

"Papa said Old Zoltai said you'd been asking him about the mountains."

By now she had let go of his arm and was looking down at her dress, smoothing and straightening out folds in it. "Oh, *that*! Nothing special. I…I've asked lots of Chelks questions, about lots of things. Ever since I was a little girl I can remember standing in a window in my father's study and looking up at the mountains and being absolutely fascinated by them." She laughed. "You know, the stories about Ogre and all. So, naturally, I was curious about what people over here thought. Someone said Old Zoltai was the best to ask about Ogre and the mountains, so I did."

She stood, brushing off the back of her dress as she did. "I'd better go back inside now. Your parents will think I'm terribly rude."

He started to stand, but she was already walking away with quick steps and in a plaintive voice he called after her, "No they won't. They'd never think anything bad of you."

At the corner she stopped and looked back. "You're sweet. I'm glad we talked." And with a smile and a little wave, she was gone.

"I'm glad we talked, too," he said, but only quietly, more to himself than to her. The resentment had returned already. Yes, he was something special in her life. Just not special enough to be told the truth.

CHAPTER 39

# A Yellowtail Run and a Red-haired Baby

Though Togai had fished several days in a row while Old Exl was hurt, Togl had treated him as a 'learner,' as a little boy. But now he was expected to be a full-fledged-fisher, a man, and Togl treated him as such. He was expected to make as many throws, catch as many fish, paddle as hard as any other fisher, and Togai was soon sore all over, especially his shoulders, from the paddling and throwing, and his weak left leg from bracing against the roll of the canoe and in throwing the net. He sometimes dreaded going to bed because he knew how much those first paddle strokes and net throws would hurt next morning.

To make matters worse, the fish hadn't been running for a while and Togl was pushing them all to fish harder, even with urgency, not just to catch enough for what they and the Zaps would eat day-to-day but to catch enough to replenish their dwindling supplies of smoked and pickled fish.

Though nothing happened to ease the work, by the start of his second moon as a fisher Togai was sleeping easier. His arm and back muscles stopped their constant aching, and he found he could, even while throwing his net, listen to and be amused by the never-ending banter between fishers. To his surprise, he found he was even enjoying the trading. Watching, that is.

Though he was sure he'd never even want to talk to Zaps, and though he continued to stand by the canoe and hand fish to Togl, he was beginning to like watching the Zaps and fishers as they bargained and haggled. What really amused him, tickled him, was the faces of Zaps when they realized that—with catches down and the Chelks needing to build up their supplies of preserved fish—the fishers weren't willing to take just about anything offered for fish and were driving harder bargains than ever before.

One day well into his third moon as a fisher, he saw a man he'd never seen before. Going by the man's leathery skin and simple, work-worn clothes, Togai guessed the man was a farmer. Since most farmers bought from peddlers or sent their wives, Togai had been told, and since this man had been moving slowly along the bank, watching others trade, Togai guessed this might be the first time he'd ever traded directly. The man had now come to stand just slightly behind a well-to-do-looking townsman who had been haggling with Togl over the price of a long and full-bodied sea bass, one sure to have huge slabs of tasty white meat. Just as Togl seemed ready to agree to the townsman's offered shirt and loaf of bread, the farmer took a half step forward and said, "I'll give a basket of apples. Nice apples. Big ones."

The townsman gave the farmer a hard look. "I beg your pardon. This is my fish. We Zaps don't bargain against one another."

"Well, that's good for us, isn't it?" the farmer said. "But this fisher here? He might have worked as hard for that fish as I did for my apples."

The townsman gave the farmer a condescending smile. "Well, yes, but even if that were true, we don't..."

"Tell you what," the farmer said. "If you think that fish is worth more than an old shirt and a loaf of stale bread, offer more."

"Hmpf," the townsman said, and looked at the Zaps behind him waiting their turn to trade. "What say we leave this farmer and fisher to their trading and find our bargains elsewhere?"

Some nodded, some shrugged, but they all began to move.

"I'll get my apples," the farmer said, but he had taken only a few steps when he paused and looked back. "Uh, you willing to move upstream a little, give me more room to get my horse and wagon close to the water?"

"Glad to," Togl said. He turned to Togai and smiled. "Hmm. Must be a big basket."

Togai laughed.

The man backed the horse and cart up to where they'd pulled the canoe in and as he came to open the tailgate, Togl held the fish up. "I appreciate what you did back there."

The man ignored the fish. "I work too."

He opened the tailgate. Turtles, Togai thought. In the wagon were at least one basket each of yams, potatoes, apples, and pears— and a bag of flour, maybe corn.

The man squatted in front of Togl and pointed into the back of wagon. "Let's talk a new trade." He leaned to look past Togl. "What you take for the whole boatload?"

"I...I don't know. I'd have to think."

"Take your time. Reason I asked you to come up here is so we could talk, private like. You see, I like bargains as much as the next fellow, and, to be honest, I figure now's the time to get one."

Togl shook his head. "I...I guess I don't understand."

The man hunched a little closer to Togl and said in a low voice, "For a while now my cows have been giving less milk—and now, what little there is is almost worthless. Watery, bad tastin' stuff. Some of my neighbors are noticin' the same thing. Some kind of disease, probably, and if it spreads—and it probably will—there's not going to be much milk or butter or cheese. And it won't be long, I'm thinkin', before people will be willing to give an old shirt, a loaf of bread *and* a basket of apples for a nice fish like that. So, I want to stock up now, before the cost goes go up."

Even before they were in their canoes and the last of the Zaps had left, the other fishers were asking Togl about his good fortune. Never had anyone seen a canoe so full of goods from Zaphyr. But Togl waited until they were paddling toward Chelekai before he told what the farmer had said.

Though the young fisher Gadlu slapped the water with his paddle and said, "We'll clean up," most of the fishers showed somber faces. They knew they needed to replenish their own stores and that catches were down. And they all agreed with Togl when he said, "If we ever needed a run of yellowtail we need it now."

Yellowtail was practically everybody's favorite fish, both sides of the river. Had to be, Togai thought. Yellowtail were maybe three times as large as any other fish the fishers caught. The great slabs of meat that fell easily from their sides had a yellow color and people said that, even smoked or pickled, the meat had a taste like that of butter. Even in normal times Zaps were willing to pay more for yellowtail, and if a shortage of milk and, especially, cheese came, who knew what yellowtail might bring?

Trouble was, there was a run of yellowtail only every three or four years. Oh, the fishers would catch one now and then, but that was rare. Only when the current was right, to pull the yellowtail in from what Togl and others guessed was an every-year migration from the south to some northern feeding ground, was there a good run. And since three years had elapsed since the last such 'pull,' many were saying they were almost sure to have one this year. Togl said there was no way to tell. His father had told him many times about a long stretch of eight years without a catch of yellowtail.

The day after the farmer's warning about the cow disease and drop in milk production, the fishers saw neither him nor any other farmer and neither saw nor heard any concern among the townspeople and peddlers there. Trading seemed normal—and again the next day. But that day there was excitement amongst the fishers. As they were making their last casts, Galu pulled in a yellowtail.

The next day the fishers went to work eagerly and threw each net with an interest and anticipation they hadn't felt in over three years. But when no yellowtail were caught, the paddle in seemed unusually long. Early the next morning, though, Kallo pulled one in, and a little before lunch time, much to his surprise, Togai felt a tugging on his net like he'd never felt before. He quickly wrapped the tow-in rope around his arm, braced his feet against the side and began to pull as hard as he could. Trying not to get excited, he said as quietly as he could to Togl, "I think I've got one."

Immediately Togl was at his side but before he could yell to the other fishers Togai heard Kallo call, "Togai's got one! Togai's got one!"—and almost immediately, from other fishers, "Pull him in, Togai. Pull him in."

Togai didn't need to be told. He was pulling as hard as he could. No doubt the fish was three times as big as he was. And just as he was thinking that the big fish might, if it wasn't tangled up in the net, pull him out of the canoe, it almost did. He came nearly upright, teetering, just about to pitch forward when the fish let up—and he fell backward, only to be jerked up again as the fish lunged forward.

"For Maker's sake," Galu yelled, "help him, Togl. Don't let the fish get away."

"No!" Togl said. "It's Togai's fish. Let him pull it in." And right away many of the fishers were reminded of why they thought Togl was such a good head fisher. He was right. It was worth the risk of losing the big fish. Worth it for Togai to have the thrill, the satisfaction, of catching that first big one all on his own. Worth it for Togai to gain not just the respect of other fishers but of himself too. It was a chance for him to grow, to take a step toward being a man. And if he lost the fish? Well, that would be a step too. Steps toward manhood weren't always pleasant.

But he didn't lose the fish, and as the big fish toppled into the boat, some fisher yelled, "Hey, Togl. How's that make you feel? Two yellowtails today—and your boys have caught both of them."

Togai quickly looked around at Togl. Togl said nothing, just smiled and winked.

Two more were caught late in the afternoon, and the fishers paddled toward Zaphyr with renewed enthusiasm. By the time they landed, they were almost giddy. Awaiting them were four farmers, wagons already backed up to the bank. And all around the farmers and along the bank were townspeople, three and four deep, none of them looking very happy.

The farmers were loaded down and easily outbid the townspeople. Each one got a yellowtail and some smaller fish. Togl had said the fishers would sell only two of the yellowtail, but when he saw what the Zaps were willing to offer, he changed his mind. On the way across the river he told Togai and the other fishers he was betting there'd be a run of yellowtail and that in the days to come they'd be able to get plenty for themselves

Next day, though, they caught only three. The day after that only two, and some of the fishers began to mutter. Most notably, Galu.

But then the number slowly began to rise—and the catch seemed to grow with the spread of the cow disease. Since the Zaps had no idea when—or even if—the cow disease would end, they were buying fish as never before and finding ways to preserve it. Some were even willing to open themselves to the jibes of their fellow Zaprians by stooping to the long ridiculed Left practices of smoking and pickling.

As a result, the fishers were taking home Zaprian goods in amounts no one had ever dreamed of—and lots of yellowtail too. The whole village was joyful. They'd never had it so good. And as the run of yellowtail continued and stores of fish and Zaprian goods went up, concerns about Prandina's coming baby went down.

Before the marriage, people both Zaprian and Chelk said there'd be no consequences. A Zaprian and a Chelk couldn't make a baby. It wouldn't happen. Maker didn't intend it. Zap farmers said a Zaprian and a Left having a baby was as unlikely as a horse and a cow having something. Some Chelk fishers said it was as unlikely as a fish and a turtle making what? A furtle?

So, as the story spread through Zaphyr, many Zaps suspected—wanted to believe—the story was a hoax. But *if* there was a baby, it would have to be a Zap. There was no way a Zaprian, certainly not one of royal birth, could give birth to a Left.

Most Chelks, especially the men, said the baby would look like a Chelk. Mix muddy water and clear water? No way it would come out clear.

By 'no-moon' of Togai's fourth moon as a fisher, not only did Chelks have more Zaprian goods than they'd ever had but also their biggest store ever of smoked and pickled fish. But it was about then that the catch began to drop and, at the same time, talk about Prandina and her baby went up.

Most fishers had always been very careful not to say anything about the marriage or the baby within Togl's or Kallo's hearing. But one unusually calm day, when the fishers had paused for lunch, there came floating through the still air what some fisher had obviously meant only for his partner to hear, "You think that since we've not as much as snagged a yellowtail this morning is a sign Maker's concerned about Prandina's baby?"

To Togai's surprise, Togl didn't get angry. "Could be the run is just coming to its natural end," Togl said calmly, but loud enough for all to hear. "Runs don't go on forever. That's why we call them *runs*. The water's cool again. That means—to me—the southern current has moved back out to where it usually is, out to where the village starts to disappear—and has taken the yellowtail with it." He glanced around and raised his voice. "Anybody want to go out near the Edge and fish?"

The only response was water gentle lapping at canoes.

That afternoon no one caught a yellowtail, and as the canoes started in, Togai saw only glum faces.

By Chelekai custom, no one—other than the mother and midwives present at birth—could see a baby before the father did. So it was that as soon as the diving raft came in sight and Lilu was on the high board waving, Togai was pretty sure what had happened. He turned to see what Togl might say or do and caught sight of the fishers in the nearest canoes. Their faces were stern and hard. They're thinking, Togai thought, *the yellowtail stopped running the day the baby was born.*

When Lilu's yelling confirmed that the baby had indeed been born, Galu said he'd drop Kallo off and trade alone. But Togl said no. Lilu could wait to see the baby. One can look at babies after dark. Work can't wait.

But when trading was done and the canoes started for Chelekai, Togl told Galu and Kallo that they could hurry ahead and that Kallo could go straight home if he wanted, he and Togai would help Galu spread his nets to dry.

Togai had been thinking for some time that he didn't want to see or be around the baby any more than he absolutely had to. He es-

pecially didn't want to be around it when it was really small and Prandina and Kallo and, especially Lilu, were all cooing over it and going
on and on about how cute it was. And he guessed that Lilu—who was
pacing up and down on the strand—expected him go with her and
Togl to see the baby as soon as he and Togl had everything put away
for the night. But he saw a way to avoid going.

After they pulled the canoe onto the strand, he said, "Papa, if
you want to go with Lilu to see the baby, I'll help Galu, then do our
stuff."

Togl glanced past him at Lilu, who wasn't far away now, taking
quick little steps back and forth and giving them impatient looks.
"All right. Your mother does seem close to the flutters. You come
when you finish?"

"Maybe. Like you said about looking after dark. No rush. It'll
still be a baby tomorrow."

Togl chuckled and started toward Lilu.

Togai worked slowly. He guessed Lilu would stay a long time,
but maybe by the time he got to the hut Togl would be there, wanting
to eat, and he'd have an excuse for not going to see the baby. But as he
neared the hut, he saw Kallo running toward him.

The words gushed out as he came to a stop, breathless. "Prandina sent me to get you."

Togai thought he had never seen Kallo so happy. "Why?"

Kallo laughed. "To see the baby, of course. You're practically its
second father."

"Oh." Togai could feel his face getting warm. "Okay." He took
a couple of steps and stopped. "Aren't you coming?"

Kallo gestured toward the hut. "No. Lilu didn't seem to be feeling very well when she and Papa left. I'm going to check on her. You
go on. I'll be there soon."

As Kallo turned toward the hut where they'd grown up, Togai
started toward Kallo's at a trot. He was almost there when he realized
he hadn't asked whether the baby was boy or girl.

Several women were gathered around the front of the hut, talking to one of the midwives just inside. He was surprised. Most Chelks

considered it bad taste to go to a hut and ask to see or, worse, try to sneak a look at a newborn. Polite people waited until they were invited or, more generally, until the mother felt strong enough to carry the baby around the village and show it off.

When the women saw him coming, they quickly moved away, giving him apprehensive, guilty looks. The midwife too, gave him an uneasy look and, with no more than a quick nod toward the bedroom, hurried to the kitchen part of the hut as if she had something urgent to do.

Togai paused outside the door, not sure what to do. He'd never been in another person's bedroom, not even Togl's and Lilu's.

He peeked in.

"Oh, Togai," Prandina said. "I'm so glad. Come in."

A small blanket-bundle was nestled between her side and slightly bent arm. He started across the floor with careful, almost tiptoe steps, and she laughed. "Don't worry. I don't think anything could wake her except hunger."

"Oh, it's a girl, is it?

Prandina laughed. "Yes. *It's* a girl." She turned slightly and reached down and moved the blanket away from the tiny face. "Have you ever seen anything so beautiful?"

"No," Togai said, but he was looking at Prandina. It was true. He had never seen anything so beautiful. He couldn't believe how happy she looked.

"If she'd been a boy we were going to name her Togai. But since she's not, we may name her Adelu, after Lilu and my grandmother, Adena. Do you like that name?"

"Yeah, sure. But, uh, were you really thinking you might name your baby after me?"

Just as she was about to answer Kallo came in. He gave Togai a sideways, one-arm hug and looked at the baby. "Isn't she pretty?"

"Yes, real pretty," Togai said, trying to make himself look at the baby.

"Want to hold her?" Kallo said.

"Me?" Togai said—and backed up a couple of steps.

Prandina laughed. "You ever hold a baby before?"

"No."

"Me either," Kallo said. "Not before today. Nothing to it."

"But what if I drop her?"

Prandina laughed. "I bet she's a lot easier to handle than a fish. Here. Just let her lie there, on your arm, kind of nestled up against your side. There's no way you can drop her. Oh...That's so sweet. I can remember the first baby I ever held. My brother." She took a deep breath. "And, well...Adelu's the second."

But Togai didn't hear. He was looking down at the baby, fascinated.

She was so small, almost weightless, and he began gently bouncing her up and down just enough to make sure she was there. All the while he held his free hand on her to make sure he didn't drop her. She seemed so helpless, yet at the same time so—what? Angry? With her little face all scrunched up, eyes tightly closed, she seemed determined to not look at the world. Or was it that she didn't want the world looking in? He sighed. Had he ever been that small, that helpless?

He glanced at Kallo, then at Prandina. In just a few short moments they had changed. Kallo no longer seemed his brother. Prandina no longer his...his what? They were parents. Like Togl and Lilu. And older. Kallo was not the boy on the next cot who'd tease him or try to awaken him by sticking a wet finger in his ear. Kallo was a father now, a man in every sense of the word. And Prandina was no longer a young girl in a pretty dress whose only worry was whether the day would be nice enough for her to ride her horse. She now had a baby to take care of. They both did. Nausea swept through Togai. They were a *couple*. A pair, man and wife, forever held together by this child.

"You feel all right?" Kallo asked. "You look kind of funny."

Togai shook his head. "No. I'm fine. I better go." He took a quick but cautious step toward Kallo and let the baby slide from his arm onto Kallo's. "Don't drop her."

Kallo laughed. "All right, *uncle*. I won't."

Togai practically ran from the hut but quickly slowed and began to walk. Why was he running? What was he running from? Himself? His feelings? He didn't know how he'd eventually feel about Kallo and Prandina—or the baby. He just knew that in that short time he'd held the baby and she had depended on him to not drop her, something had changed. The world was somehow different now. Or was it he?

When he went into the hut, he saw, as he expected, Togl and Lilu at the table. Neither spoke as he sat down, and it seemed to him that Lilu had been crying. "Something wrong?" he asked.

Lilu looked at him with red eyes. "Did you see the baby?"

"Yes."

"Did you not notice anything?"

Togai was pretty sure Lilu wanted him to say something in particular, but what? "Uh, she kept her eyes closed?"

Lilu shook her head. "I mean something about the way she looked."

"Uh...she was pink?"

Lilu gave Togl a quick glance and then looked back at Togai. "Pink? She doesn't look pink to me. She's pale. Her legs are tiny and her hair, well, it has a reddish tint." Lilu's chin quivered. "She just doesn't look like a Chelk baby ought to."

Togai slowly stood and stuck out his left leg. "She has two good eyes, two good arms, and two good legs—and you're worried because her hair's not yellow and her legs aren't fat?"

Lilu began to cry—and Togai felt guilty. But he also felt he was right. He wished his legs were simply 'thin'—and he'd gladly trade his short leg for red hair, or green or any other color. He turned and started for his room, sure that Togl was going to tell him to come back and apologize. But no words came, just the sound of Lilu crying. Had there been a door, Togai would have closed it behind him. But there was none, and he lay down on his cot and looked out into what little twilight remained.

He was about to fall asleep when he heard a whisper. "Togai? Togai? You there?"

He sat up and looked out. Just to one side in the shadows was Tatl, a finger to his lips.

"What is it?" Togai whispered.

Tatl glanced over his shoulder and took a step closer to where his face was almost in the light coming from the main room. "My mom wanted me to ask you. Is it true the baby has red hair?"

"Where'd you hear that?" Togai asked.

"A midwife told it. Everybody knows."

"Go home," Togai said. And rather than face the room where Lilu was or look out into a darkness where people talked about a baby that didn't match their ideals, he turned onto his back and closed his eyes.

CHAPTER 40

# The Avenging Witch Returns?

The next day, no sooner had Togl and Togai pulled their canoe ashore in Chelekai than Galu came striding up. Close behind him was Kallo, looking sheepish and embarrassed.

"Togl," Galu said angrily, "I want another fishing partner."

"What?" Togl said, with a tone and look that said he couldn't believe what he was hearing.

Other fishers came up. Some, Togai thought, seemed merely curious. Most had hard, determined looks.

"I said, 'I want another partner.'"

"But why?" Togl said. "You and your father asked for Kallo to be..."

"I know. But that was long before the child was born. Today I fell in the canoe and near broke my leg—and Kallo and I caught less than half the fish anybody else caught."

Togl shrugged. "We all have bad days."

"Yes. But I'm sure Maker will from now on curse any canoe that has Kallo in it."

Togl sighed. "Because of the child?"

"Yes."

Several of the fishers nodded in agreement. No one spoke up to say he didn't agree.

Togl would later say he was mad enough to bite a paddle in half, but his voice was even when he said, "I think you're wrong, but..." He gave Kallo an apologetic look. "We could try to work something out. As far as I know this is the first time a fisher has ever asked to change partners, so..." He took a deep breath and looked at Galu. "Give me some time to think about it, will you?"

"Think as much as you want," Galu said. "But I'll tell you right now, I'll not fish with Kallo again. Ever. Put him in your canoe if you want. He'll not get in mine." And he stalked off.

Though Kallo helped a sullen Galu stow their—Galu's—gear for the night, he kept as much distance between them as he could. He then waited with Togai and Togl until the last fisher had left.

After Togl's customary last look around, the three of them started toward the village and it wasn't until then that anyone spoke, and Kallo was the first.

"I'm sorry, Papa," he said, "that must have been embarrassing for you."

"Don't worry about it. It's part of being head fisher, I reckon."

Kallo shook his head. "How could people be so afraid of a little child?"

"It's not the child they're afraid of. I think it's the unknown. The new, the different. I reckon there's some of that in all of us."

Yeah, Togai thought. Most people don't want to know about the unknown. Might be different from what they think, might find out they were wrong.

Elot, a fisher a little older than Togl, was by the porch waiting for them. His son Otl, who fished with him, was on past the next hut, standing there, looking back. Watching.

Elot nodded to Togl and with a quick tip of his head toward the village said, "Otl is a good friend of Galu's, and..." He gave Kallo an uneasy look. "..agrees with everything Galu said. Out of respect for you and your father—who was a good head fisher too—I offer to let Otl fish with Galu and to let Kallo fish with me."

Togl nodded. "That's kind of you. Thanks. I accept your offer."

"Yes," Kallo said. "That's very nice of you."

Elot gave him a hard look. "But if you bring me bad luck, I'll ask for Otl back."

In most huts across the village that night adults talked about Galu's misfortunes and the other mishaps and accidents they had heard about—and agreed that Maker was showing He didn't like

Kallo's child. But they didn't say so early on. They waited until it was late, when they were alone and their children couldn't hear.

Since the Zaprians who had been at the river the day before had heard Lilu yelling, and the fishers had confirmed that Prandina had had her baby, most of Zaphyr was aware of the baby's birth by nightfall. So when the fishers had arrived at the trading bank—with Kallo and Galu's low catch and Galu ready to ask for a new partner—they were met by more than the usual number of Zaprians, many of them more interested in firsthand news of the baby than fish.

The most common questions, usually asked one right after the other, were "Is it a girl?" and "How much is it like you people?" The questions indicated that most Zaprians thought the baby would be female and Zaprian not just because Prandina's female 'Zaphyrness' would dominate but because that's the way Maker would want it.

And that night, as talk of the baby spread through Zaphyr, the Zaprians, unlike the Chelks, didn't care if children overheard. Those spreading the word said the fishers had said the princess's baby looked just awful. Some fishers had even said they were afraid the baby was cursed. And maybe it was. According to the fishers, the baby didn't have a creamy-white skin or black hair. And its face was round and kind of fat, not thin and angular the way a Zaprian's would be. So it had to be ugly. But who cared if it was cursed? It was on the Left side of the river.

Again, no one dared tell the king. Not only was there the decree to break, he was sure to be upset. He, of all Zaprian fathers, would be upset his daughter had given birth to a strange child whose father was, Maker forbid, a Left. And how would the person who told him then explain why he or she hadn't told him about the marriage so he could have taken steps to prevent the birth? Anyone foolish enough to tell him would be a double fool.

In the days that followed, the only accidents Chelks had were a few trivial ones, and talk of the baby's strange looks began to die down. But the biggest change by far, Togai thought, was in Lilu. In only a few days, in carrying out the expected grandmotherly duties of helping with the baby, she went from being concerned and worried about how the baby looked and what people might think to, "Oh, she's such a sweet baby." And in those few days, Togai became as sick of hearing about the baby as he had of hearing about Prandina and the canoe-raft Festival. Sometimes he even felt jealous. He wondered if Lilu had been that gushy over him—or Kallo.

He knew Lilu's attachment to the baby was complete when about ten days after its birth, the day before Praise Maker Day, she was on the porch when he, Togl and Kallo came up from the river. As usual, Kallo stopped to ask how her day had been.

She said, "Fine," and he said he guessed he'd get going, Prandina probably had supper waiting.

But before he could take a step, Lilu said, "You might be coming back here to eat. Prandina and I talked about it."

He laughed. "Well, I guess it's decided then." He gave her a mischievous smile. "Have a surprise for us?"

"Maybe," she said.

Kallo walked on, and as Togl followed Lilu inside, he said, "Tell us what the surprise is?"

"No. Wouldn't be a surprise if I told."

"Hmm," Togl said, looking puzzled. "Some special occasion?"

"Goodness, Togl," she said. "You forget when the boys were born? Tomorrow is Naming Day."

"Oh, yeah." He winked at Togai. "What was it they named the baby?"

Lilu shook her head, as if she couldn't believe what she was hearing, but before she could say anything Togl laughed and put his arm around her. "Oh, I know it. I know it. It's *Adelu*. A pretty name. After the two grandmothers. And at least one of them, I know for sure, is very pretty."

Lilu at first blushed but was soon beaming and moving around with, it seemed to Togai, a heightened sense of excitement and anticipation. She kept going to the door and looking up through the village, and as soon as Kallo and Prandina were in sight, she dashed into the bedroom and came out holding something behind her. Kallo and Prandina, with Adelu, were barely through the door before Lilu was in front of them holding up a small dress. "Surprise," she said. "A Naming Day dress for Adelu."

"Oh, it's so pretty," Prandina said. "Did you...Of course you made it yourself. Thank you very much."

Lilu held the dress close to the sleeping Adelu and said, "Yes, it's the right size. She'll be the prettiest baby there."

In the past, when Prandina and Kallo had been there for a meal, since there were only four chairs and the table was small, Togai would sit on the floor near the doorway to his room to eat. This night, when Lilu said everything was on the table and Prandina put the sleeping Adelu on Kallo's old bed, Togai decided he'd sit on his bed to eat. He'd be able to see and hear what was going on at the table but if that didn't interest him, and it usually didn't, he'd have someone to talk to, though he wasn't sure what he and a sleeping baby who couldn't talk would talk about.

As he expected, soon after he had filled his bowl and gone into his room, the others seemed to forget he was in the hut. But he didn't much care. Even if he was with them, no one would show any interest in what he had to say—or might say. He glanced at Adelu and an idea came. When he was finished eating he'd lie down beside her and very quietly, so no one else could hear, tell her about the mountains. And when he'd finished, even if she had heard and remembered everything he'd said, she couldn't tell anyone. He smiled. At last, he had a friend he could talk to. About anything.

But just as he was about to set his bowl on the floor, he heard Prandina say, "That was really good, Lilu. Thank you. I guess we'll be going soon, but before we do..." She glanced first at Lilu, then Togl. "I've already asked Kallo, and now I want your opinion on something."

"Oh, oh," Kallo said, and he took what Togai guessed was his last bite and pushed back from the table.

Togl chuckled. "Sounds like trouble."

"Not really," she said. "What do you think about my starting a school?"

"A *school?*" Lilu said.

"Yes. I have two moons at home before I go back to regular village work, so I was thinking about using that time to start a school. To start with, youngsters who want to could come to our hut in the afternoon—wouldn't interfere with morning work—and I could start teaching them to read and write."

"Read and write?" said Togl. "Why would anyone over here want to know how to read or write? We don't have anything to read."

"We could borrow some books from Zaphyr to get started."

When Togl frowned. she quickly added, "I know you might not want to read Zaprian books, but pretty soon you could begin to read things people over here wrote, messages say."

"Messages? If I want to give somebody a message I'll just go over to his hut and tell him."

"But if he wasn't there to talk to, you could leave a message, a *written* message. *Or*—and this is a much better example—if Chelks had been able to write, you could've had a history. A written history. You wouldn't have different stories about where you came from. You fishers say you came from an island and had to leave because the land got hot. The woodcutters aren't sure it was an island and say you had to leave because of what the fishers did. They say the fishers were always complaining that the wood used for canoes was too leaky and what was used for paddles rotted too quickly. That offended Maker and He made Mother Nature kill all the trees, so you had to leave wherever you were because you ran out of wood. So, if Chelks long ago had known how to write, even if only one had known how, you could have a written history, on paper, know which story is real."

Togl thought for a moment. "Yeah, if who wrote it wrote the truth."

At noon the next day, the entire village gathered at the Council-hut dune for two namings, the boy of Caudl and Olet and the girl of Kallo and Prandina. Togai sat in the family row at the bottom of the dune with Lilu and Togl and Caudl's and Olet's families. Three or four steps away, waiting patiently, stood Old Helu. On a bench to one side of her sat Kallo and Prandina, to the other, Caudl and Olet. The mothers held the babies.

When the crowd was still, Old Helu nodded to Caudl and Olet.

The Praise-Maker ceremony had ended under a warm sun and a blue sky, but clouds had been building from the west all morning and as Caudl and Olet moved toward Helu a gust of cool air sent up swirls of dust and fine sand. Olet stopped and turned her back to the wind but just as she bent over the baby to protect it the swirls stopped and she moved on to stand on the right side of Helu. Caudl went behind Helu to stand on her left side.

Facing the crowd, Helu spoke loudly enough for all to hear, "I will now give the child of Caudl and Olet its name." She took the baby from Olet and looked up at the sun. As she did, a cloud moved across its face. Some might have thought it a bad sign, but its leading edge was a yellow-white streak across half the sky.

"Oh, Maker," Helu intoned, "we ask Your blessings on this child and its name and that, as You always have for all of us, look over it and protect it for all its days." She looked down at the baby. "In keeping with your parents' request and in asking for Maker's continued blessing and protection, I now name you Oclo, a name given in honor of—and for you to live up to the honor of—Ocel and Letto, your two grandfathers."

Togai saw the two men bend forward and smile at each other.

Without further comment Helu gave the baby back to Olet, and as Olet and Caudl walked back to their bench, Helu glanced in the other direction and nodded.

When Kallo and Prandina were beside her, she took the baby from Prandina and looked up at the sun, or at where the sun should be. It was now completely hidden by dark clouds—and big raindrops were spattering the dust. "Oh, Maker," Helu said, "we ask Your blessings on this child and its name and that, as You always have for all of us, look over it and protect it for all its days." She looked down at Adelu. "In keeping with your parents' request and in asking for Maker's continued blessing...I...I..."

She looked more closely and her face turned to one of anguish. Hesitatingly, she looked up. "Oh, Maker, forgive me if I do something

that offends You but…" She looked back at the baby and with a quavering voice said quickly, "I now name you Adelu, in honor of your
two grandmothers."

Togai looked at Lilu. She was staring in horror at Old Helu, and
as loud talk broke out behind her she jumped up and rushed to Helu?
"What's wrong?" she asked. "What's wrong?"

Helu held out the baby and, voice and hands shaking, said, "Her
eyes. Look at her eyes. They're green!"

Though still widely scattered, raindrops were now coming down
hard and cold, thunder rumbled, and the far off mountains were lit by
flashes of lightning. And even as people went running from the dune
in the direction of their huts, Togai heard many saying Maker was
showing his displeasure with the child of the Avenging Witch.

Not long after that Togai was seated comfortably on his cot,
eating and listening to what was now a gentle rain and listening for
sounds from Adelu, again asleep on Kallo's old cot. There wasn't
much else to listen to. Out in the main room, the others were eating,
or pretending to eat, saying little.

Adelu stirred and—with a glance at the main room to see if
he was being watched—Togai slid over to her cot and sat beside her.
She was squirming and kicking her feet as if she wanted out of the
blanket. He opened it a little to give her room and with another quick
glance at the main room slid a little farther along the cot to where
he couldn't be seen and picked her up. Her face was so tiny. Still
scrunched. And her fingers! How tiny and wrinkled they were. How
could such a small and helpless thing be a witch, let alone the Avenging Witch. Slowly her eyes came open, and he bent and took a closer
look. Green? Her eyes didn't seem green to him. They looked more
gray than green. But even if they'd been bright green, how could anyone be afraid of her?

Uh, oh. Now it was she who seemed afraid. She seemed about to
cry. "Shhh," he said quietly. She grabbed his finger just as it touched
her face, and though her little fingers barely fit around its end, she
tugged on it, and began to kick and goo and wave her arms—all the
while holding tightly onto his finger as if she would never let it go. He

bent and touched his nose to hers and, to his surprise, began cooing to her. He laughed and held her close, and when he felt her heart beating close to his, he felt less alone than he had ever felt before.

He heard Prandina coming. Embarrassed by the thought she'd heard his laughing and cooing and not wanting to be caught acting silly over a baby, he quickly sat up and held Adelu out to Prandina. "She seemed to be waking up, so I...I..."

Prandina gave him a teasing look. "I know. Sometimes I can't wait for her to wake up either."

He blushed. "No. I, uh...I'm sorry people say bad things about her."

She sighed. "I...I'm just glad she's over here, where there are only words to hurt her."

Togai had no idea what she meant, but before he could ask what it meant, she was gone.

That night, before he fell asleep, the thought came that he had good reason to be growing fond of Adelu. She accepted him for what he was. Asked no questions. Made no judgments. Didn't know he had a short leg and probably wouldn't care if she did know. She just knew he had a nice finger to hold onto and eyes that looked directly into hers. He hoped that morning would not come with more rain or heavy winds or cold. That happen, Galu and others were sure to say it was a definite sign that Maker was upset over a child that looked like, maybe even was, the Avenging Witch.

To his delight the first glow in the eastern sky showed only a scarlet trimmed cloud here and there. But Galu and a few others came to the river muttering about the baby anyway, muttering plenty loud enough for Kallo and Togl to hear—and they kept looking at the mountains as if they expected to see a horde of Ogres any moment, though no cloud could be seen in that direction and the morning was unusually warm.

The day's fishing went well, and though the muttering had stopped by the time they began to paddle toward Zaphyr, the sullen looks continued. It had been a while since Togai had heard a Zaprian ask about either Prandina or her baby. He guessed the two were old news by now. And when by the end of trading no excited talk had spread along the bank he was sure that no fisher, even if asked about Prandina or Adelu, had mentioned Adelu now had green eyes to go with red hair. He guessed that even the most disgruntled fisher didn't want the Zaps thinking the fishers had a personification of the Avenging Witch living amongst them.

Togai had thought that with the really pretty day concerns about Adelu would have lessened, but as the canoes approached the Chelekai shore and he saw several of the fishers' wives there, he guessed he had been wrong.

As soon as Galu's canoe touched, his wife was beside its bow, fists on hips. "You won't believe all that's happened today. My sister's little boy fell out of a tree and broke his arm, your dad cut his foot real bad, and I broke a big crock your mother gave me when we got married. But it's not just us." She pointed along the row of canoes to where other wives were talking to their husbands and to anyone else who would listen. "Just wait till you hear."

As the stories got passed around Togai heard about a little girl who had fallen in some nettles and—lo and behold—came home with welts on her arms. Two little boys, playing, ran into each other. One chipped a tooth and the other got a gash in his head. Old Meemu lost her walking cane and Petl's gout got worse, even as he sat in the sun getting warm.

For the next few days every little bad thing that happened was blamed on Adelu or Prandina or both. But then, with fishing continuing well, in spite of no yellowtail, and with no woodcutter getting killed by a falling tree or any fish handler getting trapped in the smokehut, older Chelks began to say that the blame-it-on-Adelu had gotten out of hand. Something well out of the ordinary would have to happen—and soon—to be sure Maker really was displeased. And it was Maker they had to be concerned about.

But about the time most people stopped blaming trivial accidents on Adelu or Prandina or the Avenging Witch, the fishers began bringing in fewer and fewer fish. On top of that, the days became gloomy and windy with lots of cold rain and mist. Galu and others said this was the *real* sign Maker was displeased. Togl and some of the older fishers said it was just a matter of changing currents and changing seasons, that it wasn't at all unusual after a warm winter like they'd just had—especially with its good run of yellowtail—to have spring come cold and rainy with few fish to be caught.

One morning when even the river had whitecaps on it and a cold, stinging rain was coming down, Togl told the fishers to take the day off, go home and sit by the fire and try not to think anything was a sign of anything.

Kallo had waited to walk back with Togl and Togai and though he was shivering, he stopped at the door of the hut he had grown up in to say good morning to his mother. Lilu asked him if he and Prandina and the baby would like to come for an early supper. He said, "Yes," said since it was cold he'd even bring a chair so Togai could sit by the fire.

When they came, after Lilu had cooed a bit over Adelu, Prandina said, "She just nursed and should sleep right through the meal—once she gets good and warm." She looked teasingly at Togai. "Want to hold her by the fire awhile, then put her on Kallo's bed?" She laughed. "Be good practice for the day you have children of your own."

Others laughed too, and though Togai acted embarrassed, he was glad for the chance to hold Adelu and stand by the fire with her. He stood so close that he was soon sweating and felt that Adelu had to be getting warm, maybe even hot, and he turned to take her to the bedroom.

"I'll help you," Prandina said, "show you how to wrap her blanket around her so she won't wiggle out."

She had barely started her instructing and demonstrating when she glanced back at the main room and whispered, "I want to ask you something, but don't answer out loud. With all the talk I haven't dared say anything about starting a school. I mean, who would come? So, would you—on rainy days like this one, maybe even some at night—come and let me start teaching you to read and write?" She looked at him. "Kids in the village—parents too—look up to you. So, if you'd be my first..."

He stared at her. "*Me?* Really? Look up to me?"

"Yes. You might not think so, and although they might say some things and tease you, they really respect you for your, well, your determination and standing up for what you believe in."

"Supper's ready," Lilu called.

Prandina squeezed his hand. "So come if you can, if you want to. Then others might come."

CHAPTER 41

# Togai's Lessons Begin

About midmorning the next day—after Togl had again called off fishing because of wind and rain—the rain slackened and Togai, bored, told Togl and Lilu he was going to Kallo and Prandina's for a while.

Not seeing Kallo when he went in, not sure Kallo knew about Prandina's offer, he cautiously asked, "Where's Kallo?"

She smiled. "I'm glad you came. He's over at the carpentry hut, making an alphabet board."

Togai shook his head. "What's an alphabet board?"

"It's a board that has all the letters of the alphabet on it."

"Letters?"

"Yes. Letters are those little things—marks, squiggles, symbols—we write with, to make the words we read."

Togai felt hurt. "Kallo know how to read—and write?"

"No. He says he doesn't want to until Togl says it's okay, but he said he hoped you do—and he's being very helpful. I drew the letters on the board, but he's going to do the hard work of carving them out, starting this morning. He's already made several shallow boxes with sand in them for students so they can practice writing." She sighed. "If any ever come. Grestina gave me some paper her parents sent over, but paper's hard to come by, even in Zaphyr, so we'll start with sand. All right?"

"Sure," he said.

She put two of the shallow boxes on the table, side by side, motioned for him to sit down, then put a chair for herself next to his. From the box in front of her she took a small pointed stick and smoothed the sand. "If I didn't say it, all words can be made with let-ters. For example, the word 'can' is made with three letters—*c*, *a* and *n*—and it looks like this." Holding the stick between her thumb and first two fingers, she wrote *can* in the sand. "And the word 'Togai,' your name, looks like this," and she traced out *Togai*.

He stared. "That's my name?"

"Yes, and it has five letters in it—*t, o, g, a* and *i*. But, we'll start at the beginning of the alphabet. The first letter is *a*. But it has two forms, capital *A*, like this..." She wrote *A*. "...and small *A*, which you've already seen, like this," and she wrote *a*. She pointed to the small stick in his box. "Now you try it. Both big and little."

It had looked so easy when she did it, but the ends of his thumb and first two fingers seemed too big to hold the little sick, he didn't seem able to control where his hand went, and his first letters didn't look nearly as nice as hers—especially his little *a*, with its rounded part more of a lopsided square than a circle.

She smoothed the sand in his box and at the top of the box wrote *A* and *a*. "There," she said, "so you won't have to look over here. And try not to move your hand so much. Use your fingers, moving up and down and around to make the letters. Try it."

And Togai tried, again and again—and with her coaching— went on, to *B* and *C*. By the time they got to *G*, his hand was cramping and his head hurt, so he was not at all sorry when Prandina said she'd heard Adelu whimper and should go feed her.

"Oh, that's all right," he said. "I should go home anyway."

She patted his hand. "Thank you so much for coming. I can't tell you..." She paused and looked at him. "Please come back, when-ever you can."

"Oh, uh, sure. I will. I will."

The rain, though gentle, was cold and he began to run, thinking he couldn't wait to get home and inside to a warm fire. But as he ap-proached the hut he noticed that the dirt under his window was dry, and he stopped and knelt there. Aware of the cold rain on his neck, he bent and looked in under the low floor, and reached back and traced out *Togai*. He settled back on one heel to look at it—and a warm feeling came over him. Today, thanks to Prandina, he was probably the first Chelk who ever saw his own name written out, and now, almost surely, he was the first Chelk ever to write his own name, all on his own, without help.

Early the next morning, in another cold and driving rain, Togai was on his way to the river. Togl had already tied a long strip of yellow cloth to the corner porch post so any fisher would know to go back home, but the 'no fish' pole had to be put up so the Zaprian fish watcher could run up his 'no fish' flag, though Togai doubted any Zaprian would think there'd be any trading this day.

Normally Togai dreaded this early morning chore because it almost always meant that he'd wind up cold, wet and miserable, but today he didn't mind. Today, if he was lucky, he'd get another lesson from Prandina.

And he did. She taught him more of the alphabet, through the letter O, and showed him a few more words. One he especially liked was *Togl*, and he was pleased that he recognized that if he changed the *l* to *a* and added an *i* he could make his own name.

"Next time," she said, "we'll start with the letter *P*, the first letter in my name."

But "next time" didn't come the next day, or the next. Both were mild and sunny, and at the end of supper on the second day, Togl said to Togai, "Lilu heard that Prandina has been telling some mothers in the village, mostly those with small children, that you've been coming to their hut on rainy days to learn to read and write. That right?"

Togai noticed Lilu was giving him a hard look. He swallowed. "Yessir."

"Kallo know?"

"Yessir."

"Why didn't you tell me?"

"I don't know. I guess I...I didn't think it was important."

"Are you learning anything?"

"Yessir."

"Like what? Can you write something for me that I might know?"

Togai thought for a moment, wondering what he might try to write, then suddenly sat up straight. "Yessir, I do, but I need something to write on—and with." He looked around for a moment then said to Lilu, "Do you have a scrap of cloth, maybe white, that I could use? As big as your hand maybe?"

"Could I have it back?"

"Sure—but it may be dirty."

While she went to her sewing bag to look for a piece of cloth he went to the fireplace, knelt and took a small stick from the pile alongside and used it to reach in along the fireplace wall and drag some ashes out onto the hearth. With the stick, he sorted through the pile until he found a few, small-end charred pieces he thought he could write with and, carefully testing to make sure they weren't hot, picked up two of them.

Back at the table he asked Togl if he would stretch out the cloth flat on the table and hold it taut. Carefully then, with Togl watching every move, he wrote out *T o g l.*

"What is that?" Togl asked.

Togai turned it so Togl could look at it straight on. "That's your name, Papa. That's *Togl.*"

Togl turned his head first one way, then the other, studying the cloth. He breathed deeply. "Well split my paddle."

"Hmpf," Lilu said. "Well, I'm going to bed—and you'd better too, Togai."

"Yes, ma'am," he said and went into his room.

Once under his blanket Togai wiggled to the head of his cot and looked out. Togl was still at the table, staring at the cloth. After a few moments he very carefully folded the cloth and slid it into his inside-out shirt pocket. He stood, peeked in the pocket, and headed toward his and Lilu's bedroom.

Next morning Togai again had to run down to the river bank and put up the "no fish" pole with its yellow streamer. Midmorning he looked at Togl. "Be all right if I go over to Prandina's for another lesson?"

Togl gave him a puzzled look, as if surprised he'd ask. "Uh... sure."

Lilu looked up from her sewing. "You know how to write *Lilu* yet?"

He went over and bent and kissed her on her forehead. "No. Not yet. From the sound, I guess I need to know at least one more letter. Maybe I'll learn today."

When he got there, Prandina said, "Kallo's at the carpenter's hut again. Hopes to get the alphabet board done today, but we've done without it so far, so, want to get started? We don't have many letters left."

"Sure."

"The next letter, after *O* that we did last time, is *P*. As I told you it's the first letter in Prandina—and in ordinary words like paddle and please—and in, uh, the king's name, Praidar. Here, I'll write out Praidar."

"No. Write out Prandina." He was afraid he might blush. He looked down. "Please."

"Oh, all right."

Carefully she traced it in the sand—and Togai thought it was the prettiest word he'd ever seen. But he didn't have the courage to say that, so he said, "It's long."

"Yes—but then the sound—Prranndeena—is long. Each letter, usually, adds its own sound, and once you get the hang of it you can almost guess how to spell a word by its sound. But you need to know all the letters before you can do that, so…."

She showed him *Q* and *U*. *R* and *S* went quickly because he had already seen *r* and *s* many times in words she had shown him while teaching of other letters.

After *S* she said, "Now, the next letter you should know. You've seen in many times in other words—and it's the first letter in your name."

He bent over the sandbox, quickly traced out *Togai* in the sand and turned the box for her to see.

"Very good, Togai," she said. "Very good. Now, can you write me a word with a small *T* in it? I've shown you a few."

He thought for a moment and his face suddenly brightened. "How about a word with both little and big?"

She smiled. "Sure. If you know one."

Quickly he smoothed the sand and drew *T a t l*. "There!" he said, and he smiled and looked at her.

"Oh, Togai," she said. "That's really good. You learn so quickly."

He beamed.

She laughed. "But let's go on." She bent over her box. "We've already talked about *U*—with the *Q*. The letter after it is..."

"Is there a *u* in *Lilu*?"

"Yes. Oh..." She put her hand to her mouth. "I should have told you. Here, let me..."

"No. Let me see if I can make *Lilu* on my own," and he wrote it out.

"Oh, Togai." She patted him on the shoulder. "You really are a fast learner. Maybe we *will* finish today. The next letter is really easy to make. It's called..."

A little cry came from the bedroom.

"Oh, dear," Prandina said. "If she'd just slept a little longer." She gave Togai an apologetic look.

Togai stood. "I wouldn't want to keep Adelu from eating. Maybe we can finish next time."

Prandina, began touching the tips of her fingers to the table, counting down the letters. "..*V, W, X, Y, Z*. Yes. Only five left—and they'll go fast. They're easy to make." She looked at him. "I'm really am excited about showing you the last one, the *Z*."

"Why? Because it's last?"

She squeezed his hand and laughed. "Oh, you'll see. You'll see."

In the night he was jarred awake by a tremendous clap of thunder that was soon followed by a clattering on the roof. The clattering turned into a near-incessant din and as flashes of lightning began to light his room he turned toward the window and sat up to watch. With each flash, huts leapt out of the darkness, oversized and eerily white—and pellets of White Cold hit and went bouncing around like little white frogs. In almost no time the ground was white and he could picture the village knee-deep in White Cold—and Kallo, Prandina and Adelu being blamed. But soon the clattery-din changed to a drumming, and rain began to fall. Heavy rain. In sheets, in torrents. And within two or three lightning flashes Togai saw that the Mother of Water and Rain was sending down enough rain to wash the White Cold away. He was thankful, but she didn't stop. She kept sending it and sending it. And when there was dawn enough for him to see, the rain had practically stopped, but what he could see of the village was a near-lake of puddles. Just as he was wondering if there'd be fishing—he was pretty sure not—Togl came in.

"Glad you're awake," he said. "Hurry down to the river, will you? Get the 'no' pole up and check the river. If it's up much, come back and get me. Quick. We'll need to move the canoes to higher ground, maybe the drying racks too."

Togai ran back into the village faster than he had run out of it. When he came in sight of the hut and saw Togl standing in the doorway he stopped and, with a newly started cold and wet rain running down his face, called out, "It's up and it's rising fast, real fast. You want me to run and get the other fishers?"

Togl was coming toward him, almost running, splashing and lifting his knees as he came. "No. That'd waste time. We'll do it."

But Kallo and Old Exl must have thought about high water too for they were there right after Togai and Togl were and began to help drag the canoes away from the rising water. With the four of them working together and working hard, they were soon finished.

"I may have seen the river this high when I was a boy," Exl said, "but I've never seen it this muddy."

Kallo pointed to the diving raft. In their spare time, the village carpenter and others had been adding to it for the upcoming Festival and it was nearly twice as large as it had been. "You think we should try to get the raft in?"

Togl nodded. "We should, but I don't think the four of us could budge it. Togai..."

"Great turtles!" Togai yelled out and pointed upriver. "Look!"

They all turned to look. A huge tree, rooted end first, was being

251

swept along, barely bobbing in the fast-moving water. They watched, all hoping it would miss the raft, but it didn't. It hit the out-river corner and boards and planks splintered and leapt into the air. Some of the raft's big floor timbers stuck in and through the tree's already entangled roots, and as the trunk and top of the tree began to swing out into the current a great groaning and creaking rent the air. And just as Togl said, "It's going to tear the raft completely apart," one of the mooring ropes snapped, and in almost no time tree, debris, raft and a section of the dock attached to the raft were sliding down the river together, as peacefully and smoothly as the little leaves and sticks that bobbed alongside them.

About the time the tree and raft disappeared around the bend, the carpenter came running up with his little boy close behind him. "Great turtles," the carpenter said, "I was afraid this might happen." He looked at his son. "Run and tell your mother. Others too."

It wasn't long before nearly the entire village was there. Most stared at where the raft had been. Togai felt sorry for them. They were stunned, disbelieving. Lilu twisted her hands and asked of Togl, "What'll we do about the Festival? What'll we do?"

Lilu seemed ready to cry and Togl put his arms around her and pulled her close. "Oh, don't worry about that now. Plenty of time to build another. A small one, anyway."

A blinding bolt of lightning hit a tree across the river, and about the time Togai gasped, a great *Currrack!* pierced the air.

"Ohhh," some woman moaned, "I just know it. It's another sign. Maker and the Mother of Water and Rain aren't at all pleased with what we've let happen."

"Maybe it's just ordinary lightning and thunder," Togl said, "and we've had floods before."

"Not like this," she said. "Not any that have taken the raft away. I can understand, you being Kallo's father. But what'll it take to convince you? The whole village being washed away?"

Kallo threw up his hands. "I'm leaving," he said, and strode off toward the village.

Lilu, sobbing now, had her face buried in Togl's shoulder. "Let's go too," he said softly. "It's starting to rain harder."

"Hmpf," the woman said. "We'd all better leave before we have to swim home."

Many others had left—or were leaving—and when Togai spotted a large group close around Old Helu, he hurried to catch up and fell in at the rear. And though he didn't like what he heard, he was glad whoever was saying it was saying it loudly.

"I keep telling you," the person said, "most of us are worried. These bad things are happening because of that baby. It's plain as day. The baby was cursed from the start. Evil Spirit, probably—and is changing to a demon child of the Avenging Witch. Maker didn't know that, couldn't, till the eyes turned green. Now He's told the Mother of Water and Rain to send the storm and enough water to take the raft away. He's punishing us for letting Kallo and Prandina marry and giving the Evil Spirit a chance to bring another Avenging Witch into the world. You've got to do something."

After Togai had dried off and changed to dry clothes, he went out and as he hung his wet clothes on a rack by the fireplace he nodded toward the closed bedroom door. "Lilu?"

Togl sighed. "Yes. She's...she's not feeling well."

Togai sat by his father and, as Togl seemed to be doing, gazed into the fire. After a while, in which the only sound in the room was the crackling of the burning wood, Togai said, "Papa, why do people think that things they can see are caused by things they can't see?"

Togl turned and studied his son for a moment, then looked back at the fire. "I've been wondering something like that myself. Any other time, I think, people would think that though this is a big flood, it's just another flood and will go away. But with a baby here in the village that has the same color eyes and hair that they've *heard* a particular witch has, well, they fear things'll get worse and worse until the problem is taken care of—or goes away."

"And they want something that's more powerful than anything else to help them?"

Togl looked at Togai, puzzled. "Well, yes. That's natural, don't you think?"

Warmed by the fire—and tired, Togai guessed—Togl fell asleep, and Togai got up and tiptoed into his room. He intended to lie there and, face close to the wall, look through a crack down through the village to see a little of what was going on—if anything. But with a light rain falling and a blanket to keep him cozy, sleep came easy.

He awoke to Togl's words: "You been down to the river again?"

"Yes." It was Old Exl. "Helu asked me to go down and have a look. I want to tell you before I tell her. It's the highest I ever saw."

Togai shifted to where he could see into the main room.

"You think she and Council," Togl asked, "blame the baby for the flood?"

Exl shrugged. "Don't know what she thinks. Council does."

Togl sighed. "Well, you have to tell her what you saw."

"I know," Exl said.

He was barely off the porch when Lilu came out. Togai had never seen her look so old, so tired. She looked at Togl. "Even if the rain stops, the river will keep rising, won't it?"

Togl nodded. "I'm afraid so. A lot has fallen in the mountains and upper valley."

Lilu glanced in at Togai. "You hungry? I'm not, but I guess you and Togl might be." She put two bowls and two spoons on the table and went back into the bedroom.

They ate slowly, saying little. When they had finished, Togai wandered around for a while, getting more and more bored. He thought about wading through the puddles to get another lesson, but guessed that after what had happened at the river this morning Kallo wouldn't be much in the mood for visitors. Prandina neither, if Kallo told her.

When Togl seemed annoyed with his wanderings, Togai again sat by the fire and, a little after Togl did, dozed off. Next thing he knew, Togl was nudging him and saying, "It's clearing."

Soon all three of them were on the porch.

"Oh, good," Lilu said. "I can see streaks of sun all along the edge of the mountains. Maybe people will stop worrying now." She walked back to the fireplace and took an apron from a hook. "I'll fix us a big supper. I'm starved."

But before steam could start to rise from the black kettle she had hung over the fire, they heard the long and mournful note of a conch horn.

"Oh, my," Lilu said. "An emergency meeting."

## CHAPTER 42

# The Avenging Witch Has to Go

Though they knew that the coarse sand of the dune beside the Council hut would dry fairly quickly, especially toward the top, most villagers still brought something to sit on. Togai, Togl, Lilu, the princess, the three handmaidens and Kallo, carrying the baby, had been among the last to get there. Togai at first thought it was nice that villagers near the bottom moved to give them room to spread their mats until he realized that the villagers were doing more than giving them room. They were moving well away from them and leaving them an island unto themselves.

When she could see no one else coming, Helu rose from the bench of elders and said, "Thank you for coming on such short notice. Normally the elders and I would explain things and invite your opinions, but we think most of you know why we're here—and we've heard opinions enough already. So, will the princess—with the child—and the three handmaidens please come forward."

Togai heard Lilu gasp and a murmur ran through the crowd. They all knew that the only time a person was called forward in such a manner was to be punished.

The three handmaidens stood, looking scared and uncertain. Prandina stood too, but she looked more defiant than scared, and as she leaned down to get the baby from Kallo, he said, "I'll go with you."

"No," Togl said.

As the four young women, with Prandina carrying the baby, started forward, Old Helu turned away from them to face the mountains. Another murmur ran through the crowd. There was now no doubt. The young women from Zaphyr were to be punished. But how?

"Are the subjects in place?" Old Helu asked.

"They are," said someone, from the bench of elders.

"We of the Council of Elders," Old Helu said, "as most Chelks are, are certain that the many recent misfortunes and calamities are acts of the Evil Spirit and other vile agents. Maker let these happen to us because He was, first, displeased by the marriage of Kallo and the princess. Then the baby came, a cursed baby, which He let happen to further teach us a lesson. By the time we met today, all of us on Council felt we had learned our lesson and chose to act. What we chose to do, I'll get to, but let me say now, we *know* we made the right decision for as soon as we did the rain began to slacken and the dark clouds over the mountains began to go away. So, there is no doubt. Maker was—is—pleased."

"Glory to the Maker and Controller of All Things," said many seated on the dune.

"And that decision is...." Old Helu's voice shook. "...Because we fear that other, even worse misfortunes will occur if we let the baby stay in Chelekai and because we fear there will be other cursed babies if the handmaidens stay, we decree that the princess, her child, and the three handmaidens must leave Chelekai...*by this Praise Maker Day,* never to return."

There was a collective gasp. Kallo started to rise but Togl pulled him back.

Lilu's look was like that of the handmaidens. She couldn't believe what she'd just heard, couldn't comprehend what it meant.

"Leave?" Prandina said. "But where to? We can't go back to Zaphyr. My father has banished us."

Old Helu was still looking at the mountains. "We know that—and we of Council pray that your father will let you return."

Patya clutched Prandina's arm. "He will. He will. I know he will."

Prandina shook her head. "I don't think so. *No* king of Zaphyr has ever backed down on a decree. He might, just might let you three come back, but I...I..." She looked down and Togai saw tears, heard her voice quaver. "I could never take Adelu there. And since I could never leave her, even if my father let me return alone, she and I must prepare to leave."

"But like you asked," Grestina said, "where? Where could you possibly go?"

"I would have no choice. I would have to try to go into the mountains."

Togai sensed the shock in people all around him.

Old Helu now turned. "The mountains? You can't go into the mountains. There's no way, and besides, the Ogres of the Cold..."

Prandina ignored Helu and looked out at the people of Chelekai.

"Many of you have said that there is no way into the mountains. Is there any one out there who thinks there is?"

Togai wanted to jump up and say, "I do," but he quickly looked down to keep anyone from seeing how desperately he wanted to help.

Zoltai stood. "You have heard me say, and I tell you again, Prandina—and I swear by the Maker of All Trees—I know of no way and have heard of no way into the mountains. Not ever. And I have lived a long time. But as Helu, says, even if there was..." He let his words trail off, did not finish.

"Neither have I heard of a way," Old Helu said. "Not ever. And surely if there was a way—or even a suspicion of one—I would have heard it from the Dilkina before me. *But there is tale of an island.*"

"I know," Prandina said with sharp bitterness in her voice, "an island that *sank*. But even if it didn't, how would I get there. I know nothing of the sea, almost nothing of canoes."

"But I do," Kallo said, and he pulled free of Togl and stood.

CHAPTER 43

# Others Will Go Too—or Will They?

In a few steps Kallo was at Prandina's side. He looked up at the dune, at people he'd never been more than a shout from any night of his life. "I can't imagine any man," he said, "would ever let a daughter—especially one with a small child—be sent to sea. But I want you all to know, if she goes, I go. To banish her and my child is to banish me."

Lilu began to cry and even as people turned to look at her Colatt jumped up and, from his place high on the dune, shouted down, "And if Grestina has to go, *I'll* go with *her*." His face flushed red and glanced around nervously. "That is, if she'll have me."

Grestina, eyes filling with tears and hands clasped in a grateful, thank-you way, looked up at Colatt. But before she could say anything, Dilo stood and said, "And if *Obena* has to go, I'll go too, she want."

As Colatt and Dilo came down the dune toward the crying yet happy and relieved looking Grestina and Obena, Patya's eyes began darting about—to spot Tatl, Togai guessed. As Togai turned to look, he saw many others turning too, and heard a woman near him say, "From all I've heard about how brave and daredevilish Tatl is—and how crazy he is about Patya—you'd think he'd have been first to stand after Kallo."

Togai, helped by the direction many heads had turned, spotted Tatl—hunched with his head down as if he didn't want Patya or anyone else to see him. He peeked up, seemed to be, first, startled, then flustered by so many eyes on him. He stood, face getting redder and redder, and said haltingly, "I'll go too, with Patya…if she wants me to…" His voice cracked. "If she has to go."

As Tatl came down the dune Togai wondered if anybody on Council—in the village—had thought the cost of freeing themselves from a presumed curse might be four of their fine young men.

No sooner had he had that thought than he heard Old Helu say, "I…I must confess, I…I didn't think about the possibility of losing a loved one." Suddenly Togai remembered. Helu was Dilo's grandmother. "But in spite of that…" Tears came to her eyes and she glanced at Dilo. "…I still think we have done the right thing. As soon as we made our promise to Maker that the baby and the four young women from across the river would be gone by Praise Maker Day, Maker stopped the rain. And since time is short—Praise Maker Day is only five days away—I ask each of you to…to please go home and pray to Maker to soften the king's heart so that he will let the three handmaidens and Prandina, with her baby, back into the kingdom to live."

Togai was puzzled. If the baby was such an abomination to Maker, why should Maker care which side of the river the baby was on? And what good did Old Helu think it would do to pray to Maker to pull on the strings of the king's heart when it didn't do any good to pray to Maker to stop the rain? Does Maker not really care about what happened down here—or does He just not have the control everyone thinks He does?

Togai expected to see some remorse, even guilt, in the faces of people coming off the dune, but except in the families and closest friends of Colatt, Dilo and Tatl—and not even in all of those—he saw none. Not one person came by to say "I'm sorry" or offer to help in any way. Judging from their looks, most people now seemed relaxed. Maker was appeased. Council had done the right thing. The curse would be gone.

After some hurried talk with Prandina and the others, Kallo came to where Togl and Lilu were sitting, seemingly too numbed to move. "Old Helu—she was crying about Dilo—said, if the girls *had*

to leave, we could take anything we wanted from the village and villagers. Food, clothes, canoes. Whatever."

"That's really big of Council," Togai said. "I figured they'd
make you swim."

"Togai!" Lilu said. "That's not nice."

Kallo, ignoring the exchange, said to Lilu, "Okay if we come
over later? All of us?" He looked at Togl. "We need to plan like we'll
have to leave, so sure could use your advice."

As Lilu said, "Of course, dear," and started crying anew, Togl
stood and nodded to Kallo. "I've already been thinking. May sound
strange, but your biggest problem will almost surely be water, drink-
able water. But first..."

Thinking Togl could talk forever about what ought to be done
to prepare for long days at sea, Togai turned away, wondering what
Prandina was doing, how she was reacting.

She had been talking with the three other doubly-banished but
was now headed back into the village, still carrying Adelu. He hurried
to catch up.

"Mind if I walk with you for a while?" he said as he fell in beside
her.

"Uh, okay." Her smile was weak. Her words were with lips that
trembled. "I...I guess I *could* use a friend to talk to right now."

He glanced back to make sure no one was close enough to hear.
"You said you thought your father might let the three handmaidens
come back, maybe even you. But you said you could never *take* Adelu
there. What'd you mean?"

She seemed surprised and half turned to look at him but then
looked ahead. "Uh, well, since no Chelk has ever been allowed to even
be in Zaphyr after dark, I can't imagine my father would let one live
there, not even a half Chelk like Adelu. That's all."

"Well, I'm sure that's what most people guessed you meant. But
it seemed to me there was more to it than that. That...that you might
be *afraid* to take Adelu into Zaphyr."

She gave me a hard look. "Now why would I be afraid to take
her where...uh, take her into Zaphyr?"

"I don't know. I was just trying to be friendly. You seemed kind of scared."

"Well I wasn't."

They'd been wading carefully through puddles ankle-deep in muddy water, and Prandina now forged ahead, as if she no longer cared whether she splashed herself or Togai, maybe even wanted to splash Togai.

He hurried to keep up. "I'm curious. Why did you ask about going into the mountains?"

She shook her head. "What would you have done in my place? Remember? I didn't know Kallo would be going when I said that, and—you should know—the handmaidens and I would be absolutely helpless in canoes. So, where else could I think about going?" She looked at him. "Tell me."

"I just thought, since you asked Old Zoltai..."

"Okay, Togai, I admit it. I wasn't completely honest with you when you first asked about that. I'd read this really old Zaphyrian tale, told by one *crazy* old king, that was so farfetched *nobody* believed it. And after what Old Zoltai told me about the mountains, neither did I. So, what happened today..."

"What was the tale? I might..."

She stopped and glared at him. "Togai, you're too much. Here we are worried about our very lives and you want to talk about old tales. Kallo's always said you had a wild imagination and were fascinated with tales and old stories. Well, I can see now why he'd say that. Grow up, Togai. Grow up."

She started to turn away but he reached out and held her arm. "No. It's more than that."

She snatched her arm away. "I *know* it's more than that, Togai. But like I just told you, *grow up*. Face it. I'm *Kallo's* wife. Always will be. And he's the *man* who's going to lead me and my child and six other people to safety—*if* we have to go. But since I can't count on that *if*, please excuse me. I've got better things to do than stand here talking to you."

Togai stood there, wanting to cry, wanting to tell her it wasn't like that anymore, that he knew she was Kallo's wife and they loved each other and he'd accepted that and just wanted to help—but she was gone.

Darkness had fallen by the time the banished ones arrived at the head fisher's hut. Togl, Lilu, Kallo and Prandina, holding Adelu, took chairs. The rest sat on the floor. Talk had barely begun when they heard a loud "Pssst." Togl—puzzled—leaned back to where he could see the window in Togai's room. "That you, Exl?"

"Not gonna say," came a hushed voice, "and don't ever tell anybody I was here or who sent me. It was Old Helu. She said tell you Council wouldn't have voted the way they did if they thought it would actually happen. They thought the king might take a tough stand if it was just Prandina, but it'd be hard for him to turn his back on the handmaidens, 'specially if the handmaidens' parents went to him and pleaded for their lives. That'd give him an excuse to save them all. So, case you didn't think of it, she said you oughta get messages to the girls' parents as soon as you can."

"Kallo and I have already thought of that. But...Exl? Exl? You still there?"

His answer was a silence, broken almost immediately by Patya's crying and gurgly words, "We'll die, won't we? If we have to leave."

"Why do you say that?" Lilu asked, now looking really worried.

"Old Exl said Helu wants our parents to go to the king and *plead for our lives.*"

"Try not to worry, Patya," Togl said. "I don't believe a king would let one of his subjects be sent on such an uncertain journey. Surely no father would let that happen to a daughter."

"But how," Kallo asked, "will the king know *Prandina* has been banished? We've heard he's forbidden anyone to use her name in his presence."

Patya's chin quivered. "You mean our parents can't talk to him?"

"No, Patya," Grestina said sharply. "They can talk to him about us, not about Prandina. But somehow, some way, he has to learn about her too."

"Maybe someone could slip a message under his door," Patya said.

"Old Rono is probably our best bet," Grestina said. "You know how much she loves Prandina."

"My dad could take a message to her," Obena said. "He takes fresh milk to the castle every morning." She blushed. "The king really likes our milk."

Prandina, who had been sitting back, now sat up. "Obena's right. My father really likes fresh milk—especially with the cookies Rono makes for him almost every morning. And, I agree, if anyone could talk to him about me it would be Old Rono. She's been there since he was a child. Maybe she could take advantage of that cookie time in the morning when he'd likely be in a good mood, when no one else was around.

"The problem..." She glanced around. "...is *time*. The fishers can't deliver a message until tomorrow afternoon and..."

"I could deliver it tonight," Togai said—and immediately wished he hadn't, after what she'd said to him earlier.

"What?" Kallo said.

Lilu glared at him. "You wouldn't dare!"

Togai shrugged. "Why not? Could even be easy if Obena's parents lived close to the river."

"Hers don't, but mine do." Grestina said. "But there's nothing but a big open field between the house and the river—and there's another house close by."

Before Togai could say anything, Togl spoke. "Is there a creek—or maybe some trees—down one side? Wouldn't need much cover. Can't be that many people look out in the middle of the night, almost none I bet, to see if someone's sneaking up from the river."

"There's a small creek," Grestina said, "not many trees. But there's an orchard—behind the other house, reaches about halfway down to the river. That'd be enough, wouldn't it?"

Togl nodded. "Probably."

Lilu gave him a hard look. "You don't mean you'd approve of this?"

He shrugged. "Why not? It's been done before."

She looked at him in surprise. "It has?"

"Sure," Togl said. "When Exl's son and I were just young men..." He looked around the room. "He and my father died in a big storm when he fell overboard and Papa tried to save him. Anyway, the night before our Growing-up Day some older boys said we didn't have enough nerve to go into Zaphyr and steal some apples...but we did."

Togai looked at Kallo—who was looking at him in the same disbelief. Togl? Their father—head fisher Togl—had once snuck into Zaphyr? To *steal apples*?

Lilu shook her head. "How could you possibly do that?"

"We only took a few that were on the ground, didn't pull any off a tree."

"I wasn't talking about *stealing*. I meant, how could you dare go into Zaphyr at night?"

"Same way Togai and I are going to do it tonight..." He smiled. "Very carefully. So..." He looked around. "...if Obena and Grestina will each write for her father, and Prandina one for the cook, Togai and I—Togai mainly—will deliver. And Grestina, be sure to give us something so that your mother or father will know it's really from you."

"Wouldn't it be better—simpler—if I came with you? That way I could tell Daddy what's going on and make sure..."

"No," Togl said. "For the same reason that I'll go only about halfway up the hill with Togai. If for any reason we *have* to leave in a hurry, we'll for sure *want* to leave in a hurry, and there's no way you or I—or any Zaprian either, for that matter—could catch or keep up with Togai."

Togai felt the blood rush to his face and he looked down. Never before had he heard such words of trust and praise from Togl and he didn't want anyone to see how he was affected. But no one seemed to notice, and he later took that as a compliment—that the rest simply accepted what Togl said as fact.

"I'll go with you," Kallo said. "The river's still way up, and though I know you'll stick to eddies close to shore, the going will still be hard and three can make better time than two."

"And four better than three," Colatt said. "I'll come."

Both Tatl and Dilo seemed about to volunteer to come but Togl said, "No. Four's plenty—and Colatt, being a paddle maker, ought to know how to handle a paddle pretty well."

Togai stopped beside the trunk of the tree at the orchard's upper corner. Though the moon was only three-quarters or so full and about halfway down, it was halfway down a perfectly clear sky and open spaces were nearly day bright. And though there were shadows under the orchard's trees, they were the wispy shadows of thin, gnarly limbs. That was why Togai had, as Togl suggested, run from trunk to trunk and paused at each to look and listen. As he looked back and again had to look closely to spot the tree Togl was under, he doubted whether either one of them would be seen by any sleepy-eyed person who just happened to look out.

Off to his right, about as far away as he could throw a small apple he guessed, was a house. Ghostly pale and partly hidden in under some tall trees, it seemed quiet. But—with his heavy breathing and pounding heart—he wondered if he'd be able to hear any movement or talk that would serve as a warning.

In the other direction, a short run away on the other side of a little creek, was the house of Grestina's parents. If it wasn't, he thought, he could be in real trouble. But it should be. The house and everything else he'd seen so far had been the way she said it'd be. He took a deep breath and tried to slow his heart. He'd been excited at the start of races, excited on going into mountains—excited by finding the chimney and going up between Ogre's horns and daring to look at, maybe, a world beyond. But tonight's excitement was different. He liked it. Enjoyed it. Found satisfaction in it. Was thrilled by it. His father was trusting *him*, had chosen *him* above all the others to get the job done. If Togl came up right now and said he'd changed his mind and wanted him to take the message right into the king's bedroom, he'd probably try it.

He touched his shirt to make sure the messages were still there—in a faded scarf Grestina had said her mother would recognize. He took a deep breath, one last precautionary look at the farmhouse above the orchard, and with a running start jumped the creek and ran as hard and as light-footed as he could toward what had better be Grestina's house.

As he ran he kept repeating, as Togl had made him do all the way up the river, the names of Grestina's parents. Gerta and Ekbar. Gerta and Ekbar. He aimed straight for a shuttered window that Grestina had said was to her parents' bedroom. As he neared the house he saw, as he had hoped, that the floor on that side was high. Barely slowing, he bent low and dived under the house. His head hit a support beam and he let out a short 'Nngg' before he bit it off. He lay there, not daring to breathe. But he heard nothing from above. No sound or movement. Letting his heart slow enough to where he could hear clearly, he wriggled around to where he could look up at the window. He reached up, gave a light tap on the shutter, and quickly ducked back under the floor. Silence. No response, no movement from above. He took a deep breath and reached up. His bolder second knock made the shutters rattle—and sent him back under the house more quickly than the first time. He held his breath.

From above, in a hushed, worried voice came, "Ekbar? Wake up, Ekbar. I think I heard something."

"Huh?"

"I think I heard something. Under the floor, first, and then the shutters banging."

"Go back to sleep. It's probably the wind."

"It's not the wind. It's me," Togai said. "Under the floor." And he began to crawl out.

He heard creaking and rustling sounds as if someone had sat up in bed.

"What did you say, woman?"

"I didn't say anything. I think it came from under the house."

"You must be dreaming."

"No," Togai said in a loud voice and stood and knocked on the shutter. "I have a message from your daughter Grestina."

The shutter burst open with unexpected violence and he fell backward onto the soggy ground. He looked up to see a man looking down on him from the window. "Cowpiles, Gerta. It's that short-legged fisherboy from Left."

CHAPTER 44

# You Have Until the Festival?

Next day, mid-morning, the king came into the castle kitchen and started to sit at a small table but, seeing it bare, looked at the gray-haired woman at a large stove just steps away.

"I'm sorry, sire," she said. "I just put the cookies in. I...I've been a bit slow today."

He stared at her for a moment, then went over and put his hands on her shoulders. He knew she could hear better if she could see the speaker's lips. "Look at me, Rono," he said more loudly than normal. "Have you been crying?"

"No, sire," she said, but the 'sire' came after a sniffle she had tried to hold back.

"You *have* been crying," he said. "Still are."

She nodded. She had been. Had been crying almost ever since Obena's father gave her the message from Prandina. But she said nothing. Prandina said to not lead the king, let him ask on his own, if he would. And he did.

"Want to tell me why?"

"Oh, sire, I...I can't talk about it."

"Come now, Rono. As many good cookies as you've made for me, as long as you've been here, you can talk to me about anything."

She gave him a cautious glance. "Anything, sire?"

"Yes, anything."

"It's about the handmaidens, the ones in Left, sire."

His face reddened, but he took a deep breath and there was no anger in his voice when he spoke. "All right. I asked for it. What is it?"

"They've been banished."

"I know they've been banished. I banished them."

"I mean from *Left*, sire."

He snorted. "Banished? The Lefts have the audacity to banish them back *here?*"

"No, sire. If I understand correctly, they just have to leave, that's all. And if you don't let them come back here, well, they have to go someplace else."

"Someplace else? Where could that possibly be?"

"To the ocean, sire, in hope of finding..."

"That's absurd. How could three young women who've never..." He tilted his head a little to one side and gave her a quizzical look. "Why are they being banished?"

She looked down. "Because of the baby, sire."

"One of the girls had a *baby?*"

"No, sire."

"Maybe I can't hear. Didn't you just say one of the handmaidens had a baby."

"No, sire."

"I'm getting tired of this." He glanced back at the table as if he were impatient to sit down. "What baby are you talking about?"

"I cannot say, sire. You have forbidden..." She let her words trail off.

"Forbidden what? I told you you could..." His eyes turned hard and he looked directly at her. "You don't mean Prandina had a baby?"

She began to cry. "Yes, sire. And she too, is being banished."

"How could she? The only boys she was ever around..." He stared at the old woman in disbelief. "You can't possibly mean a Left is...is..."

Her voice trembled. "Yes, sire. A..."

His knees gave way under him and he staggered backward, groping. His hand found the back of a chair and he practically fell into it. "Do they...do they..." His voice turned to a croak. "Do they know who did this *despicable* thing?"

"It was not a despicable thing, sire. She is married."

His face whitened. "*Married?* She married a *Left?*"

"Yes, sire."

He leaned forward, elbows on his knees, head held in his hands. After a few moments he took a deep breath and sat up. "Send someone to have Thunder saddled, then come back."

"Yes, sire."

She took a few steps to the door and, after calling out, came back to stand in front of him.

He looked up at her. "I don't understand. Why would the Lefts banish any of them because Prandina had a baby? You'd think the Lefts would be proud to have the grandchild of a king over there." He paused. He seemed afraid to look at her. "Is..." His face paled and his voice turned hoarse. "Is the child deformed in some way? Maybe even...even a monstrosity?"

"I don't think so, sire. But they do say the baby is ugly, not exactly either us or them. And they blame the recent floods and poor fishing on...."

He waved his hand. "Enough. Leave me alone. I need to think."

"But the cookies, sire."

"Let them burn."

News that the Lefts had banished the handmaidens and the princess spread from the handmaidens' parents to relatives and neighbors—and from relative to relative and neighbor to neighbor. And that afternoon when the fishers came up the Forbidden River and Togai saw the horde of Zaprians along the bank and well into the meadow, he guessed that few of them had come to trade.

"See the girls' parents, there near the middle?" Togl asked. "I'm guessing they're pretty angry with us. Can't say as I blame them. We'll aim for them. Better I should face them than anyone else."

Togai ignored the questions being thrown at them as their canoe glided toward the bank, but even as it touched and he stood to climb out and pull it onto the small strand there, someone far back in the crowd called out, "King Praidar is coming! King Praidar is coming!"

Everyone that Togai could see from his place in the bow turned to look toward the City of Light, and though all seemed to be trying to talk at the same time, one man's voice rose above the others, "I told you he'd come. I knew he wouldn't let them send Prandina away."

As Togai began to pick up the sound of hoof beats, the talk began to die down and all of a sudden both came to an abrupt halt.

"Open a way!" the king's voice rang out. "Are any of the parents of the banished handmaidens here?"

Patya's and Obena's fathers stood on tiptoes and raised their hands, and the people near them tried to move apart from one another, but the lane they were trying to form was slow in opening—and Togai stood and watched as the sweaty black stallion began to push its way through. The parents stepped aside and Togai abruptly sat down when he saw the horse coming straight at him. It stopped with its front feet on the very edge of the bank—and Togai slid back in the canoe to get away from its drool.

The king sat quietly atop Black Thunder and gazed out across the river. He wanted to appear calm. Unperturbed. Kingly. He was glad he'd had the short ride this morning and the longer one into town to collect his thoughts. For once, maybe, he could act with some foresight. Almost as soon as he'd banished Prandina he'd wished he hadn't, had known he shouldn't have. *He* needed her. *Zarian* needed her. The whole kingdom needed her. Still, he had his image and royal traditions to protect. He couldn't be seen as acting in either a weak or selfish way. He had to appear both strong and wise—seen as doing what was best for the kingdom. If he had to change a decree he could make it look as if he were being compassionate rather than weak. And he certainly didn't want to utter any decrees he'd want to take back later. He smiled to himself. He was beginning to like this planning ahead. He'd gotten off to a good start, he thought, by waiting at the start of the path and charging down as the fishers were landing. One thing he was especially glad of now was that, after his cooling-off ride this morning, he'd gone back to the castle and asked Old Rono a few questions.

He turned in the saddle and looked down at the three closest women. He guessed they must be the handmaidens' mothers. Not only was the crowd giving them space inside the respectful half circle around Black Thunder, each was looking up at him with an anxious, pleading look. One had her hands clasped under her chin. "Before I left the castle," he said, "my cook Rono told me one of you is the granddaughter of Gresta, a woman who served years ago in the castle. Did she tell me correctly?"

"Yes, sire, she did." Even if the voice hadn't been the same as the one he'd heard in the middle of the night. Togai would have known Grestina's mother from the many times she'd been at the river. Now, this plainly-dressed, dumpy woman, who'd always stayed back and watched and listened while her husband talked to Togl about Grestina, took a timid half-step forward and looked up at the king. "Yes, sire, my grandmother was Gresta. I am..."

He held up his hand. "Your name doesn't matter." He turned away from her and again gazed out across the river. "What matters is that Gresta was a loyal and devoted servant to the Good Queen Adena, my mother, and was much loved by her. For that reason, in order to save the loyal Gresta's great-granddaughter and the other two handmaidens—and the Princess Prandina—I am willing to do something no king before me has ever done."

"Oh, bless you, sire," the woman said and began to cry—as Patya's and Obena's mothers were already doing.

"But I must see my daughter first," the king said and glanced down, as if ready to give an order. But when he saw Togai, he said, "Oh. *You.*" His look hardened and he glared at Togai. "Are *you* the father?"

"No, sire," Togai said, and immediately wished he hadn't said 'sire.'

The king snorted. "Well, that's one blessing." He shifted his look to Togl and said, as if any fisher were his to command, "Bring my daughter to me."

Togai's respect for Togl, high as it already was, went up. "We'll do that," Togl said. "Not because you order it but to help Prandina and the handmaidens."

Even before Togl spoke some of the fishers had started pushing off, and soon they were all headed across the river and paddling hard. They were thinking that Old Helu might get her wish, and they wanted their families to see Praidar do what no king of Zaphyr had ever done before: eat his words.

With tears in her own eyes and with crying and excited talk breaking around her, Grestina's mother, the granddaughter of the once loyal and devoted servant of Queen Adena, looked up at the king and reached out to touch his boot. He scowled at the hand, and though she quickly pulled it back she said, "O sire, may Maker bless you forever for saving our daughters."

Immediately a voice in the crowd rang out. "He didn't say anything to the fishers about bringing the handmaidens. He doesn't care what happens to them, just Prandina."

A shocked silence fell. No one there had ever heard words spoken openly against the king, but it was true. The king hadn't told the fishers to bring the handmaidens.

The king had never heard words spoken against him either, and even as he twisted around in the saddle, he jerked on the reins. The stallion spun, knocking Grestina's mother down, and in an instant the king and horse were facing the crowd.

"Who said that?" he shouted. "Someone point the man out to me."

But no one pointed, no one called out a name.

The king looked from person to person, glaring, demanding an answer. Still none came. His face turned red, showed more and more anger. He leaned forward and seemed ready to spur the horse and send it crashing into the crowd, but slowly he straightened, and with deft movements of the reins and his knees moved the stallion back to where its front hooves were at the very edge of the bank.

And until canoes started coming back across the river, no one came near him or the stallion.

When the fishers landed on the Chelekai side of the river, they didn't have to send anyone to tell the villagers what was happening. Most of the villagers were already there. Prandina and the handmaidens had come down earlier because they were eager to learn if

Prandina's plan had borne any fruit. But they hadn't had to wait for the fishers to trade and come home. As soon as they spotted the big black horse coming at a hard gallop from the City of Light, they knew—and Patya and children playing there had run into the village to tell others.

So, as fish were being dumped from canoes into holding nets, wives, children, and friends jumped in. The many villagers who didn't find spots in the fishers' canoes dragged out old ones and paddled over on their own.

King Praidar had been the center of attention on many occasions, but never had this many eyes been this close, this watchful, this attentive.

Crowded in on both sides and from behind as closely as they could without making the closest ones bump against him or his horse, citizens of Zaphyr twisted and craned and stood on tiptoe to see. Some faces showed worry, some anger, some mere curiosity

In front of him, were the Chelks.

Directly in front, not far below the toe of his right boot and looking up from the bow of Togl's canoe, was Prandina. In her arms was Adelu, wrapped in a thin blanket. Behind her was Kallo, then came Lilu. Behind Lilu, in the stern, was Togl. In the bow of the canoe off the king's left toe, was Togai. Crowded in close behind him were the three handmaidens. Behind them came Tatl and Dilo and, in the very rear, Colatt. In the bow of the next canoe, close enough for Togai to touch, was Old Helu. Behind her were three other members of Council and two young boys who had volunteered to help paddle them over. In other canoes, in a spreading half-moon centered on the king, were almost all the other citizens of Chelekai. Some had faces expectant and optimistic. Most were drawn and anxious.

Everyone there was looking at the king—except the baby and the king. The baby was asleep. And the king? He was gazing out at the river as if he and the horse were the only creatures there.

For a few moments the only sounds were sniffles from the bank, gurgles from the river, and a few klunks as canoes bumped together.

And though he acted as if he hadn't seen anyone, the king said, "I didn't ask for anyone but Prandina to be brought over."

"Where I go, the baby goes," Prandina said.

"Can I take that to mean she is yours, of your own free choice?"

"Yes. I love her—and my husband—very much."

Trying not to show any movement of his chest and stomach, the king took a deep breath. *Careful now. Careful.* "No king has ever changed a decree, but in good conscience I cannot—and I think the people would not want me to—let you and the three handmaidens be sent onto the ocean."

A murmur of approval went up. Helu and the handmaidens' parents looked relieved.

"Therefore..." The king shifted in the saddle. "...you and the three handmaidens may return..."

Prandina's voice was loud and plaintive. "Me and the three handmaidens? What about my husband and child?"

The king glared at her, but he was glad she'd interrupted. He hadn't counted on this. He needed time to think. He stared out over the river. People would think he was letting his anger cool. Ah. He had it. A way to put pressure on Prandina to return. Return alone. Without husband or child.

He tried to keep his face stern, as he looked down at her. "You did not let me finish. I was going to address the issue of *husbands* and children. It is my understanding that the handmaidens, too, have drawn the attention of, shall we say, Left suitors. Zaphyrians and Lefts have always lived separately. I think Maker wants it that way, and..."

Murmurs of assent came from the Zaphyrians. In many canoes heads nodded.

"...I believe most Zaphyrians will want to keep it that way..." More murmurs of assent. "I suspect there is a special concern about children. I have been told that the mixed child resembles neither Zaphyrian nor Left and is ugly..."

"Ugly?" Prandina's voice cut the air. "How can you say that? You have not looked at her."

The king looked out over the river. "I do not need to look at her."

Prandina struggled to her feet and held the baby up "Look at her. She is beautiful. She's named Adelu, in part for your mother, Queen Adena."

She thrust the baby higher and yelled, "*Look at her!*"

Praidar jerked back and, without meaning to, looked at the baby.

Togai saw dismay and disbelief in the king's face—and quickly turned to look at Prandina.

As she sat, she pulled Adelu close, bent protectively over her and began gently rocking back and forth, her own body shaking with sobs.

Despite her denial, Togai thought, there really was something she was afraid of. But what? What did the king *looking* at the baby have to do with it?

Praidar was sweating. He hadn't counted on the child being a problem at all, now this. But that was a worry he could put off. Right now he had to say something. His people were watching.

He raised his riding crop. "Enough talk. Listen and listen carefully. I feel that Zaphyrians will not want Lefts or children with Left blood living in Zaphyr. How long they will take to decide, I don't know. So, my decree is: If, come Festival Day, Zaphyrians are willing to accept Lefts and children of mixed blood into Zaphyr, then the handmaidens and Prandina may return with or without husbands or children as they wish. If Zaphyrians do not want Lefts or mixeds... Prandina and any of the handmaidens—those not pregnant and none with a child—may return to Zaphyr. *But*—listen carefully—if Prandina does not return, no one does."

As an excited babble broke out, the king leaned over the horse's neck and said to Prandina, "Just think! You could live with your brother again. He loves you. He needs you."

She sighed. "So does my child."

Praidar quickly straightened and, with a point of his crop at Old Helu, said in a loud voice, "So...Until Festival Day."

Helu was trying to get to her feet, but the king turned in his saddle and pulled Black Thunder's reins hard to one side.

Grestina's mother, knocked backward, groped for something to hold onto to keep from falling. By chance she happened to grab, with one hand, a loose part of the king's pant leg and with the other the horse's mane—and, out of fear of being stepped on, quickly lifted her feet and swung with the horse as it finished its high-stepped, mincing, menacing turn.

As the king brought the horse to a stop, Old Helu, now standing, called out, "O sire, O honorable king, there's something..."

He gave an annoyed, backward wave of his crop and glared at Grestina's mother, who had just let go of his pant leg and Black Thunder's mane.

"I...I'm really sorry, sire," she said, "about holding onto your pant leg. But I really must know. Do you mean Prandina has to come back or none of the handmaidens can?"

"Yes. That is correct."

Though very much afraid to speak up, she knew the life of her child was at stake. "But, sire," she said, "Prandina may not want to leave without her child. Can't you just say you'll let the child come too?"

"No. I cannot. That will be up to your neighbors." The king pointed at the crowd with his crop. "Are you willing to have a Left living among you?" he called out.

A few yelled, "Yes." Others, "No, never."

He snorted. "Well, I guess we have some differences to work out"—and without another word or a glance backward, he spurred his horse. And even as Black Thunder began his nervous, prancing steps through the parting crowd, the king of all Zaphyr was thinking that his strategy just might work. Prandina would surely feel guilty if she didn't leave her child to save the handmaidens, and in Zaphyr there'd be pressure to let both Prandina and her child in to save the handmaidens. Either way, he'd get Prandina back. And if it turned out she and the child both came, well, he'd deal with that when he had to.

As the Zaprians began to leave, even family members were beginning to argue with one another over whether the king should let a Left or—even worse?—something that was a mix of Left and Za-phyrian into Zaphyr.

In and between the canoes headed for Chelekai, the argument was not about whether the king should let a Chelk or part Chelk into Zaphyr but whether he *would*. The people in those canoes could say whatever they wanted, as loudly as they wanted. About the handmaid-ens, Prandina, the child—or Kallo, Togl, Togai or Lilu. All of them were still on the Zaphyr side. Waiting.

As soon as Praidar had Black Thunder moving through the crowd, Gerta started toward the bank but suddenly stopped and looked back at her husband, hand to her mouth. "Oh, blessed Maker," she said. "The decree. Do you think we dare talk to Grestina?"

"I don't know if you're going to talk to Grestina," Patya's father said and stepped past, "but I'm going to talk to Patya. The king him-self let the girls sit right there in the open, where we could see them. If anyone violated his decree, he did."

With that, Togai felt the canoe rock and heard rustling and bumping sounds as the girls climbed over the side of the canoe and began splashing toward their parents, now kneeling on the very edge of the bank with outstretched arms.

Togai looked at Togl, in the canoe with Lilu and Kallo, Pran-dina and Adelu. "I guess we'll be here a while. You leaving?"

"No. We'll wait. Talk going across."

Kallo was now kneeling close behind Prandina. "Kallo," Lilu asked in a plaintive voice, "what will you do if Prandina and the baby go to Zaphyr?"

As the last bit of sun disappeared behind the mountains and shadows sped down the valley, the handmaidens said their hurried good-byes and soon the two canoes were gliding alongside each other toward Chelekai.

The handmaidens were laughing and chatting happily when Grestina realized no one else was talking. Ahead of her she saw only the backs of Tatl, Dilo and Colatt. In the other canoe, all faces were somber, serious. "Anything wrong?" she asked. "You're all so quiet."

Lilu sniffed. "I asked Kallo what he'd do if Prandina and the baby went to live in Zaphyr..."

Prandina spoke up. "I said I'd not leave him, ever."

Patya looked at her in disbelief and dismay. "You mean you'd keep us from going home?"

"You probably think," Obena said, "that most Zaprians won't want Kallo in the kingdom, but I bet it'd be okay with them if just you and the baby came. Surely Kallo could visit now and then or..."

Kallo cut in. "That's what I said,"

"And...?" Obena let the question hang.

Kallo answered. "Prandina said she'd not take Adelu into Zaphyr. Not ever. When I asked her why..."

"I said I'd tell why," Prandina said, "but I didn't want to until we were all together, so I wouldn't have to tell the story but once. It's...so shameful." She began to cry. "I want all of you to promise not to tell anyone, ever, and I mean not anyone. You'll understand why when I tell you. So, do you all promise?"

When all had promised to her satisfaction, she began.

"Leaving out a lot of details, a few years back, in my father's study, I came across some very old books, similar to diaries, written by former kings. My father never knew I found them. They had in them secret decrees, decrees to be read only by other kings, decrees that the king had to obey and pass on to the next king. In one of these books was a decree that had been put in writing for the first time ever. Before that it had been passed on only by word of mouth. The decree had started with Zaphyr's very first leader, and the decree was that if a king had a child—or if any of the king's children had a child—that had red hair and green eyes, that child had to be put to death..." She put her head down and sobbed. "...*by the king's own hand.*"

Lilu gasped, shook her head. "How could anyone? How could anyone?" Others looked at Prandina in both disbelief and sympathy.

Togai felt sorry for her, too, and could understand her anguish. But he also felt bitter. Just now she told several people—some of whom she barely knows—what just yesterday she had refused to tell him, he who had saved her life.

He had little time to stew before they landed, and as they got out, Patya said, "Does that mean kings worry about the Avenging Witch too?"

"I guess," Lilu said. "But by the time the Festival gets here, Adelu's eyes and hair might change, so the king wouldn't have reason to, uh..."

Togl cut in. "I think there's been enough sad thought for one day. Let's try to think about happy things. It seems the king really wants Prandina back, and since Council is not all that unreasonable, I'd think something can be worked out."

And from there on back up the path toward the village, the talk was happy, with Grestina going so far as to say the king might even give them—with their husbands—a place to live in the upper part of the valley, if say, the Ogres didn't object too much.

The only serious note came from Prandina. She said she'd forgotten to tell part of the story. She said she hadn't been sure her father had read the red-hair decree until just this afternoon—when she'd seen the look on his face when she showed him Adelu.

That didn't make Togai feel any better. She still should have told him when he asked. And he wasn't sure about the optimism. He remembered what Old Helu had said.

He had stayed a few steps behind Kallo and Prandina and as they came to the last turn in the path in near darkness, he almost bumped into Kallo as everyone suddenly stopped. Kallo whispered back. "Someone's at the front of the hut. With a torch."

"No need to wait here," Togl said. "Might as well go on and find out who it is—and why."

Flames on the knotty torch wafted and flickered and sent shadows darting here and there across Old Helu's face. The turtle shell scorn around her neck made it clear she was there as Dilkina. And though her voice quavered as she spoke, the words that came from the dark of the lower part of her face had a hollow note. "I have just come from a meeting with Council. As you were told yesterday, we made a promise to Maker and...and..." She looked at Dilo. "...we have no choice. We must stand by our promise to Maker and that means that by Praise-Maker sunrise, the baby, Prandina, and the three handmaidens must be gone."

"Why?" Patya blurted. "Why do we have to be gone? The king said we could..."

"No! The king said you *might* be allowed back into the kingdom, depending. But it doesn't matter. Even if he'd said you *could* return next Festival for sure, we promised Maker that if He stopped the rain you five..." She pointed at each of the banished ones. "...would be gone by *this* Praise-Maker sunrise. So, gone you must be. By then. Four mornings from now. It is not debatable."

"But, Helu," Togl said. "Council is reasonable, and surely Maker is. Can't..."

"Togl! You, you who would keep a promise to the most deceitful trader you ever dealt with, do you think we should not keep a promise to *Maker*?"

Togl looked down and shook his head. "No."

Togai, standing just outside the half circle around Helu, sensed movement and saw Tatl, who had been standing beside Patya, slide in behind her and, with a nervous glance toward the ocean, put his head down so that his face was in the shadow of her head.

Grestina's words came quickly. "If you knew you'd make us leave by Praise-Maker sunrise, why didn't you say that to the king?"

"I *tried* to tell your king, but after he'd said what *he* wanted to say, he wheeled his horse around and started to leave. He didn't care what anybody else had to say, didn't even look at me. Besides, it's obvious you got a message to him, so don't blame me if he didn't know."

Obena quickly broke in. "It was in the message I wrote my father. Prandina knows. She helped me write it—and I'm sure Daddy would have told Old Rono."

"Well," Old Helu said, "you'd better get another message to your Daddy and make it clear that he or this Old Rono or somebody has to make sure the king understands it's *this* Praise Maker Day, this Praise-Maker sunrise—and understands why it has to be that way." She looked at Obena. "Is your father a Maker-fearing man?"

"Yes. All Zaprians are."

"Good. Then he will understand that a promise to Maker is a promise that has to be kept."

"But three days is so little time," said Togl.

"Council is well aware of that and has agreed that all of you are free of work obligations and can use your time to either get yourself ready to leave or help others get ready."

Well, hug an Ogre, Togai thought.

"As said before, you may take whatever you need or want from the village or any villager. Canoes, tools, food, clothes. Anything. Every villager will be told to give you anything you ask for and to help you in any way you ask. But...all help must be done by sundown three days from now, for..." She sighed. "...the next morning you must be gone."

And with those words, the Dilkina of Chelekai walked away.

In the soft moonlight that settled in around the retreating glare of Old Helu's torch, Patya began to cry. "I'm scared," she said. "I don't want to leave"—and turned to Tatl.

But when his only response was to look the other away, Obena came over and took Patya in her arms. "That's all right, Patya, I'm scared too."

"We all are," Togl said. "But being scared and crying won't help. I still believe the king will step in and do something, but just in case he doesn't, we need to start planning—tonight."

"I agree," Kallo, "and I agree with Old Helu. We have to get another message to Obena's father. The king has to understand it's *this* Praise Maker Day."

"Maybe he does understand," Togai said. "Maybe he's just calling Old Helu's and Council's bluff. He's not used to having anybody tell him what to do."

"Whatever," Kallo said, "we need to get another message across the river." He looked at Togai. "You up to it again tonight?"

"No, don't," Prandina said. "It's too risky. And it won't matter. I'm sure he meant I'd have to return or nobody could—and since I can't let Adelu go there and would never leave her..." She shook her head and began to cry. "It just won't matter."

"But we can't stop trying," Togl said. "Like Togai said, maybe he's bluffing—or maybe he simply doesn't know. Regardless, who knows what he'll do when really put to the test?

"So, Obena, will you write another note to your father asking him to make it absolutely clear to this Old Rono that the king must understand that he must let *all* of you into the kingdom by sundown *three days from now*—or you'll all have to be gone by sunrise the next morning, Praise-Maker morning. Grestina and Patya, will you write your parents too?"

The three quickly said they would, and Togl looked at Kallo. "I know you won't be fishing tomorrow. I'll get Exl to take your place. Togai and I won't go either, of course. We'll stay and help in any way we can."

"I'll stay," Colatt said. "If I have to get in a canoe with Grestina I want to make sure it has a *lot* of food in it." He laughed. Alone.

Patya looked back at Tatl, cautiously, timidly asked, "If...if we have to go, will you..."

"Of course he'll go," Dilo said. "We all said we'd go, and we will—and help get ready too."

"Good," Togl said, and glanced at the handmaidens. "So, to-morrow, when the Zaps come to trade, I'll take your messages over. Put in everything you can think of you might need to make a, uh, whole new start in another place. Try to think of things we might not have much of here in Chelekai. Seed, ax heads, knives...saws."

"Cooking utensils," said Lilu.

"Good idea," Togl said.

"I agree," Kallo said. "So, Colatt, Tatl, Dilo, want to get some-thing to eat then join us in our hut? Grestina, Obena and Patya will already be there. We can then work on the lists. I doubt any of us would sleep much tonight anyway."

"Sure," Colatt said, and Tatl and Dilo nodded.

"But don't stay up too late," Togl said. "Get some rest. The next three days will probably be long and hard. Lilu and I will do a lot of thinking too, give you our ideas tomorrow."

Togai was angry. He resented being left out. When they needed someone to sneak a message into Zaphyr, they asked him. But when it came to ideas and planning, no one seemed to care what he might think. Fine. He'd keep his thinking to himself and go to bed. Maybe tomorrow they'd find him useful for *carrying* something.

Adelu awoke with a slight cry, and Prandina shifted her so that she, Adelu, was facing backward over Prandina's shoulder. And as they started away, Togai had the impression that Adelu was looking at him, waving good-bye. He remembered when she had held his finger and cooed and looked at him with pale green eyes that showed love and trust and asked no questions. He took a deep breath. Kallo and the others were old enough to make decisions for themselves, but he couldn't let them make one for Adelu and take her onto the open sea—not without knowing there was another choice.

He ate hurriedly and said, "You're right, Papa. The next few days will be hard. I'm going to bed."

But when the house was quiet, he climbed out his window and ran through the village to Kallo's hut.

From the porch, he peeked through the partly open door.

He saw that Kallo was standing behind Prandina, who was seated at the table with the three handmaidens, and that the handmaidens had writing paper in front of them. Close beside and a little behind them, in chairs from when the men and boys of Chelekai had built the finest hut ever for the Zaprian women, were Colatt, Tatl and Dilo. No one looked happy.

"Look, Patya," Kallo was saying as Togai started in, "we've been over this. We don't have room for frills. We need room for ourselves, extra paddles and whatever bare essentials of seed and nets and tools we'll need to get started. After that we need to put in as much food and water as we can, especially water. Not frills. What good will an extra dress do you if you die of thirst or starvation before you get somewhere to wear it?"

Kallo glanced at Togai. "Papa send you with some ideas?"

Togai bristled. "No. You ever think I might have some ideas of my own? You used to..."

"Togai," Patya said, either not knowing or not caring she had interrupted, "don't you think I should be allowed to take an extra dress or two?"

"Hmpf," Tatl said. "No need to ask him. We all know he'll agree with you."

"How do you know?" Togai said. "Maybe I would, maybe I wouldn't. But it doesn't matter. I don't want to talk about what to take—I want to talk about where to go."

Before anyone else could say anything, Prandina said, "Did you say *where* to go?"

"Yes."

"We don't have time for jokes," Kallo said.

"I get the feeling he's not joking," Prandina said. "*I'd* like to hear what he has to say."

"You *would*," Tatl said. "You're probably hoping he'll tell us to...to...." He frowned and looked at Togai. "You're not going to say we should try to go into the mountains are you?"

Togai shrugged. "I'm not saying more until everyone promises to not tell anyone outside this room what I say. Not *anyone*. Not now or ever." He glanced around. "Promise?"

"Busted ax handles," Tatl said. "We gotta go through this again?"

Kallo started to object, too, but Prandina gave him a hard look. Kallo sighed. "All right. I just hope it won't take long. I won't tell. I promise."

Togai glanced around. "And the rest of you?"

One by one they nodded or said yes. All but Tatl.

Togai looked at him.

"For Maker's sake, Tatl," Kallo said. "Say you'll not tell and let's get this over with."

"Okay, I promise. I won't tell. But I can tell you all, right now, if this has something to do with going into the mountains, he can save his breath. When I said I'd go, I thought *if* Patya had to go it would be on the ocean. That'd be bad enough. But the mountains? Forget it. The Ogres won't let anybody anywhere near the mountains."

"What if I told you that the Ogres of the Cold don't guard the mountains the way we think they do? What if even, maybe, there are no Ogres of the Cold?"

Tatl looked at him and shook his head. "Your axe has gone dull."

"I don't think so. Listen. Decide for yourself."

Prandina was the only one who showed real interest. The rest seemed, at best, impatient, at worst, angry about what Togai guessed they thought would be a waste of time .

Influenced by that impatience, Togai hurriedly told that he had stayed home that first Festival after his wrong-way race, had—on whim—followed the river up to a small waterfall and there, at the top of the waterfall, been really surprised to find himself right at the end of the first finger. But then, with much trepidation, he had gone on across the big boulder field there and on down between the first and second finger and up between them to where they joined. He'd even gone into a crack in the wall—all without seeing an Ogre or having anything bad happen to him, then hurried home.

He had, in most of the telling, looked down and only now and then, looked up afraid of the skeptical looks he was sure he'd see. Now he looked up and with a nervous laugh said, "For days, even moons after that I worried and had bad dreams about the Ogres coming to get me. But nothing bad ever happened to me or, far as I can tell, the village either."

Tatl who had been shaking his head vigorously and who seemed to be just waiting for a chance to speak, now did. "Even if you did sneak up there once—on a *Festival* day—that doesn't mean the Ogres don't..."

"But it wasn't just one trip," Togai said. "I went back."

"Huh!" Kallo said. *"You went back?"*

"Yes," Togai answered—and before anyone could object began telling about his second venture into the mountains. And though afraid he'd see skepticism, he would now and then look from person to person to be as convincing as he could.

He was encouraged, at first, because as he told about climbing up the chimney—and going onto the giant slabs of flat rock—and climbing up to look out over the valley, they all seemed to be paying very close attention, as if they were fascinated by the story and couldn't wait to hear what he would say next. But when he told about getting above Sky Falls and not seeing Mother Nature or cauldrons, just a really clear lake fed by a river that seemed to come from distant mountains, a few shook their heads looked at others as if to say, 'This is *unbelievable*.' And though they again paid close attention as he told about sneaking up to the rock ledge to take a few quick peeks at Ogre, by the time he said not only had he not seen a face but had walked right up it, the skeptical looks returned. And from there on in his story—the windy and cold walk up to the saddle, his one, quick look down the other side not to emptiness and dark but to what might be another valley—he could see that some thought he must be as crazy as Carver was.

The only one who seemed to believe at all—or was it that she *wanted* to believe?—was Prandina.

Anxious to find out what they were all thinking, Togai concluded quickly. "Not much more to the story," he said. "After that one glimpse of the 'other side,' the clouds closed in, and I hurried back the way I had come. The whole way I kept looking back, afraid the Ogres might come after me. But...."

Colatt cut in. "Togai, I don't know you as well as the others do, so I don't have to soften my words with spit or sawdust. We've all been told, all our lives, about Ogre and the Ogres of the Cold—and how mean they are. So it's hard for me to believe what you've said. My question is, if it's as easy to get up there as you say—and the Ogres didn't try to stop you—why hasn't somebody else done it? We'd surely know about it if they had."

Togai shrugged. "I don't know why we haven't heard about it, but I know one thing for sure. Somebody was up there before I was."

Prandina sat up in her chair.

Tatl snorted. "And how do you know that?"

"Because there's a scorn mark cut in the stone. Deep. Chiseled in right there at the top of the chimney."

Prandina practically leapt to her feet. "A *scorn* mark? Are you sure?"

Surprised, Togai looked at her. "Yeah. Sure. It's just like the one Old Helu..."

"Fish spit," Tatl said. "I don't believe you. I'm like Colatt. If some Chelk had been up there, we'd know about it—especially if he'd been banging around on hard rock with a hammer and chisel."

In spite of what Tatl had just said, Togai was elated by Prandina's reaction. But his elation quickly turned to anguish when she laughed and said to Tatl, "I agree, Tatl. No Chelk put a mark up there..."

As Prandina paused, Tatl looked at Togai and smirked.

"Some Zaprian did, I believe."

They all looked stunned, especially the handmaidens. "A Zaprian?" Grestina said—at the same time Colatt was saying, "A Zaprian? Why would a Zaprian put a scorn mark up there."

Prandina laughed. "I'll explain. Remember those old books I mentioned earlier. Well, in one of them—and only one—was a story written down by a king who said that though his own father told him the story, he didn't believe it—partly because his father was old and half crazy at the time but mostly because it seemed so preposterous and was so at odds with everything this king, the son, knew and had been taught.

"What this maybe crazy king told was one of these word-of-mouth stories that had to be passed on from king to king and was to be known only by kings. And the story was that Zaprians came into the valley..." She looked at Togai. "...from a place on the other side of the mountains."

Turtles, Togai thought, so this is why she was so interested in the mountains.

"That's preposterous," Tatl said.

"No, Tatl, it's not. And the reason is—and Colatt was right on this—that's no scorn mark that Togai saw up there, chiseled by some Chelk, it's a Z—put there by some Zaprian, maybe Zaphor himself, the Zaprians' first leader and, according to the story, the man who led people from the other side of the mountains to get here."

It was now Colatt who cut in. "Now, I don't know what a Z is, but it doesn't matter. Togai said it was a scorn mark."

"Ah," she said. "That's easy to explain, Colatt, and I can see from the looks on their faces that Grestina and the other handmaidens know too. Tell him, Grestina."

Grestina looked at Colatt. "Yes, it's easy. You see, your scorn mark looks just like—has the same shape as—our letter Z, the last letter of our alphabet."

"I don't believe you," Tatl said. "You could have made this up."

"No, Tatl," Kallo said. "See that board in the corner? Prandina drew all the Zap letters on it and I carved them in. And when I carved in the last one, only yesterday morning, I thought it looked like a scorn mark. I was going to ask Prandina about it but..." He started toward the board. "Here let me show you."

Tatl waved his hand impatiently. "All right. All right. But so what if this Z thing looks like a scorn? We don't really know there's a mark up there. All we have is Togai's word on it. Maybe Prandina dreamed this whole thing up, got Togai to go along with it—just to get us to *try* to go into the mountains. It's been clear from the beginning that she's *afraid* of going on the ocean."

Dilo cut in. "Maybe you're afraid to go into the mountains."

Tatl's face reddened. "I don't remember you going up there, oh brave one."

"How about tonight?" Dilo said. "Want to go tonight, see for ourselves if there's a mark up there? The moon's sure bright enough." He looked at Togai. "We have enough time?"

"Sure. We'd need to carry torches, though, for the chimney."

Colatt stood. "I can get some torches, and I'll go too. At least as far as the crack. If a couple of you go on up the chimney, take a look, that'll be enough for me."

Dilo smiled at Tatl. "I don't think I heard you. You going or not?"

Tatl gave him a withering look. "Yeah. I'll go." His face lost its anger and he looked down. "To...to the last hill, anyway. Watch some from there, maybe come on when it's...it's..." He glanced at Kallo. "You going?"

"No. I don't need to. I believe my wife. I believe my brother."

CHAPTER 45

# Three Days Till

Next morning, much earlier than usual it seemed to Togai, he was dragged from a sleep he didn't want to leave by Togl's annoyed words, "Come on, Togai. Up! The work we'll do today is far more important than any fishing we ever did."

He dressed quickly and as he stepped into the main room, Kallo came in. Lilu gave him a wistful smile, said it was nice having her three men there for breakfast once again. Togai guessed she was thinking it might be the last time. Breakfast passed in silence, and Lilu's three men left for the river to pick out canoes.

The first choice was easy—the newest and largest the fishers had, one that several fishers had tried out to make sure it was seaworthy. The next three—of five that Togl had picked to be left that day—were chosen quickly too. Togl's and Togai's, Elot's and Kallo's, and Odl's and Galu's—a pick that Galu, when he heard, said he didn't appreciate. Said it was done for spite. As soon as Kallo convinced Togl that a "supply" canoe would be more of a hazard than it was worth, especially in high seas, they went back to the village.

Togai was glad when Kallo chose Dilo and a muttering Tatl to start working with Togl gathering what was number one on Togl's list, vessels for water. Kallo told the others Togai would help him put together some odds and ends and 'think' as they worked. "Togai was always good at thinking," he said, and looked at Togai and smiled.

The women would gather dry and preserved foods that would endure a long trip.

That afternoon, when Togl judged the time about right, he went back to the strand. As he'd expected, he could see no canoes coming upriver but could see Zaprians on the other shore—and more coming. He chose a small canoe and started across at a leisurely pace but sped up when he saw the first canoe appear. He wanted to get to Zaphyr before any of the fishers did so that if any of the handmaidens' parents were there—and he thought that, surely, at least one would be—he wanted them to get the bad news from him, quietly, privately, before the fishers came and blabbed it to everyone.

As he neared shore he spotted Grestina's father watching him. He turned the canoe slightly upstream and nodded in that direction. Ekbar looked as if he didn't like having a Chelk—even a helpful one with a common interest—telling him what to do, but he—reluctantly it seemed to Togl—began to move along the bank. About halfway to the point where Togl was headed, though, Ekbar stopped and gave Togl a defiant look. Togl sighed and turned toward him.

"I'm sorry to have to tell you this," Togl said, "sorry for us all. Our Council insists on standing by its original decision. Grestina and all the others *must* be gone by Praise-Maker sunrise, *three mornings from now.*"

"What?" Ekbar said loudly—and with a quick glance at the closest Zaps, lowered himself to one knee and thrust his face close to Togl's. "The king said..."

Togl held up his hand to interrupt. "I know. I know. The king gave them until the Festival, but he didn't give our leader, Old Helu, a chance to say anything. If he had, she'd have told him yesterday. She and our Council promised Maker that if He stopped the rain they would banish those that seemed to be offending him by Praise Maker Day. Maybe the king didn't know it was this Praise Maker Day. Maybe he didn't know a promise had been made to Maker. It doesn't matter now. The important thing is that he *has* to understand it's *this* Praise-Maker sunrise, and he must understand soon. So, I've brought new messages. Written. In case I didn't get to talk to one of you."

Togl began to pull the messages from his pocket, and Ekbar said, "I'm sure the king didn't know. If he had, he'd have done something different." He snatched the papers from Togl's hand and stood.

"But he'll know this time—if I have to go with Obiah myself to make sure Old Rono understands what's going on—and will make that absolutely clear to the king."

## CHAPTER 46

# Two Days to Go

Early the next morning, Obena's father was in the castle kitchen talking to Old Rono. "What do you mean you can't remember whether you told the king that Obena and Prandina—and the other two—had to be gone from Left, completely gone, by Praise-Maker sunrise?"

"I'm sorry, Obiah. I...I just don't remember. I was so nervous and upset. And the king...he got so upset so quickly. I...I'm not sure he would have heard it even if I said it."

"But you will tell him? Today? And the baby has to come too... *before* Praise-Maker Sunrise...*two days from now?*"

She sniffed and nodded. "Yes. I'll tell him. I will."

Obiah hugged her. "Maker bless you, Rono. Maker bless you."

"Well, I hope I deserve it, but...The other day you told me the Lefts thought the baby was cursed, but you didn't say why."

"It's because she looks like..." He laughed. "...that Avenging Witch they believe in."

"Avenging Witch? What's she supposed to look like?"

"Oh, a lot like our Night Hag. Red hair, green eyes." He laughed again. "But no sign of a claw."

Old Rono's face turned ashen. "*Red hair?*"

"Yes."

"Does...does the king know that?"

"I'm sure he does. Prandina held the baby right up in front of him, insisted he look at her."

"Are you sure he saw the hair?"

"Had to. I saw it from back where I was."

"And he still...Think now, Obiah. Was it after King Praidar saw the baby that he offered to let the princess and the baby—and the others—back into the kingdom?"

"Yeah. But that offer was for the Festival, three or four moons from now, not for this...Rono, you feel all right?"

She had her hand to her throat and was clutching the corner of a table. "Yes. It's nothing. I...I just need a breath of fresh air. You go on. I'll be all right."

"You will be able to talk to the king, won't you?"

"Yes I will. But you'd better get going. You want him to be in a bad mood because the cookies he likes—with your milk—aren't ready?"

"No." he said. "Let's keep the king in a good mood." And with that, Obiah, the king's milkman and father of a handmaiden banished from both Zaphyr and Left, turned and hurried away toward the castle's front door.

When Baya, Rono's morning helper, saw Obiah leave she came back into the kitchen but said nothing. She knew Rono wouldn't hear her if she spoke. As usual about this time every morning, Rono was in a corner by the flour bin, back turned, so no one could see what ingredients she chose or in what order or how she mixed them for the king's cookie dough.

A difference this morning was that as Rono selected and blended and kneaded she leaned back to keep tears from falling into the dough. Years ago there had been talk—whispers—about a child born barely a year after Prandina. A boy. He was—maybe like Prandina's child—about three moons old when his hair began to turn red, and not long after that, early one morning, he was found dead in his crib—by Queen Irena.

Prandina was too young to have any memory of him—or his death—and no one ever told her. The day the little red-haired boy was found dead the king ordered that no one was to ever mention the boy or the incident again. In spite of that, there had been whisperings, questions. Why would—how could—a seemingly perfectly healthy child die? A few years later the rumors came back. Some said that was why Queen Irena went mad—and that was why Zarian turned out the way he did. She didn't want to have him, tried to keep him in her body, for fear he'd have red hair...and die...mysteriously. Rono didn't believe the talk, the gossip. She guessed the reason the gossip didn't spread outside the castle was that people were too afraid of what the king might do if he heard—and were too ashamed to talk about the possibility the king had done the unspeakable.

Rono didn't believe such rumors, not until the afternoon a straw fire started in the stables. The king had rushed out, and she had gone to his study to dust and tidy up. On the desk was a book. She had no idea where it came from, but it was open to its last page, and she might have paid it no attention but in dusting around it noticed it—the last page—was signed by the king's father. She paused to read it—and was stunned. Shocked. Horrified. She could hardly believe what she read. And though she didn't approve, she understood. Kings, too, had to obey decrees. They had no choice.

Well, she thought, as she began to roll balls of dough and pat them flat, *she* had a choice.

The king sat down, took a quick drink of milk and then a bite from one of the three, big fat cookies on his plate. "Um, Rono. I think they get better every day."

"You say that every day, sire."

"Yes, I guess, I do." He smiled. "Because it's true."

He was ready to take another bite when she said, "I hear you have decreed that the princess and the others can come back into the kingdom."

He put the cookie down. "Yes, that's right. Don't tell anyone, Rono, because everyone thinks I broke two decrees. But, actually, I've broken none. You see, nothing becomes a decree until I write it down. And I never did that, for either Prandina or the handmaidens."

"That must give you a clear conscience, sire," she said as he lifted the cookie toward his mouth, "not breaking a decree and all. Bet you're really looking forward to having your granddaughter on this side of the river—where she can grow up with you."

He gulped and put the cookie down. She saw his face turn slightly red.

He wiped his mouth with a napkin. "Well, I hadn't thought about it that way, but, yes."

"I had heard she was ugly, sire. Is she? Or do you think she's pretty, maybe?"

Though he usually kept his face turned so she could see his lips, he looked away from her, as if the question were of no import or as if he was wondering if the kitchen was clean. "Oh, I don't know. She looks about like any other baby, I guess."

"You did look at her, didn't you, sire?"

"Well, yes. I had to—to make sure she wasn't, uh, grotesque or something."

"Yes, sire. I can certainly understand why you'd want to do that." Her voice cracked.

He studied her for a moment. "Something bothering you, Rono? You aren't hiding something from me, are you?" He laughed. "I hope there aren't any surprise messages like the other morning. There aren't, are there?"

Her voice quavered. "No, sire. I guess I was just working up my nerve to ask...Uh, I haven't been to visit my sister in a long time and..."

"Of course you can go." He stood quickly. "I was thinking about a long ride up the valley, anyway. Feel kind of, uh, hemmed in here. So, I'll have somebody in the stable hitch up a nice mare to the cart and drive it around to the front for you. Visit as long as you like. Surely I can survive a few days of cooking by your helpers."

He left, and Rono looked at the table. Not only had he taken only one drink of milk, he'd taken only one bite from his first cookie—and hadn't asked to take any with him or for her to put some away for while she was gone.

She went into her room, reached under the bed and pulled out a small chest she'd brought her things in when she first came to live in the castle many years ago. She opened it. It now had only one object in it. A rolled-up picture. She had taken it—stolen it—when the king had ordered it destroyed right after Prandina had chosen banishment rather than let the boy who had saved her life die. She carefully unrolled the picture enough to take a glimpse. It was a portrait of Prandina and Zarian made when Zarian was three Festivals old. She had meant to give it to the king, someday when he showed regret, maybe the day he said he wanted Prandina back. Now Prandina could never come back. Not with her child, anyway. Not a red-haired child. Rono shuddered. She owed loyalty to the king, had loved him since he was a boy. But she also had loyalty and love for Prandina and would never let that dear child return with a child she surely loved.

Carefully she re-rolled the picture, put it back in the chest and closed the latch. She then lit a large candle and, holding it upside down, began dripping wax into the seam where the top and bottom halves met. Almost as important that the chest stay afloat was that no water get in and damage the picture. It was Prandina's favorite. She'd want to take it away with her or, if some miracle happened, have it with her in Left.

Waxing done, Rono quickly put on her favorite dress, a deep blue one, and her nearly new shoes. And though she guessed that by now someone from the stable was waiting for her, she took time to sit at a small desk and write for a while, stopping now and then to read what she had written to make sure it said exactly what she wanted to say.

Holding the chest by an end handle and leaning to one side to keep the other end from bumping against the floor she hurried through the castle as fast as her old, kitchen-only-exercised legs would carry her. She shoved open the castle's big front doors and blinked as she stepped into the midday sun.

From his seat on the cart, Feldar, the youngest of the stable boys, watched her come down the steps. "Want some help with your chest?"

"No," she said, "I'll put it in myself," but she set it on the ground and looked up at him.

"The king said you wanted to go to your sister's. That right?"

"That's right. I do. So why are you sitting up there?"

"Aren't I supposed to drive you?"

"No. I'll drive myself."

He looked at her uncertainly. "Are you sure you can…?"

She put her hands on her hips. "Feldar, I was driving hay wagons before either you or you daddy was born. Now get down."

"Yes ma'am," he said quickly—and climbed off the other side.

"I do have something you can do for me, though. Come around here."

As he came around behind the cart she moved to stand between him and the wax-lined chest. "You like cookies?" she asked.

He gave her a whoever-heard-such-a-dumb-question look. "Of course."

"Good," she said and pulled a small, folded piece of paper from her pocket. "Take this to Baya—and tell her I said to give you some milk and cookies."

"Thanks!" he said, and even as he took the paper he turned toward the front doors. He looked back. "What is it?"

"A recipe for cookies."

At the end of the tree-lined lane that led from the castle property she turned left, toward town. She knew she should be feeling guilty because she hadn't told the king what she'd said she would—and should be feeling guilty about withholding information from the king. But she didn't. In fact she felt good about what she'd done—and was doing. She liked being outside. She could recall many days like this when her father had let her drive the wagon all the way from the farm, through town—with its many marvels—and on down to the river to trade with the fishers. She'd been fascinated by everything she saw there: the many big and brightly colored fishes, with their white bellies and even whiter meat once they were cut open—and the fishers themselves. Those swarthy muscular men and their lack of concern standing in water long forbidden to Zaphyrians—*after* they'd just spent all day on the ocean with its many high waves and currents that ever threatened to pull them over the Edge. Against all the bad things she'd heard said about Lefts she'd thought they must be brave men and longed to be like them, to have a chance to see what it was like 'out there,' to face danger and not turn and run.

At the top of a hill she turned off the road and in a short distance through a scattered wood turned the mare across a small hillside pasture that was well out of sight of any farmhouse. As she had hoped, she found a bank that dropped away—not very high or steep or muddy—to a stretch of sand. She stopped the horse there and—with only a little tugging—soon had the chest at the water's edge.

She sighed and looked around? What to do now? She couldn't swim, of course, and she'd never been in a canoe, but she'd given this a lot of thought and she knew the main thing—the only important thing, really—was to stay afloat. She wished she'd thought ahead, put her good dress and shoes in the chest. But too late. She could take everything off and use the dress's sash to tie things to the top of the chest. No. She couldn't do that. What if she didn't get to the other side until she was near the village? Or what if someone saw her from the Zaphyrian shore? She couldn't be seen that way. No clothes on, bare, naked. No. She'd leave everything on. Shoes too. Even if she tied things to the chest they'd likely get wet, and, tender as her feet were and rocky as it was, shoes would be good for wading both in and out.

She was about to step into the water and pull the chest in after her when she thought, What if I lose my grip on the handle? The chest could float away, she'd lose it, herself too, likely. She untied the dress's color-matched deep-blue sash and knelt and tied it to one of the end handles. Securely, so it wouldn't come off. Now, what was the best way to tie it to her? She could remember seeing, way across the river, Left children swimming, wildly waving their arms. She was pretty sure she wouldn't want to try that. She'd want to hold onto the chest as much as she could, just float along with it. Surely, somewhere, it'd drift close enough to Left she could wade ashore. Ah. Tie a loop in it, right next to the handle, just big enough to slip her hand through, wrap the rest of the sash around her arm. No way the chest could get away from her, her from it—and she'd have one arm free to 'swim' with, when she wanted to, needed to.

She carefully made a loop, loosely knotted at first, checked to make sure she could—with difficulty—slip her hand in and out. She then tied and double-tied it at that size, slipped one hand through the loop, wrapped what sash was left around her arm, took hold of the handle there and securely grasped the other with her free hand. Wading backward, she dragged the chest into the water. As soon as it floated, she swung it around and slowly pushed it ahead of her.

She almost slipped in the loose gravel, but waded on into deeper water. Her dress billowed up around her—and she laughed. She felt naked from the waist down, but the cool water felt good.

In a few more steps she lost feel of the bottom—and her first desperate feeling of fear quickly gave way to elation. She was floating! For the first time in her life, maybe in any Zaphyrian's life for a long, long time, she was floating. And she'd get to see Prandina! Get to give her Zarian's picture, warn her not to return to Zaphyr no matter what.

But what then? If the Lefts changed their minds and let Prandina and the others stay, she'd plead with the Lefts to let her stay too. She couldn't go back to Zaphyr. And if the Lefts made Prandina leave, even Prandina alone, she'd go with her. Supposedly there was no place to go, but she was convinced Maker would let them find a place, a place where they could have a little farm, grow things. And if there wasn't such a place, surely He'd make one for her. In all her life she'd never done anything to offend Him. He'd not forget her.

She now saw and felt the dress starting to sink around her. She didn't feel so naked now, but the dress felt heavy.

That day, throughout the village, there had been a lot of speculation on whether the king would show up at the river—for by then it was no secret the handmaidens had, again, asked for his intervention. So, that afternoon when Togl crossed the river ready to return and get Old Helu or the handmaidens or whomever the king might want to talk to—if he came—there were many Chelks onshore behind him, watching, waiting, curious.

Another reason Togl went over—especially if the king didn't

appear—was to get any messages the handmaidens' parents might have—and all six were there, in a little group apart from the, again, more than normal number of Zaprians.

He ran his canoe aground near the parents, and though three or four looked at him, none came over. They all—as did most of the other Zaps there—kept glancing toward town. Even when the fishers came and trading began, the Zaps who actively took part would often turn and stand on tiptoe or crane to look toward town and search the path.

After a while Obiah left the circle of parents and came over to Togl and asked, "You think the king will come today—or tomorrow?"

"I don't know. He'd *better* come by tomorrow."

"Some of us think he's just playing rooster."

"Rooster?"

"Oh, you know, just acting tough, strutting, trying to make you Lefts back down first."

Togl took a deep breath. "What makes you think we—our Council—will back down?"

"Oh, you just don't seem to be uh, cruel people. Besides, if you don't…"

"What's that?" someone in the crowd called out. "Out in the river?"

Togl, as did many others, turned and looked.

"It looks like a chest," someone said.

Togl took a look toward town and, seeing no sign of the king, said, "I'll get it."

As Togl turned toward his canoe, Ekbar, who yesterday had shown so much anger at the new banishment, called out, "It's ours. We saw it first"—and he gave Togl a triumphant, defiant look.

Togl shrugged. "Fine. Go get it."

Though he heard no laughter, Togl saw a few Zaps smiling. Among them was Obiah, who kept his back toward Ekbar.

"Oh, all right," Ekbar said. "You can have half of what's in it."

Togl didn't move. He knew the chest was slowly passing, drifting toward the ocean.

"Oh, all right," Ekbar said. "You can have it all."

"I could have had it all, all along," Togl said, "just gone on across the river with it. But I'll do what I planned to do. I'll bring it back, and if we can figure out whose it was—is—they can have it."

In a short time he was back, chest sitting near his feet. He looked up at the curious crowd that had gathered. "I think somebody wanted it to float down. See how it's sealed?"

"What's that strip of blue material tied to it?" someone said.

Togl shrugged. "How would I know?"

CHAPTER 47

# One Day to Go

Deep beneath the castle, one level below its basement, down dark and usually damp steps, a spring bubbled up. The temperature there varied little from the coldest day of winter to the warmest of summer, and it was there the 'keep cool' foods of the castle were stored—the butter, eggs, fruit and fish. Canned goods, onions and potatoes and so on were stored one level up, on shelves in the basement's huge pantry-cellar. Milk—in large stone crocks, weighted with stones on top so they wouldn't float away—was stored directly in the water, which always had a cold feel to it and was said to come as directly from Mother Nature as did Sky Falls and the Forbidden River.

After Obiah had put one large crock there he went back out to his wagon and got a smaller crock—the king didn't want either old or cold 'cookie' milk—and took it to the kitchen.

When he went in he looked at a girl laboring over a big mixing bowl. He didn't know her name. The only person in the kitchen he'd ever talked to was Old Rono, and that was usually when she was alone. "Uh, where's Old Rono?" he said.

The girl looked up. She'd been crying. "Haven't you heard? She's dead."

"Dead?"

"Yes. Drowned."

He stared. Dumbfounded. All of his life he'd lived with the ban against even trying to learn to swim, told to not go near the river. So how could Old Rono . . .

"She drowned in the river. A farmer found her yesterday afternoon—when he was in a lower field picking up driftwood from the flood."

"Maker bless her." His mind raced. "Do…do you know if she talked to the king yesterday morning?"

"What did you say?" The girl's face showed real anger. "She's *dead*—and you want to know if she talked to the king?"

"Uh, I'm sorry, but it really is important. I'm Obena's father and…"

"I know who you are."

"It's really important to me, please. Do you know if she talked to the king?"

"Yes. She did. She sent me away—as usual."

"Whew. Praise Maker! Well, uh, thank you. I guess I'll be going now."

The girl shrugged. "Who cares?"

Hmpf, Obiah thought. Young people. No respect for their elders. Halfway to the big front doors the thought hit: But if Rono told the king what she was supposed to, why didn't he come to the river? He turned and went back.

"Uh, miss, I hate to bother you again, but would you take a message to the king, maybe ask him a question?"

Her eyes widened. "Absolutely not. He gave strict orders that he was not to be disturbed until after Old Rono was buried."

"But this is…"

"Look. You probably know better than I do how the king is about his orders and decrees. You want to ask him a question, I'll show you where the study is."

"Uh, no. That's all right."

At the door he paused and looked back. "When is Old Rono getting buried?"

"Tomorrow morning. Praise-Maker Sunrise."

CHAPTER 48

# Praise-Maker Sunrise

Once again Togl rolled onto his side and looked out the window. The contrasts he'd seen all night—the moonlit side of rocks and trees and dunes, pure white against their stark, black shadows—were giving way to a diffuse general light. Dawn couldn't be far away. Once again he wanted to get up and go check on Kallo and Prandina and his supposedly demon grandchild. But, again, he didn't. Council had emphatically stated they wanted all villagers to be inside their huts by sunset and to remain there until sunrise. They didn't want to add to Maker's ire by having any villager help the banished ones the night before Praise Maker Day.

The dictate meant that he and Lilu and others not only had to have given what help they wanted to but also to have said their good-byes by sunset. Now, as Togl looked out the window, he sighed. Sunrise—the deadline for the banished ones' departure—was close.

"You awake again?" Lilu asked.

"Yes."

"Me too. You hear Togai leave?"

"Yes. I hope no one saw him, certainly no one on Council. But if anyone did, maybe they'll forgive him, understand why he would want to be with his brother on his last night."

"Did he come back?"

"I don't think so. He probably helped carry last things to the canoes and stayed by the river to watch them leave. They might be leaving about now, actually. They're supposed to be clear of the river and on the sea by sunrise."

"It seems it's going to be a clear day. Calm, too. Maybe that's a sign Maker is pleased and will look kindly on them."

"I hope so," Togl said. "If Togai's at the river, I hope he's looking for a place to hide. Most of the village will be down there soon." He snorted. "The overdoers think this extra kowtowing to Maker will soften His judgment of us."

"Are you going to the river?"

"Yes, but mostly to see if they really are gone—and to find Togai. I don't feel much like praising anyone or anything today." He sighed. "I might as well get up. Can't sleep. You coming to the river?"

"No." Lilu's voice quavered. "I...I really don't feel much like praising Maker today."

Clothes in hand, Togl tiptoed out and looked into Togai's room. Empty, as he'd expected. He hoped Togai was hiding. If he tried to come back now, someone would surely see him.

He dressed quickly and took a stand in the front door to await Old Helu's signal. Council had originally said people should be in their huts until sunrise but Old Helu almost immediately realized that villagers should be at the river by sunrise and said she would use her judgment and blow the conch enough before sunrise to give everyone time to get there—if they hurried.

At the sound of the conch, Togl stepped off the porch and, best he could, began to run. He wanted to be first one to the river. As Kallo's father and head fisher, he felt he should be. At the first trees he looked back—and wondered if the many streaming down through the village behind him were hurrying to praise Maker or to see if the evil they feared was gone.

As he came to the last of the willow trees, he looked both up and down the strand and, not seeing Togai, felt good—but his heart almost stopped. The canoes he had helped Kallo load yesterday afternoon were still there! Where they'd been when he saw them just before sunset!

He hurried on and took a quick glance into each canoe. No food or seed—which Kallo had said he and the others would bring down last—had been added. All he could see were things like clothes, tools, and utensils—and the many heavy water casks he had helped Kallo so carefully place.

He glanced around wildly. Where were Kallo and the princess? Dilo and Tatl? The others? Had they decided to defy Council?

He turned back toward the village and started to run, but in the loose sand slipped and fell. Someone in the group that had been closest behind him called out, "Is something wrong?"

"Yes," he called to them as he stood. "Kallo and the others didn't leave! Their packed canoes are still here!"

And someone in that group turned and yelled, "The banished ones didn't leave!"—and soon after that, from farther and farther back along the path, were other yells. "The canoes are still here." "Nobody's gone." "The Princess and the baby didn't leave."

Most in the first group, Togl recognized, were overdoers, and as he passed them one said, "Aren't you going to stay to Praise Maker?"

Togl stopped, gave a quick nod toward the glow in the east. "Praise Maker," he said, and hurried on. Of those he could see on the path, about half were headed back to the village. Within groups hurrying toward the river, questions were flying back and forth. "What if the princess and the handmaidens didn't leave?" "What will Council do?" "What will Maker do?"—and Togl saw many worried glances at the rising sun.

He didn't bother going into his hut or even calling out as he went by. He knew Lilu would have heard the yelling and the talk and would have gone on to Kallo and Prandina's hut.

When he got to the hut the Chelks already there moved back to let him through, and even as he was stepping onto the porch Lilu was saying, "They're not here."

"You sure?"

"I peeped in and called for them, but...It's so empty it echoes."

"They're gone," came a man's voice from back in the crowd. "No doubt about it. I happened to wake up about midnight, restless I guess, glanced out, saw them."

"Me too," another man said.

Togl recognized the second voice as that of Quino, a canoe builder. "Were they headed for the river, Quino?"

"Well, they were going in that direction, but..."

"But what?" Togl's words came sharp and quick.

Quino cleared his throat. "I wasn't going to say, because I didn't want to get anybody in trouble, but...but I didn't actually see Prandina or any of the girls. There were eight people, all right. But no women. Just men. Or men and boys."

"Was one of them Togai?" Lilu asked.

"I can answer that," a woman near the porch said. "My hut is right over there, and with that full moon bearing down, I'm pretty sure Togai wasn't with them. Don't want to argue with Quino, but truth is, I believe it was who it was supposed to be. Couldn't believe my eyes at first, but there they were, Prandina and the handmaidens—in pants and shirts."

"Maker forbid," some woman said. *"Pants and shirts?"*

Tatl's father, a woodcutter, who many said was far stronger than Tatl would ever be, spoke up. "I know Prandina said something about going into the mountains, but I can't believe Tatl would let them even try that. We know they didn't leave in the canoes, so my guess is, they went up between the fingers somewhere, maybe hoping to find a little patch of ground to grow some things on—and wearing pants and shirts would make sense. Bushes, thorns and snags would tear dresses to shreds in no time. But, Maker help us, I can't believe Tatl would let them even try that. He knows there's almost nothing between the fingers, just rocky ground and no water and..." He shuddered. "...certainly knows the dangers of being close to Ogre and the Ogres of the Cold."

"What do you think, Togl?" Old Exl called from the crowd. "You think Kallo—he's probably the leader—would dare try go into the mountains? And why did Lilu ask about Togai? Is he missing?"

Togl hesitated. "We haven't seen Togai this morning. It's hard for me to believe either of my sons would go into the mountains, but I...I could get a better idea if...Is Old Helu here?'

"Yes," came her answer from the back edge of the crowd. "I just came up from the river. I felt, seeing how many of you didn't, that at least I, Dilkina, should show up at the river to properly praise Maker on this day. And I did."

"I know it's not proper to go into a person's hut when they're not home," Togl said, "but..."

"It's not their hut anymore," someone shouted. "It's the village's."

"I agree," Old Helu said in a loud voice. "Go on in, Togl."

Togl looked at Lilu. "Want to come?"

"No. I think I'll wait here. I couldn't bear to look right now."

Togl strode straight to the room the handmaidens had been using since they'd left Old Helu's place. In a loose pile were four dresses, the ones Prandina and the handmaidens had said were their most durable, the ones into whose seats Lilu had sewn extra, reinforcing layers to withstand unknown days of sitting in a canoe.

He turned back to the main room. Several times in the last few days, he'd carried things both into and out of that room, and he had a fair idea of what had been there. The stack of pants and shirts that had been in one corner—a big stack, with shirts thicker and heavier than any he'd ever seen—were missing. In a glance he saw that all the loaves of bread Prandina and the handmaidens had baked and some of the small bags of seed were missing—but, as far as he could tell, not one of the heavy crocks of pickled fish, not one of the extra nets or paddles he and Kallo had so carefully picked out was gone. And suddenly it all made sense. It had been a ruse. All of it. From the very start. All along Kallo and the others had acted as if they were going onto the ocean, had talked and gathered as if they would, but all along were planning to go up there—somewhere. He started to leave but had the annoying feeling that something else was missing. But what?

He looked around but it wasn't until he turned for the door that he remembered. Yes. That was where it had been. Near the door. Under the window. A big coil of rope. Kallo had said they needed a rope to tie the canoes together at night, but it had been Togai who had strung it out, stepping it off and measuring it by eye. Togl could remember thinking at the time: Why so much? There was enough rope there to tie half the canoes in Chelekai together.

Togl's steps were heavy as he made his way to the door. He felt as if he were dragging a full net of yellowtail.

Kallo and the others weren't just going up between the fingers. They were going to try to go the whole way. To where, he had no idea.

Once on the porch, he saw a sea of questioning faces. He took a deep breath. "I...I'm afraid they really are trying to get into the mountains...and Togai may have gone with them."

Lilu gasped and put her hand to her mouth. "Oh, I was afraid he might be up to something. A few mornings ago he got up—and his arms and legs were all scratched."

"Colatt too," Colatt's mother said. "I bet they were carrying things up during the night, getting scratched up then."

"I just don't think Tatl would risk the ire of the Ogre by trying to go into the mountains," Tatl's father said. "I bet—if they were carrying stuff up during the night—it was to a cave."

"Or up to the bottom of a cliff or something," Togl said. "To someplace where they could use a rope to get a start up, then use the rope to pull up other things—including people."

Someone yelled out, "There is no such place"—and half the people there started yelling their opinions and asking questions. The other half had their mouths half open, just waiting for the slightest chance to jump in.

About to cry, Lilu touched Togl's arm and said, "Let's go. I'm tired."

"Me too," he said. And as he helped her from the porch and led her through the crowd, various thoughts and emotions ran through him. Why had Kallo and Togai deceived him? Why hadn't they trusted their own father enough to confide in him, tell him what they planned? But the question that came most often, what puzzled him most was, why would Togai go with them? Sure. He had a lot of spunk and was a good runner but, like Kallo, a fisher. So why the mountains? Wouldn't they both have wanted to go to sea? He shook his head. None of it made sense.

They were almost to their hut when they met some overdoers just coming up from the river. One of them, a paddle maker named Allo, said, "The handmaidens' parents are across the river. They yelled and

311

asked if the banished ones were gone. We yelled back we didn't know for sure—and they asked if you'd come over and explain..."

"Thanks, Allo," Togl said. "I told them the other day I'd come over...but I forgot."

As he came back, up the path from the river he saw Old Zoltai sitting on the edge of the porch, looking up at the mountains. Lilu was in the doorway. She looked miffed, and as he came up she said, "Zoltai came just after you left. Said he had something to tell *you*."

Zoltai twisted and looked at her. "I'm sorry, Lilu. Actually, it's for both of you, but I..."

Expectation and hope lit her face and she almost jumped to the porch step and looked up at him, hand on his arm. "Is it about Togai? Is it? Is it about Togai?"

"Yes," he said, and glanced at both of them. "Togai came to see me, last night, about when the moon was overhead. Said he had something to tell me before he left."

"Before he left?" Lilu said, and began to cry. "Oh, I was afraid of that. But...but...Did he say where he..."

Zoltai interrupted. "Yes, and he wants you to know what he told me, but he asked that I tell no one else—and that you two not tell anyone either until three days from now."

"Of course," Togl said. "Whatever he wants. Now tell us."

"The reason for that is he wants them to have plenty of time to get away, not have anyone come after them." Zoltai chuckled. "Not that anyone would, not where they're going."

Zoltai then told them—with their utterances and faces changing from apprehension to disbelief and back again—about Togai's trips into the mountains, what he'd seen, and how he—with Prandina—convinced the others to look for a new place to live on the other side of the mountains rather than go onto the sea. What Zoltai didn't tell, for Togai didn't tell him, was about the chimney. Though Zoltai had asked, Togai wouldn't tell where—or how—he and the others would get to the top of a finger and from there over the mountains, over what had long been said was Ogre's backbone.

When he finished, Old Zoltai sighed and shook his head. "I

know it's hard to believe, but that's what he told me." The old woodcutter then raised his cane and jabbed it in the direction of the mountains. "I admit it. I'm still afraid of the Ogres, but know what?" He laughed. "I'm kind of jealous, wish I was up there with them."

Togl studied the old man's face for a moment. "You really mean that, Zoltai?"

"I do."

"Well, that makes me feel better. But..." He looked at the mountains. "It's such a new thought."

Zoltai stood. "I saw Allo on my way here. He said you had gone to talk to the handmaidens' parents. You bring up the mountains?"

"Didn't have to. Soon as I said the canoes were still here, right away they started thinking *mountains*. I mean, where else could it be?"

"They seem surprised? Scared?"

"More surprised than scared. But know what really surprised them? That Prandina and the girls were actually gone. They didn't think we'd actually make them leave."

"Why not?"

"For fear of what the king might do."

Old Zoltai slept little that night, and at the first hint of light he rose from his woodchip mattress and—trying to be quiet—limped along as fast as he could through the sleeping village toward the river. He was still afraid of the Ogres—in spite of all that Togai had said—and he was almost certain that when he got to the river bank and looked up the valley much of what he'd see would be blanketed with white, a sure sign that the banished ones had at least tried to get into the mountains and had angered the Ogres of the Cold. But when he came off the path and was clear of trees, the only ground whiteness he saw was a soft white that came from the setting moon. Nothing at all like the 'White Cold' he'd seen a few times. Now that he thought about it, he should have known. The morning air was warm.

Just as he was beginning to wonder if maybe the Ogres of the Cold were women or mothers and hadn't done anything because there was a mother and baby among those trying to get into the mountains, he saw a flickering light up near the City of Light, and before he could wonder why anyone from the city would be out this time of morning, he saw another light—and another and another! But it wasn't men he saw. What was it? Zoltai squinted. What was he seeing? Horses? Yes! Horses. With men on them. And men alongside, carrying torches. Lots of men! Great falling timbers. Ogre did something really bad to Zaphyr and they're on their way here to burn the village! He turned and, as well as age and injury would let him, started to limp-run back toward the village—but suddenly stopped. Why am I worried? he thought. They can't get across the river.

He turned back and, with gray light coming in the eastern sky, stood behind a willow to watch.

As the column neared the river, he guessed that the man at the head of it was the king, for he was all alone and well in front of the others, who came two-by-two. Too, there was that big black horse he was on. As soon as the leader—the king?—brought his horse to a stop, a man ran up beside them, blew a great, long blast on a horn and called out, "Looo there, men of Left. Looo, there," and blew the horn again.

Zoltai felt brave. The river was between him and them, it was barely light enough to see the other side, and he was standing behind a tree. "Looo, yourself. What do you want?"

"I have been given the honor of speaking for the king, and in his name, I ask the men of Left to bring rafts or canoes or whatever they can to help him and his searchers cross the river."

"Searchers?" Old Zoltai called back.

"Yes. Searchers. The king will lead us into the mountains to find the Princess Prandina and the three handmaidens and return them to where they are loved."

Oh, sweet song of the saw in wood, Zoltai thought. Togai can come home. He turned quickly toward the village, but while he was still trying to get his old legs up to a fast walk, he saw people streaming toward him and he stopped where he was.

Golai, a young fisher, was the first to reach him. Togl wasn't far behind. "What is it?" Golai asked. "We heard a horn."

Zoltai started to blurt out what he'd seen and heard but said,

"Wait'll Old Helu gets here." He wanted people to remember who delivered this message. When she got there, the crowd parted and let her through.

As solemnly and dramatically as he could, Old Zoltai said, "The king changed his mind. He wants to find the princess and the handmaidens and take them home. And he needs us to come and help him and his men cross the river."

"Oh, praise Maker," someone said, and Lilu and mothers of the young men who had gone with the handmaidens began to cry.

"Let's go," Golai said, and he and several others started toward the river.

"Wait!" Old Helu held up her hand. She paused and took a deep breath. "This is the first time a king of Zaphyr has ever asked us Chelks for anything. Maybe we should ask what's in it for us?"

Everyone there, including Old Zoltai himself, was surprised by his response. "I don't think that's the question," he said. "I think the question is—what's in it for us if we don't?"

Before anyone could answer, came an angry voice from across the river, "Are you coming or not?"

The absolutely still surface of the Forbidden River that had been reflecting the changing red and orange and pink hues of the eastern sky was soon being disturbed by splashes and ripples as the fishers of Chelekai launched their canoes and sent them speeding toward the waiting searchers in Zaphyr.

The searchers—save one—rode to Chelekai in the canoes while the horses—save one—swam alongside or behind. Though almost every rider had trouble coaxing his horse into the water and holding onto its reins to keep it from turning back, the horses weren't nearly as skittish or reluctant as their riders or any of the on-foot searchers, none of whom had ever before been in or above more water than a tub could hold.

The one searcher that did not come over in a canoe was King Praidar, and the one horse that did not swim was Black Thunder. They came over on a small raft the village carpenter had made for the children to dive from until the old one, the one that had been carried away by the floodwaters, could be replaced. The fishers rowing and poling it later said that the king seemed angry, not scared, and that not only did he not say anything on the way over, he didn't say anything when he got off. No even a terse "Thank you."

As Praidar led Black Thunder off the raft and onto the strand, Old Helu, with the woodcutters and Old Zoltai close behind, came to meet him. "O King," she said, "we know that neither you nor any of your men have ever been to Chelekai and, so, are unfamiliar with our land. These woodcutters know the foothills, have even been to the first big rocks where the mountains begin, and they offer to serve as guides."

The king pulled the big horse in between him and Helu and climbed onto it and looked down at her. "Why should I trust any of you to lead me to Prandina? If you cared for her at all you'd have been out there looking yesterday, not have banished her in the first place."

The king made a slight move to ride away but stopped and again looked down at Old Helu. "Tell me. From my father I heard the tale that you people came from the sea. You are fishers and have canoes, so why would your young men choose to go into the mountains, into the unknown and home to the Ogres of the Cold."

"We do not know, sire."

Praidar shook his head. "I know Prandina would have been scared of the sea, but she'd have been scared of the mountains too. Who would she—and the others—trust enough to follow into the mountains? Was it her...her..." He seemed to not want to but clenched his teeth and muttered, "...husband? Was he, maybe, a woodcutter familiar with the hills?"

"No, Sire. He was a fisher. We don't know, but his brother, Togai, may have had something to do with it. It seems he went with them."

The king thought for a moment and dread showed in his voice as he said, almost croaked, "Is he...is he the short-legged boy who pulled Prandina from the river—paddled her upriver and got the handmaidens expelled too?"

"Yes, sire. It is."

His face turned red, and he suddenly turned the horse and dug his heels into its flanks—and the powerfully muscled stallion sprayed Old Helu and those with her with sand and gravel as it sped away.

"Don't blame Togai," Zoltai called out, confident his words couldn't be heard in the loud clatter of the horse's hooves on the rocky part of the strand. "Blame yourself. Togai wouldn't have needed to lead anyone anywhere if you hadn't banished Prandina."

That day, no woodcutters cut, no seamstresses seamed, no fishers fished—and only a few cooks cooked. By mid morning—almost as soon as the last searcher had disappeared from view—most villagers were on small dunes just outside the village, talking quietly and listening for horn signals they'd heard the searchers talk about. In particular they were listening for, hoping for, triumphant blasts that indicated the banished ones had been found. More than once Tatl's father told about how, yesterday, as soon as he came to believe the banished ones really had gone into—or toward—the mountains, he went to a few of the nearby hills where he could see much of both the first and second canyons. He had looked and listened for a long time and hadn't heard or seen any sign of them. If the banished ones were found at all, he said, it would be in the afternoon, far up the third or fourth canyon. And since notes from a horn up in one of those canyons probably wouldn't get to the dunes, they might as well go home. But no one left, not even he.

Old Zoltai didn't say much. He wasn't sure he wanted the banished ones found. He feared what the king might do to Togai. Now and then, in spite of all the sadness around him, he'd chuckle to himself. Really be something if that short-legged boy did it.

By the time the sun was dropping below the mountains, no villager was waiting or listening, and most were in their huts eating supper when the crunch of hooves on gravel brought them running out. The king led a double line of horsemen—on horses with legs scratched and bloody. Trailing was a ragged column of men, one, two, and sometimes three wide, limping and muttering, some with pants and shirts torn and bloody in places.

The king brought the stallion to a stop in the middle of the village and the villagers gathered around him, hoping for some word of what had been seen—or not seen. In the failing light, the king looked down into the crowd, and when he spotted one of the fishers who had rowed him across that morning, he said, "Well?"

With a glance, that fisher and the other three who had helped him were hurrying toward the river and the raft. Close behind them were the rest of the fishers, headed for their canoes.

As the men of Zaphyr came trudging through the village, Lilu saw one she thought she recognized. She waited for him to pass near and held her hand out toward him, but cautiously, and not enough to touch him. "Kind sir," she said, "are you not the father of one of the handmaidens? Maybe Patya?"

"Yes," he said—and stopped and gave her a hard, annoyed look. "Are you the mother of the...the *Left* who went with her?"

"No, sir, I'm not. But I do have two sons out there. So, as a mother, I ask you, did you see any sign of them? A place where they might hide or get into the mountains?

The man seemed about to turn away, but with a tired sigh and look, said, "About the only place anybody saw where they might get out was at the end of the first canyon." He nodded. "Up that way. I didn't see it, but one of the horsemen said they found a split in the canyon wall with an opening that was just barely big enough for a man to crawl into. But back a short distance it was blocked with rock—freshly fallen, the man the king made crawl in there said. That could mean something—or nothing."

"And the other canyons?"

"Nothing in them either—I can assure you. The further we went, the more agitated the king got. Toward the end of the day we were looking behind bushes a bird couldn't hide behind."

With that, the man turned and began walking toward the river and Lilu hurried to get alongside him. "Sir, are you sure there wasn't some place up there they might hide? A cave or..."

"I told you, woman," came his quick retort, and he kept walking. "I told you. We've looked all over this Maker-forsaken place and if either one of your sons is as big as a bird we'd've found him. Now leave me alone."

"Please," Lilu said. "Why are you so angry? My husband is the head fisher and he said you parents were so friendly and nice."

The man stopped and gave Lilu a withering look. "Of course we were nice—when we needed to get things to our daughters. But you really expect me to be nice to you now, after you banished my dear Patya?" He looked at Lilu and the villagers near her who had been following and listening. "Well, I tell you true, if it was up to me, we'd burn this place to the ground right now."

As soon as the king and the stallion were off the raft, the two fishers who had jumped off to pull it onto the strand now started to push it back into the river. "Wait," the king said, and swung into the saddle.

The two men looked at each other. Were they about to get some payment from the king for what they—maybe all fishers—had done that day?

The king looked down at the nearer one. "The old woman who spoke to me this morning when I first crossed the river, is she still your leader?"

"Yes, sire," the man said.

"Tell her that when she knows the last of my men are safely across the river to come and talk to me. I will be waiting."

"Yes, sire."

Darkness had fallen, and the glare of flames from a torch in the bow kept Old Helu and the two fishers paddling her from seeing what was directly ahead. They had to look from side to side for signs of shore, and just as they were beginning to pick out a line of glistening stones, a commanding voice came from straight ahead, seemingly from right out of the torch: "That's close enough. Do not land."

The fisher in the stern immediately dug his paddle into the water. The bow came around, and as the strand came into full view, they saw, hovering above the strand it seemed, the glistening arms and chest of a powerful man—which, they soon saw, were below a black hood and above black pants and boots. "Great jumping turtles," the fisher in the stern said. "It's the king's executioner."

The executioner had his legs spread and his hands rested on the handle of a curve-bladed ax upright in front of him.

"I have a message from the king," he said. "Because you people of Left banished his daughter, his beloved Princess Prandina, you are hereby given—as Prandina was—three days to leave the valley. If the fourth morning hence, the village is not burning and all of you gone, the king and men of Zaphyr will by some means—perhaps on logs, perhaps on rafts not yet built—cross the river, torch the village, and with pitchforks, knives, hammers, and axes force however many of you remain from the valley."

"But there's so many of us. Where...where will we go?"

"The king said if you asked that, to remind you that you have the same choices you gave Prandina."

As the farmers and tradesmen of Zaphyr left their homes that fourth morning with the sky still dark, they were almost certain they'd not need the implements and tools they carried either for weapons or for building rafts, for the glow in the sky told them the village was already afire. Still, they came on, for the king had so ordered.

And as many expected, when they reached the river they were told by the Captain of the Guard they could return home. They were told he and the king had been there since midnight, had watched the Lefts load their canoes, had heard them cry and wail as flames leapt above the trees and they boarded their canoes...had heard their cries fade far downriver.

Most of the farmers and tradesmen stayed, though, to watch the smoke grow faint, as if—with the last wisp—the Lefts would be gone forever.

A little after sunup, with the king still sitting quietly atop his black stallion, as he had been since first light, staring out across the river and showing no inclination to move or to give an order, ten or so men who had begun talking quietly off to one side now came toward him. They stopped three or four steps away, and from the group, which included all three handmaidens' fathers, Obena's father took a half step forward. With his hat clutched nervously in front of him, he looked up and said, "O King, since we are already here and…"

"No," the king said, without shifting his gaze. "You cannot build a raft. There will be no more searching, no reason to go over and see if all the Lefts are gone. The Captain of the Guard will post a man night and day for a few days, hidden back in the trees, to watch for any sign of life."

Silent for a few moment, reflective, the king turned and said loudly enough for all to hear, "I know I ordered differently the other day, but the law still applies. The penalty to anyone who crosses the Forbidden River is death."

After that, no one in the Kingdom of Zaphyr ever again saw or heard from any Left or any of the young people who had been banished, but it is said that when King Praidar grew old, he would sit in his study high in the castle, read old books, think about a dream an aged cook once told him—and wonder if a short-legged fisher boy from the Land of Left had found a way over the mountains and taken the kingdom's greatest treasure with him.